Arthur Martin Wheeler

Sketches From English History

Arthur Martin Wheeler

Sketches From English History

ISBN/EAN: 9783337096434

Printed in Europe, USA, Canada, Australia, Japan

Cover: Foto ©Andreas Hilbeck / pixelio.de

More available books at **www.hansebooks.com**

SKETCHES

FROM

ENGLISH HISTORY,

SELECTED AND EDITED

WITH AN

INTRODUCTION,

(FROM THE ROMAN CONQUEST TO THE REVOLUTION OF 1688.)

BY

ARTHUR M. WHEELER,

PROFESSOR OF HISTORY IN YALE COLLEGE.

TWO PARTS IN ONE VOLUME.

NEW YORK:
PHILLIPS & HUNT.
CINCINNATI:
CRANSTON & STOWE.
1886.

INTRODUCTION.

THE history of England really begins with the conquest of the island of Britain, in the fifth and sixth centuries of our era, by some German tribes known as the Jutes, the Saxons, and the Angles —the last ultimately giving their name to the whole country—Angleland, Engla-land, England. It is necessary, however, to go back a little in order to understand the condition of both the conquered and conquerors at the time of the invasion.

Britain, at the opening of its history, was inhabited by the Celts, a race which, at that time, was spread over a large portion of western Europe. During the first century of the Christian era, the greater part of it was conquered by the Romans, and was held by them as a province of the empire for about three hundred and fifty years. In spite of this long occupation, however, the Roman civilization did not strike deep root in the island. Perhaps because it was her latest conquest in the west, perhaps because she did not find it worth her while to make the effort, Rome, in fact, never succeeded in incorporating the Celts of Britain into her system, as she had succeeded in incorporating the Celts of Gaul. The inhabitants of Britain, while they accepted Christianity, the religion of the conquerors, and submitted to the Roman rule, kept for the most part their native customs, and above all their native speech, which is still spoken in some portions of the island. When Rome, pressed by dangers nearer home, was compelled to withdraw her army from Britain, about the year 402, the Romanized Britons were left to defend themselves. They succeeded in maintaining their independence for a time; but, long accustomed as they had been to rely on foreign protection, and apparently without any national organization, they were unable to resist either the attacks of the Picts from the north, who had never come under the Roman sway, or the inroads of the German tribes from the east. The latter proved to be the more dangerous, and, in the end, the successful enemy.

The German invaders came from the Baltic lands lying about the mouths of the Elbe and the Weser. They were heathen, and, unlike their brethren who invaded the continental provinces of Rome, they had never been brought into contact with the Roman civilization. They had, therefore, no reverence either for the religion or the institutions which they found in Britain; and, as the Britons, though unorganized, were brave, and defended their homes with the greatest obstinacy, the war was necessarily a war of extermination. The invaders were forced to win the land bit by bit by hard fighting. They destroyed cities, and towns, and churches; the natives were either driven back or killed; and the Roman civilization was obliterated. The English conquest, as far as it extended, was a well-nigh complete displacement of one people by another.

Thus, during a century and a half (449–600) the invaders succeeded in establishing a number of petty states on the soil of Britain, seven or eight of which soon became prominent. They retained their own language, they brought with them their own laws and customs, and, excepting such modifications as were necessary in consequence of their new surroundings, they organized themselves in their new home as they had been organized in the old one. A king at the head; local assemblies for local purposes, general assemblies for general purposes, each of which all freemen of each tribe or state had the right to attend; an armed force made up of all freemen capable of bearing arms; these were the general features of their organization (see p. 32, ff.). It contained nearly all the germs of the later system of self-government, and its development has been continuous from that day to this.

At the close of the sixth century the Britons still held all of the land beyond the Forth, and a belt of territory extending up the western coast; the rest of the country was in the hands of the intruders. And now a change began which was to exert a vast influence on the destinies of England. This was the conversion of the heathen English to Christianity.

The work of conversion was accomplished in the south by missionaries from the Church of Rome, and in the north by missionaries from the Irish Church. There were some ritualistic differences between the two Churches which, however, were happily adjusted at the synod of Whitby (664), where the Roman influence prevailed; and, five years later, Archbishop Theodore began the ecclesiastical organization of the country on the Roman model, and "converted what had been a missionary station into an established Church." England thus acquired ecclesiastical unity as a daughter of the Church of Rome, and was brought through her into direct contact with all the civilization and culture of the time. Moreover, the example of unity in the Church had a direct influence in bringing about unity in the state. It was impossible that so many petty kingdoms, without natural boundaries, should long remain independent; the work of consolidation began early, and, helped by the example of the Church, was continued with varying success until Ecgberht, king of Wessex (800–839), succeeded in extending his authority over all the English-speaking peoples of the island.

But the work of consolidation was still incomplete when the country was confronted with a new and formidable danger. The Danes, or Northmen, who were of the same German stock as the English, but who were still heathen, and but little farther advanced in civilization than the English had been three hundred years before, had earlier begun their terrible inroads, and now came in ever-increasing numbers. They devastated the north and center of the country with fire and sword, and even broke into Wessex itself. It seemed as if the new Church and State in England were to go down before this fresh onslaught of heathenism, when, in the very crisis of peril, King Alfred appeared. He could not drive out the Danes, but he succeeded in re-establishing the boundaries of Wessex, and, by abandoning to the intruders nearly half of England, induced them to make peace (878). The Danish leader, Guthrum, embraced the Christian faith, and his example was soon imitated by his followers. The successors of Alfred on the West Saxon throne set to work to recover the lost supremacy. Their progress was slow, but in the end they succeeded. The peace and prosperity of Eadgar's reign (959–975) was largely due to Dunstan's wise and vigorous administration, but also to the fact that there had been no fresh Danish inroads for nearly a century because the Danish energies had been directed elsewhere.

Thus far, aside from the general devastation and misery they had caused, the chief result of the Danish invasions had been to check the growth of English unity, and to interrupt the progress of education and culture. Now the Danish settlers were gradually absorbed by the larger English population, without adding much to the strength of the nation. Meanwhile, however, in Skandinavia, the home of the Northmen, the same process of unification and consolidation had been going on which had earlier taken place in England itself. Great kings had risen to power there, and the petty leaders who opposed the national movement were forced to seek refuge in other lands. The isolated attacks on England began again, but they soon passed under the control of Swegen, the king of all Denmark, who now attempted the conquest of England. After many failures he succeeded. The weak king, Æthelred the Unready, was driven out, Swegen was accepted as king by the English people, and handed on his power to his son Cnut. The reign of Cnut was of great political importance, "because it produced, on a small scale, the same tendencies which were to be developed on a large scale by the Norman conquest;" but the misrule and the early death of his two sons led to the restoration of the old West Saxon line of kings in Eadward the Confessor.

England was now to be brought into closer contact with the land and the people that were destined to exert such a vast influence upon her future. The Normans or Northmen, of the same race as the Danes and the English, had conquered Normandy, a province of France, about one hundred and fifty years before this time. They had speedily accepted the religion, the language, and the institutions of the conquered province, were now farther advanced in civilization than their English neighbors, and were noted for their energy, their boldness, their love of war and of distant foreign enterprises. Their present duke, William, had been left, at the death of his father, a boy of eight years of age, in circumstances of great difficulty and danger, out of which he had extricated himself with rare ability, and he had already won a European reputation by the vigor and wisdom of his rule. He was second cousin to the new English king. Eadward himself had spent his earlier years at the Norman court, where he had acquired strong predilections for French ways of thinking and living, and it was natural, now that he was on the throne, that he should surround himself with French influences by appointing Normans to high offices in Church and State. Opposed to this foreign tendency stood the national party headed by Earl Godwine, whose daughter the king had married. The fact that Eadward was childless, and that the only direct heir to the crown was an exile, living in remote Hungary, doubtless suggested to the ambitious duke of the Normans the idea that he might, one day, add a royal crown to his ducal coronet. He visited England in 1051, and is said to have received from Eadward the assurance that he should be his successor. Such a promise, however, Eadward had no right to make. The disposal of the crown was in the hands of the national assembly of wise men—the Witenagemot. William's sole rival was Godwine's son, Earl Harold, who, since his father's death, had become the first subject in the land. Chance placed him, later, in William's power for a time, and the duke did not release him until he had exacted from him a pledge made, if Norman writers are to be believed, in the most solemn form, that he would marry William's daughter, and support his claim to the English throne. At the death of Eadward (January, 1066) the national assembly promptly chose Earl Harold as king. William at once proclaimed Harold as a perjurer ; by adroit representations he succeeded in making men believe that he had been defrauded of his rights ; he persuaded his Norman nobles to assist him in recovering what he represented as his own ; at his call volunteers from many lands flocked to his standard ; he even obtained the papal sanction to his enterprise ; and, in September, 1066, he landed, at the head of a large army, on the English coast.

The moment was opportune. The English fleet, which had been watching his movements all the summer, had temporarily retired, and Harold, himself, was in the north engaged in repelling a dangerous attack headed by his rebellious brother and the Norwegian king. At the news of William's landing he hurried southward, gathering his forces as he went, and met his rival on the hill of Senlac. The terrible battle which was fought there, lasting all day, in which Harold, two of his brothers, and the chief of the English nobility were slain, practically decided the fate of England.

The immediate changes wrought by the Norman conquest were few, yet of immense significance. As the new king claimed to be the legitimate successor of Eadward, he could treat all those who had opposed him as rebels and traitors. The vast estates of Harold and his supporters were, therefore, confiscated, and were either held by William or bestowed upon the chiefs of his army; and within a few years all the high offices in Church and State were in the hands of Normans. The classes that had hitherto ruled in England were thus forced to take a subordinate position, and that change, of itself, was pregnant with meaning to the English people. But a still greater change was in the spirit and tone of the new order of things, a change which grew out of the personal views and character of the new sovereign. William regarded kingship as a possession rather than as an office, and the kingdom as a private estate to be managed primarily in the interests of the king rather than as a trust to be administered for the good of the nation. But the old laws were continued in force, and under them the rights of the conquered were strictly maintained; the old institutions were preserved, and were modified only so far as the conqueror thought necessary in order to establish a strong centralized government, which was the great need of the time.

The indirect influence of the conquest can be traced in all the subsequent history of the country. It made itself felt in manifold ways on the judicial, legislative, and administrative systems, on foreign and ecclesiastical relations, on language, literature, architecture, and society. The energy and vigor infused by the Norman nobles into the English people prevented them from falling into a state of stagnation and isolation toward which they were tending, and ultimately enabled them to recover the liberties which they had temporarily lost.

Under the Conqueror Normandy was naturally regarded as the chief possession, and England as a dependency; under his sons this relation was reversed. The kingdom became the basis of their power, and the duchy an appendage of the English crown. In the disputes with their brother Robert, as well as in their conflicts with the turbulent feudal nobility, both the Red King and the first Henry relied for support upon the conquered English. Henry, who was born in England, strengthened his position among the conquered race by marrying an English wife, and in all his measures showed a determination to mete out strict justice to Norman and Englishman alike. His chief aim, like that of his father, was to build up and extend the royal authority, and to make its influence felt in every corner of the land. The imperative need of such an authority was made more manifest than ever by the anarchy of Stephen's reign. At the close of that terrible score of years, so full of confusion and bloodshed, all men in England who loved law and order were ready to join hands in hearty support of the new sovereign. Fortunately Henry the Second was in many ways eminently qualified for his high position. The general success of his administration stamps him as a man who was born to rule. He destroyed a great multitude of the feudal castles which had been illegally erected and were centers of oppression. He diminished the military strength of the nobles by his law of *scutage*, which allowed them to substitute a money payment in place of the personal service in the field, which they were bound to render as the condition on which they held their lands. By his *assize of arms* he revived and reorganized the old English militia system, and made it an effective means of national defense. He sent out his judges, at regular intervals, to hold court in every county, thus securing to all his subjects a uniform, cheap, and prompt administration of justice. He revolutionized the methods of judicial procedure then in vogue by substituting the sworn testimony of twelve men, both in civil and criminal cases, for the crude and clumsy ordeal and trial by battle. He failed, indeed, to gain the points at issue in the quarrel with Becket, yet the contest aroused a spirit in the nation which proved fatal to papal claims and exactions in the later years. In all these measures Henry seems to have had the steady support and sympathy of the great mass of the people. It is evident that all distinctions of race were rapidly disappearing. The nobles, themselves, began to feel that they were Englishmen, and that their interests lay chiefly in England. Henry's system, with their support, proved strong enough to bear the strain to which it was subjected during the reign of the absentee Richard, and, a few years later, we see the descendants of the men who had fought for the Conqueror uniting with the conquered race to wrest the Great Charter from the tyrant John.

The Great Charter, at the time it received the royal signature, was the supreme constitutional effort of the nation. Clergy and laymen, nobles and commoners, had united to obtain it. It embodied all that men had regarded as good law and custom for the last hundred years. It was direct and practical, free from political abstractions, designed to meet wants which actually existed or which were likely to arise in the immediate future. The fact that it was afterward so often appealed to, and so often re-affirmed, proves that it was, on the whole, well adapted to accomplish the objects which its framers had in view. Yet it did not, and could not, in the very nature of the case, embody a complete constitutional system. The political machinery for such a system did not then exist. The highest judicial, legislative, and administrative body in the land was the king's council, which was composed exclusively of the higher clergy and the baronage. These were the men who framed the Charter, and it did not enter their thoughts to change the composition and character of their own assembly. Just then their interests coincided with those of the nation ; but the time might come when, under other circumstances and influences, they might combine with the king against the liberties of the people. If the nation was ever to govern itself, it must have a really national assembly through which it could act, one in which all classes should be represented, in which chosen men from the shires and from the cities and boroughs should be associated with the higher clergy and the baronage ; in a word, it must have a Parliament.

The principle of representation had long been familiar to the English mind. It had been applied for ages in the local assemblies, in shire court and hundred court, and therefore it was now comparatively easy to extend it to the national assembly. Already, on rare occasions, the shires, and, again, the cities and boroughs, had been summoned to send chosen men to the king to consult with him and his council; but the great merit of having, for the first time, united all the elements of the future Parliament—prelates, nobles, knights, citizens, and burgesses—in one assembly belongs to Earl Simon de Montfort. The famous body which he summoned in 1265 was not, however, a complete Parliament. Besides being imperfect in the mode of summons, it was made up chiefly of the earl's supporters, and, moreover, was called in opposition to the king; it was a revolutionary rather than a legal body. A national Parliament, if it was ever to become a permanent feature of the constitutional system, must, necessarily, have the sanction of the king as the constitutional head. But De Montfort's example was not forgotten. Thirty years later (1295) the work which he had left unfinished was completed by King Edward I.

In yielding to the demand for a national Parliament Edward proved himself a really great as well as a thoroughly English king. That his action was prompted largely by his pecuniary necessities does not detract from his greatness. He knew that it would be impossible to accomplish the great enterprises he had in hand without the hearty support of the entire nation, and he clearly saw that the best and simplest way to gain that support was through an assembly in which all classes of the nation were represented. A little later, when under still greater pecuniary stress, he yielded to the Parliament the sole right of taxation, and thus placed in its hands a perpetual check on the power of the crown.

At the close of his reign Parliament consisted of one assembly; in the course of a generation it divided into two. The prelates and barons united to form the House of Lords, the other component parts crystallized into the House of Commons. That the knights of the shire, that is, the country gentlemen, coalesced with the citizens and burgesses—the trading classes—rather than with the barons, with whom they were much more closely connected by birth and social position, was due, far more than to any other one cause, to the fact that they had, for ages, acted with the citizens and burgesses in the local assemblies. Their political union with the classes below them gave to the House of Commons a dignity and importance which it could not otherwise have acquired. The Parliament thus constituted soon made its influence felt in all departments of the government, and, in a few years, we see it exercising the highest of parliamentary functions, that of deposing the king (Edward II.).

In the next reign the nation, at length conscious of its unity, plunged into a war with France. The war was a truly national one,

1*

although it was conducted by a sovereign who was half French by birth, and who was under the influence of French ideas (Edward III.). Since the days of the Conqueror, the situation had been completely reversed. Then a French people had conquered England; now the English nation goes forth to the conquest of France. The great successes of the war (Crecy and Poitiers) were won by the English archers, who were drawn from the middle classes. It was only natural that these classes should claim, as a reward for such service, a larger share in the government of the country. The influence of the Parliament, and especially of the Lower House, steadily increased. Besides the right of taxation, it acquired a voice in general legislation and in all affairs of state. It obtained control over the appointment of the king's ministers; it acquired the right of appropriating money to specific objects, and of examining into the public accounts. It established the principle that no law was valid without its own consent; it surrounded itself with a code of rules to guide its conduct; it made itself an integrant part of the constitutional system; and soon, for the second time within three quarters of a century, it exercised a paramount authority in the deposition of an intractable king (Richard II.).

As Henry IV., the first of the Lancastrian kings, owed his crown to an act of Parliament, it was inevitable that, under him, that body should establish more firmly the great powers it had already acquired. In a certain sense, the Parliament was now complete; it was invested with all the authority which it wields to-day, and in some respects its influence was, perhaps, more potent because more direct. But the Parliament was essentially an aristocratic body. The balance of power lay in the Upper House, which was composed exclusively of the great land-holders; and in the Lower House the land-holding interest, represented by the country gentlemen (knights of the shire), was largely predominant. The representatives of the trading classes were overawed by their aristocratic associates. The towns, indeed, were rapidly growing in importance, but in them the tendency was toward the formation of an aristocracy of wealth which was gathering into its own hands whatever political power and influence the towns possessed. At this stage of parliamentary development, then, the lower half of the nation was without any direct representation in the national assembly.

Moreover, causes were now at work which tended to increase the political influence of the great land-holders. Wool-growing had long been one of the leading industries of the country. From the time of Edward I. the woolen mills of Flanders had drawn their supply of the raw material, to a great extent, from England. In the reign of Edward III. a terrible pestilence swept away more than half of the laboring population. Owing to the consequent scarcity of labor, the rate of wages rose so high that the great land-holders preferred to turn those portions of their lands which had been under tillage into pasturage for sheep, since sheep-farms could be managed with comparatively few laborers. The large class of laborers who had hitherto gained a living by tilling the great estates of the nobles were now turned adrift to become vagabonds and beggars. Furthermore, the profits of wool-growing tempted the nobles to add to their already vast estates by buying up small farms, and by fencing in the great tracts of common lands adjoining their properties, from which the peasantry had drawn, in part, their subsistence. The peasants, cut off from their means of livelihood, oppressed by harsh laws, and inflamed by the preaching of some of Wyclif's followers, rose in revolt. But the insurrection was crushed; the nobles retained all they had, and, moreover, they secured the enactment of laws which guaranteed to them the hereditary possession of their enormous estates intact. Their power was now disproportionately great, and might have proved destructive to the constitutional system, had it not been greatly diminished by subsequent events.

Henry V. renewed the struggle with the old enemy across the Channel. Though the war was utterly unjust, and though it could not be successful in the end, yet, as the king was popular, the nation obeyed his call. For many years the energies of England were expended in a vain attempt to effect the conquest of France. So long as Henry lived, his military genius and his statesmanship made the war a succession of triumphs; but, soon after his death (1422), in spite of the great ability of his brother, the duke of Bedford, it took a disastrous turn. At last the French had found a leader in the Maid of Orleans. The spirit of nationality awoke among them; and the English, though fighting desperately, were steadily forced back, and at length driven from the country. The leaders with their large bands of lawless retainers returned home demoralized by a war which they had entered into for plunder and glory, and thoroughly disappointed at its failure. It was natural that the House of Lancaster, now represented by the weak and unfortunate Henry VI., should be held responsible for the disasters which had overtaken the English arms. The government was also intensely unpopular on other grounds; and now the rival claim of the House of York, which had lain dormant for fifty years, was revived by Richard, duke of York, the most popular nobleman of his day; and the partisans of the two claimants soon began an open conflict, which lasted, with short intervals of truce, for thirty years. When the struggle ended, it was found that the balance of the constitution was changed; the old nobility had been nearly destroyed; their vast estates had been confiscated to the crown, and the remnant of the baronage was unable to offer any effectual resistance to the arbitrary power of the sovereign. Moreover, the Church, which, in the earlier ages, had often helped to keep the royal authority in check, had lost her hold upon the nation; and, no longer able to rely for support upon the papacy, whose influence, especially in England, had been steadily declining, she now, in order to retain her great possessions, allied herself with the king. The only remaining barrier was the Commons; but they, too, had lost ground during the civil war, and were now too weak to battle alone successfully with the crown. The nation, too, was weary of strife, and ready to welcome a strong centralized government. Thus the ground was prepared for the practically unlimited despotism of the first two Tudors.

The sovereigns of the Tudor line were unquestionably gifted; they all showed far more than the average ability of princely houses. Though differing widely in personal appearance and personal characteristics, they all had the same inexorable will, the same irresistible impulse to rule as autocrats; and they all showed, though in unequal degree, a marvelous skill in recognizing and using the moments when their own personal interests and wishes coincided with those of the nation. At the close of the mediæval period they found England prostrate, suffering terribly from the effects of civil war, near to inward dissolution; without influence abroad, and threatened on her northern border with a ruinous invasion from Scotland, whom she had so often made to tremble. They left to the Stuarts a kingdom strengthened and developed internally in every direction, freed from its subjugation to Rome, in union with Scotland, on the high road to the formation of the British Empire of our day, while on the Continent it had set limits to the imperious ambition of the great Spanish monarchy, and had laid, both in the east and in the west, the foundations of its colonial greatness. Much of this wondrous change was certainly due to general causes which were working every-where in Europe during the 16th century—to the revival of learning, the invention of printing, and of the mariner's compass—but much, also, was due to the energy, the ability, the fostering care, the tack and skill of the Tudor sovereigns.

For England the central fact of the period was the great political and religious revolution which brought about her separation from the Church of Rome. Whatever the motives of Henry VIII. may have been, and some of them were certainly base, he could never have accomplished such a work, had it not been for the deep-seated and wide-spread feeling of dissatisfaction toward Rome which had existed for ages among the English people. The opposition to Rome had begun away back in the days of the Red King, and had manifested itself in a long series of statutes against papal exactions and aggressions. Wyclif, in his day, had struck the key-note of English feeling in his attack upon the organization and discipline of the Church, and, though the nation was not ready to follow him in his attack upon her doctrines, yet the example he had set was not forgotten. The opposition was intensified rather by the alliance of the papacy with France during a portion of the Hundred Years' War, by the growing corruption of the clergy, by their enormous and, in part, ill-gotten wealth, and by the fact that, although they maintained all their high pretensions, they had ceased to perform conscientiously and fully the duties of their office. The English clergy stood as a body by itself, divorced from the nation, and owing allegiance primarily to a foreign power. The antagonism between Church and State in England had reached its limit.

Henry now made use of this situation in order to accomplish his own objects and in his own way. But reckless as he was by nature, and intense as his personal interest was in the dispute with Pope Clement VII. over the divorce question, he moved forward slowly, and cautiously felt his way. More than six years elapsed after the divorce was first mooted, before final action was taken on his side. The succession of measures which severed the connection with Rome and broke up the monastic system in England met with surprisingly little opposition, and that was easily crushed. The nation looked on in silence while blow after blow was struck at the papal supremacy. The Parliament acquiesced in every thing, even in the most despotic measures of the king; its power seemed to be in abeyance. The new nobles, in fact, were entirely dependent on the sovereign; and, moreover, they were soon gorged with the plunder of the monasteries, and so were bound by the strongest tie, that of self-interest, to the new *régime*. The Commons, even if they wished to oppose, were too weak to do so; they were apparently content to merely preserve the constitutional forms out of which the spirit had temporarily vanished. Henry, however, made no important changes in the doctrines of the old Church. The ecclesiastical system which he established was simply " popery without the pope ;" or, rather, it was popery with himself as pope. He gave, indeed, the English Bible to his subjects, but he himself was to be its interpreter. As the creed of the prince so the creed of the people was a principle somewhat widely accepted in those days ; but Henry was the first secular prince, and also the last, who arrogated to himself the sole right of shaping the creed. It was impossible that such a state of things should continue long. It was certain that the nation would either go forward or go back. Though the king arranged in his will to perpetuate his system, the will was broken before he was in his grave. Under his son doctrinal changes followed each other in quick succession. Under his daughter Mary the nation swung back, for a brief period, to the old faith ; it had not yet fully made up its mind. But under Elizabeth it again moved onward, and within a year after her accession the new creed assumed definite shape, and the Church of England was separated, forever, as it proved, from the Church of Rome.

The English Church was now the State Church, established by law, and, in theory, the whole nation was included in it ; but, in fact, the Catholics, who still composed nearly half of the nation, already stood outside of it ; and within it there was a small, but growing, opposition party—the later Puritans—who advocated still further change. Between these two extremes the government of Elizabeth attempted to steer a middle course, and to make the Catholics and Puritans conform to the established system. The principle of toleration was then acknowledged by no sect or party. The mediæval idea that Church and State were inseparable, that those who stood outside of the one stood outside of the other, and were, therefore, not only heretics, but also rebels and traitors, was still prevalent in the minds of men. In attempting to enforce conformity, the ministers of Elizabeth were acting in accordance with the accepted ideas of the age. But neither the English Catholics nor the Church of Rome were inclined to accept the situation and give up the struggle. They still hoped that England might yet be recovered to the papal see, and the temptation to undertake its recovery was well-nigh irresistible. Elizabeth stood alone, the last of her race in the direct line. In the eyes of the Catholics her title was worthless. They regarded her Catholic rival, Mary Stuart, as the rightful queen. To dethrone Elizabeth and put Mary in her place seemed to them simple and feasible, and the most direct way to secure the restoration of Catholicism in England. The personal rivalry between the two queens soon divided the nation, and ultimately broadened out into a struggle between Protestant England and Catholic Europe, a struggle which was brought to a close by the execution of Mary and the defeat of the Armada.

Meanwhile the Puritans had been increasing in numbers and influence. They did not at first propose to go out of the established Church, but, remaining in it, to introduce a simpler and, in their view, a purer form of worship. Possibly, if a few concessions as to outward forms and ceremonies had been promptly made, a schism might have been prevented. But the government showed an uncompromising spirit, and the Puritans passed from outward forms to attack the very basis of the established Church. They denied the right of the State to coerce in matters of religion. They formed separate assemblies, and at length organized separate Churches, worshiping in their own way, and growing apace in spite of penal laws. They began to appear in considerable numbers in the House of Commons, and their influence in that body was relatively all the greater because the Catholics had already been, by law, excluded from it. Since the days of Henry VIII. the Commons had been gradually recovering their lost prestige and power. Their growing importance is evidenced by the various devices to which the government resorted to keep them under control. The Puritan element added largely to their strength, for the Puritans, unlike the Anglicans, thoroughly believed in the right and duty of resisting the encroachments of arbitrary power. They often came into collision with Elizabeth, but she never allowed a quarrel to go too far; her unerring tact told her when and how to yield. Above all, she never challenged them to a combat over the disputed ground. Moreover, she was greatly beloved, and the Commons themselves, now that she was growing old, were not inclined to force her hand. But they stood ready, as soon as the grave closed over her, to assert and maintain their rights and privileges against her successor.

James met the Commons with the peculiarly Stuart doctrine of the divine right of kings. That doctrine was the cardinal point in his political creed. He also firmly believed that the Established Church was an indispensable support of the monarchy. "No bishop, no king," was his favorite saying. He told the Puritan clergy that they must conform, or he would harry them out of the land. He told the Commons that his prerogative was above the law, and could not be touched; that their so-called rights and privileges were merely matters of grace, conceded to them by former sovereigns, and revocable at his pleasure. He forbade them to meddle with affairs of state, as these were matters too high for their comprehension. He presumed to tax the country without the authority of Parliament, and he pursued a foreign policy which he knew to be highly distasteful to the nation. By dismissing Chief-Justice Coke, the greatest lawyer of his day, from his high position, because he showed a spirit of independence, he taught the judges that he would brook no opposition from them. He silenced the bar by imprisoning some of its most prominent members, and he alienated the House of Lords, which had regained a portion of its earlier power, by a wanton attack upon its rights. And withal, in sharp contrast with his lofty pretensions and arbitrary acts, he was defective in body and mind, lacking in courage, low in his tastes, and thoroughly unkingly in all his ways.

Among all the natural and constitutional barriers which then existed against the power of the crown—the church, the bench, the bar, the House of Lords, and the House of Commons—the last was the only one that had both the ability and the inclination to offer any effectual resistance. The Commons met the encroachments of James with becoming spirit; they protested in firm, but temperate, language, and in a thoroughly loyal tone, against his violations of their privileges and of the rights of the nation. They successfully asserted their right to withhold grants of money until grievances were redressed; they impeached two of his ministers; and in other points they managed to hold their own against James. But in his son, Charles I., they had to deal with a far more dangerous antagonist. In him they found a man who, though conscientious in private life, was, in all his public acts, and especially in his dealings with his Parliaments, false to the core; who was capable of making a solemn public promise, of putting his name to a statute, without any realizing sense of the moral obligation thus assumed. They found it impossible to control such a king by strictly constitutional means; and, as he persisted in his arbitrary courses, and, as the conflict between him and them developed, they were fairly forced to encroach on his lawful prerogative, to make him harmless by depriving him even of those powers which a constitutional king ought to wield. In the first three Parliaments of the reign which were called, quarreled with, and dissolved in quick succession, and in the fourth, which came together after a long interval of arbitrary power, the Commons presented a united front against the king. Even in the famous Long Parliament itself, which met when the situation was already revolutionary, they at first stood together as one man in the assertion of their rights. The attainder of Strafford (May, 1641) was the first measure on which the House divided, and on that there was only a small minority in favor of the earl. But from this time on, the minority steadily increased. In revolutions, men and parties are generally driven beyond the goal at which they originally aimed. In this revolution the Commons had started with the idea of compelling the king to exercise his sovereign power within constitutional limits, and now, whether they were distinctly conscious of it or not, they were, in reality, seeking to transfer the sovereign power to themselves. This they regarded as the only way in which they could secure the nation's liberties against such an inveterate cozener as Charles. They had already shorn him of much of his prerogative, and when they now proceeded to take away the rest, and make him a king merely in name, many of those who had hitherto acted with them drew back. Some were moved to pity by his defenseless condition; others were sincerely attached to the established Church, whose very existence was threatened by the Puritan party; others still were actuated by a feeling of loyalty to the reigning house. And so, as the dispute drifted into civil war, nearly half of the Parliament and of the nation sided with the king.

On the parliamentary side the war was, at first, conducted in a lame and spiritless way. The Presbyterians, who were the conservative wing of the Puritan party, predominated both in the House of Commons and in the army. They, in union with the Scots, wished to establish their own religious system in place of Anglicanism, and to beat the king just enough to bring him to their own terms, but, in no case, to depose him or overthrow the monarchy. The Independents, on the other hand, who were the radical Puritans, believed in religious toleration and in the right of each separate congregation to organize itself in its own way; and they were ready, in case of necessity, to get rid of Charles and of the monarchy as well. The wonderful success of their leader, Oliver Cromwell, and of his famous cavalry, the Ironsides, soon brought them to the front. They got control of the army, reorganized it, under Fairfax and Cromwell, in accordance with their own ideas, and practically ended the war by their great victory over the king's forces at Naseby (1645). The king took refuge with the Scots (May, 1646). The Scots, failing to convert him to Presbyterianism, delivered him over to the English Presbyterians (January, 1647), and a little later he was seized by the army (June, 1647). The Presbyterians, who were still a majority in the Parliament, thereupon attempted to get rid of the army by disbanding it; and the army, refusing to disband until it had secured the great object for which it had entered the war, liberty of conscience, marched upon London, and expelled from the Parliament some of the obnoxious Presbyterian leaders. Thus the independence of the Parliament was destroyed.

The army leaders, with Cromwell at the head, now made an honest, but ineffectual, attempt to come to terms with the king. Charles intrigued with all parties, and was false toward all. His intrigues, however, soon led to a combination between the Scots and the English Presbyterians and royalists against the Independent army, and the result was a renewal of the civil war (1648). Before marching out to battle the army resolved, in case it should be successful in suppressing this new movement, to call "Charles Stuart, that man of blood," to a strict account for his misdeeds. The combination was speedily crushed, and the army at once proceeded to bring the king to justice. It weeded out the Presbyterians from the Parliament, leaving "the Rump," which was composed entirely of Independents. That body established an extraordinary tribunal which tried and condemned the king; it voted the House of Lords to be useless, declared that all power rested with the Commons, abolished the monarchy, and set up a republic or commonwealth in its place.

But the situation of the new government was exceedingly precarious. Nine tenths of the English people were opposed to it, Ireland and Scotland rejected it altogether, while abroad it encountered at once the bitter hostility of foreign powers. It owed its existence entirely to the army, and by the army alone it could be maintained. The task of establishing firmly its authority was intrusted to Cromwell. His brilliant campaigns in Ireland (1649) and Scotland (1650) reduced those countries to obedience, and made organized resistance in England impossible. At the same time they made him predominant in the new commonwealth, and he now used his great influence in trying to bring the country back as speedily as possible to a constitutional basis. He wanted a new Parliament, freely chosen, which should represent the three nations; he wanted reforms in the law and in the Church; and, above all, he wanted liberty of conscience. The Rump Parliament, on the other hand, already distrustful of the successful general and fearing a military dictatorship, sought to perpetuate its own power; and when it refused to fix a limit to its sessions, Cromwell drove it out (April, 1653). He then called a convention, composed of prominent men of his own party, to whom he intrusted the work of reconstructing the government. After a few months of trial, they resigned their authority back into his hands, and a Protectorate was established with him at the head (December, 1653). In a constitution which was drawn up, his power was limited by a council and a Parliament. Cromwell earnestly strove to rule within the limits imposed, and to prevent his government from degenerating into a military despotism. But he met with opposition on every side; many of his own party distrusted him; the new Parliament refused to recognize his authority, and had to be dissolved; the royalists and radicals intrigued against him; and he was forced, for a time, to rule as a despot. Yet his despotism was of a different kind from that of Charles. Cromwell used his power for the good of the nation, not for the destruction of its liberties. By his brilliant foreign policy he made the influence of England in Europe far greater than it had ever been before. The energy and ability he displayed surprised and dazzled even his enemies. A part of the nation, at last, began to realize, in some degree, at least, the inestimable value of the man as a ruler. A new constitution was drawn up, making him protector for life, and empowering him to name his successor. A new Parliament was called, and it seemed for the moment as if harmony would be restored, as if Parliament would become reconciled with Protectorate, and the proper limits of power be assigned to each. Many of the leading men of the nation urged Cromwell to take the title of king, but this he refused out of deference to the feelings of the army. In other matters, however, he complied with the wishes of those who were trying to work back to the forms of the old constitution. But the temporary harmony was destroyed by the establishment of a new House of Lords, a measure which aroused strong opposition among the well-meaning, but fanatical, republicans of the Lower House, and Cromwell was forced to dissolve this his last Parliament. His power still rested on the support of the army, and all his efforts to secure for it a legal and constitutional basis proved unavailing. For a few months after his death, the different factions were held in awe by the influence of his name; then party spirit broke forth, and, after a brief interval of chaos, the mass of the nation hastened with feverish anxiety to welcome back the returning Stuarts.

The Restoration was followed by a period of degradation without a parallel in the nation's history. In the earlier years of the reign of Charles the Second the reaction against Puritan England was extreme; the men and the measures of the commonwealth and of the protectorate were cast aside; even the Presbyterians, who had helped to restore the monarchy, were subjected to a bitter persecution. The royal palace was little better than a brothel. Every thing that savored of morality was laughed at. The literature of the day, with some noble exceptions, reeked with sensuality. The Church, content with her recovered wealth, made little effort to stem the tide of corruption. The government was brought, by the royal extravagance, to the verge of bankruptcy. The Parliament was subservient, and pandered to the vices of the sovereign. The king became the tool and pensioner of France. Both he and his ministers seemed alike destitute of political honor. The influence of England abroad, which had been so great in Cromwell's time, was almost annihilated, and important changes, directly affecting her interests, went forward on the Continent with as little regard for her as if she had been blotted from the map of Europe. But the reaction gradually spent its force, and then it appeared that the work of Cromwell and his associates had not been done in vain.   Slowly, but surely, an opposition to the prevailing *régime* arose and grew both in the Parliament and in the nation.   It culminated in the formation of the great Whig party (1679), while the supporters of the king took the name of Tories. The Whigs were temporarily overthrown in consequence of the factious spirit of their leaders in fomenting the Popish Plot and in trying to exclude the popish duke of York, later James the Second, from the succession to the crown.   But they rose again under James, and when that monarch attempted to subvert the laws by means of a standing army, a packed bench of judges, and a packed House of Commons, Whigs and Tories united in inviting William, prince of Orange, to invade the country and assist in restoring the ancient liberties of the nation.   Soon after William's landing James, deserted by all parties, fled to France, and the Convention Parliament, which was called, declared that he had abdicated, and elected William and Mary to fill the vacant throne.   The Declaration of Right, which took the form of a statute in the Bill of Rights, fixed in definite terms the relations between king and Parliament and between Parliament and the people; and a later statute, the Act of Settlement (1700), "made the English sovereign as much the creature of an act of Parliament as the pettiest tax-gatherer in his realm."

Thus the revolution of 1688 was accomplished, "the least violent and the most beneficent of all revolutions."   The result of causes which had been in operation for centuries, it definitely established the leading principles of the constitution, both in theory and in practice. The change of sovereign was one of the lesser benefits it conferred. It swept away forever, besides much other political rubbish, the doctrines of the divine right of kings, of absolute royal authority, and of the passive obedience of the subject, which had so long obstructed constitutional progress.   It transferred the paramount authority in the State from the king to the House of Commons, and gave the nation guarantees of liberty so simple, broad, and strong that they could neither be evaded nor revoked.   It fitly closed a long era of constitutional struggle, and at the same time prepared the way for a new development.

YALE COLLEGE, *May* 29, 1886.

CONTENTS.

PART I.

PART II.

Illustrations.

PART I.

SKETCHES

FROM

ENGLISH HISTORY.

I.

THE ROMAN OCCUPATION.—GREEN.

[At the time of Cæsar's invasion of Britain, B.C. 55, the land was inhabited by the Celts, who were members of the great Aryan family of nations to which the Romans themselves belonged. The natives were in a semi-barbarous condition, and, though they fought bravely for their homes, were no match for the trained legions of the Empire. Cæsar himself made no systematic attempt to subjugate the island ; but about a hundred years after him the work of conquest was begun in earnest and pushed steadily until all the country south of the Forth had submitted to the Roman arms. Britain remained a province of the Empire for three hundred and fifty years.]

THE island of Britain was the latest of Rome's conquests in the west. Though it had been twice attacked by Julius Cæsar, his withdrawal and the inaction of the earlier emperors promised it a continued freedom ; but a hundred years after Cæsar's landing, Claudius undertook its conquest, and so swiftly was the work carried out by his generals, and those of his successors, that before thirty years were over, the bulk of the country had passed beneath the Roman sway. The island was thus fortunate in the moment of its conquest. It was spared the pillage and exactions which ruined the provinces of Rome under the Republic, while it felt little of the evils which still clung to their administration under the earlier Empire. The age in which its organization was actively carried out was the age of the Antonines, when the provinces

2

became objects of special care on the part of the central government, and when the efforts of its administration were aided by peace without and a profound tranquillity within. The absence of all record of the change indicates the quietness and ease with which Britain was transformed into a ·Roman province. A census and a land-survey must have formed here, as elsewhere, indispensable preliminaries for the exactions of the poll-tax and the land-tax, which were the main burdens of Rome's fiscal system. Within the province the population would, in accordance with her invariable policy, be disarmed ; while a force of three legions was stationed, partly in the north to guard against the unconquered Britons, and partly in the west to watch over the tribes which still remained half-subdued. Though the towns were left in some measure to their own self-government, the bulk of the island seems to have been ruled by military and financial administrators, whose powers were practically unlimited. But, rough as their rule may have been, it secured peace and good order; and peace and good order were all that was needed to insure material development. This development soon made itself felt. Commerce sprang up in the ports of Britain. Its harvests became so abundant that it was able at need to supply the necessities of Gaul. Tin mines were worked in Cornwall, lead mines in Somerset and Northumberland, and iron mines in the Forest of Dean. The villas and homesteads which, as the spade of our archæologists prove, lay scattered over the whole face of the country, show the general prosperity of the island.

The extension of its road system, and the upgrowth of its towns, tell above all how rapidly Britain was incorporated into the general body of the empire. It is easy, however, to exaggerate the civilization of Britain. Even within the province south of the firths the evidence of inscriptions shows that large tracts of country lay practically outside the Roman life. Though no district was richer or more peopled than the south-west, our Devonshire and our Cornwall seem to have remained almost wholly Celtic. Wales was never really Romanized; its tribes were held in check by the legionaries at Chester and Caerleon, but as late as the beginning of the third century they called for repression from the Emperor Severus as much as the Picts. The valleys of the Thames and of the Severn were fairly inhabited, but there are fewer proofs of Roman settlement in the valley of the Trent; and, though the southern part of Yorkshire was rich and populous, Northern Britain, as a whole, was little touched by the new civilization. And even in the south this civilization can have had but little depth or vitality. Large and important as were some of its towns, hardly any inscriptions have been found to tell of the presence of a vigorous municipal life. Unlike its neighbor, Gaul, Britain contributed nothing to the intellectual riches of the empire; and not one of the poets or rhetoricians of the time is of British origin. Even moral movements found little foothold in the island. When Christianity became the religion of the empire, under the house of Constantine, Britain must have become nominally Christian; and the presence of British bishops at ecclesiastical councils is enough to prove that its Christianity was organized in the ordinary form. But as yet no Christian inscription or ornament has been found in any remains of earlier date than the close of the Roman rule; and the undoubted existence of churches at such places as Canterbury, or London, or St. Albans, only gives greater weight to the fact that no trace of such buildings has been found in the sites of other cities which have been laid open by archæological research.

Far, indeed, as was Britain from the center of the empire, had the Roman energy wielded its full force in the island it would have Romanized Britain as completely as it Romanized the bulk of Gaul. But there was little in the province to urge Rome to such an effort. It was not only the most distant of her western provinces, but it had little natural wealth, and it was vexed by a ceaseless border warfare with the unconquered Britons, the Picts, or Caledonians, beyond the northern firths. There was little in its material resources to tempt men to that immigration from the older provinces of the empire which was the main agent in civilizing a new conquest. On the contrary, the harshness of a climate that knew neither olive nor vine deterred men of the south from such a settlement.. The care with which every villa is furnished with its elaborate system of hot-air flues shows that the climate of Britain was as intolerable to the Roman provincial as that of India, in spite of punkahs and verandas, is to the English civilian or the English planter. The result was that the province remained a mere military department of the empire. It is a significant fact that the bulk of the monuments which have been found in Britain relate to military life. Its inscriptions on tombs are mostly those of soldiers. Its mightiest work was the great wall and line of legionary stations which guarded the province from the Picts. Its only historic records are records of border forays against the barbarians.

It was not merely its distance from the seat of rule, or the later date of its conquest that hindered the province from passing completely into the general body of the empire. Its physical and its social circumstances offered yet greater obstacles to any effectual civilization. In spite of its roads, its towns, and its mining works, it remained, even at the close of the Roman rule, an "isle of blowing woodland," a wild and half-reclaimed country, the bulk of whose surface was occupied by forest and waste. The rich and lower soil of the river valleys, indeed, what is now the favorite home of agriculture, had, in the earliest times, been densely covered with primæval scrub; and the only open spaces were those whose nature fitted them less for the growth of trees, the chalk downs and oolitic uplands that stretched in long lines across the face of Britain from the Channel to the Northern Sea. It is mainly in the natural

clearings of the uplands that the population concentrated itself
at the close of the Roman rule, and it is over these districts
that the ruins of the villas or country houses of the Roman
land-owner are most thickly scattered.

The cities of the province were, indeed, thoroughly
Romanized. Within the walls of towns such as Lincoln
or York, towns governed by their own municipal officers
guarded by massive walls, and linked together by the net-
work of roads which reached from one end of the island to
the other, law, language, political and social life, all were of
Rome. But if the towns were thoroughly Romanized, it seems
doubtful, from the few facts that remain to us, whether Roman civilization had made much impression on the bulk of the
provincials, or whether the serf-like husbandmen, whose cab-
ins clustered round the luxurious villas of the provincial
land-owners, or the yet more servile miners of Northumbria,
and the Forest of Dean, were touched by the arts and knowledge of their masters. The use of the Roman language may
be roughly taken as marking the progress of the Roman civilization; and, though Latin had all but wholly superseded
the languages of the conquered peoples in Spain and Gaul, its
use was probably limited in Britain to the townsfolk, and to
the wealthier proprietors without the towns. Over large
tracts of country the rural Britons seem to have remained
apart from their conquerors, not only speaking their own
language, and owning some traditional allegiance to their
native chiefs, but retaining their native system of law. Imperial edicts had long since extended Roman citizenship to
every dweller within the empire; but the wilder provincials
may have been suffered to retain in some measure their own
usages, as the Zulu or Maori is suffered to retain them, though
subject in theory to British law, and entitled to the full privileges of British subjects. The Welsh laws, which we possess in
a later shape, are undoubtedly, in the main, the same system of
early customs which Rome found existing among the Britons

in the days of Claudius and Cæsar; and the fact that they remained a living law when her legions withdrew proves their continuance throughout the four hundred years of her rule, as it proves the practical isolation from Roman life and Roman civilization of the native communities which preserved them.

II.

THE ENGLISH CONQUEST AND SETTLEMENT.—GARDINER.

[At the beginning of the fifth century the Roman Empire was in a state of dissolution. The barbarian tribes had broken into it in many directions, and in 410 the Goths, under Alaric, took and sacked Rome itself. In the following year the government, needing all its available forces at home, withdrew its army of occupation from Britain. The Britons, thus left to themselves, remained nominally independent for sixty years. But, accustomed as they had so long been to imperial protection, they were unable to defend themselves. They were attacked from the north by the Picts and Scots, who had never been brought under the Roman sway, as well as by the Teutonic or German pirates from the south. The latter they invited to assist them against their northern enemies. Quarrels arose between them and their allies. The Teutons, among whom the Angles predominated, came in ever-increasing numbers. The natives made a desperate resistance. The struggle lasted a hundred and fifty years. At the end of that period the invaders had succeeded in establishing ten or twelve petty kingdoms on the soil of Britain.]

WHEN, in the middle of the fifth century, our Teutonic ancestors landed on the shores of Britain, they carved out settlements for themselves; they were Jutes and Saxons and Angles from the coast which stretches from Jutland to the mouths of the Elbe and Weser. Over the horror of the struggle a thick darkness has settled down, and, with the exception of one lightning-flash from a Celtic writer, it was only by its leading features, by a battle or a siege traditionally remembered, that any portion of it could be recovered when civilization and its power of recording events again spread over the land. At the end of a century and a half the Teutonic settlers occupied the whole of the eastern half of the land, from the Forth to the Straits of Dover, and from the coast of the German Ocean to the Severn. Over all this tract the Low German speech of the invaders was to be heard. To what extent the British population had disappeared is a matter of controversy. It is a point on which no certain knowledge is attainable. The invaders did not enter the island impressed with the dignity of Roman civilization. They knew nothing of the Roman speech. They seized upon the lands of the Britons. They stormed and sacked their cities. They probably carried off their daughters to be their wives or concubines. The men who resisted were slain as wild beasts are slain, without thought of mercy. Of the rest, some were reduced to slavery, some may have kept up a precarious independence in the woods. Under such circumstances a population suffers fearful diminution from misery and starvation. The weak and the old, with the young child, the hope of future generations, perish for lack of food. Yet, whatever the numerical amount of the survivors may have been, the general result is certain. The Teutonic speech, save in a few words used principally by women and slaves, prevailed every-where. The Teutonic law, the Teutonic way of life, was the rule of the land. The Teutonic heathenism was unchanged. The Celtic element, whether it was larger or smaller, was absorbed, and left scarcely a trace behind.

If the history of the settlement is to be gathered from scanty tradition, the character and institutions of the settlers have to be inferred from that which is known of them in their own land, and from that which is known of them later in the land of their adoption. Fierce and masterful as they were, they were not barbarians, except in antithesis to the civilization of Rome. The stage which they had reached was very much that of the Homeric Greeks, if we allow for the greater inclemency of a northern sky. Each tribe was complete in itself. It had its own assembly of freemen, whose voice was decisive in regulating its actions. At its head was a chief, the ealdorman, as he was named, who guided its deliberations, and who, after its arrival in England at least, headed it in war. The freemen themselves were composed of two ranks, eorls and ceorls. The eorls, or nobles by birth, whose origin is lost in the mists of the past, had an honorary pre-eminence. Their voice was of greater weight, their life was of greater value, their share of booty larger. But they did not make the State, though they had, doubtless, much to do with its direction. In fact, there was nothing that we should now call political life in existence. New legislation there was none. The old customs, handed down from father to son in Germany, were adhered to in England, and the only question which could arise for deliberation was whether some new expedition should be undertaken against the enemy. Outside the assembly, as well as within it, all freemen were equal, however much they might differ in influence or wealth. Each man had his own share of the conquered land, and his share of pasturage or wood-cutting in the folkland—the common land that had been left undivided. The organization of which he formed a part did not, as in the empire, reach from the State to the individual, but from the individual to the State. Each township which, in an ecclesiastical form, became the parish of modern days, made its appearance once a month, in the hundred mote, to decide quarrels and to witness contracts ; while the members of the tribe met twice a year to decide matters of more general importance. As every man was a judge—unless, indeed, the practice of attending the hundred mote by a deputation of the reeve, or head man, and four best men of the township, had already been adopted—so every man was a soldier. The assembly was, in truth, the tribe in arms, and the eorls and the ealdormen could but lead, they could not constrain, the will of their fellow-tribesmen.

Left in the positions they had originally occupied, the tribes might have retained these institutions unaltered for centuries. The progress of the war necessitated expansion and amalgamation in order that greater force might be brought to bear on the enemy. As it had been with Rome so it was now with the English tribe. The system of popular assemblies had reached its limit. The men of Dorset or the men of Norfolk could come up without difficulty to the place of meeting. The men of a State reaching from the Severn to the borders of Sussex could not come up. The idea of delegation, if it had as yet existed at all, had not acquired sufficient strength to suggest the idea of a general collective council. Recourse was had to a different factor in the commonwealth. Of all human occupations war requires the most complete discipline and the most prompt obedience to a single chief. Naturally, therefore, it was the chief, the ealdorman, who gained most by the changes wrought by war. Every-where he took the higher title of king, and in taking its title he gained a higher standing-point. He was the bond of union between many tribes. The ealdorman who now presided in the tribal assembly derived his authority from him, even if he owed his position to an older tribal authority. At the end of the sixth century some ten or twelve kingdoms existed, and the authority of the kings would, doubtless, tend to increase in civil matters as they grew more successful as leaders in war.

Yet, growing as it was, the king's authority was by no means absolute. The power which the king wielded could only be exercised in accordance with the wishes of the armed force, and that armed force was still, in great measure, composed of the contingents of the freemen of the several tribes. It is true that it was not so altogether. By an old German custom a great man had been accustomed to entertain a body of followers—gesiths, as they were called in England—who attached themselves, not to the tribe, but to the person of
2*

him whom they followed, and upon whose bounty they lived. For him they fought, and for him they were ready to die. They held it disgraceful to forsake him in battle, or even to leave the field alive if he were lying dead upon it. No doubt, if we possessed a history of those times, we should find that these two component parts of the king's army were also component parts of his council, and the witan, or wise men, without whose advice he did not venture to act in any important matter, were, some of them, the chief men of his personal following; some of them leading eorls, or land-owners, from the various populations which were blended together under his rule. But, however this council may have been formed, it had no immediate organic connection with the people. Its members were not elected from beneath. They became councilors either from their own position in life, or as selected by the king. As long as there was a powerful enemy in the field this breach in the continuity of the constitution might not be felt; but it was, none the less, a source of danger.

The judicial arrangements of our ancestors were those of a strong-handed but law-loving race, in which each man was ready to do himself right with his own hand, but in which there was a general understanding that feuds should not be perpetual. The notion that it was the duty of the State to punish crime, and the notion that the criminal himself was any the worse for the crime which he had committed, would have been alike unintelligible to them. All that they saw was that it was in their power to enforce upon the kindred of a murdered man, or upon him who had suffered a loss of property, the acceptance of a weregild, or money payment, in satisfaction of the injury done to them, which they might otherwise have avenged by the slaughter of the aggressor. As, again, the power of taking vengeance was different in different ranks—as the relations of a murdered king were more likely to take effectual vengeance than the relations of an eorl or a simple ceorl, and as they, therefore, required more to induce them to draw back—a larger money payment was enforced in proportion to the rank of the person injured. As, too, the State had no interest in the matter, excepting to prevent continual private warfare, it had no trained police to seize the criminal, and no trained advocates or judges to investigate evidence. It looked to the kindred of the accused person to present him before the popular assembly at which he was to be tried, or to pay his weregild in his stead. If he denied his guilt he had to bring others to swear that he was innocent, and the declaration of the belief of these compurgators in his favor was accepted as satisfactory. If he failed to find compurgators he had still the resource of appealing to the ordeal, doubtless performed, in heathen times, in some specially sacred spot. The assembled people, who acted as his judges, contented themselves with seeing that the provisions of ancient customs were duly carried out.

III.

CONVERSION OF THE ENGLISH.—Milman.

[The conquerors had scarcely established themselves in the land when a contest began between the different English kingdoms for supremacy. To the war between Britons and Englishmen was added a war between Englishmen and Englishmen. The struggle went on for two hundred years, and culminated in the final supremacy of Wessex. Long before the end of this period, however, an event had occurred which contributed powerfully to the work of consolidation and unification. This was the conversion of the heathen English to Christianity. The work was accomplished in the south by Roman, in the north by Irish, missionaries. The two tides of Christian influence met in the center of England. After a brief struggle the Roman party triumphed, in 664, at the Synod of Whitby, and Archbishop Theodore organized the new Church on the Roman model.]

Nothing certain is known concerning the first promulgation of the Gospel in Roman Britain. There can be no doubt, however, that conquered and half-civilized Britain, like the rest of the Roman Empire, gradually received, during the second and third centuries, the faith of Christ. The depth of her Christian cultivation appears from her fertility in saints, and in heretics. But all were swept away, the worshipers of the saints and the followers of the heretics, by the Teutonic conquest. The German races which overran the island came from a remote quarter yet unpenetrated by the missionaries of the Gospel. They knew nothing of Christianity but as the religion of that abject people whom they were driving before them into their mountains and fortresses. Christianity receded, with the conquered Britons, into the mountains of Wales, or toward the borders of Scotland, or took refuge among the peaceful and flourishing monasteries of Ireland. The clergy fled, perhaps fought, with their flocks, and neither sought nor found opportunities of amicable intercourse, which might have led to the propagation of their faith; while the savage pagans demolished the churches and monasteries, with the other vestiges of Roman civilization. They were little disposed to worship the God of a conquered people or to adopt the religion of a race whom they either despised as weak and unwarlike, or held as stubborn and implacable enemies. Nor was there sufficient charity in the British Christians to enlighten the paganism of their conquerors.

Happily Christianity appeared in an opposite quarter. Its missionaries from Rome were unaccompanied by any of these causes of mistrust and dislike. It came into that part of the kingdom the farthest removed from the hostile Britons. It was the religion of the powerful kingdom of the Franks; the influence of Bertha, the Frankish princess, the wife of King Ethelbert, wrought, no doubt, more powerfully for the reception of the faith than the zeal and eloquence of Augustine.

Gregory the Great, it has been said, before his accession to the papacy, had set out on the sublime though desperate mission of the reconquest of Britain from idolatry. It was Gregory who commissioned the monk Augustine to venture on this glorious service. Yet so fierce and savage, according to the common rumor, were the Anglo-Saxon inhabitants of Britain, that Augustine shrank from the wild and desperate enterprise; he hesitated before he would throw himself into the midst of a race of barbarous unbelievers, of whose language he was ignorant. Gregory would allow no retreat from a mission which he had himself been prepared to undertake, and which would not have appalled, even under less favorable circumstances, his firmer courage.

The fears of Augustine as to this wild and unknown land proved exaggerated. The monk and his forty followers landed without opposition on the shores of Britain. They sent to announce themselves as a solemn embassage from Rome, to offer to the King of Kent the everlasting bliss of heaven, an eternal kingdom in the presence of the true and living God. To Ethelbert, though not unacquainted with Christianity, for, by the terms of his marriage, Bertha, the Frankish princess, had stipulated for the free exercise of her religion, there must have been something strange and imposing in the landing of these peaceful missionaries on a shore still constantly swarming with fierce pirates, who came to plunder or to settle among their German kindred. The name of Rome must have sounded, though vague, yet awful, to the ear of the barbarian. Any dim knowledge of Christianity which he had acquired from his Frankish wife would be blended with mysterious veneration for the pope, the great high-priest, the vicar of Christ and of God upon earth. With the cunning suspicion which mingles with the dread of the barbarian, the king insisted that the first meeting should be in the open air, as giving less scope for magic arts, and not under the roof of a house. Augustine and his followers met the king with all the pomp which they could command, with a crucifix of silver in the van of their procession, a picture of the Redeemer borne aloft, and chanting their litanies for the salvation of the king and his people. "Your words and offers," replied the king, "are fair; but they are new to me, and, as yet, unproved; I cannot abandon at once the faith of my Anglian ancestors." But the missionaries were entertained with courteous hospitality. Their severely monastic lives, their constant prayers, fastings, and vigils, with their confident demeanor, impressed more and more favorably the barbaric mind. Rumor attributed to them many miracles. Before long the king of Kent was an avowed convert; his example was followed by many of his noblest subjects. No compulsion was used, but it was manifest that the royal favor inclined to those who received the royal faith.

The British Church, secluded in the fastnesses of Wales, could not but hear of the arrival of the Roman missionaries, and of their success in the conversion of the Saxons. Augustine and his followers could not but inquire with deep interest concerning their Christian brethren in the remote parts of the island. It was natural that they should enter into communication; unhappily they met to dispute on points of difference, not to join in harmonious fellowship on the broad grounds of their common Christianity. The British Church followed the Greek usage in the celebration of Easter; they had some other points of ceremonial, which, with their descent, they traced to the East; and the zealous missionaries of Gregory could not comprehend the uncharitable inactivity of the British Christians, which had withheld the blessings of the Gospel from their pagan conquerors. The Roman and the British clergy met, it is said, in solemn synod. The Romans demanded submission to their discipline, and the implicit adoption of the western ceremonial on the contested points. The British bishops demurred; Augustine proposed to place the issue of the dispute on the decision of a miracle. The miracle was duly performed—a blind man brought forward and restored to sight. But the miracle made not the slightest impression on the obdurate Britons. They demanded a second meeting and resolved to put the Christianity of the strangers to a singular test, a moral proof with them more convincing than an apparent miracle. True Christianity, they said, "is meek and lowly of heart. Such will be this man (Augustine), if he be a man of God. If he be haughty and ungentle he is not of God, and we may disregard his words. Let the Romans arrive first at the synod. If on our approach he rises from his seat to receive us with meekness and humility, he is the servant of Christ, and we will obey him. If he despises us and remains seated, let us despise him." Augustine sat, as they drew near, in unbending dignity. The Britons at once refused obedience to his commands, and disclaimed him as their metropolitan. The indignant Augustine (to prove his more genuine Christianity) burst out into stern denunciations of their guilt in not having preached the Gospel to their enemies. He prophesied—a prophecy which could hardly fail to hasten its own fulfillment —the divine vengeance by the arms of the Saxons. So complete was the alienation, so entirely did the Anglo-Saxon clergy espouse the fierce animosities of the Anglo-Saxons, and even imbitter them by their theologic hatred, that the gentle Beda relates with triumph, as a manifest proof of the divine wrath against the refractory Britons, a great victory over that wicked race, preceded by a massacre of twelve hundred British clergy, chiefly monks of Bangor, who stood aloof on an eminence praying for the success of their countrymen.

IV.

THE EARLY MONASTERIES.—ALLEN.

[The religious activity of the time showed itself mainly in the planting
and endowment of monastic colonies, which gradually transformed the
face of the country. " In this monastic movement two strangely contrasted
impulses worked together to change the very aspect of the new England
and the new English society. The one was the passion for solitude, the
first outcome of the religious impulse given by the conversion ; a passion
for communing apart with themselves and with God, which drove men into
waste and woodland and desolate fen. The other was the equally new
passion for social life on the part of the nation at large; the outcome of its
settlement and well-doing on the conquered soil, and yet more of the influence of the new religion, coming as it did from the social civilization of
the older world, and invariably drawing men together by the very form of
its worship and its belief."]

IT was mainly by means of the monasteries that Christianity
became a great civilizing and teaching agency in England.
Those who judge monastic institutions only by their later and
worst days, when they had, perhaps, ceased to perform any
useful function, are apt to forget the benefits which they conferred upon the people in the earlier stages of their existence. The state of England during this first Christian
period was one of chronic and bloody warfare. There was
no regular army, but every freeman was a soldier, and raids
of one English tribe upon another were every-day occur-
rences ; while pillaging frays on the part of the Welsh, followed by savage reprisals on the part of the English, were
still more frequent. We catch glimpses, from time to time,
of the unceasing strife between each folk and its neighbors,
besides many hints of intestine struggles between prince
and prince, or of rivalries between one petty shire and others of the same kingdom.

With such a state of affairs as this it became a matter of
deep importance that there should be some one institution

where the arts of peace might be carried on in safety, where agriculture might be sure of its reward, where literature and science might be studied, and where civilizing influences might be safe from interruption or rapine. The monasteries gave an opportunity for such an ameliorating influence to spring up. They were spared, even in war, by the reverence of the people for the Church; and they became places where peaceful minds might retire for honest work and learning and thinking, away from the fierce turmoil of a still essentially barbaric and predatory community. At the same time they encouraged the development of this very type of mind by turning the reproach of cowardice, which it would have carried with it in heathen times, into an honor and a mark of holiness. Every monastery became a center of light and of struggling culture for the surrounding district. They were at once, to the early English recluse, universities and refuges, places of education, of retirement, and of peace in the midst of a jarring and discordant world.

In the Roman south many, if not all, of the monasteries seem to have been planned on the regular models; but in the north, where the Irish missionaries had borne the largest share in the work of conversion, the monasteries were irregular bodies on the Irish plan, where an abbot or abbess ruled over a mixed community of monks and nuns. Hild, a member of the Northumbrian princely family, founded such an abbey at Streoneshalch (Whitby), made memorable by numbering among its members the first known English poet, Caedmon. St. John of Beverley, Bishop of Hexham, set up a similar monastery at the place with which his name is so closely associated. The Irish monks themselves founded others at Lindisfarne and elsewhere. Even in the south some Irish abbeys existed. In process of time, however, as the union with Rome grew stronger, all these houses conformed to the more regular usage, and became monasteries of the ordinary Benedictine type.

The civilizing value of the monasteries can hardly be over-rated.   Secure in the peace conferred upon them by a religious sanction, the monks became the builders of schools, the drainers of marsh-land, the clearers of forest, the tillers of heath. Many of the earliest religious houses rose in the midst of what had been trackless wilds.   Peterborough and Ely grew up on islands of the fen county.   Crowland gathered round the cell of Guthlac in the midst of a desolate mere.   Evesham occupied a glade in the wild forests of the western march. Glastonbury, an old Welsh foundation, stood on a solitary islet where the abrupt knoll of the Tor looks down upon the broad waste of the Somersetshire marshes.   Beverley, as its name imports, had been a haunt of beavers before the monks began to till its fruitful dingles.   In every case agriculture soon turned the wild lands into orchards and corn-fields, or drove drains through the fens which converted their marshes into meadows and pastures for the long-horned English cat-tle.   Roman architecture, too, came with the Roman Church. We hear nothing before of stone buildings; but Eadwine erected a church of stone at York, under the direction of Paulinus ; and Bishop Wilfrith, a generation later, restored and decorated it, covering the roof with lead and filling the windows with panes of glass.   Masons had already been set-tled in Kent, though Benedict, the founder of Wearmouth and Jarrow, found it desirable to bring over others from the Franks.   Metal-working had always been a special gift of the English, and their gold jewelry was well made even be-fore the conversion, but it became still more noticeable after the monks took the craft into their own hands.   Beda men-tions mines of copper, iron, lead, silver, and jet.   Abbot Benedict not only brought manuscripts from Rome, which were copied and imitated in his monasteries at Wearmouth and Jarrow, but he also brought over glass-blowers, who in-troduced the art of glass-making into England.   Cuthbreht, Beda's scholar, writes to Lull, asking for workmen who can make glass vessels. Bells appear to have been equally early introductions. Roman music, of course, accompanied the Roman liturgy. The connection established with the clergy of the continent favored the dispersion of European goods throughout England. We constantly hear of presents, consisting of skilled handicraft, passing from the civilized south to the rude and barbaric north. Wilfrith and Benedict journeyed several times to and from Rome, enlarging their own minds by intercourse with Roman society, and returning laden with works of art or manuscripts of value. Beda was acquainted with the writings of all the chief classical poets and philosophers, whom he often quotes. We can only liken the results of such intercourse to those which, in our own time, have proceeded from the opening of Japan to western ideas, or of the Hawaiian Islands to European civilization and European missionaries. The English school, which soon sprang up at Rome, and the Latin schools, which soon sprang up at York and Canterbury, are precise equivalents of the educational movements in both those countries which we see in our own day. The monks were to learn Latin and Greek " as well as they learned their own tongue," and were so to be given the key of all the literature and all the science that the world then possessed.

The monasteries thus became real manufacturing, agricultural, and literary centers on a small scale. The monks boiled down the salt of the brine-pits; they copied and illuminated manuscripts in the library; they painted pictures not without rude merit of their own; they ran rhines through the marshy moorlands; they tilled the soil with vigor and success. A new culture began to occupy the land —the culture whose fully-developed form we now see around us. But it must never be forgotten that in its origin it is wholly Roman and not at all Anglo-Saxon. Our people showed themselves singularly apt at embracing it, like the modern Polynesians, and unlike the American Indians; but they did not invent it for themselves. Our existing culture is not home-bred at all; it is simply the inherited and widened culture of Greece and Italy.

V.

ALFRED'S EARLY YEARS.—FREEMAN.

[It was in the reign of Ecgberht, king of Wessex, that all the English kingdoms were united for the first time under one ruler. But the young State was no sooner formed than it was forced to face a new danger in the invasion of the Northmen or Danes. These people came from the Scandinavian kingdoms of the north of Europe, were of the same blood as the English, but were far behind them in civilization, and were still heathen. They began to land in England, to harry the country, and to carry off their spoil. At first as robbers, then as settleis, and finally as conquerors, for two centuries they occupy a large space in English history. In the midst of their invasions Alfred ascended the West-Saxon throne, and a large portion of his life was devoted to beating off their attacks.]

WE now come to our great King Alfred, the best and greatest of all our kings. We know quite enough of his history to be able to say that he really deserves to be so called, though I must warn you that, just because he left so great a name behind him, people have been fond of attributing to him things which really belonged to others. Thus you may sometimes see nearly all our laws and customs attributed to Alfred, as if he had invented them all for himself. You will sometimes hear that Alfred founded trial by jury, divided England into counties, and did all kinds of other things. Now the real truth is that the roots and beginnings of most of these things are very much older than the time of Alfred, while the particular forms in which we have them now are very much later. But people have a way of fancying that every thing must have been invented by some particular man, and, as Alfred was more famous than any body else, they hit upon

Alfred as the most likely person to have invented them. But, putting aside fables, there is quite enough to show that there have been very few kings, and very few men of any sort, so great and good as King Alfred. Perhaps the only equally good king we read of is Saint Lewis of France; and, though he was quite as good, we cannot set him down as being so great and wise as Alfred. Certainly no king ever gave himself up more thoroughly than Alfred did fully to do the duties of his office. His whole life seems to have been spent in doing all he could for the good of his people in every way. And it is wonderful in how many ways his powers showed themselves. That he was a brave warrior is in itself no particular praise in an age when almost every man was the same. But it is a great thing for a prince, so large a part of whose time was spent in fighting, to be able to say that all his wars were waged to set free his country from the most cruel enemies. And we may admire, too, the wonderful way in which he kept his mind always straight and firm, never either giving way to bad luck or being puffed up by good luck. We read of nothing like pride or cruelty or injustice of any kind either toward his own people or toward his enemies. And if he was a brave warrior, he was many other things besides. He was a lawgiver; at least he collected and arranged the laws, and caused them to be most carefully administered. He was a scholar, and wrote and translated many books for the good of his people. He encouraged trade and enterprise of all kinds, and sent men to visit distant parts of the world and bring home accounts of what they saw. And he was a thoroughly good man and a devout Christian in all relations of life. In short, one hardly knows any other character in all history so perfect, there is so much that is good in so many different ways; and, though no doubt Alfred had his faults, like other people, yet he clearly had none, at any rate in the greater part of his life, which took away at all seriously from his general goodness.

One wonders that such a man was never canonized as a saint; most certainly many people have received that name who did not deserve it nearly so well as he did.

Alfred, or, as his name should really be spelled, Ælfred, was the youngest son of King Æthelwulf, and was born at Wantage, in Berkshire, in 849. His mother was Osburh, the first, or perhaps the second, wife of Æthelwulf, She was the daughter of Oslac, the king's cup-bearer, who came of the royal house of the Jutes in Wight. Now a story is told of Alfred and his mother, which you may, perhaps, have heard already, and which is such a beautiful tale that I am really sorry to have to say that it cannot possibly be true. We are told that up to the age of twelve years Alfred was fond of hunting and other sports, but that he had not been taught any sort of learning, not so much as to read his own tongue. But he loved the old English songs; and one day his mother had a beautiful book of songs, with rich pictures and fine painted initial letters, such as you may often see in ancient books. And she said to her children, "I will give this beautiful book to the one of you who shall first be able to read it." And Alfred said, "Mother, will you really give me the book when I have learned to read it?" And Osburh said, "Yes, my son." So Alfred went and found a master, and soon learned to read. Then he came to his mother and read the songs in the beautiful book, and took the book for his own.

Now it is a great pity that so pretty a story cannot be true, and I must tell you why it cannot. Alfred was sent to Rome to the pope when he was four years old; and if the pope took him as his "bishop-son," and anointed him to be king, one cannot help thinking that he would have taught him to read, and to learn Latin. And it is quite certain that he could do both very well in after life. Still this is not quite certain proof, as he might have learned afterward. But one thing is quite certain. Alfred was not twelve years old till 861. By that time his brothers were not children playing round their mother, but grown men and kings, and two of them, Æthelstan and Æthelbald, were dead. Moreover, in 861 Alfred's father, Æthelwulf, was dead, and his mother must have been dead also, as Æthelwulf married Judith in 856, when Alfred was only seven years old. If, then, any thing of the kind happened, it could not have been when Alfred was twelve years old, but before he was four. For in that year he went to Rome, and could never have seen his mother again, even if she were alive when he went. And for a child of four years old not to be able to read, is not so very wonderful a thing, even in our own time.*

In 871, on Æthelred's death, Alfred came to the crown, and he had at once to fight for his kingdom. The battle was at Wilton, near Salisbury, and does not seem to have been a very decisive one, as we read that the Danes were put to flight, and yet that they kept possession of the place of battle. And after the battle the Danes seem to have been tired : we read that they made peace with the West-Saxons, and there was peace, as far as Wessex was concerned, for a few years.

---

* I have seen in different books two attempts to get out of this difficulty, but I do not think either of them will do.

First, some suggest that Osburh was not dead when Æthelwulf married Judith, but that he had put her away, and that she might still have had her children about her. But of this there is no sort of proof, and when we read that a man, and especially a good man like Æthelwulf, married a second wife, we are bound to suppose that his first wife was dead, unless we have some clear proof that she was alive. And granting this, we still have the difficulty that, when Alfred was twelve years old, his brothers were not, as the story clearly implies, boys, but grown men and kings, and that some of them were dead.

Secondly, some suggest that the story really belongs, not to Alfred's mother, Osburh, but to his step-mother, Judith. Now it is really ridiculous to fancy that this young foreign girl would act as a careful mother to Æthelwulf's sons, some of whom must have been older than herself, and one of whom (Æthelbald) she was unprincipled enough to marry. Moreover, in 861 Æthelbald was already dead, and Judith had gone back into Gaul.

But they were all the while fighting and plundering and set-
tling in other parts of Britain, and in 876 they came again into
Wessex. We thus come to that part of Alfred's life which is
at once the saddest and the brightest. It was the time when
his luck was lowest and his spirit was highest. The army
under Guthrum, the Danish king of East-Anglia, came suddenly to Wareham, in Dorsetshire. The "Chronicle" says
that they "bestole"—that is, came secretly, or escaped—
from the West-Saxon army, which seems to have been
waiting for them. This time Alfred made peace with the
Danes, and they gave him some of their chief men for hos-
tages, and they swore to go out of the land, but they did not
keep their oath. . . .

And now we come to the terrible year 878, the greatest
and saddest and most glorious in all Alfred's life. In the
very beginning of the year, just after Twelfth-night, the Danish host again came suddenly—"bestole," as the Chronicle
says—to Chippenham. Then "they rode through the West-
Saxon's land, and there sat down, and mickle of the folk over
sea they drove, and of the others the most deal they rode
over, all but the King Alfred; he with a little band hardly
fared (went) after the woods and on the moor-fastnesses."
How can I tell you this better than in the words of the
Chronicle itself, only altering some words into their modern
shape, that you may the better understand them? But it is
quite certain that this time of utter distress lasted only a
very little while, for in a few months Alfred was again at the
head of an army and able to fight against the Danes. It must
have been at this time that the story of the cakes happened,
if it ever happened at all. The tale is quite possible, but
there is no proof of it being true. It is said that Alfred went
and stayed in the hut of a neatherd or swineherd of his, who
knew who he was, though his wife did not know him. One
day the woman set some cakes to bake, and bade the king,
who was sitting by the fire mending his bow and arrows, to

Alfred in the Herdsman's Hut.

tend them. Alfred thought more of his bow and arrows than he did of the cakes, and let them burn. Then the woman ran in, and cried out: "There, don't you see the cakes on fire? Then wherefore turn them not? You're glad enough to eat them when they're piping hot!"*

It is almost more strange when we are told by some that this swineherd or neatherd afterward became Bishop of Winchester. They say that his name was Denewulf, and that the king said that, though he was in so lowly a rank, he was naturally a very wise man. So he had him taught, and at last gave him the bishopric. But it is hard to believe this, especially as Denewulf, Bishop of Winchester, became bishop the very next year.

━━━━━━━•━━━━━━━

VI.

DUNSTAN, THE ECCLESIASTICAL STATESMAN.—GREEN.

[The struggle with the Danes gave a new direction to the growth of Wessex. By the Treaty of Wedmore (878) England was divided between Alfred and the Danish leader. Wessex lost her external supremacy, but her immediate territory was largely increased. The impulse, thus given, continued under Alfred's son and grandsons, until, in the reign of Eadgar, the boundaries of Wessex became co-extensive with those of the kingdom of England. This result seems to have been largely due to the able administration of Archbishop Dunstan.]

THE completion of the West-Saxon realm was, in fact, reserved for the hands, not of a king or warrior, but of a priest. Dunstan stands first in the line of ecclesiastical statesmen, who counted among them Lanfranc and Wolsey, and ended in Laud. He is still more remarkable in himself, in his own vivid personality, after eight centuries of revolution and change. He was born in the little hamlet of Glastonbury, the home of his father, Heorstan, a man of wealth and

---

* The woman's speech is put into two Latin verses. Most likely the whole-story comes from a ballad.

3

brother of the Bishop of Wells and of Winchester. It must have
been in his father's hall that the fair, diminutive boy, with his
scant but beautiful hair, caught his love for "the vain songs
of heathendom, the trifling legends, the funeral chaunts,"
which afterward roused against him the charge of sorcery.
Thence, too, he might have derived his passionate love of
music, and his custom of carrying his harp in hand on journey
or visit. Wandering scholars of Ireland had left their books
in the monastery of Glastonbury, as they left them along the
Rhine and the Danube; and Dunstan plunged into the study
of sacred and profane letters till his brain broke down in
delirium. So famous became his knowledge in the neighborhood that news of it reached the Court of Æthelstan; but
his appearance there was the signal for a burst of ill-will
among the courtiers. They drove him from the king's train,
threw him from his horse as he passed through the marshes,
and, with the wild passion of their age, trampled him under
foot in the mire. The outrage ended in fever, and Dunstan
rose from his sick-bed a monk. But the monastic profession
was then little more than a vow of celibacy, and his devotion
took no ascetic turn. His nature, in fact, was sunny, versatile,
artistic, full of strong affections, and capable of inspiring
others with affections as strong. Quick-witted, of tenacious
memory, a ready and fluent speaker, gay and genial in address, an artist, a musician, he was at the same time an inde-
fatigable worker at books, at building, at handicraft. As his
sphere began to widen we see him followed by a train of
pupils, busy with literature, writing, harping, painting, design-
ing. One morning a lady summons him to her house to
design a robe which she is embroidering, and as he bends
with her maidens over their toil, his harp, hung upon the
wall, sounds, without mortal touch, tones which the excited
ears around frame into a joyous antiphon.

From this scholar-life Dunstan was called to a wider sphere
of activity by the accession of Eadmund. But the old jeal-

St. Dunstan

ousies revived at his re-appearance at court, and, counting the game lost, Dunstan preferred again to withdraw. The king had spent the day in the chase; the red deer which he was pursuing dashed over Cheddar cliffs, and his horse only checked itself on the brink of the ravine at the moment when Eadmund, in the bitterness of death, was repenting of his injustice to Dunstan. He was at once summoned on the king's return. "Saddle your horse," said Eadmund, "and ride with me." The royal train swept over the marshes to his home; and the king, bestowing on him the kiss of peace, seated him in the abbot's chair as Abbot of Glastonbury. Dunstan became one of Eadmund's councilors, and his hand was seen in the settlement of the North. The league between Scot and Briton was finally broken up, and the fidelity of the Scots secured by their need of help in holding down their former ally. The settlement was soon troubled by the young king's death. As he feasted at Pucklechurch, in the May of 946, Leofa, a robber whom Eadmund had banished from the land, entered the hall, seated himself at the royal board, and drew sword on the cup-bearer when he bade him retire. The king sprang in wrath to his thane's aid, and seizing Leofa by the hair, flung him to the ground; but in the struggle the robber drove his dagger to Eadmund's heart. His death at once stirred fresh troubles in the North; the Danelagh rose against his brother and successor, Eadred, and some years of hard fighting were needed before it was again driven to own the English supremacy. But with its submission, in 954, the work of conquest was done. Dogged as his fight had been, the Northman at last owned himself beaten. From the moment of Eadred's final triumph all resistance came to an end. The Danelagh ceased to be a force in English politics. North might part anew from South; men of Yorkshire might again cross swords with men of Hampshire, but their strife was henceforth a local strife between men of the same people; it was a strife of

Englishmen with Englishmen, and not of Englishmen with Northmen.

The death of Eadred, in 955, handed over the realm to a child-king, his nephew, Eadwig. Eadwig was swayed by a woman of high lineage, Æthelgifu; and the quarrel between her and the older councilors of Eadred broke into open strife at the coronation feast. On the young king's insolent withdrawal to her chamber, Dunstan, at the bidding of the Witan, drew him roughly back to his seat. But the feast was no sooner ended than a sentence of outlawry drove the abbot over sea, while the triumph of Æthelgifu was crowned, in 957, by the marriage of her daughter to the king, and the spoliation of the monasteries which Dunstan had befriended. As the new queen was Eadwig's kinswoman, the religious opinion of the day regarded his marriage as incestuous, and it was followed by a revolution. At the opening of 958 Archbishop Odo parted the king from his wife by solemn sentence; while the Mercians and Northumbrians rose in revolt, proclaimed Eadwig's brother Eadgar their king, and recalled Dunstan. The death of Eadwig, a few months later, restored the unity of the realm; but his successor, Eadgar, was only a boy of fourteen, and throughout his reign the actual direction of affairs lay in the hands of Dunstan, whose elevation to the see of Canterbury set him at the head of the Church as of the State. The noblest tribute to his rule lies in the silence of our chroniclers. His work, indeed, was a work of settlement, and such a work was best done by the simple enforcement of peace. During the years of rest in which the stern hand of the Primate enforced justice and order, Northmen and Englishmen drew together into a single people. Their union was the result of no direct policy of fusion; on the contrary, Dunstan's policy preserved to the conquered Danelagh its local rights and local usages. But he recognized the men of the Danelagh as Englishmen: he employed Northmen in the royal service, and promoted them to high posts in Church and State. For the rest he trusted to time, and time justified his trust. The fusion was marked by a memorable change in the name of the land. Slowly as the conquering tribes had learned to know themselves by the one national name of Englishmen, they learned yet more slowly to stamp their name on the land they had won. It was not till Eadgar's day that the name of Britain passed into the name of Englaland, the land of Englishmen, England. The same vigorous rule which secured rest for the country during these years of national union, told on the growth of material prosperity. Commerce sprang into a wider life. The laws of Æthelred, which provide for the protection and regulation of foreign trade, only recognize a state of things which grew up under Eadgar. It was in Eadgar's day that London rose to commercial greatness.

———◆———

VII.

CNUT, THE GREAT DANISH KING.—Freeman.

[On the accession of the second Æthelred, named the Unready, the Danish wars began again, and soon passed into their third phase—an attempt on the part of the King of all Denmark to subjugate the kingdom of England. The fatal policy was adopted of buying off the invaders. This led to more frequent invasions, and to ever-increasing demands for money, until at length the country was exhausted and could pay no more ; while, under the enervating influences of the time, the English military system seems to have utterly broken down. The Conquest, nearly finished by Swegen, was completed by his son Cnut, who thus became King of all England. He won his success by unscrupulous means, but a great change came over him as soon as his power was firmly established.]

THIS gradual change in the disposition of Cnut makes him one of the most remarkable, and, to an Englishman, one of the most interesting, characters in history. There is no other instance—unless Rolf, in Normandy, be admitted as a forerunner on a smaller scale—of a barbarian conqueror, en-

tering a country simply as a ruthless pirate, plundering, burning, mutilating, slaughtering, without remorse, and then, as
soon as he is seated on the throne of the invaded land,
changing into a beneficent ruler and lawgiver, and winning
for himself a place side by side with the best and greatest of
its native sovereigns.   Cnut never became a perfect prince
like Ælfred.   An insatiable ambition possessed him throughout life, and occasional acts of both craft and violence disfig-
ure the whole of his career.   He always found some means,
by death, by banishment, by distant promotion, of getting rid
of any one who had once awakened his suspicions.   Reasons
of State were as powerful with him, and led him into as many
unscrupulous actions as any more civilized despot of later
times.   But Englishmen were not disposed to canvass the
justice of wars in which they won fame and plunder, while no
enemy ever set foot on their own shores.   They were as little
disposed to canvass the justice of banishments and executions
when, for many years, it was invariably a Dane, never an
Englishmen, who was the victim.   The law by which the
Dane settled in England presently became an Englishman,
received its highest carrying out in the person of the illustrious Danish king.   As far as England and Englishmen were
concerned, Cnut might seem to have acted on the principle
of the Greek poet, that unrighteousness might be fittingly
practiced in order to obtain a crown, but that righteousness
should be practiced in all other times and places.   The throne
of Cnut, established by devastating wars, by unrighteous executions, perhaps even by treacherous assassinations, was, when
once established, emphatically the throne of righteousness and
peace.   As an English king, he fairly ranks among the noblest
of his predecessors.

His best epitaph is his famous letter to his people on his
Roman pilgrimage.   Such a pilgrimage was an ordinary de-
votional observance, according to the creed of those times.
But in the eyes of Cnut it was clearly much more than a mere

perfunctory ceremony. The sight of the holy places stirred him to good resolves in matters both public and private, and, as a patriotic king, he employed his meeting with the pope, the emperor, and the Burgundian king, to win from all of them concessions which were profitable to the people of his various realms. No man could have written in the style in which Cnut writes to all classes of his English subjects, unless he were fully convinced that he possessed and deserved the love of his people. The tone of the letter is that of an absent father writing to his children. In all simplicity and confidence, he tells them the events of his journey, with what honors he had been received, and with what presents he had been loaded by the two chiefs of Christendom, and what privileges for his subjects, both English and Danish, he had obtained at their hands. He confesses the errors of his youth, and promises reformation of any thing which may still be amiss. All grievances shall be redressed; no extortions shall be allowed; King Cnut needs no money raised by injustice. These are surely no mere formal or hypocritical professions; every word plainly comes from the heart.

The same spirit reigns in the opening of his laws. The precept to fear God and honor the king here takes a more personal and affectionate form. First, above all things, are men one God ever to love and worship, and one Christendom with one consent to hold, and Cnut king to love with right truthfulness. The laws themselves embrace the usual subjects, the reformation of manners, the administration of justice, the strict discharge of all ecclesiastical duties, and the strict payment of all ecclesiastical dues. The feasts of the two new national saints, Eadward the King and Dunstan the Primate, are again ordered to be observed, and the observance of the former is again made to rest in a marked way on the authority of the Witan. The observance of the Lord's Day is also strongly insisted on; on that day there is to be no marketing, no hunting; even the holding of folkmotes is forbidden, except in cases of absolute necessity. All heathen superstition is to be forsaken, and the slave-trade is again denounced. The whole fabric of English society is strictly preserved. The king legislates only with the consent of his Witan. The old assemblies, the old tribunals, the old magistrates, retain their rights and powers. The king, as well as all inferior lords, is to enjoy all that is due to him ; the royal rights, differing somewhat in the West-Saxon and the Danish portions of the kingdom, are to be carefully preserved, and neither extended nor diminished in either country. No distinction, except the old local one, is made between Danes and Englishmen, and no sort of preference is made in favor of Cnut's own Danish followers.

And as Cnut's theory was, so was his practice. No king was more active in what was then held to be the first duty of kingship, that of constantly going through every portion of his realm to see with his own eyes whether the laws which he enacted were duly put in force. In short, after Cnut's power was once fully established, we hear no complaint against his government from any trustworthy English source. His hold upon the popular affection is shown by the number of personal anecdotes of which he is the hero. The man who is said, in the traditions of other lands, to have ordered the cold-blooded murder of his brother-in-law, and that in a church at the holy season of Christmas, appears in English tradition as a prince whose main characteristic is devotion mingled with good-humor. In the best-known tale of all, he rebukes the impious flattery of his courtiers, and hangs his crown on the image of the crucified Saviour. He bursts into song as he hears the chant of the monks of Ely, and rejoices to keep the festivals of the Church among them. He bountifully rewards the sturdy peasant who proves the thickness of the ice over which the royal sledge has to pass.

In ecclesiastical matters Cnut mainly, though not exclusively, favored the monks. His ecclesiastical appointments, especially that of the excellent Archbishop Æthelnoth, who had baptized or confirmed him, do him high honor. He was also, after the custom of the age, a liberal benefactor to various ecclesiastical foundations. He made provision for all the holy places which had in any way suffered during his own or his father's wars. Nor was his bounty confined to England, or even to his own dominions. On his Roman pilgrimage the poor and the churches of every land through which he passed shared his bountiful alms.

Such, then, was Cnut's internal government of England. The conqueror had, indeed, changed into a home-born king. At no earlier time had the land ever enjoyed so long a term of such unmixed prosperity.

VIII.

THE CLERGY IN THE EARLY MIDDLE AGES.—Stevenson.

[It is almost impossible to estimate too highly the influence of the clergy during the five hundred years that followed the conversion of the English to Christianity. Foremost in Church and State, they were the civilizers and educators of the English people. They fostered agriculture and the arts; they protected the poor and weak against the rich and powerful; they were the only barrier against the brute force of the times, and in a thousand channels they made their influence felt for good. Their very success, however, demoralized them, and we shall find them, in the later ages, working rather for the interests of their own order than for the good of the nation.]

THROUGHOUT the earlier ages the clergy represented the true principles of democracy. In the best sense of the word they were popular. They were of the people and for the people. They mediated between the commonalty and the nobles; they were a barrier and a protection of the weak against the strong at a time when the throne was none. But for that interposition there would have been more grinding oppression, and more revolting cruelty. Men who laughed

3*

at the laws enacted by the State, trembled at the censure of an ecclesiastical judge. That an independent power should be recognized as existing somewhere in the midst of the general anarchy, was an advantage; that it should be in the hands of those whose position secured them from abusing it, as the nobles did, was a blessing.

The Church did what the crown could not do; it enforced its own decisions. It established a system of legislation, and its sanctions reached the noble no less than the peasant. To give free scope to this system, it reconstructed society by introducing a new classification of ranks and dignities. The world and the Church had each their peculiar system; the rank which a man occupied in the State was not necessarily that which he occupied in the Church. No sooner did he cross the threshold of the sacred building than he was measured by a standard different from that which prevailed outside the fabric. Here worldly rank and power and influence went for nothing; he took his place, whoever he might be, according to his moral worth and his religious education. The Church exercised her authority over the serf and the sovereign equally, and this authority was not to be gainsaid. The system of public penance placed in the hands of the priesthood an authority from the operation of which no state, no condition of life, was exempted. It was for them to specify the nature of the temporal punishment due to the transgression of the law, to limit its application, and to fix its continuance. Except in a few extreme cases, its severity might be modified, or it might be withdrawn altogether, at the discretion of the bishop. ·In cases of extraordinary guilt the penitent was forbidden to enter the church, a distinctive dress was assigned him; he walked barefoot, his food was bread, water, and herbs. Mere worldly rank could plead no exemption for the guilty.

At a time when every man went armed, when human life was little valued, when it was considered meritorious to avenge upon the spot every wrong, imaginary or real, when the opportunities of escape from the pursuit of justice were many, when the law was slow of foot and weak of hand, originated the privilege of sanctuary. It was a revival of that earlier law which had provided a place of refuge, "that the slayer might flee thither that should kill his neighbor unawares, and hated him not in times past, and that fleeing thither he might live." What the cities of refuge had been to the Jew, the Church was to the Christian. For centuries the clergy were the only representatives of the principle, now so generally acknowledged in all free states, that, until a man has been proved to be guilty, he shall be considered to be innocent. They went a step further, and declared that no man should be accuser, witness, advocate, judge, and executioner in his own cause. They preached and wrote against the dangerous theory, always apt to become dominant in an imperfect degree of civilization, that the survivor must avenge the blood of the slain. They refused to join in the cry which deifies "the wild justice of revenge." By extending its protection over those who fled to it for safety, the Church afforded time for the first burst of passion to subside, and the voice of reason to be heard, and all must have seen that, in mediating between the offender and the offended, it did so for the good of both.

The middle classes, to which England is indebted for a very large share of the wealth, intelligence, and independence which have made her what she is, originated in that fusion of ranks which constituted the clergy. In the earlier ages of society the two great divisions of the people are the noble and the ignoble, and the Church afforded the only common ground of approximation. Here, and here only, their interests met, blended, and harmonized. Recognizing, as has already been stated, none of the distinctions which prevailed in the world, the Church welcomed the highest and the lowest. It offered the same advantages and the same rewards to both. If the son of the poor man could rise above the condition of his father, and emerge from the degradation to which feudalism had consigned the class to which he belonged, it was through the agency of the Church. The history of the Middle Ages shows how frequently the highest dignities which the State had to offer have been attained by ecclesiastics of the humblest parentage. If we have examples of kings, like Offa and Ceadwalla, Ceolwulf and Ini, who became monks, we have instances of monks, like Dunstan and Anselm, who became archbishops, and as such governed kingdoms and kings. Nicholas Breakspear, from a poor serving-lad at St. Albans, became pope of Rome. If the Church of the poor man opened up to him and his the road to fame and honor, we cannot wonder that it had his respect and his affection in return, and, as a thank-offering, the best that he had to give.

Again, the clergy of the Middle Ages secured no small accession of strength in public estimation from the struggle which they carried on against slavery. Here they fought the battle of the weak against the powerful, and in the end they were victorious through the force of public opinion. The circumstances of the times afforded ample scope for the exercise of this active benevolence. According to the spirit in which war was then conducted, the goods, the person, and the life of the vanquished were at the disposal of the victor. If he sacrificed his defeated enemy to the war-god of his nation, it was justice; if he sold him into captivity, or made him labor in his own service, it was clemency. Further, men might become slaves as a punishment for certain crimes, or they might be born in a state of slavery. Against this system in all its forms the clergy protested upon principles of pure and genuine philanthropy. They opposed it because they regarded it, as all good men will ever regard it, as affecting the dignity, the happiness, and the welfare, temporal and spiritual, of all who fall under its power; and the Church, by its laws and its example, its wealth and its influence, succeeded first in mitigating, and then in suppressing, the crime of slavery, which for centuries polluted every nation of Europe.

Intimately connected with this subject, and with the whole condition of society in those early times, is the care with which the clergy watched over the poor, the widow, and the orphan. These they regarded as their especial inheritance, and upon them they spent willingly and liberally the funds which had been placed at their disposal.

But, more lasting still, as outliving all change of society, was the care taken by the clergy for the education of the people. For a long time they were the only teachers of the entire population of England. Instruction was nowhere to be had but from them. They collected, preserved, and transmitted the scattered fragments of learning which had descended to their own time. The monastery was the only school, the monk or the cleric the only teacher. The education which they could give was no trifling boon ; and the laity could not fail to notice that it led to the substantial prizes of wealth, honor, and influence. With no better advantages than those which the school of the monastery at Wearmouth afforded, Beda achieved a reputation which carried his name over Europe. Alcuin, educated within the monastery of York, was competent to teach the teachers of Charlemagne, and he obtained from that monarch the proud title of the restorer of letters in France. The bishop in his palace, the monk in his monastery, and the parish priest in his parsonage, each contributed to the great work of education. Ecclesiastical laws were enacted to secure for the people the advantages which it was believed would result from a system so comprehensive. Nor were these schools instituted for professional purposes only. The benefits they conferred were not limited to those persons who were intended to recruit the ranks of the priesthood ; for, although these schools were founded by the clergy, supported by the clergy, and conducted by the clergy, yet free access was afforded to all who chose to profit by the advantages which they offered. Persons of different ranks of life were thus instructed in secular and religious learning, who might afterward marry and enter the world as laymen.

From these considerations it appears that during the early period there existed a remarkable unity of sentiment and interest between the clergy and the people. We have seen that the bishop and the parish priest cared as well for the temporal happiness as the spiritual progress of all sorts and conditions of men. They could help the Saxon serf and the Norman villein and his family in various ways, and they did not hesitate to lend a helping hand. By their influence the chain of the bondman's slavery was made less galling; his children were educated and advanced in life. They stood between him and the oppression of his feudal superior; and, if this were not enough, through them his wrongs found a way to the ear of the sovereign. They were his advocates in the courts of law, in prison they visited and comforted him. If he had been plundered, they (if any one could) obtained for him the restitution of his property. In sickness they were the physician of the body as well as of the soul, for the little skill in the art of healing which then existed was in the hands of the clergy. If the disease was of long continuance, the monastery was at once dispensary and hospital. The various offices of charity, kindness, usefulness, and brotherly love which were discharged by Churchmen alone for centuries, are now parceled out among a variety of religious and benevolent societies, each of which stands high in public estimation. They did the work of Scripture readers at home and of missionaries abroad. Their system, so long as it existed, rendered it unnecessary to tax the country for the support of the poor. For a long period, the monastery was the only inn; there the traveler was welcomed, housed, and fed; if overtaken by sickness he was tended there with unpaid skill and watchfulness until he could proceed upon his journey.

Their ready benevolence and untiring zeal originated and carried on the machinery which in our day requires the support of thousands of voluntary subscribers, and millions of involuntary taxpayers.

IX.

BATTLE OF SENLAC OR HASTINGS.—Freeman.

[The two sons of Cnut, Harold and Harthacnut, died childless, after brief and disgraceful reigns, and the nation restored the old line of kings in the person of Eadward, called the Confessor, son of Æthelred the Unready and a Norman princess. He had spent most of his youth at the Norman court. Weak, pious, well-intentioned, he was better fitted for a Norman monastery than for the English throne. His court became a gathering-place for Norman courtiers and ecclesiastics, whose influence, however, was largely counteracted by Earl Godwine, who had risen to power in the days of Cnut, and who had the chief management of affairs under Eadward, with one brief interval, until his death, in 1053. He was succeeded by his son, Earl Harold, who had married the king's sister. On the death of Eadward, without issue, early in 1066, Harold was elected to the vacant throne. His right was at once disputed by William, Duke of the Normans, on the ground that Eadward had promised him the crown, and that Harold had sworn to maintain William's claim. Though William's title had no legal basis, he determined to enforce it with the sword, and the two rivals met on the field of Hastings.]

MEANWHILE King Harold marshaled his army on the hill, to defend their strong post against the attack of the Normans. All were on foot; those who had horses made use of them only to carry them to the field, and got down when the time came for actual fighting. The army was made up of soldiers of two very different kinds. There was the king's personal following, his housecarls, his own thanes, and the picked troops generally, among them the men of London, who claimed to be the king's special guards, and the men of Kent, who claimed to strike the first blow in the battle. They had armor much the same as that of the Normans, with jave-lins to hurl first of all, and for the close fight either the sword, the older English weapon, or more commonly the great Danish ax, which had been brought in by Cnut. This was wielded with both hands, and was the most fearful of all weapons if the blow reached its mark, but it left its bearer specially exposed while dealing the blow The men were ranged as closely together as the space needed for wielding their arms would let them; and, besides the palisade, the front ranks made a kind of inner defense with their shields, called the *shield-wall*. The Norman writers were specially struck with the close array of the English, and they speak of them as standing like trees in a wood. Besides these choice troops there were also the general levies of the neighboring lands, who came armed anyhow, with such weapons as they could get, the bow being the rarest of all. These inferior troops were placed to the right, on the least exposed part of the hill, while the king, with his choice troops, stood ready to meet Duke William himself. The king stood between his two ensigns, the national badge, the dragon of Wessex, and his own standard, a great flag with the figure of a fighting man wrought on it in gold. Close by the king stood his brothers, Gyrth and Leofwine, and his other kinsfolk.

By nine in the morning the Normans had reached the hill of Senlac, and the fight began. But before the real attack was made a juggler, or minstrel, in the Norman army, known as *Taillefer*, that is, the Cleaver of Iron, asked the duke's leave to strike the first blow. So he rode out, singing songs of Charlemagne, as the French call the Emperor Charles the Great, and of Roland, his paladin. Then he threw his sword up in the air and caught it again; he cut down two English-men, and then was cut down himself. After this mere bravado came the real work. First came a flight of arrows from each division of the Norman army. Then the heavy-armed foot pressed on, to make their way up the hill and to

break down the palisade. But the English hurled their jave-
lins at them as they came up, and cut them down with their
axes when they came near enough for hand-strokes. The
Normans shouted, "God help us!" the English shouted,
"God Almighty!" and the king's own war-cry of "Holy
Cross"—the Holy Cross of Waltham. William's heavy-
armed foot pressed on along the whole line, the native Normans having to face King Harold's chosen troops in the
center. The attack was vain; they were beaten back, and
they could not break down the palisade. Then the horsemen
themselves, the duke at their head, pressed on up the hill-
side. But all was in vain; the English kept their strong
ground; the Normans had to fall back; the Bretons on the
left actually turned and fled. Then the worse-armed and
less-disciplined English troops could not withstand the
temptation to come down from the hill and chase them. The
whole line of the Norman army began to waver, and in many
parts to give way. A tale spread that the duke was killed.
William showed himself to his troops, and, with his words,
looks, and blows, helped by his brother, the bishop, he
brought them back to the fight. The flying Bretons now
took heart; they turned and cut in pieces the English who
were chasing them. Thus far the resistance of the English
had been thoroughly successful, wherever they had obeyed
the king's orders, and kept within their defenses. But the
fault of those who had gone down to follow the enemy had
weakened the line of defense, and had shown the Normans
the true way of winning the day.

Now came the fiercest struggle of the whole day. The
duke and his immediate following tried to break their way
into the English inclosure at the very point where the king
stood by his standard with his brothers. The two rivals
were near coming face to face. At that moment Earl Gyrth
hurled his spear, which missed the duke, but killed his horse
and brought his rider to the ground. William then pressed

to the barricade on foot, and slew Gyrth in hand-to-hand fight. At the same time the king's other brother, Earl Leofwine, was killed. The duke mounted another horse, and again pressed on ; but the barricade and the shield-wall withstood all attempts. On the right the attack of the French division had been more lucky ; the palisade was partly broken down, But the English, with their axes and shields, still kept their ground, and the Normans were still unable to gain the top of the hill or to come near the standard.

The battle had now gone on for several hours, and Duke William saw that, unless he quite changed his tactics, he had no hope of overcoming the resistance of the English. They had suffered a great loss in the death of the two earls, and their defenses were weakened at some points ; but the army, as a whole, held its ground as firmly as ever. William then tried a most dangerous stratagem, his taking to which shows how little hope he now had of gaining the day by any direct attack. He saw that his only way was to bring the English down from the hill, as part of them had already come down. He, therefore, bade his men feign flight. The Normans obeyed ; the whole host seemed to be flying. The irregular levies of the English on the right again broke their line ; they ran down the hill, and left the part where its ascent was most easy open to the invaders. The Normans now turned on their pursuers, put most of them to flight, and were able to ride up the part of the hill which was left undefended, seemingly about three o'clock in the afternoon. The English had thus lost the advantage of the ground ; they had now, on foot, with only the bulwark of their shields, to withstand the horsemen. This, however, they still did for some hours longer. But the advantage was now on the Norman side, and the battle changed into a series of single combats. The great object of the Normans was to cut their way to the standard, where King Harold still fought. Many men were killed in the attempt ; the resistance of the English grew slacker, but yet, when evening was coming on, they still fought on with their king at their head, and a new device of the duke's was needed to bring the battle to an end.

This new device was to bid his archers shoot in the air, that their arrows might fall, as he said, like bolts from heaven. They were, of course, bidden specially to aim at those who fought around the standard. Meanwhile twenty knights bound themselves to lower or bear off the standard itself. The archers shot; the knights pressed on; and one arrow had the deadliest effect of all; it pierced the right eye of King Harold. He sank down by the standard; most of the twenty knights were killed, but four reached the king while he still breathed, slew him with many wounds, and carried off the two ensigns. It was now evening; but though the king was dead, the fight still went on. Of the king's own chosen troops it would seem that not a man either fled or was taken prisoner. All died at their posts, save a few wounded men who were cast aside as dead, but found strength to get away on the morrow. But the irregular levies fled, some of them on the horses of the slain men. Yet even in this last moment they knew how to revenge themselves on their conquerors. The Normans, ignorant of the country, pursued in the dark. The English were thus able to draw them to the dangerous place behind the hill, where not a few Normans were slain. But the duke himself came back to the hill, pitched his tent there, held his midnight feast, and watched there with his host all night.

X.

THE CONQUEROR AND HIS POLICY.—GREEN.

[Although the great victory at Senlac did not put William in possession of the whole country, it, nevertheless, decided the fate of England. He advanced upon the capital, and, two months after the battle, was elected and crowned as king. Even then he was in real possession of only a third of the kingdom. But he met, henceforth, with no general, organized resistance. Revolts here and there were easily crushed, and gradually his authority was extended over the whole land. In three years the Conquest was complete. It was not a conquest in the ordinary sense. It was not the complete subjugation of one people by another people. The Norman duke had taken the place of the English king, and he had taken it by force ; but he presented himself to the conquered nation as its legitimate ruler. The ultimate results of the change were almost incalculable, but the immediate results were few. The old laws and customs were preserved, and the continuity of English history remained unbroken.]

IT is to the stern discipline of our foreign kings that we owe not merely English wealth and English freedom, but England herself. And of these foreign masters the greatest was William of Normandy. In William the wild impulses of the Northman's blood mingled strangely with the cool temper of the modern statesman. As he was the last, so he was the most terrible outcome of the northern race. The very spirit of the sea-robbers, from whom he sprang, seemed embodied in his gigantic form, his enormous strength, his savage countenance, his desperate bravery, the fury of his wrath, the ruthlessness of his revenge. "No knight under heaven," his enemies owned, "was William's peer." Boy as he was at Val-ès-dunes, horse and man went down before his lance. All the fierce gayety of his nature broke out in the warfare of his youth. No man could bend William's bow. His mace crashed its way through a ring of English warriors to the foot of the standard. He rose to his greatest height at moments when other men despaired. His voice rang out as a trumpet when his soldiers fled before the English charge at Senlac, and his rally turned the flight into a means of victory. ·In his winter march on Chester he strode at the head of his fainting troops, and helped with his own hand to clear a road through the snow-drifts. And with the Northman's daring broke out the Northman's pitilessness. When the townsmen of Alençon hung raw hides along their walls, in scorn of the "tanner's" grandson, William tore out his prisoners' eyes, hewed off their hands and feet, and flung them into the town. Hundreds of Hampshire men were driven from their homes to make him a hunting-ground, and his harrying of Northumbria left Northern England a desolate waste. Of men's love or hate he recked little. His grim look, his pride, his silence, his wild outbursts of passion, left William lonely even in his court. His subjects trembled as he passed. "Stark man he was," writes the English chronicler, "and great awe men had of him." His very wrath was solitary. "To no man spake he, and no man dared speak to him," when the news reached him of Harold's seizure of the throne. It was only when he passed from his palace to the loneliness of the woods that the king's temper unbent. "He loved the wild deer as though he had been their father."

It was the genius of William which lifted him out of this mere Northman into a great general and a great statesman. The wary strategy of his French campaigns, the organization of his attack upon England, the victory of Senlac, the quick resource, the steady perseverance which achieved the Conquest, showed the wide range of his generalship. His political ability had shown itself from the first moment of his accession to the ducal throne. William had the instinct of government. He had hardly reached manhood when Normandy lay peaceful at his feet. Revolt was crushed; discord was trampled under foot. The Duke "could never love a robber," be he baron or knave. The sternness of his temper stamped itself throughout upon his rule. "Stark he was to men that withstood him," says the chronicler of his English system of government; "so harsh and cruel was he that none dared withstand his will. Earls that did aught against his bidding he cast into bondage. If a man would live and hold his lands, need it were he followed the king's will." Stern as such a rule was, it gave rest to the land. Even amid the sufferings which necessarily sprang from the circumstances of the Conquest itself, from the erection of castles or the inclosure of forests or the exactions which built up William's hoard at Winchester, Englishmen were unable to forget "the good peace he made in the land, so that a man might fare over his realm with a bosom full of gold." Strange touches, too, of a humanity far in advance of his age contrasted with this general temper of the Conqueror's government. One of the strongest traits in his character was an aversion to shed blood by process of law; he formally abolished the punishment of death, and only a single execution stains the annals of his reign. An edict yet more honorable to his humanity put an end to the slave-trade which had, till then, been carried on at the port of Bristol. The contrast between the ruthlessness and pitifulness of his public acts sprang, indeed, from a contrast within his temper itself. The pitiless warrior, the stern and awful king, was a tender and faithful husband, an affectionate father. The lonely silence of his bearing broke into gracious converse with pure and sacred souls like Anselm. If William was "stark" to rebel and baron, men noted that he was "mild to those that loved God."

But the greatness of the Conqueror was seen in more than the order and peace which he imposed upon the land. Fortune had given him one of the greatest opportunities ever offered to a king of stamping his own genius on the destinies of a people; and it is the way in which he seized on this opportunity which has set William among the foremost statesmen of the world. The struggle which ended in the fens of Ely had wholly changed his position. He no longer held the land merely as its national and elected king. To his elective right he added the right of conquest. It is the way in which William grasped and employed this double power that marks the originality of his political genius, for the system of government which he devised was, in fact, the result of this double origin of his rule. It represented neither the purely feudal system of the Continent nor the system of the older English royalty; more truly, perhaps, it may be said to have represented both. As the conqueror of England, William developed the military organization of feudalism so far as was necessary for the secure possession of his conquests. The ground was already prepared for such an organization. We have watched the beginnings of English feudalism in the warriors, the "companions" or "thegns" who were personally attached to the king's war-band and received estates from the folkland in reward for their personal services. In later times this feudal distribution of estates had greatly increased, as the bulk of the nobles followed the king's example, and bound their tenants to themselves by a similar process of sub-infeudation. The pure freeholders, on the other hand, the class which formed the basis of the original English society, had been gradually reduced in number, partly through imitation of the class above them, but more through the pressure of the Danish wars and the social disturbances consequent upon them which forced these freemen to seek protection among the thegns at the cost of their independence. Even before the reign of William, therefore, feudalism was superseding the older freedom in England as it had already superseded it in Germany and France. But the tendency was quickened and intensified by the Conquest. The desperate and universal resistance of the country forced William to hold by the sword what the sword had won; and an army strong enough to crush at any moment a national revolt, was needful for the preservation of his throne. Such an army could only be maintained by a vast confiscation of the soil, and the failure of the English risings cleared the ground for its establishment. The greater part of the higher nobility fell in battle or fled into exile, while the lower thegnhood either forfeited the whole of their lands or redeemed a portion by the surrender of the rest. We see the completeness of the confiscation in the vast estates which William was enabled to grant to his more powerful followers. Two hundred manors in Kent, with more than an equal number elsewhere, rewarded the services of his brother Odo, and grants almost as large fell to William's counselors, Fitz-Osborn and Montgomery, or to barons like the Mowbrays and the Clares. But the poorest soldier of fortune found his part in the spoil. The meanest Norman rose to wealth and power in this new dominion of his lord. Great or small, each manor thus granted was granted on condition of its holder's service at the king's call; a whole army was by this means encamped upon the soil, and William's summons could at any hour gather an overwhelming force around his standard.

Such a force, however, effective as it was against the conquered English, was hardly less formidable to the crown itself. When once it was established, William found himself fronted in his new realm by a feudal baronage, by the men he had so hardly bent to his will in Normandy, and who were as impatient of law, as jealous of the royal power, as eager for an unbridled military and judicial independence within their own manors here as there. The political genius of the Conqueror was shown in his appreciation of this danger and in the skill with which he met it. Large as the estates he granted were, they were scattered over the country in such a way as to render union between the great landholders, or the hereditary attachment of great areas of population to any one separate lord, equally impossible. A yet wiser measure struck at the very root of feudalism. When the larger holdings were divided by their owners into smaller sub-tenancies, the under-tenants were bound by the same conditions of service to their lord as he to the Crown. "Hear, my lord," swore the vassal, as kneeling bareheaded and without arms he placed his hands within those of his superior, "I become liege man of yours for life and limb and earthly regard; and I will keep faith and loyalty to you for life and death, God help me!" Then the kiss of his lord invested him with land as a "fief" to descend to him and his heirs forever. In other countries such a vassal owed fealty to his lord against all foes, be they king or no. By the usage, however, which William enacted in England each sub-tenant, in addition to his oath of fealty to his lord, swore fealty directly to the Crown, and loyalty to the king was thus established as the supreme and universal duty of all Englishmen.

XI.

THE RED KING.—HUNT.

[On the death of the Conqueror, and in accordance with his wishes, the duchy of Normandy went to his eldest son, Robert, while England fell to his second son, William Rufus. William succeeded in making good his claim to the kingdom, notwithstanding the opposition of Robert and the Norman nobles, who did not like to have their hereditary estates in Normandy separated from their conquered estates in England. After a few years Robert pledged Normandy to William in order to raise money with which to join in the first Crusade, so that the duchy and the kingdom were again virtually united under one ruler. The Red King, as he was called, had great energy and ability, but he was utterly reckless and unscrupulous, and a man of the foulest life. "Never day dawned," says his chronicler, "but he was a worse man than when he lay down; never sun set, but he lay down a worse man than he had risen."]

No form of election seems to have preceded the coronation of William Rufus. His accession to the throne was the work of Archbishop Lanfranc, acting on the instructions of the Conqueror. Conscious of the character of Rufus, who had been his pupil, Lanfranc made him, in addition to the ordinary coronation oath, give a special promise that he would govern well, and would in all things be ruled by him.

4

For, as he had knighted him, and had brought him up, Lanfranc had a claim on his reverence, besides that which the archbishop derived from his office, and from having been the chief minister of his father.   Promises had little sanctity in the eyes of Rufus, unless they concerned some matter of military honor. "Who is there that can do all he promises?" was his wrathful answer to the archbishop, when he reminded the king of his own words.   In 1089 the death of Lanfranc freed him from a restraint which he regarded with impatience.   From this date his true character showed itself.   Unlike his father, William Rufus put no check on his evil nature.   Of no other can it be more truly said that he feared not God, neither regarded man.   The hideous depravity of his life reveals the depth to which man can sink when, owning no law, he gives himself up to work all uncleanness with greediness.   The special form of his immorality was, perhaps, an effect of the connection of the Normans with the people of the south and east of Europe, which arose from the conquest of Sicily.   Thence, too, it may be, came that habit of speaking evil of God and his saints, in which he constantly indulged.   When he recovered, for instance, from an illness in which, with the fear of death before him, he promised to live a better life, he swore that "God should never find him a good man in return for the ill He had done him."   And when certain men, accused of deerstealing, were acquitted by the ordeal, he loudly impugned the justice of God's judgment.   For such offenses men were, in his reign, condemned to death, for he set aside the law of his father, which forbade capital punishment.   Although he was not guilty of delighting in the bodily suffering of others, he was utterly careless of the welfare of his subjects.   He rejoiced in hurting men's feelings, and in shocking their prejudices.   He took a bribe from the Jews of Rouen to make some of their people who had become Christians turn back to their old religion.   In a spirit of mockery he made the bishops in England hold a set disputation with the Jews, and declared that if they were worsted he would become a Jew himself. William Rufus was a dutiful son to his father while he lived, and ever held his memory in honor. His filial admiration led him to try to imitate his father's dignity, and his boastful insolence was a travesty of his father's majesty. The mighty oath of the Conqueror gave place to the adjuration, " By the holy face of Lucca!'' or the yet more senseless form, " By this and by that." He loved to boast of his power, and to talk of his kingly dignity; but there was, in truth, nothing kingly in him. An assumed scowl and a blustering tone were the means by which he sought to make men feel the fear inspired by the fierceness of his father's mien and his terrific voice. At the same time Rufus loved to jest with his companions, and to make his own wickedness the subject of their laughter. Men bandied words with him as they would not have dared to do with his father. They even played tricks upon him. Thus one day it chanced, as he was putting on some new boots, that he asked his chamberlain how much they cost, and when he said, " three shillings," Rufus abused him, for he held them to be too cheap for a king's use. The man went and fetched a cheaper pair, telling him that they cost more. - " Ay," said he, " these are fit for a king's majesty." Not so, we may be sure, did his servants treat his father. The story is told by William of Malmesbury to illustrate the king's wastefulness. New fashions of effeminate luxury prevailed in his court. Men went about with long hair and flowing robes, and long, pointed shoes. Extravagance and folly were encouraged by the example and by the prodigal gifts of the king. His empty treasury was supplied by the devices of his low-born minister, Ranulf Flambard, who oppressed all alike, caring for no man's hatred if only he might please his master. These extortions were the more galling because they were committed under the guise of law, for every court was made by the justiciary the means of pressing the claims of the Crown.

Chief among the causes of the extravagance of Rufus was his love of all that pertained to arms. From his youth he excelled in all knightly exercises. A man-at-arms was to him something different from the rest of mankind. The word of such a one was more worthy of belief than that of others, and to such a one he held that a man should keep his word. To speak "as a good soldier" was to give another the highest assurance of truth. Some relation there was between such ideas and the arbitrary and imperfect code of chivalry. Yet, while chivalry exalted certain virtues to the neglect of others, and regarded a certain part of mankind as alone worthy of consideration, the system was founded on the idea that this regard was paid to the members of an order on the ground that they were pledged to exercise the virtues which were thus honored. Rufus, on the other hand, exalted no virtue, and honored men, not because they spoke the truth, but because they belonged to a profession which he loved. For this reason he held them to be entitled to privileges which he would not extend to others, and was careful to attach them to his service. When Rufus rewarded and enlisted a soldier who unhorsed him at St. Michael's Mount, or when he refused to believe that the knights at Ballon could break their word, he seems to exhibit the spirit of Francesco Sforza when, in 1424, he spared the lives of the captains whom his father bade him put to death, rather than to resemble Bayard, who, imperfect as were his ideas of right, poured scorn with his dying breath on the greatest captain of his age because he was "false to his country, his king, and his oath." Nor do the ideas of Rufus seem to me to have much in common with those of his ancestor, Richard the Good; for the king made his privileged class of soldiers, while an accident of birth was the sole recommendation for promotion at the court of the duke. Rufus would have made no bad captain of mercenaries, and these troops flocked to him in great numbers. He paid them highly, and if sometimes his treasury was empty, still their services were not unrequited, for he let them do as they liked. The license extended to these men caused much suffering to his people. In other cases he was stern enough. Death was a common penalty, until he found it more profitable to make men give him money than to hang them.

No dependence could be placed on the word of Rufus. Three times he promised that he would govern well, and three times those who believed him were deceived. The first of these promises he made to Lanfranc. Again, in 1088, when the Normans rebelled against him, and he was driven to seek the support of the English, "he promised them the best laws that ever were before in this land; and every unjust geld he forbade, and granted them their woods and hunting, but it stood no while." The third time he made such a promise was in 1093, when he was sick, and this, too, he broke when he recovered from his sickness. Great as the help was that he gained from the English *fyrd*, on one notable occasion he shamefully betrayed the loyalty of the people. In his war with Robert, in 1094, he sent over from Normandy to Flambard and bade him levy twenty thousand Englishmen to come over to him. The English then, as ever, obeyed the call of their king. The host came together at Hastings, each man with ten shillings given him by his shire for his expenses on the campaign. Then Flambard came and took this money away, and dismissed the men. So the king gained £10,000 by this transaction, and used the money in buying off the French king from his brother's side. Impetuous at the beginning of all his undertakings, Rufus lacked the steadfastness to carry them out to a distinct issue. Unstable as water, he never made a great war or a firm peace. In his attempt, in 1098, to bring Maine again under the Norman power, he took Le Mans, and then left the country unsubdued. Before he finished his work there, he began a war in the French Vexin, and that also, after a while, ceased without any definite ending. The vague and spasmodic character of his foreign relations make them of no real importance. At last the life of foul depravity and the reign of great undertakings and of small achievements came to an end; the tongue that boasted great things was silenced; the time of military license and administrative iniquity was cut short; the Red King was slain in the place made desolate by his father's cruel selfishness, and was carted away like one of those high deer which the Conqueror loved so well.

XII.

HENRY I., THE SCHOLAR-KING.—PEARSON.

[The tragic death of the Red King summoned his younger brother, Henry, to the throne. The claim of the elder brother, Robert, who was still absent in the east, was simply ignored. Robert, on his return, attempted to assert his rights in England, but without success. Weak, vacillating, and extravagant, he was soon unable to maintain his ground against the powerful barons in his own duchy. Henry, on pretext of being alarmed for the safety of his continental possessions, invaded Normandy, met Robert in battle, captured him, and kept him in prison until his death, in 1134. Henry's rule both in Normandy and England was stern, but, perhaps, no sterner than the times demanded.]

THE Conqueror's youngest son had the stature and general features of his family; but the high forehead, inherited from his father, the dark complexion and quiet, thoughtful eyes peculiar to himself, indicated a statesman rather than a soldier. Thrown early upon the world, Henry had been trained in a rough school. He had spent a large portion of his inheritance in buying the government of the Cotentin from Robert, who discharged the obligation by throwing him into prison. A reconciliation was effected, and Henry did good service in the revolt of Rouen, recovering the town when the duke fled from it in a panic. A few weeks passed, and the fickle Robert had united with William to besiege Henry in his castle of

Mont St. Michel. That Robert behaved with knightly courtesy, in refusing to starve his brother out, is true; but he continued the siege till the castle was surrendered; and Henry spent the next few years of his life without money or men, with a beggarly household of one squire and a priest. He was, probably, the better scholar, but not the milder man, for these experiences. As king he soon made himself respected; he was a pleasant companion at times; but no man could withstand "the imperious thunder of his voice;" and it was remarked that he was inscrutable; his praise was often a sure sign that he meant to ruin. He brooked no rivalry, and forgave no insult; the old favorite, who had boasted that he could build as grand a monastery as the king, was ruined by suits at law, and died broken-hearted. The foreign knight, who satirized Henry in songs, was blinded, in spite of the Earl of Flanders' intercession, and dashed out his brains in despair. When the king's ambition was interested, he was careless what suffering he caused; he oppressed the people with intolerable taxes; and punished one of his own daughters for rebellion by dragging her through a frozen moat.

Yet Henry possessed merits of a high order. He was not moral, but he was not shamelessly vicious; he was moderate in dress and food; his conversation was pure, and his court decorous. He honored learning and talent, formed a menagerie at Woodstock, and promoted the formation of a vernacular Norman literature. He advanced the fortunes of Robert the Great, whom he had chosen chaplain for his skill in hurrying through the mass, but who proved a first-rate justiciary, and adorned his see with the splendid cathedral of Salisbury. He brought over Gilbert the Universal, the first scholar north of the Alps, to be bishop of London. A great historical school flourished in his reign, and the zeal of his son, the Earl of Gloucester, for these studies, may well have been derived from a father who looked back with affection on his own " tumultuary " scholarship through all the troubles of his life. Nor was he indifferent to religion; he preferred being served by good men if good men would do his will. He was clear-sighted enough to perceive the importance of uniformity in standards. He fixed the length of the English yard, it is said, by his own arm; and at some immediate hardship he substituted payments in coin, which was instantly smelted down, for payments in kind by which the taxes had been discharged. Above all, he had a statesmanlike love of order; and devoted himself to the cares of government, when his ambition was satisfied by the conquest of Normandy. He was called by one who survived him: " The peace of his country, and the father of his people." . . .

It is difficult to say whether Henry introduced any new principles into his government; but he struck vigorously at the great abuses. The most monstrous of all, the purveyance of the royal officers, was repressed. The coinage had been debased until the king's soldiers in Normandy were unable to use it. Accordingly the coiners throughout England were summoned to Winchester, and were there one by one blinded and otherwise mutilated. It does not seem that any trial was held; it was mere Lynch law; but the people applauded it. A new coinage was issued, and the old withdrawn. The stern measure dealt out to outlaws was less popular. Henry revived the punishment of death; in 1124 the grand justiciary was sent down into Leicester, which had been peculiarly infested with thieves, and forty-four men, accused of burglary, were hanged, and six mutilated, at a single session. The sympathies of the people were with the sufferers, of whom several were said to be innocent, while the guilty had probably practiced upon the rich. These executions, however, effected their purpose; the land was restored to complete order, and Henry obtained the title of the Lion of Justice. . .

Henry's marvelous prosperity was darkened by one great loss. His only legitimate son, William, had already received the barons' oath of homage as their future king, when he accompanied Henry on a visit to Normandy (1120). When they were about to return by the port of Barfleur, a Norman captain, Thomas Fitz-Stephen, appeared, and claimed the right of taking them in his ship, on the ground that his father had been captain of the *Mora* in which the Conqueror crossed to invade England. The king did not care to alter his own arrangements, but agreed that his son should sail in the *Blanche Nef* with Fitz-Stephen. William Ætheling, as the English called him, was accompanied by a large train of unruly courtiers, who amused themselves by making the sailors drink hard before they started, and dismissed the priests who came to bless the voyage with a chorus of scoffing laughter. It was evening before they left the shore, and there was no moon; a few of the more prudent quitted the ship, but there remained nearly three hundred—a dangerous freight for a small vessel. However, fifty rowers flushed with wine made good way in the waters; but the helmsman was less fit for his work, and the vessel struck suddenly on a sunken rock, the Ras de Catte. The water rushed in, but there was time to lower a boat, which put off with the prince. When in safety, he heard the cries of his sister, the Countess of Perche, and returned to save her. A crowd of desperate men leaped into the boat; it was swamped, and all perished. As the ship settled down, all but three of those on board were washed away. One of these, Fitz-Stephen, drowned himself when he learned that the prince was lost; one perished from cold; the third, a common sailor, was kept warm by his thick sheep-skin dress, and survived to tell the tale. It was a fresh horror of this tragedy that scarcely any bodies were found to receive Christian burial. For more than a day no one dared to tell the king of his loss; at last a page was sent weeping to his feet. Three of Henry's children, but, above all, the heir of all his hopes, for whom he had plotted and shed blood, were taken from him at a blow. It is said that from that hour he was never known to smile.

4*

XIII.

THE ASSASSINATION OF BECKET.—Milman.

[The untimely death of Prince William seemed certain to involve the country in all the miseries of a disputed succession. Henry I. made every effort to secure the succession to his only remaining legitimate child, his daughter Matilda. She had married the German emperor, Henry V., and, after his death, in 1125, she became the wife of Geoffrey Plantagenet, count of Anjou. This second marriage was displeasing to the English barons, who feared the influence of a foreign prince in England ; and, moreover, it was repugnant to feudal principles that a woman should wear the crown. At Henry's death the throne was seized by Stephen, count of Blois, who was the third son of Adela, fourth daughter of the Conqueror. Matilda attempted to make good her claim, and the result was civil war. The barons divided between the two claimants, or went from one to the other, as their own interests demanded. For nearly twenty years the feudal spirit was rampant in England. At length the ruinous contest was stopped by the treaty of Wallingford (1153), brought about by the influence of the clergy, by which it was agreed that Stephen should remain king during his life-time, and that Henry, son of Matilda, should succeed him. In less than a year after the treaty was ratified Stephen died.

The young Henry—the first of the Plantagenets—stood pledged to reform. He proved equal, on the whole, to the gigantic problem which he had to solve, that of bringing order out of chaos, and of establishing a strong centralized government, which was the greatest need of his time. He had difficulties to meet such as had confronted no other English king. By inheritance and by marriage he was ruler over many heterogeneous peoples, with varied and often conflicting interests. His dominions stretched from the Scottish borders to the Pyrenees.

In the work of governing his vast dominions Henry was ably assisted, during the first few years, by his chancellor, Thomas Becket. One of the king's chief objects was to bring all classes of his subjects, rich and poor, high and low, clergy and laity alike, under the rule of the common law. In furtherance of this object, he determined to make Becket archbishop of the realm. This was a great mistake. As chancellor, Becket had steadily upheld the royal authority ; as archbishop he felt it his duty to uphold the authority of the Church. The antagonism between Church and State was such as to make a collision between them inevitable. It soon came. Becket fled from the country. Henry, whose aims were largely right, resorted to unwise and unwarrantable means to bring him to terms, and the archbishop retaliated by measures equally unwise. At length a partial reconciliation was effected, and Becket returned to England. But his temper was unchanged; he seemed to have a veritable passion for the glory of martyrdom, and it may be fairly said that he forced the issue between himself and the king. Henry lost patience. In his rage he uttered some hasty words, which were interpreted too literally by a few of his attendants. They hastened to England, sought out the archbishop in his own cathedral, and entered into an angry altercation with him, which resulted in his death.]

THE assassination of Becket has something appalling, with all its terrible circumstances seen in the remote past. What was it in its own age? The most distinguished churchman in Christendom, the champion of the great sacerdotal order, almost in the hour of his triumph over the most powerful king in Europe; a man, besides the awful sanctity inherent in the person of every ecclesiastic, of most saintly holiness; soon after the most solemn festival of the Church, in his own cathedral, not only sacrilegiously but cruelly murdered, with every mark of hatred and insult. Becket had all the dauntlessness, none of the meekness, of the martyr; but while his dauntlessness would command boundless admiration, few, if any, would seek the more genuine sign of Christian martyrdom.

The four knights do not seem to have deliberately determined on their proceedings, or to have resolved, except in extremity, on the murder. They entered, but unarmed, the outer chamber. The archbishop had just dined, and withdrawn from the hall. They were offered food, as was the usage; they declined, thirsting, says one of the biographers, for blood. The archbishop obeyed the summons to hear a message from the king; they were admitted to his presence. As they entered there was no salutation on either side, till the primate, having surveyed, perhaps recognized them, moved to them with cold courtesy. Fitz-Urse was the spokesman in the fierce altercation which ensued. Becket replied with haughty firmness. Fitz-Urse began by reproaching him with his ingratitude and seditious disloyalty in opposing the coronation of the king's son, and commanded him, in instant obedience to the king, to absölve the prelates. Becket protested, that so far from wishing to diminish the power of the king's son, he would have given him three crowns and the most splendid realm. For the excommunicated bishops he persisted in his usual evasion, that they had been suspended by the pope, by the pope alone could they be absolved; nor had they yet offered proper satisfaction. "It is the king's command," spake Fitz-Urse, "that you and the rest of your disloyal followers leave the kingdom." "It becomes not the king to utter such command: henceforth no power on earth shall separate me from my flock." "You have presumed to excommunicate without consulting the king, the king's servants and officers." "Nor will I ever spare the man who violates the canons of Rome, or the rights of the Church." "From whom do you hold your archbishopric?" "My spirituals from God and the pope, my temporals from the king." "Do you not hold all from the king?" "Render unto Cæsar the things that are Cæsar's, and unto God the things that are God's." "You speak in peril of your life!" "Come ye to murder me? I defy you, and will meet you front to front in the battle of the Lord." He added that some among them had sworn fealty to him. At this, it is said, they grew furious, and gnashed with their teeth. The prudent John of Salisbury heard, with regret, this intemperate language: "Would it may end well!" Fitz-Urse shouted aloud, "In the king's name I enjoin you all, clerks and monks, to arrest this man till the king shall have done justice on his body." They rushed out, calling for their arms.

His friends had more fear for Becket than Becket for himself. The gates were closed and barred, but presently sounds were heard of those without, striving to break in. The lawless Randulph de Broc was hewing at the door with an ax. All around Becket was the confusion of terror; he only was calm. Again spoke John of Salisbury with his cold prudence: "Thou wilt never take counsel: they seek thy life." "I am prepared to die." "We who are sinners are not so weary of life." "God's will be done." The sounds without grew wilder. All around him entreated Becket to seek sanctuary in the church. He refused, whether from religious reluctance that the holy place should be stained with his blood, or from the nobler motive of sparing his assassins this deep aggravation of their crime. They urged that the bell was already tolling for vespers. He seemed to give a reluctant consent; but he would not move without the dignity of his crozier carried before him. With gentle compulsion they half-drew, half-carried him through a private chamber, they in all the hasty agony of terror, he striving to maintain his solemn state, into the church. The din of the armed men was ringing in the cloister. The affrighted monks broke off the service; some hastened to close the doors; Becket commanded them to desist: " No one should be debarred from entering the house of God." John of Salisbury and the rest fled and hid themselves behind the altars and in other dark places. The archbishop might have escaped into the dark and intricate crypt, or into a chapel in the roof. There remained only the canon, Robert (of Merton), Fitz-Stephen, and the faithful Edward Grim. Becket stood between the altar of St. Benedict and that of the Virgin. It was thought that Becket contemplated taking his seat on his archiepiscopal throne, near the high altar.

Through the open door of the cloister came rushing in the four, fully armed, some with axes in their hands, with two or three wild followers, through the dim and bewildering twilight. The knights shouted aloud, " Where is the traitor ? " No answer came back. "Where is the archbishop ? " " Behold me, no traitor, but a priest of God." Another fierce and rapid altercation followed: they demanded the absolution of the bishops, his own surrender to the king's justice. They strove to seize him and to drag him forth from the church (even they had awe of the holy place), either to kill him without, or carry him in bonds to the king. He clung to the pillar. In the struggle he grappled with De Tracy, and with desperate strength dashed him on the pavement. His passion rose; he called Fitz-Urse by a foul name, a pander. These were almost his last words (how unlike those of Stephen and the greater than Stephen!) He taunted Fitz-Urse with his fealty sworn to himself. "I owe no fealty but to my king!" returned the maddened soldier, and struck the first blow. Edward Grim interposed his arm, which was almost severed off. The sword struck Becket, but slightly, on the head. Becket received it in an attitude of prayer—"Lord, receive my spirit," with an ejaculation to the saints of the Church. Blow followed blow (Tracy seems to have dealt the first mortal wound), till all, unless perhaps De Morville, had wreaked their vengeance. The last, that of Richard de Brito, smote off a piece of his skull. Hugh of Horsea, their follower, a renegade priest, surnamed Mauclerk, set his heel upon his neck and crushed out the blood and brains. "Away!" said the brutal ruffian, "it is time that we were gone." They rushed out to plunder the archiepiscopal palace.

The mangled body was left on the pavement; and when his affrighted followers ventured to approach, to perform their last offices, an incident occurred which, however incongruous, is too characteristic to be suppressed. Amid their adoring awe at his courage and constancy, their profound sorrow for his loss, they broke out into a rapture of wonder and delight on discovering not merely that his whole body was swathed in the coarsest sackcloth, but that his lower garments were swarming with vermin. From that moment miracles began. Even the populace had before been divided; voices had been heard among the crowd denying him to be a martyr; he was but the victim of his own obstinacy. The archbishop of York, even after this, dared to preach that it was a judgment of God against Becket—that "he perished, like Pharaoh, in his pride." But the torrent swept away at once all this resistance. The government inhibited the miracles, but faith in miracles scorns obedience to human laws. The Passion of the martyr, Thomas, was saddened and glorified every day with new incidents of its atrocity, of his holy firmness, of wonders wrought by his remains.

The horror of Becket's murder ran throughout Christendom. At first, of course, it was attributed to Henry's direct orders. Universal hatred branded the king of England with a kind of outlawry, a spontaneous excommunication. William of Sens, though the attached friend of Becket, probably does not exaggerate the public sentiment when he describes this deed as surpassing the cruelty of Herod, the perfidy of Julian, the sacrilege of the traitor Judas.

It were injustice to King Henry not to suppose that with the dread as to the consequences of this act must have mingled some reminiscence of the gallant friend and companion of his youth and of the faithful minister, as well as religious horror at a cruel murder, so savagely and impiously executed. He shut himself for three days in his chamber, obstinately refused all food and comfort, till his attendants began to fear for his life. He issued orders for the apprehension of the murderers, and dispatched envoys to the pope to exculpate himself from all participation or cognizance of the crime. His embassadors found the pope at Tusculum; they were at first sternly refused an audience. The afflicted and indignant pope was hardly prevailed on to permit the execrated name of the king of England to be uttered before him. The cardinals still friendly to the king with difficulty obtained knowledge of Alexander's determination. It was, on a fixed day, to pronounce, with the utmost solemnity, excommunication against the king by name, and an interdict on all his dominions, on the continent as well as in England. The embassadors hardly obtained the abandonment of this fearful purpose, by swearing that the king would submit in all things to the judgment of his Holiness. With difficulty the terms of reconciliation were arranged.

XIV.

DEATH OF HENRY II.—STUBBS.

[Political and domestic troubles brooded over the last years of Henry's reign. With the former he would have been able to cope, but the latter weighed heavily upon him, and ultimately broke him down. His own wife and children made common cause with his enemies against him. Their disaffection was partly due, no doubt, to his own injudicious management and conduct ; yet he was an indulgent father, and had striven to do his best for his children. Only Geoffrey, his natural son, remained faithful to him to the last. Worn-out with chagrin and disappointment and ceaseless toil, he died at the age of fifty-six.]

AND now Henry nerved himself for an interview which he knew could have but one issue. Ill as he was, he moved from Saumur to Azai, and in the plain of Colombieres met Philip and Richard on the day after the capture of Tours.

Henry, notwithstanding his fistula and his fever, was able to sit on horseback. His son Geoffrey had begged leave of absence, that he might not see the humiliation of his father ; but many of his other nobles, and probably two of his three archbishops, rode beside him. The terms which he had come to ratify had been settled beforehand. He had but to signify his acceptance of them by word of mouth. They met face to face, the unhappy father and the undutiful son. It was a clear, sultry day, a cloudless sky, and still air. As the kings advanced toward one another a clap of thunder was heard, and each drew back. Again they advanced, and again it thundered louder than before. Henry, wearied and excited, was ready to faint. His attendants held him up on his horse, and so he made his submission. He had but one request to make ; it was for a list of the conspirators who had joined with Richard to forsake and betray him. The list was promised, and he returned to Azai. Before he parted with Richard he had to give him the kiss of peace ; he did so, but the rebellious son heard his father whisper, and was not ashamed to repeat it, as a jest, to Philip's ribald courtiers, " May God not let me die until I have taken me due vengeance on thee."

But not even his submission and humiliation procured him rest. Among the minor vexations of the last months had been the pertinacious refusal of the monks of Canterbury to obey the archbishop in certain matters in which they believed their privileges to be infringed. Henry had, as usual with him in questions of ecclesiastical law, taken a personal interest in the matter, and had not scrupled to back the archbishop with arms at Canterbury and support of a still more effective kind at Rome. A deputation from the convent, sent out in the vain idea that Henry's present misfortunes would soften his heart toward them, had been looking for him for some days. They found him at Azai, most probably on his return from the field of Colombieres. " The convent of Canterbury salute you as their lord," was the greeting of the monks. " Their lord I have been, and am still, and will be yet," was the king's answer ; " small thanks to you, ye traitors," he added, below his breath. One of his clerks prevented him from adding more invective. He bethought himself, probably, that even now the justiciar was asking the convent for money toward the expenses of the war ; he would temporize, as he had always seemed to do with them. " Go away, and I will speak with my faithful," he said, when he had heard their plea. He called William, of S. Mere l'Eglise, one of the chiefs of the chancery, and ordered him to write in his name. The letter is extant, and is dated at Azai. It is probably the last document he ever issued. It begins, " Henry, by the grace of God, king of England, duke of Normandy and Aquitaine, and count of Anjou, to the convent of Christ Church, Canterbury, greeting, and by God's mercy on his return to England, peace." The substance of the letter is, that the monks should take advantage of the delay in his return to reconsider their position and the things that make for peace, that they might find an easier way out of their difficulties when he should come.

The monks, delighted with their success, retired, and the king lay down to rest. It was then, probably, that the fatal schedule was brought him, which he had so unwisely demanded at Colombieres. It was drawn up in the form of a release from allegiance ; all who had adhered to Richard were allowed to attach themselves henceforth to him, in renunciation of the father's right over them. He ordered the names to be read. The first on the list was that of John. The sound of the beloved name startled him at once. He leaped up from his bed, as one beside himself, and, looking round him with a quick, troubled glance, exclaimed, " Is it true that John, my very heart, the best-beloved of all my sons, for whose advancement I have brought upon me all this misery, has forsaken me ? " The reader had no other answer to make than to repeat the name. Henry saw that it was on the list, and threw himself back on the couch. He turned his face to the wall, and groaned deeply. " Now," he said, " let all things go what way they may ; I care no more for myself nor for the world." His heart was broken, and his death-blow struck.

He could not, however, remain at Azai. His people carried him in a litter to Chinon, where Geoffrey was waiting for him. It was the fifth day of the fever, and, in all probability, he was delirious with the excitement of the morning. It was remembered and reported in England that after he was brought to Chinon he cursed the day on which he was born, and implored God's malison on his sons; the bishops and priests about him implored him to revoke the curse, but he refused. But Giraldus, bitter enemy as he was, somewhat softened by his misfortune, tells a different tale. He draws the picture of the dying king leaning on Geoffrey's shoulder, while one of his knights held his feet in his lap. Geoffrey was fanning the flies from the king's face, as he seemed to be sleeping. As they watched, the king revived and opened his eyes. He looked at Geoffrey and blessed him. "My son," he said "my dearest, for that thou hast ever striven to show toward me such faithfulness and gratitude as son could show to father, if by God's mercy I shall recover of this sickness, I will of a surety do to thee the duty of the best of fathers, and I will set thee among the greatest and mightiest men of my dominion. But if I am to die without requiting thee, may God, who is the author and rewarder of all good, reward thee, because in every fortune alike thou hast shown thyself to me so true a son." Geoffrey, of whose sincere sorrow there can be no doubt, was overwhelmed with tears; he could but reply that all he prayed for was his father's health and prosperity. Another day passed, and the king's strength visibly waned. He kept crying at intervals, "Shame, shame on a conquered king." At last, when Geoffrey was again by his side, the poor king kept telling him how he had destined him for the see of York, or, if not York, Winchester; but now he knew that he was dying. He drew off his best gold ring, with the device of the panther, and bade him send it to his son-in-law, the king of Castile; and another very precious ring, with a sapphire of great price and virtue, he ordered to be delivered out of his treasure. Then he desired that his bed should be carried into the chapel and placed before the altar. He had strength still to say some words of confession, and received the "Communion of the Body and Blood of the Lord with devotion." And so he died, on the seventh day of the fever, on the sixth of July, the octave of the apostles Peter and Paul.

XV.

HOW THE GREAT CHARTER WAS WON.—Pearson.

[Richard, the Crusader, was remarkable for his personal prowess, but lacked the essential characteristics of a great military leader. As king, he spent but a brief period in England, and cared nothing for English interests. His exploits in the East, his captivity, and the tragic circumstances of his death, have surrounded his name with a halo of romance ; but he was selfish, cruel, tyrannical, vicious, a bad son, and a bad husband. During his reign the strong administrative system which his father had built up was successfully maintained by such statesmen as William Longchamp and Hubert Walter, in spite of the intrigues of his brother John.

John began his reign under favorable auspices, but the essential badness of the man soon displayed itself. He quarreled with his suzerain, the king of France, and thereby lost a large portion of his continental possessions. He quarreled with the Church, brought an interdict upon England and excommunication on himself, and then pusillanimously yielded up his kingdom, to be held as a fief from the Holy See He quarreled with his barons, and at length united nine tenths of the English people against him. It was this last quarrel which led to the signing of Magna Charta.]

ALTHOUGH John had been able to keep an army and a contingent in the field, many of his barons had remained behind in England, and those of the north especially had again put forward their plea of exemption from all service except on the marches. As it was certain from the first that the king would try, on his return, to revenge himself, and as the government of Peter des Roches, bishop of Winchester, who had succeeded Geoffrey Fitz-Petre as justiciary, was intolerably oppressive, the nobles resolved on resistance ; and, within a few days after John had landed and begun to levy scutage on all who had neglected to follow him, a meeting of nobles was held at Bury St. Edmunds, under pretext of celebrating the saint's festival (November 20). The charter of Henry I. and the laws of Edward the Confessor were read aloud, and the barons swore, one by one, on the high altar, to demand the observance of these liberties from the king, and to constrain him by arms and the withdrawal of fealty if he refused a peaceable consent. As men, however, who knew the risk of their enterprise, at a time when every fortress in England was garrisoned by royal mercenaries, they agreed to collect men and arms, and to meet after the approaching Christmas and urge their petition with an army at their back. The precaution was the more necessary as John, vaguely sensible that there was thunder in the air, and alarmed by the recall of his partisan, the legate, tried to detach the clergy from the national cause by granting them absolute liberty of election.

This remarkable charter was issued the very day after the barons' meeting at Bury St. Edmunds, and it reflects the highest credit on Stephen Langton and his followers that the enormous bribe to their feelings as churchmen, backed, as it was in many cases, by restitution of honor and estates, failed to make them forget that they were citizens. To the barons, of course, the new charter was of no interest, except as an item in John's degradation, and a declaration of war against themselves. Accordingly, as soon as John came from Worcester, where he had held his Christmas court, to London, the confederates, in unwonted military array, waited upon him, and claimed that he should perform the oath which he had sworn at Stephen Langton's bidding in Winchester, and confirm the constitution as defined by the charter of Henry I. The king feared to refuse compliance with the ‘demand of armed men, ready for action, and begged for time, that he might think the matter over and give his answer at Easter. The barons reluctantly consented, their cause being as yet espoused only by about half of the nobility, and the primate, the bishop of Ely, and the earl-marshal, were persuaded to become sponsors for the king's good faith.

The pledge was a perilous one, for John meditated nothing less than observance of his word. He was singularly destitute of counselors and supporters, for the legate had left the country in disgrace for maladministration, and Geof-frey Fitz-Petre and the bishop of Norwich were dead ; but he took instant steps to procure the release of the earl of Salisbury, abstained for a time from any gross act of op-pression, and sent commissioners to the different counties to explain his quarrel with the lords and enforce new oaths of homage on the free tenants. But he counted too much, in a time of popular excitement, on the silent, unceasing feuds between gentry and baronage. Men generally refused to take the oath with the new clause inserted, that they would support the king against " the now talked-of charter," and John was obliged to desist from the attempt. He had thought of bringing over troops from Poitou, but the tidings of disaffection alarmed him, and he hastily recalled his or-ders. Nothing now remained but to claim the protection of the Church, and hold his castles till the barons were wearied out, or till a royal party arose. That no precaution might be omitted, he assumed the white cross, in the hope of investing himself with the inviolable character of a crusader. But his chief trust was in Innocent. The pope had been applied to by Eustace de Vesci, as the barons' agent, in the preceding autumn, and had sternly admonished them not to disturb the course of royal justice. The cruel irony fell upon deaf ears. Both parties now sent commissioners to Rome, and Innocent unhesitatingly supported his vassal. He blamed the barons, who demanded, sword in hand, the rights they ought to have, prayed humbly and devoutly of " our dearest son in Christ, the illustrious King John," and he blamed the bishops who had sympathized with the barons. But the apostolical coun-sels reached England when the whole nation was in revolt.

By Easter the party of reform, numbering four earls and forty great barons, had assembled a large and well-appointed army. They halted at Brackley, in Northamptonshire, to re-ceive the primate and earl-marshal, who came as royal com-missioners to learn their demands. When these were reported to John, who was then at Oxford, he asked, with a bitter laugh, why the barons did not at once ask for the kingdom, and swore that he would never yield liberties which would leave himself in the position of a slave. As soon as his answer was known, the barons declared Robert Fitz-Walter "Marshal of the Army of God and of Holy Church," and proceeded to invest Northampton. But, wanting all engines of war, they could effect nothing, and accordingly marched on London, receiving admittance, by the way, into Bedford from the governor, William Beauchamp. London was opened to their advance-guard by a friendly party among the citizens (May 24), and the royal troops were easily overpowered, though the garrison of the Tower held out to the last. The soldiers of the Church filled their purses with the spoil of royal partisans and of the Jews, who always suffered in time of civil commotion, and who saw the very stones of their houses taken away to strengthen the city walls. The metropolis became the center of operations; but the whole country was in rebellion. Alexander of Scotland and Llewellyn of Wales were said to favor the revolt, and it often happened that where the father was royalist the son was in the camp of the insurgents. Presently one party seized Exeter, another Lincoln, and a riot took place in the streets of Northampton, in which many of the king's garrison were slain, the remainder retaliating by burning part of the town. As always happened in civil wars, the royal parks and forests were among the first objects of attack.

John had tried in vain to induce the primate to excommunicate the rebels, and the letters of Innocent were mere waste paper. In his extremity the king resorted to his favorite expedient, and called over his mercenaries from Poitou and other parts. The unpopular act probably contributed to detach the remainder of his adherents, and he found himself, by the beginning of June, with scarcely seven horsemen in his train. Even the bishops, who were nominally on his side, except the deeply injured Giles de Braose of Hereford, were of doubtful loyalty, and the earl-marshal himself had a son, his eldest, among the insurgents. In this extremity, fearing to be overpowered and dreading the arrival of the northern barons, who were known to be on their way, and who were his bitterest foes, John consented to a conference between Staines and Windsor. The army of the barons encamped on the broad plain of Runnimede, on the southern bank of the Thames; the royal forces were on the north, and the negotiations were carried on in an island. John came prepared to concede every thing, and the Great Charter was agreed to and received the royal seal in a day.

XVI.

DEATH OF KING JOHN.—Pearson.

[John at once sought to break away from the obligations of the Great Charter. He summoned mercenaries to his aid, and displayed so much ability and energy that the barons were forced to look abroad for assistance. They invited Lewis, son of the king of France, to become king of England. It was a dangerous move, and would probably have resulted in a hopeless division of the baronial party, had not the timely death of John relieved it from its embarrassing situation.

As soon as he had effected the object of relieving Lincoln and learned that the barons were not in pursuit of him, John decided to march southward again. In passing over the Wash, between the Cross-keys and the Foss-dike, he marched too near the sea at a time when the tide was still high, and lost many of his sumpter-mules and household retinue, with his jewels, including the crown, and a shrine containing relics which he especially prized. At the abbey of Swineshead, where he passed the night, he is said, by the more credible account, to have eaten peaches in excess;

vexation, fatigue, and the surfeit bringing on a dysentery. Later legends declared that a monk, who heard him boast he would raise the price of the loaf from a half-penny to a shilling, devoted himself for his country and poisoned the fruit he presented, eating of it himself, to inspire confidence, and dying. The illness, however caused, did not hinder John from proceeding the next day, to Sleaford, where he learned that Dover still held out and had obtained a truce till Easter, but was probably bound to surrender if it were not relieved by that date.

The news was bad medicine for a sick spirit, and the king's next stage, to Newark, was his last. His last acts were to write a letter to Pope Honorius (Oct. 15), recommending his young son to him, and to dictate a short will, by which he constituted what may be called a council of regency, with the legate Gualo at its head. But its provisions are chiefly the work of a craven conscience, desiring to purchase pardon of heaven by alms to the poor, and to religious houses, by " aid to the land of Jerusalem," and " by making satisfaction to God and holy Church for the damage and injury done them." The sacrilege wrought in Croyland monastery, where Savary de Mauléon's men had carried off spoils and captives in mid-mass, not three weeks before, may, perhaps, have risen up accusingly before the king's fevered fancy. On whom the furies should wait, if not on John, may indeed well be questioned. We seem to trace his gradual depravation in his history. The fair boy, his father's darling, who lets his courtiers pull the beards of his Irish lords, in the very wantonness of youthful arrogance, and bandies rough jokes with Giraldus Cambrensis, grows up reckless of all self-restraint, of all honorable sentiment, false to his father, false to his brother, false to his associates in treason, casting off the wife who has made his fortunes, slaying the nephew whom he has sworn to spare. He has all the lower talent of his family, is a pleasant boon companion, fond of

5

books and of learned men, irresistible among women. A few friends held by him to the last, with more of what seems personal regard than Edward II. or Richard II. conciliated. He has partisans in London at the time of his deepest humiliation, and is welcomed rapturously in Lynne a few days before his death. The Cinque-ports seem to have been steadily faithful to his interests. It is evident that, while his clergy and his nobles hated him, a portion of the towns were with him, either grateful for past favors or liking his enemies less. The loss of Normandy was chiefly due to his quarrel with his English subjects; he held England against the pope with singular success; and his last campaigns prove that he had organized his tyranny till he was an overmatch for half the realm, and could still do something when France had succored the rebellion.

Yet, allowing all this, which has, perhaps, been too often overlooked, it may be doubted if it be not an aggravation of the infamy that clings to John's name. He favored the cities, not in the interest of freedom, but to gain money by the sale of charters, or to set class against class. His power was based on the systematic employment of foreign merce- naries; he tortured to extort wealth, and murdered freely when his avarice was disappointed. His great struggle against Innocent began in the attempt to usurp the rights of a corporate body, and was carried on by confiscations and violence. Lastly, like all voluptuaries, John perpetually broke down at the critical moment of his fortunes. He scoffed at religion, and was cowed by a strolling prophet's utterances. Bearing to be excommunicated for years, giving churches freely to be plundered, he yet attached a supersti- tious reverence to the relics he carried with him. Perhaps the best summary of his life is the simple record of the great facts of his reign, that he lost Normandy, that he became the pope's vassal, and that he died fighting against Magna Charta. Never, probably, was there an English king who would more cordially have indorsed the Roman tyrant's wish : " When I am dead let the earth be consumed in fire ; " never one of whom the poet might have said, with greater truth, that " he wearied God."

XVII.

ENGLAND IN THE THIRTEENTH CENTURY.—LONGMAN.

[John left, as his heir and successor, a little boy nine years old—Henry III. His long reign covers more than half of the thirteenth century, one of the most brilliant and eventful periods of the world's history. It was the age of great statesmen, great scholars, and great architects. It was, for England, an age of great constitutional progress; but in this the king himself had little share. He was essentially weak and untrustworthy—a mere figure-head; during his minority under the control of able ministers; then the tool of foreign favorites; while, later, he became involved in a fateful struggle with the baronial party. Some idea of the condition of England at this period may be obtained from the following sketch of domestic life and manners.]

ABOUT twenty years before Edward became king, more than seventy woods and forests belonged to the Crown ; and this was one of the great grievances of the people. These woods were full of game of all kinds : wolves were far from uncommon ; wild cattle were found so near London as in Osterly Wood, in Middlesex ; and the fens and marshes were the abode of cranes, storks, and bitterns.

Besides these woods belonging to the Crown, the whole land was scattered over with forest. Between London and St. Albans the country was so thickly wooded, and the woods were so much frequented by lawless freebooters, who robbed the passing travelers, that the abbots of St. Albans kept armed men to guard the road to London. Throughout the whole country, indeed, the woods were so much the haunts of robbers, that, in 1285, a law was passed, ordering that all highways leading from one market-town to another, should be widened, so that there might be no bushes, woods, or dikes within two hundred feet of each side of the road; and those owners of land who refused to cut down underwoods close to the high-roads were held answerable for all crimes committed by men lurking in them. Even the boundaries of parks were to be set farther back when they approached too near the highway.

This was the state of the high-roads; but there were cross-roads, from one town to another, so little known that guides—shepherds and men of like degree—were hired to show the way to travelers. There were but few bridges, and guides, therefore, were needed to show the fords across the streams and rivers.

Such were the roads; let us now see how men traveled on them. There were no carriages in those days; or, at least, they were so uncommon, and their use so completely confined to ladies of rank, that they cannot be looked upon as the means by which people got from one place to another. Such as were to be found, were a kind of covered car, fitted with a weather-tight roof, from which hung curtains of leather, or of heavy silk; the wood-work was painted, and the nail-heads and wheels were often gilt; there were plenty of cushions inside, but there were no springs. Edward's queen, Eleanor of Castile, and his daughter, the duchess of Brabant, each had a carriage of this kind. Henry III. had "a house of deal" made for him, which ran on six wheels, and was roofed with lead. In all likelihood this was meant for traveling, but it must have been ill-suited to the roads of those days. Litters, or covered couches, supported by horses, were also made use of, and must have been more convenient than wagons on wheels, on most of the roads.

The usual mode of traveling, therefore, was on horseback, and the number of horses wanted by the nobles was very great. Thus, in the year 1265, when Simon de Montfort was at Odiham with his wife, the countess of Leicester, he had the surprising number of three hundred and thirty-four horses in his stables for himself and his retinue, and not for military purposes. Those who had no horses of their own hired horses of "hackney-men." Thus, a traveler going from London to Dover hired one horse as far as Rochester, for which he paid one shilling four pence, being about sixteen shillings of our money; the same from Rochester to Canterbury, and so on, in like proportion, to Dover. It was far from uncommon for travelers to steal these horses, and to cut off their ears and tails to prevent their being recognized. This practice was carried to such a length that, in the following century, a law was passed to put a stop to it.

There were other men who let out carts for carrying luggage; but the state of the roads, in some districts, was so bad that the cattle had to rest four days after traveling two. The general custom was to travel for four days, and then rest for three. At night travelers used to lodge at farms, or religious houses, where they were able to buy any food they wanted.

As an illustration of the traveling at this time, I may describe the way in which a large sum of money was carried from Chester to London. The sum of one thousand pounds, which meant one thousand pounds weight of silver, was due to Prince Edward from his barony of Chester. It was packed, by the prince's cook, in ten panniers, which were put on five horses, and thus carried to London, under the charge of two knights, attended by sixteen armed men on foot. Two cooks went with them to provide them with food, for there were no inns except in towns. It took the guard eight days to reach London, and six days to return without the heavy weight.

The houses of the barons, and, indeed, the king's palaces, were, most of them, very simply built. The hall was the great place of assembly, where all ate together, and, except at the dais, where the nobles sat, the dwelling-rooms on the ground-story were seldom boarded over, the floor being nothing more than the natural soil, well rammed down, with litter spread over it. The tables were stuck into the ground. This part of the hall was, therefore, often damp, and it was sometimes called the marsh of the hall, a name it, no doubt, well deserved. An idea of its state, even in a royal residence, may be gathered from the fact that at the king's palace at Winchester the door-way was widened to let in carts. This rude condition of the houses is very remarkable considering the luxury and splendor with which the ladies were often dressed.

The upper floors were generally boarded, but carpets were uncommon, and were looked on as a luxurious innovation. Thus, on the arrival of Eleanor of Castile, to be married to Edward, the Londoners were angry "at the very floors being covered with costly carpets."

As a general rule, the houses were built of timber, but sometimes of wood and stone. Bricks were very uncommon. In the hall the fire was in the middle, and the smoke escaped through the roof, but in the kitchen the fires were in large fire-places built in the walls, and there was a hole in the roof to let out the smoke.

Whether the houses were built of wood, stone, or rubble, they were almost all plastered and whitewashed, both inside and out. Wainscoting was not much used in domestic buildings, but the royal chambers and chapels, and probably also the large and wealthy monasteries, were generally wainscoted. Fir was generally used for this purpose, and Norway planks were brought into England in great quantities. The wainscoting was sometimes worked in patterns, but it was usually painted with subjects from sacred or profane history.

To the king's houses there were always attached apartments called "wardrobes," where the heavy and costly stuffs and cloths wanted for the dress of the king and his household were kept; and where, also, the royal tailors worked. When it is remembered that the summer and winter dresses of the king's attendants were furnished at his cost, and made under his roof, and that it was difficult to buy any large quantity of the cloths and furs necessary for the clothing of a numerous retinue, except at the great fairs, it is easy to see that the wardrobes needed ample room. In the wardrobes were also kept the rare productions of the East, which then found their way to England; such as almonds, ginger, the rosy and violet-colored sugars of Alexandria, and other " stomachics," as they were called.

Glass for windows was but little used. The windows were usually simply closed by wooden shutters, iron stanchions being sometimes added for greater safety. Canvas, or some such material, was often used to keep out the weather, and to admit a dim light. Glass for windows was a luxury, barely known to kings ; and it seems that no glass was made in this country until much later times. Window-glass was one of the things we got from the Flemings in exchange for our wool ; and so scarce was it, even in the next century, that the king ordered as much glass as was needed for the repairs of the windows of one of his chapels, to be searched for in the counties of Norfolk, Northampton, Leicester, and Lincoln. The wooden shutters cannot have afforded much defense against rough weather, and charges were often made for "making the windows shut better than usual." Draughts of cold air were somewhat prevented by putting the windows nearer the roof than the floor of the room.

The entrance to the manor-houses was usually by an outer staircase, shielded from the weather by an overhanging shed or pent-house ; but the way from the hall to the first story was sometimes through a trap-door. From this it seems that the chief dwelling-rooms in these manor-houses were on the first story, and the ground floor was probably used only as the hall.

I will now try to give you a sketch of the way in which people lived inside their houses. Let us imagine ourselves in one of them, as lookers-on, and that we see a lord sitting down to dinner with his guests and his vassals. All are gathered together in the hall. At the upper end, on the dais, where the ground is somewhat raised and boarded over, sit the lord and his chief guests. They are protected by a covering which, as our host is a great man, is made of silk. Below, in "the marsh," sit the vassals, farm-servants, and others. The door, which has lately been widened to let in carts more easily, is closed, to keep out the wind; a dim light is let in through the canvas windows, and "the marsh" is made tolerably dry and clean by litter and rushes. Fish in plenty is served up; eels and pike, and even whale, grampus, porpoise, and "sea-wolves" may be had. There is plenty of beef, and plenty of mutton, but it is nearly all salted; and the bread is rather black. Vegetables are plentiful enough; there are no potatoes, but there are peas, beans, onions, garlic and leeks, pot-herbs and sweet herbs. There is fruit enough, though not equal to what we now have. There are pears, and particularly one sort grown by the monks of Wardon, in Bedfordshire, which are made into Wardon pies. Then there are apples, particularly of the sort called "costard." These cost one shilling per hundred, or about twelve shillings of our money. Peaches, and cherries, and mulberries, too, are not wanting. If we suppose the entertainment to be given in London, the garden of the earl of Lincoln, in Holborn, would be ready to furnish a good supply, for the fruit out of it was sold for above one hundred pounds of our money in one year alone. There is plenty of claret, or clairets—so called because the wine was sweetened with honey, and afterward strained till it became clear — from our possessions in Gascony, and some sort of sherry from Spain, for those who sit on the dais; and beer and cider enough for those who sit in "the marsh." But the beer is made of a mixture of barley, wheat, and oats, without hops, which have not yet been "found out." The insipidity of the beer is taken off by spices. There is wine, too, made from English vineyards, but it must be sour stuff, and fit only for "the marsh." Nobody but the king has glass to drink out of, and he has none to spare for his friends; but he has cups made of cocoa-nuts, of gourds, of buffalo horns, and of beautiful agates for his principal guests. The wooden bowl, the earthen jug, and the leathern jack, serve well enough for the great bulk of the assemblage. The tables are pretty firm, for their legs are well stuck into the mud floor. Now that the guests are seated, and ready for their repast, up comes the meat on a spit, served round by the servants, and each man cuts off a bit with his knife, and puts it into his wooden bowl or on his trencher. Most of the people have wooden spoons, but nobody has a fork. The pitchers and jugs are made of earthenware, but the plates or dishes are all of wood.

XVIII.

THE MENDICANT FRIARS.—GEIKIE.

[With the increase of wealth and power corruption crept into the Church, and she lost much of her early purity and influence. At the end of the twelfth century many eminent men recognized the necessity of making some great effort to arrest her downward progress, and recover the lost ground. For this purpose the various orders of mendicant friars were established. Their special mission was to carry the Gospel to the poor. The most important of these orders were the Dominicans, or Black Friars; the Franciscans, or Gray Friars; and the Carmelites, or White Friars. The Dominicans and Franciscans exercised great influence in the social and political development of England.]

THE thirteenth century saw the Church rise to its most extravagant pretensions and sink to its deepest corruption. Its worldly splendor was at its height, but its spiritual condition was appalling. All its institutions had been noble in their first years, but success had ruined them. The vast

5*

cathedrals had once been the pride of the serf, who felt himself on a level with his oppressors when within their walls, and saw the sons of his despised class set above barons and princes as their ministers. But their clergy had gradually secured independence of the bishops, and now transferred their duties to vicars, preferring worldly indulgence for themselves. The appointment of titular bishops had, in the same way, enabled the wealthier prelates to find substitutes, and few of them any longer troubled themselves about their sees, further than to draw the revenues.

The independent episcopal courts, in their early history, had been a bulwark to the weak and oppressed in rough and lawless ages, against civil misrule and injustice. To the Church, Europe had owed the Truce of God, which sought, though vainly, to establish a cessation of private and national wars, then universal, for three days a week; it had aided emancipation of the slave in many ways in earlier times; the legislation of its courts against piracy, wrecking, incendiarism, usury, false coinage, tournaments, trial by ordeal, and much else, was of benefit to the nation and to morality. But ere long its claims became so excessive, and its tribunals so venal, that they lost all credit, and became a public scandal and oppression.

The efforts to enforce the celibacy of the clergy, which had been made unceasingly since Dunstan's day, through more than three hundred years, had only resulted in wide-spread immorality. The Church laws against married or immoral clergy could not be carried out from the number of offenders. This immorality of the clergy, their worldliness, their avarice, and notorious simony, were by turns rebuked with solemn earnestness by the few faithful men left in the Church, or upbraided with biting sarcasm by the wits of the age. Ecclesiastics, high and low, had, in fact, well-nigh lost the respect of the laity. "You are a worthy man, though you be a priest," says a female speaker in one of the poems of the time.   Nothing could be more bitter than the language in which ecclesiastical persons, as a class, are described by the writers of the day.

The enormous wealth of the Church had, in great measure, led to this state of things.   The laity had gradually submitted to the demand for tithes ; wills of all kinds, and all suits respecting them, were ecclesiastical matters ; dispensations for marriage were needed, at heavy cost, on every hand , possession of ready money facilitated purchases of land, often at a nominal value ; the safety of property held by the Church led many to make over their possessions to it, and rent them again from it, and a thriving trade in mortgages added to the whole.

The monks, also, had gradually become as corrupt as the rest.   There was no end of orders—Carthusians, Cistercians, Carmelites, Benedictines, and a host besides.   Exemption from episcopal authority and growth in wealth had done their work.   The abbots obtained, in many cases, episcopal privileges, and in many others forged the right to them.   Many parishes were united to monasteries to escape the oversight of the bishops.   There were convents for both sexes under the same roof, and men, like Bernard in the century before, denounced the pride and luxury of abbots and monks alike. Bernard had, indeed, founded a stricter rule among the Cistercians, which, for a time, gave them great popularity, but they, too, after a while, became as corrupt as the others.

It was under these circumstances that the mendicant orders were founded, to try if the laity, scandalized by the corruption of the monks and clergy, could not be won back to the Church.   From the year 1207 Francis of Assisi had first begun to gather round him a society which should reproduce apostolic life and labor, in strict obedience to Rome ; and such had been the effect of his saintly life, disinterested love, transparent sincerity, and simple preaching, in an age of hypocrisy and vice, that before his death, in 1226, many thousands had joined his order. " The Lord added, not so much a new order," says a contemporary (in the foundation of the " Begging Friars "), " as renewed the old, raised the fallen, and revived religion, now almost dead, in the evening of the world, hastening to its end, in the near time of the Son of Perdition ; that He might prepare new athletes against the dangerous times of Antichrist, and might protect the Church by fortifying it beforehand. The Lord Pope confirmed their rule, and gave them authority to preach in any churches, the bishop of the diocese permitting. They are sent two by two to preach, as before the face of the Lord and before His second Advent. These paupers of Christ carry neither purse, nor scrip, nor bread, and have no shoes on their feet, for no brother of this order can own any thing. They have no monasteries or churches, no fields, or vines, or beasts, or houses, or lands, or even where they may lay their head. They do not wear furs or linen, but only woolen gowns with a hood: no head-coverings, or cloaks, or mantles, or any other garments have they. If any one invite them, they eat and drink what is set before them. If any one, in charity, give them any thing, they keep nothing of it to the morrow. Yet, not by preaching only, but also by the example of a holy life and blameless conversation, do they attract many, not of the poor alone, but of the rich and noble, to despise the world, forsaking their towns, and houses, and great possessions, and giving up earthly wealth, by a happy exchange, for spiritual—to put on the habit of the ' lesser brethren '— a tunic of no value—and to gird themselves with their cord. For, in a short time they have so increased that there is no Christian land in which some are not found, for they let all join them, if unmarried, and not already under a vow. All but these they welcome, committing themselves to the providence and love of God, and not fearing for support."

Beginning with professions so noble and, at first, so sincere, it was found desirable, in 1212, to found a Franciscan sister-

hood as well, and to this was added, in 1221, a third order—
the Tertiaries—of both sexes, who were not required to take
the vows of the order or to live apart, but were rather Associates, carrying out, as far as might be, the spirit of the order without leaving their ordinary callings or their place in
life. The order of Dominican Friars, founded at first for the
conversion of the Albigenses (1205)—who were soon, however, to be given over to pitiless massacre, when found obstinate—grew, also, apace. A generation later came the Car-
melite Friars (1245) and the Augustines (1256); and all
these, like the Franciscans, had their sisterhoods and their
countless associates, or tertiaries, of both sexes.

The friars were, in fact, the Methodists, or revivalists of
six hundred years ago; but it would have been well for them
if they had been as permanently faithful to their mission as
Wesley's great communion. The people flocked every-where
to their preaching. It was like a new Gospel. Seeing their
power to work on the masses, the pope soon granted them
privileges which speedily corrupted them. Bishops were ordered to secure them a hearty reception, to urge all to come
to their preaching, and personally to help them in every way;
nor were they to be hindered from confessing those who attended their services. They were to be independent of
episcopal supervision, and had the right to bury any who desired it in their churches and inclosures. The door was
thus opened for their gaining wealth, and wealth brought
spiritual ruin.

Meanwhile they streamed into England—hailed by the
people, hated and feared, in anticipation, by the clergy and
monks. Foreigners, they had to beg their way, with only
their rags and their mission to recommend them. But they
soon learned English enough to begin their vocation actively,
and, ere long, every parish priest found them unwelcome intruders on his bounds, for they set up their movable pulpit
at any cross, without consulting him, and carried the multi-

tude away by their enthusiasm and the novelty and nobility of their principles and mission. Self-sacrificing love, for the sake of Christ, was the sum of their lives, and the only reward they asked, food and shelter. For a time they kept nobly true to the spirit of their rule. The towns of the Middle Ages were wretched in the extreme ; fever and pestilence were permanently established in them, as in modern cities of the East ; leprosy had its special houses, and little care was taken of the wretched inmates. But the Gray Brothers at once betook themselves to the most miserable quarters of the boroughs and to the foul leper houses, to alleviate suffering, and, if possible, remove it. Barefooted by day, they lay without a pillow by night. Their houses were as mean as the wretched hovels around them. True work, honestly done, had its ample reward in enthusiastic admiration.

Their preaching, ready, fluent, and familiar, was no less a wonder. The ignorant mass-priest, who depended on his fees, had been almost the only ecclesiastic with whom the lower towns-people had hitherto come in contact. The services of the Church were in an unknown language, the ritual was unmeaning, and the pictures or statues on the church walls needed an explanation which they did not receive. In contrast with this the friar addressed the crowd with fervid appeals, rough wit, or telling anecdote, as best suited the moment, with no attempt at studied harangues. It was a religious revolution, and gave the Church another lease of popular favor.

But they did not long confine themselves to preaching or tending the sick ; they soon aimed also at higher flights. The universities were in their first glory : humble enough compared with their state to-day, but immensely popular. Thirty thousand students are said to have attended Oxford at one time. The revival of mental activity, however, was dangerous, and the friars resolved to check, or at least to direct, it. Their care of the sick had soon drawn them to study the physical sciences, and their preaching led them to study theology. In 1230 the Dominicans had already gained a theological professorship in the University of Paris, and the Franciscans soon after secured another. The schools of both, at both the English universities, became famous. Theology resumed its old supremacy, and for a time such men as Roger Bacon, Duns Scotus, and Ockham gave a true glory to the new orders.

But the corruption of the rest of the Church ere long invaded the ranks of the Brethren, and speedily brought them to its own miserable level. Even so early as 1243 Matthew Paris writes of them : " It is only twenty-four years since they built their first houses in England, and now they raise buildings like palaces, and show their boundless wealth by making them daily more sumptuous, with great rooms and lofty ceilings, impudently transgressing the vows of poverty which are the very basis of their order. If a great or rich man is like to die, they take care to crowd in, to the injury and slight of the clergy, that they may hunt up money, extort confessions, and make secret wills, always seeking the good of their order as their one end. They have got it believed that no one can hope to be saved if he do not follow the Dominicans or Franciscans. They are restless in trying to get privileges, to get the ear of kings and princes, to be chamberlains, treasurers, bridesmen, match-makers, and agents of papal extortion. In their preaching they either flatter or abuse without bounds, or reveal confessions, or gabble nonsense." The monks and the clergy soon came to regard them as their mutual enemies, and the peace of the towns was often disturbed by riots caused by their mutual hatreds.

XIX.

DEATH OF DE MONTFORT.—Gardiner.

[The weakness and incapacity of Henry III., and his reliance upon foreign favorites, led gradually to the development of an opposition baronial
party. The nobles were the natural leaders of the people ; but they were
disorganized, and powerless, without a leader, to withstand the wretched
system of government that prevailed.

At length they found a leader in Earl Simon de Montfort, himself a
foreigner. He became the head of the national party. Under his direction, the opposition culminated in the Mad Parliament (1258), which forced
upon the king the constitution known as the " Provisions of Oxford." It
practically substituted a baronial oligarchy for the royal power. De Montfort, however, was not content with this, for he had wider plans of popular
government. His attempt to realize these led to a division of the national
party itself ; recourse was had to arms, and the combatants met on the field
of Lewes in 1264. Here the royalist party was overthrown, the king and
Prince Edward were taken prisoners, and all the power passed into De
Montfort's hands. His triumph led to the famous Parliament of 1265, to
which he summoned representatives from the towns as well as from the
shires, and a new constitution was drawn up, which put the government
into the hands of the commonalty of the realm. A reaction followed against
De Montfort. Prince Edward escaped from captivity, gathered an army,
destroyed a large force under De Montfort's son, and defeated the earl
himself in the battle of Evesham.]

IF the great barons were weary of Simon, he had full confidence in himself, and he determined to show that he could
do without them. When the Parliament which contained for
the first time representatives of the towns met, very few of
the great men had been asked to attend. Simon seems to
have felt that he could not trust many of them. He attempted
to do everything himself, and to rule the kingdom as if all
men in it were his subjects. His sons were more arrogant
and more unwise than he was. Even while Parliament was sitting news was brought that the young men and their friends
had arranged to engage in a tournament against the earl of

Gloucester and his supporters. A tournament was intended to be an imitation of a fight, in which knights rode at one another and attempted to thrust one another off their horses. But it might easily lead to a real fight, and Simon sent orders to stop it. Gloucester was angry with Simon for interfering with his amusement; and he was still more angry with him for keeping the king's castles in his hands. Gloucester was himself one of the three electors, and he may very well have thought himself aggrieved when he was treated as a man of little importance. Before long he was preparing to attack Simon, as soon as he could find a favorable opportunity.

Gloucester was not likely to have any lack of followers. Before the end of May he obtained help in an unexpected way. Prince Edward had been kept as a prisoner ever since the battle of Lewes. One evening he went out with his guards, and invited them to try which of them had the swiftest horse. As soon as they had tired their horses by galloping them one against another, he rode off, and was once more at liberty.

At once Prince Edward summoned to his aid all Simon's enemies. He was soon at the head of a large army. Gloucester and his friends, who had fought by Simon's side at Lewes, now followed the prince. Simon's supporters were but few, and he had little to trust to but his own skill. If Edward behaved as he had behaved at Lewes, a victory might yet be won. Edward, however, had learned much since the day when in hot haste he galloped after the Londoners, and left his father a prey to the enemy. He was one of those who was made wiser and better by adversity, and he was now as skillful a general as Simon himself. In the meanwhile Simon had been gathering forces in Wales, and was still on the western side of the Severn when he summoned one of his sons, a younger Simon, to join him with all the troops he could collect in London and the South. The young man after some delay arrived at his father's strong castle of Kenilworth. He and his men took no precautions against surprise, and even slept outside the castle walls. Early in the morning of August 1, Prince Edward and his men were upon them while they were still asleep. Young Simon and a few others escaped into the castle, which was too well fortified to be easily taken, but the greater part of his troops were obliged to surrender. The elder Simon would hardly have had a sufficient force if his son's army had joined him ; he was now terribly outnumbered.

Of this disaster he knew nothing when, on the following morning, he crossed the Severn, and marched toward Kenilworth, where he expected to find his son. On the 4th he arrived at Evesham, bringing King Henry with him under guard. Before long he was told that a body of armed men was coming toward him. He heard the news with joy, as he believed the soldiers to be his son's ; and, in order to be sure of the truth, he sent his barber, who was a long-sighted man, to the top of the abbey tower. The barber's intelligence was encouraging. He saw young Simon's banners floating at the head of the advancing troops. As they drew nearer Simon learned that he had been bitterly deceived. The banners were indeed his son's, but they were in the hands of the enemy. That enemy was too strong to be overcome, and even flight was impossible for a whole army. Evesham lies within a loop of the winding river Avon, some miles below the town of Stratford, where the great Shakespeare was afterward born. Edward had men enough to spare, and he had sent a detachment round to block the way of retreat over the bridge at the end of the loop. He himself bore down upon the town across the fields.

No one knew better than the old warrior that he had no hope of escape. "May the Lord have mercy on our souls," he prayed, "for our bodies are undone ! " He himself would stand and perish where he was ; but a few might fly, and keep themselves for better times. One and all refused to live when their captain and their leader was dead. "Come, then," said Simon, "and let us die like men; for we have fasted here, and we shall breakfast in heaven." Simon and his faithful band knelt down to ask forgiveness of their sins, and, in God's name, the bishop of Worcester declared them to be absolved. Then Simon rose, and with his whole force dashed forward to meet the foe. "By the arm of St. James!" he said, as he saw the orderly advance of the enemy, "they come on well; they learned that not of themselves, but of me."

The battle, if indeed it deserves the name, could not be of long duration. Prince Edward bore down upon Simon's little army in front, Gloucester charged upon its flank, a third force which had been sent to watch the bridge charged it in the rear. Simon's band of heroes was surrounded and outnumbered. Henry de Montfort, Simon's eldest son, was one of the first to be struck down. "Is it so?" said the father, when the news was brought to him. "Then, indeed, it is time for me to die." He rushed into the thickest ranks of the enemy, slashing, as he went, with his sword. Prince Edward's men pressed round him, and one, coming behind him, lifted his coat of mail, and stabbed him in the back with a mortal wound.

The noblest heart in England had ceased to beat. Edward, barbarous in his triumph, allowed the body of the great leader to be brutally mutilated in scorn, and his comrades to be pitilessly slaughtered. The common people indeed reverenced him as a martyr and a saint, and believed that miracles were wrought at his tomb. Poets sang how the precious flower of warriors had faded away, and how the land wept for the loss of him who had been victorious even in death.

It seems a strange thing to speak of him whose torn and bleeding corpse had lain upon the field at Evesham as victorious in his death. Yet no words could be more true. In the pages of history, as in our own experience, we sometimes meet with men who accomplish some great work which they have undertaken, and who die full of years and honors amid the grateful thanks of those who have enjoyed the fruit of their labors. But there are others who specially call for our gratitude, whose whole life seems at the time to have been thrown away, who have aimed at that which they could not win, and who have struggled always against the stream, to be swept away in the end in some dark day of storm. These are, indeed, the heroes of the earth. It is not what a man accomplishes, but what he aims at, which is the measure of his greatness, for it is the noble aim which makes him great and good.

> " That low man seeks a little thing to do,
>   Sees it and does it ;
> This high man, with a great thing to pursue,
>   Dies ere he knows it."

Simon had sought to accomplish no less a thing than to make England self-governing, that it might no longer be the prey of a spendthrift king, and of his foreign hangers-on who flocked across the Channel, like vultures to the carcass. When he died he left the country in the hands of that king who had done the wrong, and who seemed likely to return to his evil ways. Yet it was not so. By the side of Henry was now his son Edward, firm of will, and victorious in war. Edward had learned other things from Simon than the military art. He had learned to do justice, and to seek for justice by seeking to know the opinions of every class of the people. During the remainder of Henry's reign, Edward took care that wise laws should be made, and that Englishmen should have the mastery in England. When he himself came to be king, he upheld the principle that what was for the good of all should be consulted on by all. He gathered round him Parliaments even more complete than that which Simon had summoned, and there he strove to do justice to all. The spirit of the slain leader seemed to have passed into his conqueror.

It is given to no man, not even to Simon or to Edward, to make a free country. England is free, because for centuries before Simon was born Englishmen had been in the habit of discussing their own concerns, at least in their local assemblies, in meetings in town and country. But Simon is none the less worthy to be held in remembrance because he found followers ready to support him. His immediate failure may, in part indeed, be attributed to his own faults, his quick temper, and his contempt of men who were less in earnest than himself; but it was far more to be attributed to the jealousies of the great men, and to the unpreparedness of the middle class to combine permanently in his support. He needs no monument of marble to be remembered by. Wherever a free Parliament meets and gives laws in the English tongue, there is Earl Simon's monument.

XX.

WALLACE, THE SCOTCH PATRIOT.—Pearson.

[Edward I., son of Henry III., had profited by the troubles of his father's reign. He realized the needs of his people, and sought to meet them by enacting wise and just laws. His maxim was, "What concerns all should be approved by all." He was brave and prudent, and, above all, faithful to his word. He completed the parliamentary system, re-organized the courts of law, improved the system of police, and developed the resources of the country. In many ways he was really a great king.

His kingly pride and love of order led him to wish to extend the supremacy of England over the entire island. He, no doubt, honestly believed that the action of the Scottish nobles, in inviting him to decide between the different claimants to the Scottish crown, gave him tho right to exercise a paramount authority over Scotland. This explains his policy toward that country; it also explains, though it does not justify, his savage treatment of the patriot leader, William Wallace.]

In the spring of 1303 Edward at last saw all difficulties removed. The treaty with France only awaited signature;

the pope was occupied with troubles in Italy; the English estates were thoroughly reconciled to the crown. Edward summoned an overpowering army to Roxburgh, and, disregarding the Scotch borderers, who ravaged Cumberland behind him, he carried fire and sword through the whole country, penetrating even to Caithness. Debarred of all hope of foreign assistance, the Scotch nobles lost heart, and were only anxious to make terms. Two years before they had demanded that their lands in England should be restored, and the king had indignantly refused the request. They now stipulated only for the recovery of their Scotch estates, on the payment of reasonable fines, and Edward admitted them, by a general amnesty, to his peace. Probably the English earls, who had received grants of Scotch forfeitures, were bought off, or easily consented to renounce dangerous titles of doubtful value. John de Soulis, with a noble constancy, refused these terms, and retired to die, beggared and free, in France; but there was only one exception to the king's clemency. William Wallace, who had taken part in the earlier negotiations, applied, like others, for the king's grace and for permission to hold the lands he had acquired. The expression points to transactions, now unknown, by which his services had been rewarded with manors, so that he was, nominally at least, an estated gentleman. But Edward would not recognize the titles derived from war against himself, or could not bring himself to pardon the adventurer who had held all the force of England at bay. He would only agree that Wallace should come in and make his peace, that is to say, should make unconditional submission, with the understanding that he should be tenderly handled. Wallace refused these terms, and was proclaimed an outlaw, with a price set upon his head.

Unhappily for Edward and England, the measures taken to apprehend Wallace were crowned with a fatal success. By the late peace Wallace was debarred his old refuge in France.

After a long vagrancy in the moors and fens, where he supported himself by plunder, he incautiously ventured to Glasgow, and was taken in the house of his mistress, through the
treachery of his servant, Jack Short, who bore a grudge
against him for the death of a brother. The earl of Monteith, then governor of Dunbarton, and one of the few Scotch
nobles who had served Edward with fidelity, shares with his
brother, Sir John Monteith, the discredit of a service to his
country's enemy against his country's defender. The large
rewards showered upon the captors, and the strong escort under which Wallace was hurried through the lowlands, attest
the importance which Edward attached to his capture.
Faithful to his maxim, that he would not see any one to
whom he would not show grace, the king sent his great antagonist to London (August 22, 1305), where he was taken
through the streets in a mock procession, with a crown of
laurel on his head, and tried by a special commission, consisting of three judges, the lord mayor, and John de Segrave, the
beaten general of Roslyn. By strict law, as soon as the fact
of Wallace's outlawry was proved against him by record of
the coroner's roll, he was to be hanged, and his property
forfeited to the crown ; but this summary process would not
have suited the English policy, which desired, before it slew
its victim, to brand him as a felon. Accordingly the forms
of trial were observed, and Wallace was indicted for treason,
for murders and robberies, for sacrilege in churches, and for
not having come to the king's peace. It is said that Wallace
answered to the first count, denying that he was a traitor, as
he had never sworn allegiance to the king of England. By
the ideas of that time the defense was valid, for allegiance
was a personal tie rendered in return for certain advantages,
and which gentlemen at least might withhold at pleasure, so
that Wallace was not necessarily bound by the acts of his
countrymen. His refusal exposed him to forfeiture of his
land, and might put him out of the king's peace, but did not

make him a traitor. If, however, this plea was overruled Wallace had no answer, as he seems, in fact, to have made none, to the other counts of the indictment. He had undoubtedly headed a war in which men and women had been slain under circumstances of great ferocity, and churches burned or plundered by his followers. He had certainly not been worse, and probably had been more merciful, than other Scotch leaders; but he was not justified by ancestral rank in putting himself at the head of a national movement, and English pride could not forgive the mere squire who had defeated nobles and knights with burghers and Highland kerns. To Edward and his people—as even to Philip of France, and perhaps to some Scotchmen of the day—Wallace was no better than a brigand leading an armed rabble against their natural lords, and subverting the foundations of a political order more valuable to every statesman than a mere principle of nationality. Accordingly the sentence pronounced, though it struck men who remembered better times as horrible, did not seem to them unjust. By a new refinement of cruelty, Wallace was not only to be dragged to the gallows and hanged, but to be cut down while yet living, and disemboweled. This atrocious sentence was actually carried out.

Those who remember how Henry II. had spared the promoters of a wanton rebellion; how King Richard had acted by his brother John and his followers; how John himself had been compelled to plead at the bar of public opinion for the murder of the younger De Braose, and never dared to bring a rebel to formal trial; how Fawkes de Breautè was suffered to leave the country, and William de Marsh only hanged for complicity in rebellion and assassination, will understand what the clemency of our old judicial practice to all offenders in the rank of gentlemen had been, and how completely it was transformed, under Edward, into an impartial barbarity. The early lenity was, perhaps, excessive, but it did not demoralize, like the executions which are henceforth crowded thickly into the king's bitter old age.

It is possible that Wallace's fame has been better served by his death than it could have been by his life. Though a man of rare capacity, who called the first army of independence, as it were, out of the earth, and who gave body and enthusiasm to the war, he was unfitted by position to command the allegiance of the great nobles, who could alone insure success. He would probably have weakened Bruce by dividing the patriotic interest, or else have degenerated into a mere partisan leader. From the little we know of him, he was no faultless hero of romance, or absolutely without reproach among bloody and faithless men. It is probable that he permitted a savage license before he was sobered by success and a high position; and he seems to have lost heart in the last campaign, and to have wished to renounce a struggle which he was left to maintain alone. But these frailties, dearly expiated, cannot detract from the great facts of his life : that he was the first man who fought, not to support a dynasty, but to free Scotland; and the first general who showed that citizens could be an overmatch for trained soldiers; that no reproach of cruelty or self-seeking attaches to his term of government; and that the enemy of his country selected him as its first martyr.

6

XXI.

BRUCE AND BANNOCKBURN.—LONGMAN.

[Edward II. was as weak and cowardly as his father was brave and noble. He fell at once under the influence of favorites and parasites, and the greater part of his reign was occupied with struggles between him and his barons, whose object was to secure good government, and save the king from the consequences of his own folly. He undertook to carry out his father's policy in Scotland, but his overwhelming and disgraceful defeat at Bannockburn robbed him of the little influence he possessed. He was at length deposed, and the crown was given to his son. Though his fate is somewhat doubtful, it is generally supposed that he was secretly murdered in Berkeley Castle in 1327.]

THE almost inaccessible castle of Stirling was nearly the last fortress of importance which still held out against the Scots, and Bruce's brother, Sir Edward Bruce, now laid siege to it. Its goverror, Philip de Mowbray, was hard pressed, and feared his garrison would be starved out before it was possible to get help from England. He therefore concluded a truce with Sir Edward Bruce, on the condition of surrendering the castle by the 24th of June, the feast of St. John the Baptist, in the following year, if it were not previously relieved by an English army. Bruce justly blamed his brother for making so disadvantageous an agreement, but he did not attempt to break it.

King Edward, having made a kind of peace with his barons, was now able to turn his mind seriously to the war with Scotland. Had he not now roused himself from his supineness, he would, in fact, have left Scotland to its fate. But, on learning De Mowbray's agreement about Stirling Castle, he made immense preparations for its relief. He summoned the whole military force of the kingdom to meet him at Berwick on the 11th of June, 1314. To this general muster ninety-three barons were commanded to repair, with horse and arms, while the different counties of England and Wales were ordered to raise a body of twenty-seven thousand foot-soldiers. The whole army is said to have exceeded one hundred thousand men, of whom forty thousand were cavalry, three thousand of these being, man and horse, in complete armor, and fifty thousand were archers. A fleet of about fifty ships was appointed to co-operate with the army; ample stores of provisions for the troops, and forage for the horses, were collected from all quarters; smiths, carpenters, masons, and armorers joined the grand array; and numerous wagons and carts, for the conveyance of the tents, pavilions, and baggage, formed a necessary part of the well-appointed army.

Bruce on his side was not idle. But he found he could not muster above forty thousand fighting men, and his horses were not equal to those of the English. He therefore determined to fight principally on foot, and to choose ground where the English cavalry could not act with advantage. His soldiers were armed with battle-axes, long spears, knives or daggers, and bows and arrows. The formidable weapons, called Lochaber-axes, spiked flails, and claymores, are, however, said to have been also used at the time.

Stirling is situated on the south side of the river Forth, which winds round it, in a very devious course, on all sides but the south. On the north and east this river formed in those days a strong natural defense of the town; but on the west it was not near enough to protect it. The castle, however, stands on a precipitous rock, which is, for all military purposes, inaccessible on the western and southern sides. The only side, therefore, from which a successful attack could be made was the south-east. It was from that side that the English were approaching, but they could reach the castle only by crossing the little river Bannock. The Bannock, from Milton Marsh as far as the village of Bannockburn, runs through a deep ravine, which the English could not pass in the face of the Scotch army; below the village it turns to the north, and flows into the Forth. The ground in this direction, lying between the Forth and the Bannockburn, was a level marsh, unfit for the passage of a large army, but practicable for a small body of troops.

Bruce, therefore, seeing that the English must advance by the Falkirk road, expected that they would cross the Bannock at a ford on the Kilsyth road, and consequently posted his army across it, on sloping ground to the north of the Halbert and Milton Marshes. The right of his army rested on a deep marshy hollow, lying on the west and north sides of the Coxe Hill, and through which ran a little stream. The left rested on the Bannock, at Milton Mill, where the river runs through the deep ravine already mentioned. In order, however, to strengthen his position further, he caused a number of pits to be dug in the ground from the Halbert Marsh to the marshy hollow under Coxe Hill. In these pits sharp stakes were placed, and they were then covered over with turf. On the Coxe Hill Bruce placed a body of men to observe the movements of the enemy, and to resist any treacherous attack from Stirling Castle, the garrison of which was bound by the truce to take no part in the battle. Lastly, he placed a body of wild, undisciplined Highlanders, with the sutlers and camp followers, concealed in a valley which divides a hill, called the Gillies' Hill, from east to west. These men might be very useful in an irregular fight, or in case of any reverse to Bruce's army, but would have done more harm than good in a well-arranged plan of battle. His reserved forces were placed in the rear.

Bruce, having thus made all his plans with great skill, reviewed his troops, and declared himself satisfied with their appearance and equipment. The leaders of his army were, his brother, Sir Edward Bruce; Sir James Douglas; Randolph, earl of Moray; and Walter, the high steward of Scotland. To them he fully explained his intended order of battle, and then quietly awaited the approach of the enemy. He soon received intelligence that the English had lain all night at

PLAN OF THE
BATTLE OF BANNOCKBURN

Edinburgh. This was on Saturday, the 22d of June. On the following day, Sunday, the soldiers heard mass and confessed themselves with great solemnity. They were fully impressed with the importance of the coming fight, and of the superior numbers likely to be opposed to them, but they were determined to overcome the English or die in the attempt.

Bruce now, expecting the approach of the English, arranged his army in order of battle. He divided his soldiers into three masses and a reserve. Sir Edward Bruce commanded the right division; Sir James Douglas and Walter, the steward, the left; Randolph the center; and Bruce himself took charge of the reserve, placing himself on a hill called the Caldon Hill. He fixed the staff of his standard into a massive stone in front of the reserve. This stone still remains in its original position.

Bruce then sent out messengers to reconnoiter, and they soon returned saying that the English army was advancing in great strength, and making a very warlike appearance. Edward was evidently well informed of the position of Bruce's army, and saw that, if a body of cavalry could cross the Bannockburn, to the left of the Scotch, he might get to their rear, enter Sterling, relieve the garrison, and thus enable them to take part in the battle. Bruce had seemingly relied on the marshy nature of the ground beyond the ravine through which the little river flowed, as a sufficient protection to his army, and had made no preparation to resist this flank movement. In order, therefore, to gain the rear of the Scotch army, Edward, early in the morning, had sent forward a body of eight hundred horse, led by Sir Robert Clifford, to cross the Bannock and relieve the castle. Clifford succeeded in crossing the stream, his forces being concealed by a bank which lies on the west side of the carse, or marshy plain, and was making his way to the castle, when Bruce discovered the movement of his troops, and dispatched Randolph, with a select body of foot-soldiers, to intercept them. So soon as Clifford saw the approach of the Scotch he ordered his soldiers to wheel round and charge. Randolph formed his men into a square, and received the shock of the English horse without wavering, and at length, after desperate attempts on the part of the English, and determined resistance on the part of the Scots, the English were compelled to retreat.

In the meantime the English army had steadily advanced, till Edward ordered a halt to consult with his leaders, whether they should give battle at once, or wait till the following day, in order to let the soldiers have a night's rest. By some mistake, the English center continued to advance, and Bruce, therefore, rode forward to make some fresh arrangements. An English knight, Sir Henry De Bohun, or Boune, well mounted, seeing that Bruce was alone, rode forward to attack him. Bruce was mounted only on a weak horse, but was too brave to shun the conflict. The English knight galloped forward at great speed, charging with his lance, but Bruce parried the attack, and, as the knight passed him, he raised his battle-ax, and, with one blow, laid him dead at his feet.

> "High in his stirrups stood the king,
> And gave his battle-ax the swing.
> Right on De Boune, the whiles he passed,
> Fell that stern dint—the first—the last!
> Such strength upon the blow was put,
> The helmet crashed like hazel-nut;
> The ax-shaft, with its brazen clasp,
> Was shivered to the gauntlet's grasp.
> Springs from the blow the startled horse,
> Drops to the plain the lifeless corse;
> First of that fatal field, how soon,
> How sudden, fell the fierce De Boune."
> —*Scott's "Lord of the Isles," Canto vi*, 15.

The Scotch now rushed forward with great fury, and drove back the English in confusion; but Bruce, fearing to disarrange his order of battle, called his soldiers back, and both sides tacitly determined to delay the battle till the next day.

On the following morning, Monday, June 24th, the Scottish king confessed, and, along with his army, heard mass; and the soldiers then arranged themselves in battle-array. The English advanced, led on by the king in person, who had with him a chosen body-guard of five hundred horse. As they approached, the Scotch all knelt down, in reverence to a crucifix carried through their ranks by the Abbot of Inchaffray. "See," cried Edward, "they are kneeling; they ask mercy." "They do, my liege," answered Sir Ingram Umfraville, "but it is from God, and not from us. Trust me, yon men will win the day, or die upon the field." "Be it so, then," replied the king, and ordered the charge to be sounded. The English, owing to a dispute among their leaders, charged irregularly, but with great fury. The Scotch received their attack with steady courage, and the English fell in great numbers. But the Scotch were terribly galled by the showers of arrows poured upon them by the English bowmen. Bruce, therefore, ordered Sir Robert Keith to take a body of five hundred horse, the only cavalry in the Scotch army, around Milton Marsh, and charge the English archers. The archers had no weapons but their bows and arrows, and their quivers being emptied, they were unable to resist the attack of the Scotch cavalry and fled. Bruce now saw signs of wavering among the English, and, bringing up his whole reserve, charged the English with his entire army in one line. At this critical moment, by Bruce's orders, the Highlanders made their appearance on the top of Gillies' Hill, and the English, supposing them to be a fresh army advancing to the attack, fled in confusion. This last charge of Bruce decided the fate of the day, and the Scots now obtained a complete victory over their opponents. Thirty thousand of the English are said to have been left dead on the field, but Edward escaped in safety, and took refuge in Berwick.

It was still many years before the wars between England and Scotland ceased, but the battle of Bannockburn had the effect of securely establishing Bruce and his successors as kings of Scotland.

XXII.

BATTLE OF CRECY.—FROISSART.

[The real cause of the Hundred Years' War, begun by Edward III., was an attempt on the part of the French king, Philip of Valois, to annex Edward's province of Aquitaine to the crown of France. The preposterous claim of Edward to the French throne was urged mainly as a pretext for the war. The age of Edward was pre-eminently the age of chivalry, and he made war in the spirit of a knight-errant, without much plan or purpose, for personal glory. After having undertaken several expeditions against France, he landed at La Hogue, in Normandy, in July, 1346, intending to join the Flemings. But the French king, with a large army, lay between him and Flanders, on the right bank of the Seine. By a feint upon Paris, however, Edward succeeded in crossing the river, and advanced toward the Somme, which he also crossed, near Abbeville, and there won the great victory of Crecy (August 6, 1346), against enormous odds. But even this surprising success brought no permanent advantage to England ; nevertheless it was a "glorious" victory.]

THAT night the English king lay in the fields with his host, and made a supper to all his chief lords of his host and made them good cheer. And when they were all departed to take their rest, then the king entered into his oratory, and kneeled down before the altar, praying God devoutly that if he fought the next day, that he might achieve the journey to his honor. Then, about midnight, he laid him down to rest, and in the morning he rose betimes, and heard mass, and the prince, his son (the Black Prince), with him, and the most part of his company were confessed and houseled. And, after the mass said, he commanded every man to be armed, and to draw to the field, to the same place before appointed. Then the king caused a park to be made by the wood-side, behind his host, and there was set all carts and carriages, and within the park were all their horses, for every man was afoot; and into this park there was but one entry. After arranging the army in three battalions, the king leapt on a hobby, with a white rod in his hand, one of his marshals on the one hand, and the other on the other hand; he rode from rank to rank, desiring every man to take heed that day to his right and honor; he spake it so sweetly, and with so good countenance and merry cheer, that all such as were discomfited took courage in the seeing and hearing of him. And when he had thus visited all his battles (battalions) it was then nine of the day: then he caused every man to eat and drink a little, and so they did at their leisure; and afterward they ordered again their battles. Then every man lay down on the earth, and by him his salet and bow, to be the more fresher when their enemies should come. It was in

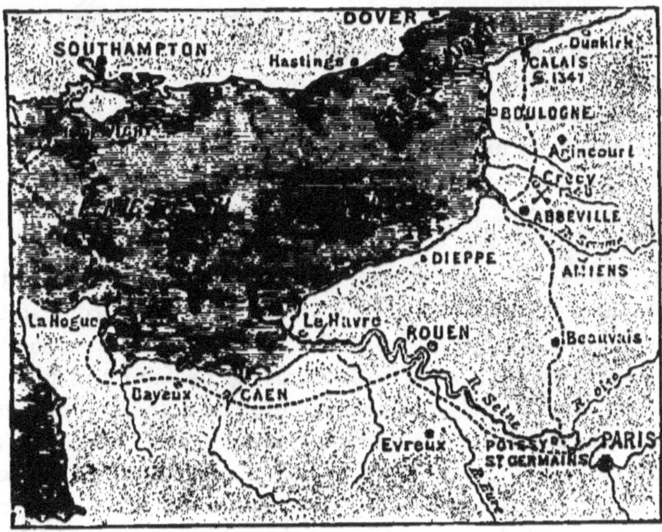

BATTLE OF CRECY.

6*

this position that they were found by the tumultuous French army, which came rushing on, crying "Down with them," "Let us slay them." in such a manner, that, says Froissart, there was no man, though he were present at the journey, that could imagine or show the truth of the evil order that was among them. The day of this meeting was Saturday, August 6, 1346.

The Englishmen, who were in three battles, lying on the ground to rest them, as soon as they saw the Frenchmen approach, they rose upon their feet, fair and easily, without any haste, and arranged their battles: the first, which was the prince's battle; the archers there stood in the manner of a herse (harrow), and the men-of-arms in the bottom of the battle. The earl of Northampton and the earl of Arundel, with the second battle, were on a wing in good order, ready to comfort the prince's battle, if need were. The lords and knights of France came not to the assembly together in good order; for some came before, and some came after, in such haste and evil order that one of them did trouble another. When the French king saw the Englishmen, his blood changed, and (he) said to his marshals, " Make the Genoese go on before, and begin the battle in the name of God and St. Denis." There were of the Genoese cross-bows about fifteen thousand; but they were so weary of going a-foot that day a six league, armed with their cross-bows, that they said to their constables, " We be not well ordered to fight this day, for we be not in the case to do any great deed of arms, as we have more need of rest." These words came to the duke of Alençon, who said, "A man is well at ease to be charged with such a sort of rascals, to be faint and fail now at most need." Also at the same season there fell a great rain and eclipse, with a terrible thunder; and before the rain there came flying over both battles a great number of crows, for fear of the tempest coming. Then anon the air began to wax clear and the sun to shine fair and bright, the which was

right in the Frenchmen's eyes and on the Englishmen's
backs. When the Genoese were assembled together, and began to approach, they made a great leap and cry to abash the
Englishmen, but they stood still, and stirred not for all that.
Then the Genoese again the second time made another leap,
and a fell cry. and stept forward a little, and the Englishmen
removed not one foot; thirdly, again they leaped and cried,
and went forth till they came within shot, then they shot
fiercely with their cross-bows. Then the English archers
stept forth one pass (pace), and let fly their arrows so wholly,
and so thick, that it seemed snow. When the Genoese felt
the arrows pressing through heads, arms, and breasts, many
of them cast down their cross-bows, and did cut their
strings, and returned discomfited. When the French king saw
them flee away, he said, " Kill me these rascals; for they
shall lett (hinder) and trouble us without reason." Then ye
should have seen the men-of-arms dash in among them, and
kill a great number of them; and ever still the Englishmen
shot whereas they saw thickest press; the sharp arrows ran
into the men-of-arms and into their horses, and many fell,
horse and men, among the Genoese; and when they were
down, they could not relyne again, the press was so thick
that one overthrew another. And also among the Englishmen there were certain rascals that went on foot, with great
knives, and they went in among the men-of-arms, and slew
and murdered many as they lay on the ground, both earls,
barons, knights, and squires, whereof the king of England
was after displeased, for he had rather they had been taken
prisoners.

The valiant king of Bohemia, called Charles of Luxenbourg, son to the noble Emperor Henry of Luxenbourg, for
all that he was nigh blind, when he understood the order of
the battle, he said to them about him, " Where is the Lord
Charles, my son ? " His men said, " Sir, we cannot tell, we
think he be fighting." Then he said, " Sirs, ye are my men,

my companions and friends in this journey; I require you bring me so forward that I may strike one stroke with my sword." They said they would do his commandment; and to the intent that they might not lose him in the press, they tied all the reins of their bridles each to other, and set the king before to accomplish his desire, and so they went on their enemies. The Lord Charles of Bohemia, his son, who wrote himself king of Bohemia, and bare the arms, he came in good order to the battle; but when he saw that the matter went awry on their party, he departed, I cannot tell you which way. The king, his father, was so far forward, that he struck a stroke with his sword, yea, and more than four, and fought valiantly, and so did his company, and they adventured themselves so forward that they were all slain, and the next day they were found in the place about the king, and all their horses tied to each other.

The prince's battalion at one period was very hard pressed; and they with the prince sent a messenger to the king, who was on a little windmill-hill; then the knight said to the king, "Sir, the earl of Warwick, and the earl of Oxford, Sir Reynold Cobham, and others, such as be about the prince, your son, are fiercely fought withal, and are sore handled, wherefore they desire you that you and your battle will come and aid them, for if the Frenchmen increase, as they doubt they will, your son and they will have much ado." Then the king said, "Is my son dead or hurt, or on the earth felled?" "No, sir," quote the knight, "but he is hardly matched, wherefore he hath need of your aid." "Well," said the king, "return to him and to them that sent you hither, and say to them, that they send no more to me for any adventure that faileth, as long as my son is alive; and also say to them, that they suffer him this day to win his spurs, for if God be pleased, I will this journey be his, and the honor thereof, and to them that be about him." Then the knight returned again to them, and showed the king's words, *the which greatly encouraged them*, and they repined in that they had sent to the king as they did. The king of France stayed till the last. It was not until the evening that he could be induced to acknowledge that all was lost. Then, when he had left about him no more than a threescore persons, one and other, whereof Sir John of Heynault was one, who had remounted once the king—for his horse was slain with an arrow—then he said to the king, " Sir, depart hence, for it is time ; lose not yourself willfully ; if ye have loss this time, ye shall recover it again another season ; " and so he took the king's horse by the bridle and led him away in a manner per force. Then the king rode till he came to the castle of La Broyes ; the gate was closed, because it was by that time dark ; then the king called the captain, who came to the walls, and said, " Open your gate quickly, for this is the fortune of France." The captain knew. then it was the king, and opened the gate and let down the bridge ; then the king entered, and he had with him but five barons, Sir John of Heynault and four others. The unhappy king, however, could not rest there, but drank and departed thence about midnight.

XXIII.

THE BLACK DEATH.—WARBURTON.

[The great pestilence which swept over England in 1348–49 was by far the most important event of Edward III.'s reign. It destroyed nearly half of the population, and raged most fiercely among the working classes. It more than doubled the rate of wages, in spite of the stringent laws enacted to keep the price of labor at its former standard. It led to the rising of the peasants in the next reign, to the re-organization of the agricultural system of the time, and ultimately to the emancipation of the peasant class from serfdom or villeinage.]

In the interval between the capture of Calais and this attempt to recover it, a visitation occurred which turned all the gay prosperity of England into mourning, and brought the French nation to the very brink of ruin. The outbreak of the Plague, or the " Black Death," as it was then called, has been left comparatively in the background by contemporary historians ; but it is undoubtedly the central fact of the reign of Edward III. and of the fourteenth century, and, in the opinion of some writers, the most important economic fact in modern history. Among its consequences may be reckoned an immense advance in the social condition of the working classes, owing to the scarcity of labor, and consequent increase in its value as a commodity ; the substitution of what we should call tenant-farming for landlord occupation ; and a " strike " of fifty years' duration, which culminated in the rebellion of Wat Tyler in the following reign, and, though then cruelly and treacherously put down, resulted at last in the emancipation of the English peasantry.

The local origin of the Plague is mysterious, and it has, therefore, perhaps, been traced to Cathay, the land of mystery ; but it is an ascertained fact that all the most devastating epidemics which have visited Europe have had their cradle in the far East. Tidings of the Plague's ravages in

Central Asia had reached England as far back as the year 1333; but the western peoples thought little of it as long as it was talked of only as one of the many scourges of imperfectly known and half-barbarous nations. Constantinople was then, as now, the great frontier city between European civilization and the far East, and through it flowed one of the three principal tides of Oriental traffic. Thither, in 1347, the destroyer came, along with the caravans laden with Asiatic produce, and followed the westward course of commerce by easy stages along the shores and islands of the Mediterranean, sometimes pausing, sometimes doubling back, but always gaining ground, till it reached the uttermost north-western boundary of Europe, not sparing Iceland, and even leaping over to Greenland—where it probably extirpated the European colony—and returning by Norway and Sweden, through Russia, in 1351.

In Provence the chief cities were almost depopulated. At Avignon, where Pope Clement VI. held the most extravagant and dissolute court in Europe, three fourths of the people died. The pope shut himself up a close prisoner in his palace-fortress, and kept huge fires burning day and night.

In Cypress, Sicily, and Florence the Plague was felt with extraordinary severity. In the last place only it would seem that some efforts, though ineffectual, were made by the authorities to check the spread of the disease, among the victims of which was Petrarch's "Laura." During its ravages in that city a number of ladies and gentlemen withdrew together from all communication with the outer world, diverting themselves with music and dancing and other in-door entertainments, eating and drinking of the best, and never listening to or thinking about any thing which might check their good spirits or disturb their serenity. Stories by which they are supposed to have amused each other have been preserved, or invented, in the " Decameron " of Boccaccio, the effect of whose gay and festive pictures is heightened by contrast with the somber background on which they are drawn.

The Black Death, which made the tour of Europe in 1349–51, is undoubtedly the same disease as the Plague, now, or till quite lately, endemic on the shores of the Levant and in Egypt, having been, as it were, domesticated there by the lazy, filthy, and fatalistic habits of the people. Its specific causes are as much unknown as its original seat. The opinion of the time and some modern authorities agree in connecting its appearance with contemporary physical phenomena of a very remarkable kind; but it would seem as if these phenomena must have been of too limited and local a character to account for a pestilence which spread over a whole continent. Parching droughts, as it is said, were succeeded by convulsions of the earth and crackings of its surface, from which a fetid and poisonous vapor was projected into the atmosphere, the corruption of which was afterward increased by malarious exhalations from swamps caused by incessant deluges of rain. To the panic-struck imagination of the people the Black Death seemed to be advancing to their destruction in the palpable form of a " thick, stinking mist."

In some rare and frightful cases of seizure the victims fell down and died without premonitory symptoms, but in the majority of instances the attack began with shiverings and bristling of the hair, succeeded by burning internal fever with a cold skin, and the rapid formation of boils, first in the *axillae* and the groin, and afterward in the internal organs. The appearance of these boils was the most characteristic of all the symptoms of the Black Death, but the advance of dissolution was often so rapid as to outstrip these forerunners, which were, indeed, due to a strong effort of nature to expel the matter of the disease from the blood.

The terror of the Plague was every-where, inviting death ; men's vital powers were so depressed by anticipation that they were already half-dead before they were attacked ; the throat parched, the pulse quickened, by nervous anxiety, were taken for the fatal symptoms of seizure. And next to the fear of death was that of previous desertion. Men and women feared to look in each other's faces lest they should be betrayed by the "muddy glistening" of the eye, or detected in feeling with feverish finger for "the little hard kernel, no bigger than a pea, which moved with the touch under the skin of the armpit," the sure precursor, as it was thought, of doom inevitable, irremediable, inexorable, and irrespective of persons, ages, or conditions of life. To imaginations morbid with terror pestilence indeed seemed to lurk in every thing—in every morsel eaten, in every rag that fluttered in the wind. But who would be so fool-hardy and irrational as to "throw good life after bad," by nursing a dying friend, when Black Death was in the breathing of his last sigh or the farewell pressure of his hand? So the nearest and dearest ties were dissolved, the calls of kindred and humanity neglected, and the sick were left to die and then be carted to the grave by hirelings. Numbers were driven, by an unreasoning terror, away from human habitations, and perished miserably in the solitude of the fields.

In England, however, by far the most memorable results of the Black Death were its social and economical effects. It made its appearance in Dorsetshire, in the month of August of the fatal year 1348, but it was three months before it had reached London. Knyghton, who lived at the time, says that "many villages and hamlets were desolated, without a house being left in them, all those who dwelt in them being dead." The country places which the Plague attacked were soon silenced, for the pestilence did not even spare the brute creation ; and the carcasses of sheep, horses, and oxen lay putrefying in the fields, untouched by dogs or birds of prey. But in London the streets and public places were, for a time at least, all alive and brisk with funerals—"alive with death."

First single biers, and then cart-loads of corpses hurried along to the grave-yards : no time was to be lost, for there would soon be too few left living to bury the dead.

It is said on contemporary authority—and the statement is confirmed by modern research—that no less than one-half of the population perished. The immediate consequence was an enormous increase in the value of labor, and a corresponding depreciation in the value of land. In the winter which followed the Plague "flocks and herds wandered about the fields and corn without any that could drive them." Landlords excused their tenants' rents for one, two, or three years, lest they should desert their holdings, and leave them uncultivated on their owners' hands. Wages were so high as to swallow up the farmer's profit, and it frequently became a question whether it would be more ruinous to leave the crops ungathered or to comply with the extravagant demands of the laborers.

XXIV.

JOHN WYCLIF.—SHIRLEY.

[The career of Wyclif, as a reformer, included the later years of Edward III., and the earlier years of his grandson and immediate successor, Richard II. He attacked both the discipline and doctrine of the Church of his time, and in many points anticipated the great Reformation of the sixteenth century. When he first rose into prominence the papal court was at Avignon, in France. A few years later occurred what is known as the Great Schism. Two popes were elected, one at Rome and the other at Avignon, and Europe was divided between them. The schism caused great scandal and corruption, and did much to destroy the influence of the papacy. In England the French pope was regarded as an enemy ; hence, to a large extent, the popular sympathy for Wyclif.]

Of all external events perhaps the great schism of the West exercised the most important influence on the career of the reformer ; it strengthened his theological, but it undermined his political, position. He may not have been aware, certainly John of Gaunt, if we may judge by his acts, was not aware, how large a portion of the antipathy of Englishmen to the papal court was due to its residence at Avignon. The pope was, to Englishmen of the time of Edward III., the obedient slave of France, through whose coffers the treasure of this country passed to feed the war against herself, whose partisans, especially among the mendicant friars, were perpetually engaged in fostering an unpatriotic, unnational feeling, and who appeared, an advocate in the garb of mediator, to throw the weight of his influence in every negotiation into the scale of the enemies of England.

With the great schism all this was changed. Not only did the common feeling of reverence for the head of the Church naturally return when the causes which had for a time destroyed it were removed, but the nation must have witnessed, with novel delight, the " king's adversary of France " falling under the ban of the papacy. The violence of the Lancastrian government, and its mad defiance of popular feeling, hastened the reaction, and thus before long Wyclif, sanguine as he was, had probably abandoned all serious hope of any practical reform of the Church.

From this time the theological element, in our modern and narrower sense of the word, becomes predominant in his works ; he begins to write English tracts, to speak of the translation of the Bible, which was probably in progress at this time, and lastly, arriving at a conclusion to which he had long been tending, he put out, in the spring of 1381, a paper containing twelve propositions, in which he denied the doctrine of transubstantiation.

It was on these propositions that his prosecution by the archbishop was framed—a prosecution which, unlike that of four years before, was really theological, not political, in its object. Whatever share old party feeling may have had in stirring Courtney's theological zeal, no archbishop of Canterbury,

even if inclined, could safely have neglected to proceed
against the author of opinions so profoundly at variance with
the ecclesiastical, even more than with the theological, principles of the day.

Yet the first attack on the new doctrine was not made by
him. Almost immediately after its appearance it was condemned by the chancellor of the university and a select
meeting of doctors. Wyclif appealed to John of Gaunt, who
came down to Oxford, and, caring little to be embroiled in a
theological dispute, confirmed the sentence of the chancellor
by an injunction to the reformer not to speak further on the
subject of the eucharist. A political partisan would have
been silenced : Wyclif replied by his memorable confession.
Help came to him from a quarter whence, perhaps, it was
little expected.

The popular cry of heresy, then as ever, was far less telling within the university than in the country at large. The
theological alarms of John of Gaunt were little felt by the
masters of arts. Their common enmity to the religious, and
especially to the mendicant, orders, attached the secular
clergy of Oxford, as a body, to the cause of Wyclif. They
did not forget that three years before the monks, in gratify-
ing their animosity against him, had sacrificed the independent pride of the university, and they could not but foresee,
in the new prosecutions which were preparing, fresh sources
of humiliation for her. This feeling, re-enforcing the strength
of Wyclif's own party, told in the university elections. In the
annual change of officers, the incoming chancellor and proc-
tors were all more or less inclined to his cause, and the university troubled him no more

Thus checked, the leaders of the movement turned to the
archbishop, and, in consequence of their representations, in
May, 1382, a provincial council was assembled at the Black
Friars, in London.

The form of the proceedings was remarkable. Wyclif

himself was never summoned before the council, but twenty-four conclusions, extracted from his writings, were condemned, search was ordered to be made in Oxford for copies of his works, and he himself was banished from the university. For his followers severer measures were in store. The Lollard chancellor, Rigge, after a bold but short resistance, was compelled to submit; the heads of the party were made to recant, and the whole party in Oxford received a blow from which it seems to have never thoroughly recovered.

LUTTERWORTH—WYCLIF'S CHURCH.

Wyclif's enemies, however, were not satisfied. From his retreat at Lutterworth they summoned him before the papal court. The citation did not reach him till 1384. But he was then dying of paralysis. His reply to the pope, excusing himself from attendance, is preserved to us. From its half-enigmatical language we could scarcely guess, what we know from another source, that his failing strength was unequal to the journey. On the 29th of December, of the same year, as he was hearing mass in his parish church, a fatal stroke deprived him of speech, and on the 31st he breathed his last.

No friendly hand has left us any, even the slightest, memorial of the life and death of the great reformer. A spare, frail, emaciated frame, a quick temper, a conversation "most innocent," the charm of every rank ; such are the scanty but significant fragments we glean of the personal portraiture of one who possessed, as few ever did, the qualities which give men power over their fellows. His enemies ascribed it to the magic of an ascetic habit ; the fact remains engraven upon every line of his life.

To the memory of one of the greatest of Englishmen his country has been singularly and painfully ungrateful. On most of us the dim image looks down, like the portrait of the first of a long line of kings, without personality or expression —he is the first of the reformers. To some he is the watchword of a theological controversy, invoked most loudly by those whom he would most have condemned. Of his works, the greatest, "one of the most thoughtful of the Middle Ages," has twice been printed abroad, in England never. Of his original English works nothing beyond one or two short tracts has seen the light.* If considered only as the father of English prose, the great reformer might claim more reverential treatment at our hands. It is not by his translation of the Bible, remarkable as that work is, that Wyclif can be judged as a writer. It is in his original tracts that the exquisite pathos, the keen, delicate irony, the manly passion of his short, nervous sentences fairly overmasters the weakness of the unformed language, and gives us English which cannot be read without a feeling of its beauty to this hour.

* Since this was written (1858) the English works of Wyclif have been printed, with a very able and interesting introduction by F. D. Matthew (1880).

As it is in the light of subsequent events that we see the greatness of Wyclif as a reformer, so it is from the later growth of the language that we best learn to appreciate the beauty of his writing. But it was less the reformer, or the master of English prose, than the great schoolman, that inspired the respect of his contemporaries ; and, next to the deep influence of personal holiness and the attractive greatness of his moral character, it was to his supreme command of the weapons of scholastic discussion that he owed his astonishing influence.

XXV.

DEPOSITION OF RICHARD II.—YORK POWELL.

[During the first twelve years of Richard II.'s reign, the conduct of affairs was largely in the hands of his uncle, the duke of Lancaster, and, after him, of another uncle, the duke of Gloucester. Richard however, was allowed to choose his own ministers. In 1387, through the efforts of Gloucester and four other nobles, called Lords Appellant, the ministers were impeached in Parliament and condemned to death. Two years later the king suddenly assumed sole authority, and for nearly eight years ruled wisely and successfully. In 1389 he entered upon a course of arbitrary government which led to his deposition. His cousin, Henry of Bolingbroke, duke of Hereford, took the vacant throne, with the title of Henry IV.]

THE earl of March had been killed by the "wild Irish" at Kenlys, July 20, 1398, and now, that all was outwardly at peace in England, Richard was minded to go over to Ireland, and stay there till he had established good government once for all. He made his will, leaving all his money to his heir, on condition that he up-

RICHARD II.

held the acts of the last two Parliaments, appointed his uncle, the duke of York, Keeper of the Realm, and then sailed, with many of his nobles, May, 1399. As soon as Henry heard that he was gone, he set out from Brittany with Archbishop Arundel and his nephew (the dead earl's son), Sir Thomas Erpingham, and forty men, and landed at Ravenspur, July 4, swearing to the northern lords who joined him that he was come to claim his heritage, and to put an end to the bad rule of the king's friends, but not to touch the crown. The Keeper was won over July 27, Bristol surrendered, and the king's friends there were hanged. Richard sent Salisbury to gather troops at Conway, promising to follow him at once; yet he did not come for three weeks, when he landed at Beaumaris. But there his own men fled from him, and he fell into despair, and cursed the untruth of England, saying, "Alas! what faith is there in this false world?" and, instead of going to Bordeaux, where he would have found help and welcome, left his treasure and fled, in disguise, to Conway. He found no help there; Salisbury's levies had gone home, tired of waiting for him. Ere he could make fresh plans, he was lured, by Northumberland's false oath, out of his stronghold and brought to Flint. "Fool that I was!" he cried, when he found himself betrayed, "to have saved the life of this Henry of Lancaster three times, as I have, yea, when his own father would have had him die for his treason and wickedness! 'Tis a true saying, indeed, 'Your worst foe is him you free from the gallows.'"

When he saw Lancaster, he smiled and said, "Welcome, fair cousin!" "I am come home before my time, sir," answered Lancaster, bowing, "for your people complain that you have ruled them harshly for a score of years or more, but now, if it please God, I will help you to rule better." "If it please you, it pleaseth us well," replied Richard. They then started for London.

At Lichfield the king tried to escape, but was retaken,

and henceforth strictly guarded. The Londoners welcomed Henry with joy, but hooted and groaned as the king was led to the Tower. Before the Parliament that had been called could meet, Richard, seeing no present hope, agreed, in writing, to give up the crown. When the Parliament met, the resignation was read in English and Latin, and accepted. Thirty-three charges against Richard were then read, which accused him of having acted wrongfully toward Archbishop Arundel and the appellants; of having packed Parliaments by means of the sheriffs, and got them to give up their lawful rights to him; of having lowered the free crown of England by seeking the pope's approval of acts of Parliament; of having raised unlawful taxes, loans, purveyance, and ransoms; of having broken the laws as to the sheriffs, and royal officers, and judges; of having made an unrighteous will; of having said and held that the laws lay in his own mouth, and that he could change them as he liked, and that the life, lands, and goods of every man were at his mercy without trial.

The Parliament voted these charges true, and sufficient grounds for setting the king aside, and sent seven commissioners to tell him so. Only one man, Thomas Marks, bishop of Carlisle, spoke up for his master, and asked for a fair trial, but he was not listened to. As soon as the throne was declared vacant, the duke of Lancaster rose, and, crossing himself, said, "In the name of God, I, Henry of Lancaster, claim this realm, and the crown thereof, with all the members and appurtenances thereto, as coming of the right blood of King Henry, and through that right which God, of his grace, hath sent me, with the help of my kin and of my friends, to recover it, the which realm was in point to be undone for default of governance and undoing of laws." And with that he showed the signet which Richard had given him at Flint.

Whereon the Three Estates, severally and together, agreed
7

to take him as king. Then Henry, having knelt down and prayed a while in their midst, was handed to the throne by the two archbishops. After a sermon by Arundel, on the text, "Behold the man whom I spake to thee of, the same shall rule over my people," Henry spoke again: "Sirs, I thank you, both spiritual and temporal, and all the estates of the land, and I do you to wit that it is not my will that any man should think that by way of conquest I would disinherit any man of his heritage, liberties, or other rights that he ought to have, or put him out of that he hath and hath had by the good laws of this realm, save those that have been against the good state and common profit of the realm." And on the morrow, October 1st, Sir William Thirning, as the spokesman of the Seven Commissioners, went to the Tower and addressed Richard, saying, "Sir, ye remember you well that ye renounced and put off the state of king and lordship, and of all the dignity that belongeth thereto." "Yea," said Richard, "but not the ghostly honor of the royal anointing, which I could not renounce or put off." But Thirning went on to say that "his renunciation and cession was plainly accepted and agreed to by all the estates and people. And besides this, sir, at the instance of all the estates and people, there were certain articles of default in your governance there read, and there well heard and plainly understood by all the the estates aforesaid, and by them thought so true and notorious and well-known that for these two causes, and for others also, as they said, and having consideration to your own words in your renunciation and cession, that ye were not worthy nor sufficient nor able for to govern because of your own demerits (as it is more fully declared therein), they therefore thought that it was reasonable and cause for to depose you." "Nay, nay," cried Richard, "not for any lack of power, but because my rule did not please the people." "I am but using your words, sir," answered Thirning. "Well," said Richard, smiling, "I look for no more, but, after all this, I hope that my cousin will be good lord to me." This was the imprisoned king's last free utterance. On the 27th he was condemned by the Lords and Council to perpetual imprisonment, and two days after sent from the Tower to Pomfret. His after fate is as yet unknown.

Richard was ruined, as William Langland says, by *redcless-ness*, or lack of good counsel. He was not an idle trifler, like Edward II., nor a shiftless spendthrift, like Henry III.; but a singularly gifted man, handsome, brave, generous, intelligent, merciful, and able to act boldly and quickly when he chose. His path was never free from difficulty and danger, family quarrels, foreign hatred, and English discontent, a heritage of trouble that came to him with his crown; but he was on the verge of safety when he ruined himself by two or three false steps taken in the interest of his friends, rather than of himself or his people. He was ill-advised when, for the sake of peace, he let the irritating misdeeds of his brothers, his officers, and his guard go unpunished; ill-advised when, out of love for art, splendor, and a fair life, he kept up a grand court, and was the patron of poets, painters, and architects, though he knew that his people grudged spending money on any thing but war; ill-advised when, impatient at the ceaseless falsehood and plots of his kinsmen, he used haughty language, and spoke of his royal rights as above the law; and still more ill-advised when he tried to govern well without consulting the likes and dislikes of the people he had to rule, banishing their favorites, breaking down their privileges, mocking at their cherished beliefs, and overriding the rights to which they clung. But Richard was no brutal or heartless tyrant, and if his luck had not left him, he might have put away the follies, set right the mistakes into which his youth and his young counselors had led him, and so reigned more happily than his supplanter. However, he had had his chance and failed, and the English people, perhaps rightly, would not give him another, though he had a few warm friends who could not forget his fair face and open hand, and pitied his fate.

> " Ah, Richard, with the eyes of heavy mind
> I see thy glory like a shooting star
> Fall to the bare earth from the firmament.
> Thy sun sets weeping in the lowly west,
> Witnessing storms to come, war, and unrest."

XXVI.

BATTLE OF AZINCOURT.—MARTIN.

[The reign of Henry IV., the first of the Lancastrian kings, was a constant struggle against treason and revolt. His son, Henry V., strong in his position at home, renewed the old quarrel with France. In 1415 he landed with an army in Normandy, captured Harfleur, after a hard siege, and then marched to Calais. On his way thither he encountered and overthrew the French army at Azincourt.]

On Thursday evening, October 24, the English were encamped in and around the little village of Maisoncelle; the French lay in the open fields near the village of Azincourt, through which ran the road to Calais. The night was cold, dark, and rainy. The French, with feet in the mud, and bodies exposed to the rain, gathered around large fires which had been built near the banners of their chiefs, and awaited the tardy coming of an autumnal dawn. Among them there was a great noise of pages, varlets, and " all sorts of fellows," calling and shouting; " but they had few musical instruments to cheer them, and few of the horses neighed during the night, a fact which many marveled at, and thought full of omen. The English, on the other hand, though weary, hungry, and cold, kept their trumpets and various musical instruments sounding all night long, so that the whole region round about was filled with the noise; and they made their peace with God, confessing their sins with tears, and many partaking of the sacrament, for they expected certain death on the morrow." But not a shout, not a useless word, was heard among them; the men-at-arms refitted the lacings of their armor, and the archers put new strings to their bows.

At length morning dawned. The French army drew up on the narrow plain of Azincourt, in three deep lines of battle, each directly behind the other, so that neither could render the others any assistance. The little English army presented a front of equal extent to this great multitude, which gained no advantage from the depth of its lines. Nearly all the princes, lords, and great nobles had insisted on placing themselves in the advance-guard, sending to the rear the infantry, the bowmen, and probably the artillery also, as there is no mention of it during the day. Eight thousand gentlemen, magnificently arrayed, pressed into the front line of battle, with the constable, the dukes of Orleans and Bourbon, the counts of Eu and Richemont, and the Marshal Boucicaut, grand-master of the cross-bowmen. Five hundred of these eight thousand nobles, including the duke of Orleans and the count of Nevers, had had themselves invested with knighthood the preceding day. The dukes of Alençon and Bar, and the count of Nevers had very reluctantly consented to take command of the second line; the rear-guard had been intrusted to the counts of Dammartin, Marle, and Fauquemberg; but these noblemen and their followers immediately abandoned their posts, and, rushing on, helped to encumber the advance-guard. With the exception of the two wings, each composed of several hundred lancers, and destined "to strike" the English archers and "break their fire," all the men-at-arms of the first two lines had dismounted, and had shortened their lances so as to fight on foot. These warriors, heavily armed as they were, sank half-way to the knee in the freshly-plowed ground, which was soaked with rain, and had been trampled into mud by the horses during the night. They could not move, and so resolved, instead of attacking the enemy, to await his attack. A vague feeling of sadness spread through the ranks; affecting scenes took place. Gentlemen "pardoned each other for the hatreds they had cherished, many embraced and made peace, which was a touching sight to see." The solemnity of the situation awakened kindly feelings in the souls of even these men, steeped, as they were, in pride and sensuality; they became serious in the presence of death.

The English had arrayed themselves by placing the mass of their archers in front; behind these came the men-at-arms on foot, and on the wings were men-at-arms and bowmen intermingled. The archers were protected by a movable palisade, each man carrying a stake sharpened at both ends, which he fixed in the ground in front of him, with the point inclined toward the enemy. The English presented a strange contrast to the French nobles, who were all resplendent in their steel breast-plates, and their coats of mail, embroidered with gold and silver, and variegated with brilliant colors. The archers had suffered so much in this campaign that they looked like a troop of vagabonds and beggars; many of them were barefoot and without helmets; others had head-pieces of waxed leather or of willow, guarded only by a cross-piece of iron, and most of them were without mailed doublets; but they were all the more active for fighting on this muddy and slippery ground, and though their "jackets" were worn-out, and their breeches in tatters, their weapons were in good condition, as they speedily proved.

King Henry had begun the day by hearing three masses in succession; then he put on his helmet, surmounted by a crown of gold, mounted a charger, and ordered his men forward into a field of young grain, where the soil was less soaked than elsewhere. He rode along the lines, and reminded them of the "fine affairs which the kings, his predecessors, had won over the French. . . . Moreover he told them that the French boasted they would take all the archers prisoners, and cut off the three fingers of the right hand." The English answered, with a great shout, "Sire, God give you long life and victory."

The two armies were within bow-shot. But Henry hesitated to begin a conflict with thirteen or fourteen thousand combatants against fifty thousand. Conferences had already taken place in the preceding days; and he now sent a message to the chiefs of the French army, offering, it is said, to give up his claim to the French crown, and to surrender Harfleur, if they would restore to him the county of Ponthieu and five cities, which ought to belong to his duchy of Guyenne, and give him in marriage the Princess Catherine of France, with eight hundred thousand crowns of gold. The French demanded Harfleur, and renunciation of the crown, without compensation. They consented to leave to the English only Calais, and what they actually held in Guyenne. The English refused.

It was now eleven o'clock in the morning; and, as soon as the conference was broken off, the marshal of the English army, Sir Thomas Erpingham, exhorted his troops again to fight well, then, throwing his staff in the air, cried out, " Ne strecke!" (Now strike!) The English army raised a great shout, and advanced several paces. The French remained motionless; they were nearly knee-deep in mud. The English gave another shout, advanced nearer, and the archers began the battle with a volley of ten thousand arrows, which was followed by many more. The French at last began to move, and, bowing their heads so that the arrows might not penetrate the openings in their visors, they struggled laboriously against the enemy's line, and forced it back a little, while at the same time the men-at-arms on the two wings, who had remained mounted, started from Azincourt and Tramecourt to take the archers in flank.

This cavalry charge, if it could have been properly executed, would have decided the fortune of the day; but the condition of the ground was such that it failed completely. Most of the cavalry stumbled and fell in the furrows of the newly-plowed fields; not more than one in ten succeeded in reaching the enemy. A few of the bravest and best-mounted came on against the pointed stakes of the archers, and were slain; the others, recoiling before the hail of arrows, struggled out of the mud in which they were nearly mired, fell back on the first line of battle, and their horses, wounded, and furious with pain, plunged into the ranks, causing frightful disorder. The line of the advance-guard was broken; the men-at-arms fell one upon the other, and were unable to rise; "many got out of the *mêlée*, and fled."

The archers seeing these breaks in the French line, threw down their bows and arrows, and, seizing their swords, hatchets, loaded clubs, and *hawk-bills*, charged through their palisade of stakes into the gaps of the opposing ranks. The French men-at-arms, weighed down by their armor, sinking at every step into the spongy soil, and already exhausted before having fought at all, were so crowded together that they could scarcely raise their arms to strike. "The archers smote them down in heaps; it seemed as if they were hammering on anvils; and the French nobles fell one upon another, some being suffocated, the rest killed or captured."

The archers broke through to the second line of battle, opening a way for King Henry and his men-at-arms, who followed and supported them with the greatest energy. The second line met the fate of the first, which it had been unable to assist, and was now involved with it in irretrievable disaster. Desperate efforts were made to dispute the victory, but any general maneuver on the part of the French was impossible; the flower of their nobility could only sell their lives or their liberty as dearly as possible. Lefevre, an eye-witness, reports that eighteen French knights had solemnly sworn to get at the English king and strike the crown from his head, or lose their lives in the attempt. They did, in fact, get so near him that one of them, with a blow of his ax, struck one of the jewels from the crown ; but he and all the rest were speedily cut down and killed. The duke of Alençon, with his men, forced his way nearly through the English line, killed the duke of York, the king's cousin, close by his side, but was cut down by the royal guard just as Henry advanced to spare his life. Duke Antoine de Brabant, who was hastening up by forced marches to join the French army, reached the field at this juncture with the best-mounted of his men. Without stopping even to put on his coat of mail, he seized an emblazoned banner from one of his trumpeters, cut a hole in it, slipped it over his head, and, with drawn sword, rushed upon the English. He was at once unhorsed and slain. The English archers and men-at-arms advanced steadily, always in good order, "fighting, killing, and taking prisoners," without ever breaking their lines to pursue the fugitives, until they were face to face with the French rear-guard, which had remained mounted. The latter did not await their onset; they broke and fled, with the exception of the leaders and some six hundred lancers, who perished in a last charge against the victorious foe.

The English were already complete masters of the field when it was announced to the English king that a new enemy had appeared in his rear, and was plundering his baggage. Henry, alarmed at this unexpected attack, and seeing, in the distance, the fugitives of the French rear-guard gathering again in companies, gave orders, at the sound of the trumpet, for every Englishman to slay his prisoners. The English refused to obey, not from any feeling of humanity, but for fear of losing the great ransoms they expected to get from their captives. Henry then detailed a knight and two hundred archers to do the "business, and there, in cold blood, all that French nobility was killed and cut to pieces, a pitiable sight to see." A multitude of persons had been slaughtered when the king, seeing that the men who had attacked

7*

the baggage were fleeing with their booty, revoked his barbarous order. The attack had been made by only a few
hundred soldiers and peasants, under the command of the
lord of Azincourt. The men of the French rear-guard, who
had tried to rally, fled as soon as they saw that the English
were ready to fight them.

The English remained till evening, plundering the dead
and succoring those of the wounded from whom they hoped
to receive a ransom. The next morning they returned to
finish their work and turned over all the heaps of wounded
that lay scattered about the plain, choosing whom to kill and
whom to take away.

Never had the French nobility experienced a disaster com-
parable to that of Azincourt. Courtrai, Crecy, and Poitiers
had been surpassed. Of the ten thousand dead, there were
counted more than eight thousand nobles, a great part of
whom had been massacred after they had surrendered, when
Henry V. gave orders to slay the prisoners. Among these
were the dukes of Alençon and Brabant, the duke of Bar
and his two brothers, the Constable d'Albret, the counts of
Nevers, Marle, Fauquemberg, and others, the warlike bishop
of Sens, about one hundred and twenty great barons, etc.
The duke of Orleans was drawn out, alive, from a heap of
dead and wounded, and remained a prisoner, together with
the duke of Bourbon, the counts of Eu, Vendôme, and
Richemont, the Marshal Boucicaut, and fifteen hundred
knights and esquires. The English lost the duke of York,
the earl of Suffolk, and about sixteen hundred men.

XXVII.

JEANNE DARC.—GUEST.

[Henry V. pursued his French conquests until his death, in 1422. He left to his brother, the duke of Bedford, the care of his French dominions. At that time France was in a deplorable condition, rent with faction, and a prey to anarchy. Her imbecile king, Charles VI., died, and his son, the dauphin, was unable to unite the nation, restore order, and drive out the English. What was needed was a leader, and one came at last in the peasant girl, Jeanne Darc. At the time of her appearance, the English were engaged in besieging the city of Orleans.]

THERE is no story in all the long history of the world more strange and beautiful than the story of the Maid of Orleans. She was born in a wild and woody country, on the borders of Lorraine and Champagne. Her father, Jacques Darc, was a poor laborer. His little Joan, or Jeanne, was bred up like any other poor man's child ; but before we can understand either the maiden or her story, we must try to realize a little, if we can, the world she lived in, and how different it was from our world. When she was taken to the little country church, on Sundays and holy days, she would, doubtless, see on the walls the images of crowned saints and angels, of Christ, and the Virgin Mary. They might be very roughly painted, but to the poor village people they would seem beautiful and glorious ; nor would they be looked upon as mere pictures. Jeanne and all the others in the church thought they were actually like the real saints and angels in heaven, and would kneel and pray before them without a moment's doubt that they would hear and answer. If the world seemed cold and bleak, the poor cottages rude and bare, and men were rough and miserable, they would like to think of the happy, glorious world, where their friends the saints sat in glory, with a kind thought of pity for them and their troubles. Jeanne loved going to church above all other things.

But when she walked in the great oak forests, near her home, she would have a visionary world about her there, too. Where we should only see trees and streams and grass and flowers, and might half fancy, from their beauty and brightness, that they must be alive and happy in a way of their own, every body then thought that there were fairies and wood-spirits. In England, indeed, it was believed that the elves and fairies had been driven away by priests and friars, and that that was the reason they could no longer be seen, as they used to be, dancing in the green meadows. In the forests where Jeanne lived the priest used to drive the fairies away, too; he came to say mass every year beside their favorite fountain, and under a great tree, on which the children would hang garlands to please the "ladies," as they called them. The priests, like every body else, believed in the fairies, but as the tales of them had come down from the old heathen times, they considered them unchristian, and that they ought to be banished.

Thus these people did really and truly seem to live in two worlds, the visible and the invisible; and though the commonplace, the busy, and the dull would half forget the invisible world, the gentle and quiet and thoughtful ones would live in it more than in the visible. Jeanne, besides being a good and pious girl, was full of poetry and imagination; when she was not sewing or spinning by her mother's side she loved dearly to go and pray in the quiet church where the saints were, or to wander in the woods, feeding the wild birds and listening to the church bells.

As she was growing up, this peaceful, visionary life was disturbed by the same miseries which disturbed the rest of the country. Sometimes poor fugitives, who had been driven out of their homes by the war, came through the village; sometimes her own people had to flee, and when they came back would find every thing destroyed or burned. Thus she began to think about the war and her unhappy country, and her whole heart was filled with pity and sorrow. She did what she could to help the sufferers; when the poor refugees came by she gave them up her own bed, and went to sleep in the barn. She prayed and fasted; and as she brooded over these sad things, and longed to do more, she seemed to be lifted out of herself and the little world about her. The saints seemed to come nearer to her; she began to see bright lights, and to hear strange voices, which no one else could see or hear. From out of the bright light a noble figure with shining wings spoke, and told her it was she who was to help the king of France, and to give him back his kingdom. The poor child was frightened; she was now seventeen or eighteen years old; she said she knew nothing about riding on horseback or leading soldiers. But as time went on she saw more and more visions, heard more and more voices, all bidding her rise and rescue her country.

No one believed her at first; her father and mother were angry, and forbade her leaving home; they even tried to marry her to an honest man of the village. But the impulse was too strong; she felt that she must go. At last she persuaded an old village wheelwright, her uncle, to take her to the nearest town, where she would find soldiers and a captain, who would send her to the dauphin. The captain was greatly puzzled when he saw this village girl arrive, and heard her say that the Lord had sent her to the aid of the dauphin. He was quite ready to think there was something supernatural in the matter, but he was by no means sure that it might not be the work of the devil instead of the saints; for, besides believing in the agency of the invisible saints and angels, every one believed, also, quite as firmly in the power of evil spirits, wizards, and witches; and to the end of her life half the world believed that poor Jeanne Darc was a sorceress inspired by the devil. The parish priest was sent for to sprinkle holy water, and to drive away the evil spirit, if there was one.

But Jeanne was so gentle, so modest, and so firm in declaring that she was sent by God, that people began to believe in her. The captain decided that he would send her to the king, or the dauphin, as she called him, for he had not yet been crowned. She was dressed in armor, and five or six armed men were appointed to attend her, though they did not know what to think about it, and were half afraid she might be a witch after all. But she stopped to pray at every church she passed, and at last arrived safely at the French court. When she saw the king, whom she recognized at once among the crowd of courtiers, she knelt down before him, saying : "Gentle dauphin, I am called Jeanne the Maid. The King of Heaven sends to tell you, by me, that you shall be consecrated and crowned in the city of Reims." It was in Reims Cathedral that all the kings of France were crowned, and the French people thought as much of that sacred city as the English did of Westminster Abbey.

Whether Charles believed in her divine inspiration or not, it seemed as if there was no other way of saving Orleans, and that this last desperate chance had better be tried. But, before that, it should be inquired into once more whether she might not be influenced by the devil, instead of by God. Four or five bishops examined her this time, but they could find nothing against her. When they desired that she would show a sign to prove that God had sent her, she said : " My sign will be to raise the siege of Orleans." Every one in the whole region declared that she was a saint ; the defenders of Orleans had heard that a miraculous virgin was coming to help them, and sent earnestly entreating for her aid.

At last she was allowed to go. She rode forth, no longer like a poor peasant girl, but fully clad in beautiful white armor, mounted on a splendid black horse, and bearing a sacred sword, called the sword of St. Katherine, which, it was said, she had miraculously discovered in the church. Before her was carried a white standard, on which was the picture of God holding the world in his hands, and two angels, each with a lily-flower.

It is easy to imagine what an effect this wonderful sight would produce both on friend and foe. The poor discouraged French roused up suddenly to hope and confidence. Here was this beautiful girl, this beautiful saint, sent expressly by God, to lead them to victory; and if God were for them, who could be against them? As she marched to Orleans, followed by her troop of soldiers, she had an altar set up in the open air, and they all received the sacrament. These wild, fierce men, who would obey no one else, would have followed the maid to the end of the world.

The English, on the other hand, lost heart. They, too, believed Jeanne was miraculously inspired. If it were God fighting against them, what could they do? But in their hearts many of them thought she was a witch and led by the devil. This seemed more terrible still. They were ready enough to fight against men—against the Frenchmen, whom they had beaten so often; but how could they resist the spells of a sorceress?

It was no wonder that it all ended as it did. When Jeanne led the French soldiers against the besiegers, the English, brave as they were, were terrified; they began to see visions, too. Sometimes they saw white butterflies fluttering around her sacred banner; sometimes they saw the saints or Michael, the archangel, among her troops. The siege of Orleans had lasted seven months; in ten days all the English forts were in the hands of the French, and the city was free. It was on a Sunday morning that the English retreated. The maiden caused an altar to be raised in the plain, and before the enemy was well out of sight the rescued people were kneeling around it giving God thanks.

Thus Jeanne had given the "sign" she had promised, and Orleans was delivered. Now she turned to the great work she had at heart—the coronation of the dauphin. It was a long journey to Reims, and a great part of the country through which they must pass was in the hands of the English or the

Burgundians. But the French knew no fears now ; they crowded around the maid ; always more and more of them followed her standard as she led the king to Reims. Wherever they went they were successful. They took one town after another—even Troyes, where Henry V. had been married ; they defeated the English in the battle of Patay. At last they reached Reims, and in its venerable cathedral Charles was anointed, crowned, and consecrated king of France.

XXVIII.

WARS OF THE ROSES.—GUEST.

[After the raising of the siege of Orleans and the death of the duke of Bedford, the English were rapidly expelled from France. In England a child, Henry VI., was on the throne. The lawless habits acquired by the English nobles during the French war could not be restrained when they returned home. They divided into two factions, one rallying around the house of York and the other around the house of Lancaster, and they soon drifted into civil war. The struggle was ostensibly for the possession of the crown, but there were many causes at work to produce discontent.]

EDWARD IV.

IT is hardly necessary to study and recollect all about the twelve battles that were fought, and all the changes and chances of the war. Sometimes one side conquered, and sometimes the other. In the end we may say *neither*, or perhaps *both*, conquered, since a member of the house of Lancaster, marrying a member of the house of York, became undisputed king. But though we may be inclined to say, then, that the wars were all for nothing, and nothing came of them, they had in reality a very great effect on the whole future history and state of England. After those wars were over England was much more like what she is now than she ever could have been without them.

In all the past history we have seen what an enormous power the nobles possessed; how they could help or hinder the king and government just as they chose; how they rebelled and led armies about, fighting each other or fighting the king, just as it happened; or, if they had a strong, clever king, whom they respected, following him and fighting for him. How different all that is from any thing we ever see or hear of now! Imagine now if we were to hear that some great duke or earl was going to lead an army against the government!

We all know it is impossible. Dukes and earls have no armies now. They may give their opinions and advice and votes and money, they may serve in the queen's army, as any other gentleman may, and that is all they can do. But up till this time the great lords had always little armies, or even rather large armies sometimes, of their own. They were bound, indeed, to have them; it was on that very condition that they held their estates. The theory of the feudal system was, that the vassals of the king were obliged to furnish so many men to help him in his wars. But when they did not like the king it was quite probable that they would fit out those said men to oppose him; and, if there was a rival claimant to the throne, some of the nobles would take one side and some the other, according as it suited their interest, or, perhaps, according as they thought was their duty.

In such times a rich nobleman, who had a large following, who could make himself popular, and perhaps hire many other soldiers besides his own under-vassals and tenants, would be very powerful indeed, even more powerful than the king himself, like Warwick, the king-maker. In those days there was no regular standing army, such as we have now.

At that time every body was a soldier, and nobody was a soldier. So, when the nobles went to muster up an army, the plowmen, the weavers, the laborers of all sorts, would leave their work and follow them to fight. They were, doubtless, better soldiers than such men would be at present, for they were regularly trained and practiced at certain times, and every man knew, more or less, how to fight, though they were not like the disciplined regiments we have now. In a little while, after a battle or two perhaps, they would go back again to their work, to their plows or their looms. There were some regular soldiers, too, whose regular profession was war, "companions," as they were called, who were trained men, but who belonged to no side and no chief, and who could be hired by any party, city, or rich man who wanted them ; and who, when wanted by no one, generally became brigands.

At the time of the Wars of the Roses all the principal nobles of the kingdom took one side or the other, either that of York or Lancaster; each brought his little army behind him, and it was they who fought those twelve battles. At the end of the wars they were nearly all gone—all killed. The family feeling was very strong in those times, and it was a point of honor for a man to revenge the deaths of his relations; then the other side would revenge themselves in return, till we can hardly believe the men who worked these cruel deeds could have called themselves Christians at all. Thus the war became bitterly cruel and savage.

In looking over the pedigrees of those great old families it is quite startling to see how many times we read "killed at Tewkesbury," "killed at St. Albans," "beheaded after Wakefield," and the like. No less than four dukes of Somerset, one after the other, perished in these wars. The end of it all was that the old nobility was almost destroyed, and the feudal system vanished forever. Things began to be much more like what they are now; so this period is generally looked on as the end of the Middle Ages, and the beginning of modern times.

We cannot suppose the great nobles, or any body else, would have taken all this trouble, raised their armies, and hurried about all over the country, fighting, killing, and being killed, all for love of Henry or Edward, Lancaster or York. Had there not been some grave causes of discontent, it is pretty certain both York and Mortimer would have been forgotten, now that the Lancasters had been sitting on the throne for fifty years, whatever their exact rights might have been at the outset. But there was, in fact, a great deal of discontent, and a spirit of entire disaffaction spread abroad among the nation. Every one was ashamed and disgusted at the disgraceful end of the French war, and the pride of the people was not much comforted by the death of the duke of Suffolk or the bishop of Chichester. The state of England itself was also unsatisfactory. Jack Cade and the Kentish men, as we saw, had complained about the way Parliaments were elected. A great many people who formerly used to vote for members were no longer allowed to do so at all, and many of those who still had votes had to give them according to orders, and not according to their own wishes. And Parliament very seldom met at all. Nor was the government strong enough to keep the country quiet and peaceful. High and low were able to defy the law with impunity; the great families were continually carrying on little wars of their own; innumerable robbers ranged over the land, keeping the people in constant alarm and distress, and nobody had power to punish the evil-doers or protect the helpless and innocent.

Moreover the house of Lancaster, both Henry IV. and Henry V., had, in a mistaken zeal for religion, made common cause with the Church, and had persecuted and burnt the Lollards. But, though the Lollards appeared to be quite crushed and put down, in the bottom of their hearts immense numbers of people believed them to be right and sympathized with them; so that when they had time to think, and were not dazzled and absorbed by Henry's splendid victories, it caused a vast deal of hidden discontent, and turned men's hearts away from their rulers.

Thus with all these grievances, either spoken or unspoken, a great many people were ready for a change. Not that the princes of the house of York were at all likely to remedy any of these things, or ever did so, but that when people are dissatisfied they are willing to hope that any change will be for the better; though it had need to be very, very much better indeed, to make up for the misery of a civil war. We have seen how cruel and hard-hearted the nobles became toward one another; what their followers were obliged to suffer we may imagine. In one beautiful passage which Shakespeare added to the old play of *Henry VI.* he paints it for us very vividly. He shows us how, in one of these battles, a father has unknowingly killed his own son, and a son his own father, who were fighting in opposite ranks; and, as they both lament their cruel fortunes, they think of what is so often forgotten, of the poor wife and mother at home, to whom they must carry the bitter news.

But, though sad and terrible things like this must often have happened, and though the nobles, many of them, became little better than murderers, there is a great consolation in knowing that, on the whole, the mass of the people did not suffer so much as might have been expected. In some of the battles the leaders on both sides gave orders that the poorer people were to be spared, and that only the principal men were to be killed. For the most part the people, except those who were dependent upon the nobles, took no part at all. The merchants and shopkeepers went on with their business; the judges went on circuit and held their assizes, as if nothing was the matter. No towns, no churches, were destroyed, and we have the comfort of thinking that those who made the quarrel bore the brunt of the punishment.

There is good reason to believe, in fact, that the poor people were better off than they ever were before; for while Edward IV. was king new laws were made to prevent them from spending too much money on their clothes. This subject seems to be always cropping up; we are perpetually having sermons and laws against finery, and very little good they seem to have done. In the very midst of the war a law was passed beginning in this way: "The commons, as well men as women, have worn, and daily do wear, excessive and inordinate array and apparel, to the great displeasure of God, and impoverishing of this realm of England." It goes on to command that common laborers and servants, and their wives, are never to wear cloth costing more than two shillings a yard; nor are they to wear girdles ornamented with silver. Another law was passed forbidding the wives to get their veils and handkerchiefs too fine. Thus it is evident they must have been well off and receiving good wages, or they would never have thought of wanting expensive things of this kind.

But, though the emancipation of the serfs had done a great deal of good and the laborers were in this prosperous condition, some evil had come with it too, and that was that there were now a great many people who had no work and no wages at all. As we saw, after the plague of the Black Death, when there were so few men, and wages rose so high, many landlords would not, or could not, pay them. They left off tilling the land, and turned it into great sheep-farms. Then only two or three men would be wanted, instead of a great many, and the sheep were very profitable, both for food and for their wool. Now there was this to be said in favor of villeinage, that the owner of the land had at least to feed, clothe, and shelter all his villeins, or to see that they had land enough to support them. Even when they were ill or old they still had to be maintained, and we never hear that they were badly treated in this respect.

But now that was all over; they were free and their own masters, and it was nobody's duty to look after them any longer. They had to try how they liked "a crust of bread and liberty." There began to be a great many beggars; some "sturdy beggars," who would not work; others old and feeble, who could not work; others who could find no work to do. It was very hard to know what to do with all of them; there was always the fear that many of them might turn thieves, as, indeed, they often did. The government did its utmost, and passed a great many laws, many of them very harsh and cruel, about vagabonds and beggars; but it was a long time before it found out any thing like a reasonable way of dealing with them.

We must now see how some of the more distinguished people, the kings and princes, were behaving. The reign of Henry VI., if it can be called a reign, is generally reckoned to have ended after the battle of Towton (1461), which was one of the most cruel and bloody of all the twelve, and in which the Lancastrians were utterly defeated. Henry and Margaret fled, and Edward IV. was crowned king. But the Wars of the Roses were by no means over yet, and it was not very long before he in his turn had to flee, and Henry, who had been caught and imprisoned in the Tower, came forth again a king. For, though Edward was so clever, handsome, and popular, he contrived to give dire offense to the nobles who supported him, and, above all, to the earl of Warwick, the king-maker. The way in which he did this was in choosing to make a love-match instead of marrying according to prudence or policy. The marriage he made was very much beneath his position, since, though his wife was a lady by birth and breeding, she was only the widow of an obscure gentleman, and, to make it still worse, her husband had been on the Lancastrian side.

In these wars it was the practice that whichever side conquered took revenge on the other by depriving all the lords
and gentlemen of their estates (even if they escaped with
their lives) and dividing them among their own party; so that
many great lords and gentlemen were reduced to literal beg-
gary. They might be seen wandering about barefoot and begging their bread in France, while their enemies at home were
sitting in their fine houses, eating their bread, and spending
their money. Among others there was one John Grey, of
whom we read that " King Henry made him knight at the
last battle of St. Albans, but little while he enjoyed his
knighthood, for in the same field he was slain." His property had been confiscated, and his children were left destitute.
His widow, who was young and beautiful, appeared before
Edward to implore his compassion. The king was also
young, and always ready to fall in love. The lady behaved
very modestly and very cleverly; she quite won his heart;
and, casting away all thought of prudence or worldly wisdom, Edward determined to marry her.

The English had been very angry at Henry VI.'s marrying
a princess who brought no dowry and no high alliances; but
assuredly this match would seem worse still, as Margaret had
at least been a princess of royal blood. Moreover, Edward
had half promised to marry a French princess himself, a sister of the queen of France; and Warwick, who, besides being
king-maker, would have wished to be queen-maker also, was
very keen in promoting that alliance. He, likewise, wished
Edward to give his sister in marriage to a French prince,
but he chose to marry her to the duke of Burgundy instead.
It was also believed that Warwick would have desired Edward, if he married an English woman at all, to have married
one of his own daughters.

Thus he was quite alienated from Edward, though he did
not, as yet, take part with Henry. He first made friends
with Edward's brother, George, the duke of Clarence, and

gave him the daughter, Isabel, whom he had, perhaps, intended for the king. Through all these wars the nobles were constantly changing sides and betraying one another. Even the royal family itself was not faithful, and Clarence now conspired to betray his brother. Afterward he changed again, and betrayed his father-in-law. He himself was finally betrayed and murdered.

Perhaps the king thought, as he had married greatly beneath his dignity, and his wife and her relations were looked down upon by all the aristocracy of the land, that it would set things right to make them noble now. Accordingly, all the greatest honors and riches were poured out upon them. Her father and her brothers received great titles and estates ; her son was married to the heiress of the duke of Exeter, whom Warwick wanted for his own nephew ; her sisters were married to the richest young men who could be found, heirs of earls and dukes, whom the lords would have liked to marry their own daughters. All this, therefore, instead of setting things right, angered the earl of Warwick and the rest of the old nobility beyond bearing.

Except for their being "upstarts," however, there was nothing to be said against these relations of the queen. One of them in particular, her brother, Lord Rivers, was good, accomplished, and faithful. But their glory was short-lived, and they paid very dear for it. At last things came to an open rupture, and Warwick, forsaking Edward, allied himself with his most bitter enemy, Margaret of Anjou, who had never ceased stirring and striving to reinstate her husband and son. He now married his other daughter to her son, Edward, so that he had, we may say, two strings to his bow— two daughters who might, in the changes of that changing time, come to be queens of England. This second daughter, Anne, was, indeed, queen for a short time, though not at all by the means her father expected.

As soon as Warwick appeared in England the people, who

loved and admired him, flocked around him in crowds. Edward had to flee out of the country, and to flee in such haste that he took nothing with him, and had no means of paying the captain of the ship which carried him across but by giving him a cloak lined with sable. As to his poor wife, whom he left behind him, as well as his luggage, she took refuge with her young daughters in the sanctuary at Westminster.

Here the poor queen remained, and here her unhappy little son, Edward V., was born. Shakespeare makes her say, " Small joy have I in being England's queen." Katherine of France, who was so despised for descending to marry a private gentleman, was, perhaps, a good deal wiser and happier than poor Elizabeth Woodville, who rose from being a private lady to marry a king. However, it was not very long before Edward returned. His brother Clarence was treacherous again, and deserted Warwick. Two great battles were fought, in both of which Edward was victorious. The first was at Barnet (1471), and there Warwick, the king-maker, was slain ; the second was at Tewkesbury, and it utterly ruined the Lancastrian house. The poor young Prince Edward, son of Henry and Margaret, was brutally murdered, it is said by Edward's two brothers, Clarence and Gloucester. Margaret was made prisoner, and Henry was taken back to the Tower, where he very soon after died. The Yorkists gave out that he died of a broken heart, but every body believed that he was murdered, and Richard, duke of Gloucester, had all the credit of it, whether he really deserved it or not. The people soon began to look on poor King Henry as a saint, and said that wonderful miracles were worked at his tomb.

8

XXIX.

BOSWORTH FIELD.—GAIRDNER.

[Edward IV. left two young sons, Edward V. and Richard, duke of York. Their uncle, Richard, duke of Gloucester, was appointed Protector of the Realm, and then claimed the crown on the ground that his nephews were illegitimate. He was crowned July 6, 1483, and soon afterward the young princes disappeared. Though nothing absolutely certain is known as to their fate, it is exceedingly probable that they were murdered by Richard's order. As king, he pursued a conciliatory policy; but there was much disaffection, and it gradually centered around Henry, earl of Richmond, the representative of the Lancastrian line. In 1485 Henry invaded the kingdom, and the two rivals met on Bosworth Field.]

RICHARD III.

By repeated proclamations Richard called upon his subjects to resist the intended invasion of Richmond with all their force. He denounced the earl and his followers as men who had forsaken their true allegiance, and put themselves in subjection to the French king. He pointed out that, owing to the illegitimacy of the Beauforts, Henry could have no claim to the crown, and that even on the father's side he was come of bastard blood. He declared that he had bargained to give up forever all claims hitherto made by the kings of England either to the crown of France, the duchy of Normandy, Gascony, or even Calais. Richmond, however, had sent messages into England by which he was assured of a considerable amount of support; and he borrowed money from the king of France with which he fitted out a small fleet at Harfleur, and embarked for Wales, where his uncle, Jasper Tudor, earl of Pembroke, possessed great influence.

Richard, knowing of the intended invasion, but being uncertain where his enemy might land, had taken up his position
in the center of the kingdom. Following a plan first put in
use by his brother, Edward, during the Scotch war, he had
stationed messengers at intervals of twenty miles along all the
principal roads to the coast to bring him early intelligence.
But Henry landed at Milford Haven, at the farthest extremity
of South Wales, where, perhaps, Richard had least expected
him ; and so small was the force by which he was accompanied, that the news did not, at first, give the king very much
anxiety. He professed great satisfaction that his adversary
was now coming to bring matters to the test of battle. The
earl, however, was among friends from the moment he landed.
Pembroke was his native town, and the inhabitants expressed
their willingnesss to serve his uncle, the earl of Pembroke,
as their natural and immediate lord. The very men whom
Richard had placed to keep the country against him at once
joined his party, and he passed on to Shrewsbury with little
or no opposition.

The king's "unsteadfast friendships," on the other hand,
were now rapidly working his ruin. His own attorney-general, Morgan Kidwelly, had been in communication with the
enemy before he landed. Richard, however, was very naturally suspicious of Lord Stanley, his rival's step-father, who,
though he was steward of the royal household, had asked
leave, shortly before the invasion, to go home and visit his
family in Lancashire. This the king granted only on condition that he would send his son George, Lord Strange, to
him at Nottingham in his place. Lord Strange was, accordingly, sent to the king ; but when the news arrived of Henry's
landing, Richard desired the presence of his father also.
Stanley pretended illness, an excuse which could not fail to
increase the king's suspicions. His son at the same time
made an attempt to escape, and, being captured, confessed
that he himself and his uncle, Sir William Stanley, had formed

a project, with others, to go over to the enemy; but he protested his father's innocence, and assured the king that he would obey his summons. He was made to understand that his own life depended on his doing so, and he wrote a letter to his father accordingly.

Richard, having mustered his followers at Nottingham, went on to Leicester to meet his antagonist, and encamped at Bosworth on the night of August 21. The earl of Richmond had arrived near the same place with an army of 5,000 men, which is supposed to have been not more than half that of the king. That day, however, Lord Stanley had come to the earl secretly at Atherstone to assure him of his support in the coming battle. He and his brother, Sir William, were at the head of a force not far off, and were only temporizing to save the life of his son, Lord Strange. This information relieved Henry's mind of much anxiety, for at various times since he landed he had felt serious misgivings about the success of the enterprise. The issue was now to be decided on the following day.

Early in the morning both parties prepared for the battle. Richard arose before day-break, much agitated, it is said, by dreadful dreams that had haunted his imagination in the night-time. But he entered the field wearing his crown upon his head, and encouraged his troops with an eloquent harangue. There was, however, treason in his camp, and many of his followers were only seeking an opportunity to desert and take part with the enemy. A warning, indeed, had been conveyed by an unknown hand to his foremost supporter, the duke of Norfolk, in the following rhyme, which was discovered the night before, written on the door of his tent:

> "Jack of Norfolk, be not too bold,
> For Dickon, thy master, is bought and sold."

Lord Stanley, who had drawn up his men at about equal distance from both armies, received messages early in the morning from both leaders desiring his immediate assistance.

His policy, however, was to stand aloof to the very last moment; and he replied, in each case, that he would come at a convenient opportunity. Dissatisfied with this answer, Richard ordered his son to be beheaded, but was persuaded to suspend the execution of the order till the day should be decided.

After a discharge of arrows on both sides the armies soon came to a hand-to-hand encounter. Lord Stanley joined the earl in the midst of the engagement, and the earl of Northumberland, on whose support Richard had relied, stood still with all his followers and looked on. The day was going hard against the king. Norfolk fell in the thickest of the fight, and his son, the earl of Surrey, after fighting with great valor, was surrounded and taken prisoner. Richard endeavored to single out his adversary, whose position on the field was pointed out to him. He suddenly rushed upon Henry's body-guard, and unhorsed successively two of his attendants, one of whom, the earl's standard-bearer, fell dead to the ground. The earl himself was in great danger, but that Sir William Stanley, who had hitherto abstained from joining the combat, now endeavored to surround the king with his force of 3,000 men. Richard perceived that he was betrayed, and crying out, "Treason, Treason!" endeavored only to sell his life as dearly as possible. Overpowered by numbers, he fell dead in the midst of his enemies.

The battered crown that had fallen from Richard's head was picked up upon the field of battle, and Sir William Stanley placed it upon the head of the conqueror, who was saluted as king by his whole army. The body of Richard, on the other hand, was treated with a degree of indignity which expressed but too plainly the disgust excited in the minds of the people by his inhuman tyranny. It was stripped naked and thrown upon a horse, a halter being placed round the neck, and in that fashion carried into Leicester, where it was buried with little honor in the Grey Friars' church.

Such was the end of the last king of England of the line of

the Plantagenets.   In warlike qualities he was not inferior to the best of his predecessors, but his rule was such as alienated the hearts of the greater part of his subjects, and caused him to be remembered as a monster.   In person, too, he is represented to have been deformed, with the right shoulder higher than the left; and he is traditionally regarded as a hunchback. But it may be that even his bodily defects were exaggerated after he was gone.   Stories got abroad that he was born with teeth, and hair coming down to the shoulders, and that his birth was attended by other circumstances altogether repugnant to the order of nature.   One fact that can hardly be a misstatement is, that he was small of stature—which makes it all the more remarkable, that in this last battle he overthrew, in personal encounter, a man of great size and strength named Sir John Cheyney.   He was, in fact, a great soldier-king, in whom alike the valor and the violence of his race had been matured and brought to a climax by civil wars and family dissensions.

Chapel and Tomb of Henry VII.

PART II.

XXX.

THE CARDINAL'S LAST JOURNEY.—BREWER

[Henry VII. was really the founder of a new dynasty, and his efforts were mainly directed to securing the throne for himself and his family. This he did by strong rule at home, and by skillful diplomacy abroad. His son, Henry VIII., under the guidance of his famous minister, Cardinal Wolsey, took a much more active part in European politics. In 1527 he determined, from a variety of motives, to obtain a divorce from his queen, Catherine of Aragon. This brought him into collision with the papal power. Wolsey, having promised to gratify the king in the matter of the divorce, and having failed to do so, was deprived of nearly all his offices in 1529, and, a little later, arrested on a charge of high treason.]

ON Sunday, after dinner, as it drew toward night, he was conducted to Pomfret with five of his attendants only. At his departure, which had now got wind, a multitude of the country people assembled to testify their grief at his arrest, praying that " the foul fiend might catch " all those who had taken the cardinal from them. From the Abbey of Pomfret he

HENRY VIII.

proceeded next day to Doncaster where he lodged with the Black Friars; the day after, to Sheffield Park, where he was received by the earl and countess of Shrewsbury with great affability. There he remained for eighteen days, and was treated by his host with great consideration and generosity. Once every day he was visited by the earl, who sought to comfort his unfortunate prisoner. But he resolutely repelled all the efforts that were made to console him, applying himself wholly to devotion, and renouncing all earthly pleasure. Though he was not more than fifty-nine years of age, his health and strength had been completely broken down by his

8*

long and laborious occupations, and the incessant vexations to which he had been exposed since his disgrace. Even in his most prosperous days he had never been a strong man: now his great anxiety of mind, and the enormous pressure upon his faculties during the progress of the divorce, had wholly undermined his constitution.

The final and heaviest blow was reserved for his last moments. The reasons for his arrest had been studiously kept from him, but as upon all occasions when the king had resolved to strike he struck once and never wavered, so it was now. When Henry had abandoned himself to his resentment, he was borne along its current with the blind impetuosity of fate. No doubt was allowed to enter his mind. No question of the wisdom or justice of his own determination, no feeling of pity, no sense of past services, however great, were allowed to arrest his hand. He had ordered Sir William Kingston, the keeper of the Tower, to proceed to Sheffield to receive the earl's prisoner, and bring him to the Tower. It required the greatest delicacy to break the dreadful news to the unhappy cardinal. For this purpose, the earl, who seems to have been unusually humane and considerate, hit upon the following expedient. During his conversations with Wolsey, when the latter expressed his apprehensions lest he should be condemned unheard, the earl either took, or pretended to take, an opportunity of writing to the king in Wolsey's behalf. Then, calling Cavendish to him, he said:

" My lord, your master, has often desired me to write to the king, that he might answer his accusers in the king's presence. Even so have I done; and this day I have received letters from his grace, by Sir William Kingston, by which I perceive that the king holds the cardinal in very good estimation, and has sent for him by Sir William, who is now here, to come up and make his answer. But do you play the part of a wise man, and break the matter unto him warily; for he is always so full of sorrow when he is in my company that I am afraid he will not take it quietly."

Cavendish proceeded to break the news. "I found him," he says, "sitting at the upper end of the gallery upon a trussing chest of his own, with his beads and staff in hand."

"What news?" said he, seeing Cavendish come from the earl.

"Forsooth, sir," he replied, assuming the best appearance of cheerfulness he could muster, though his voice sadly belied his words, "I bring you the best news that ever came to you in your life."

"I pray God it be so," said Wolsey. "What is it?"

"Forsooth, sir," replied Cavendish, "my lord of Shrewsbury, perceiving how desirous you were to come before the king, has so exerted himself that the king has sent Master Kingston with twenty-four of his guard to bring you into his presence."

"Master Kingston! Master Kingston!" exclaimed the unhappy cardinal, musing for a time, as if to recollect himself, and then, clapping his hand on his thigh, he gave a deep sigh. Cavendish endeavored to cheer him. He urged the old argument that the king had no other intention by this act than to bring Wolsey into his presence, and had sent the constable with a guard of honor out of consideration for Wolsey's high estate, and he had no reason, therefore, to mistrust his master's kindness. All his efforts were useless. The cardinal knew too well the king's temper to be deceived. He had not served him so long without being fully aware how implacable and immovable were his resentments.

"I perceive," he said, with very significant words, "more than you can imagine or can know. *Experience of old has taught me.*"

It was the sentence of death, and he knew it full well; but his despondency and waning health anticipated the sword of the executioner, and disappointed the malice of his enemies.

That night his disease increased rapidly; he became very weak and was scarce able to move.

The next day he commenced his journey, and lodged at night, still very sick, at Hardwick Hall. The day after he rode to Nottingham, his sickness and infirmity increasing at every stage. On Saturday, November 26, he rode his last stage to Leicester Abbey, "and by the way he waxed so sick that he was divers times likely to have fallen from his mule."

As the journey was necessarily impeded by these delays, Sir William and his prisoner did not reach Leicester until late at night; where, on his entering the gates, the abbot with all his convent went out to meet him, with the light of many torches, and received him with great demonstrations of respect. "To whom my lord said: 'Father Abbot, I am come hither to leave my bones among you.'"

They then brought him on his mule to the stair's foot of his chamber, where Kingston took him by the arm and led him up. Immediately he went to his bed. On the Monday morning, "as I stood by his bedside," says Cavendish, "about eight of the clock, the windows being close shut, having lights burning upon the cupboard, I beheld him, as meseemed, drawing fast to his end. He, perceiving my shadow upon the wall by his bedside, asked who was there; and inquiring what was the clock, 'Sir,' said Cavendish, 'it is past eight of the clock in the morning.' 'Eight of the clock, eight of the clock,' slowly repeated the dying man; 'nay, that cannot be, for by eight of the clock you must lose your master. My time draweth nigh.'"

But even in these last faltering moments he was not allowed to remain unmolested. The king had received information from Northumberland that by an account found in Cawood the cardinal had in his possession £1,500, of which no portion could be found. Anxious to obtain the money, the king's impatience could brook no delay, although the cardinal was now on his way to the Tower. He sent a special messenger to

Kingston, commanding him to examine the cardinal, and discover where this money was deposited. The commission would have been immediately executed, but the weakness of the cardinal was so great, and increased so rapidly, that Kingston was obliged to put off the examination till the next day. The same night Wolsey was very sick, and swooned often, but rallied a little at four the next morning. About seven Kingston entered the room, intending to fulfill the king's command respecting the money. But seeing the feeble condition of the patient, he endeavored to encourage him with the usual topic, telling the cardinal he was sad and pensive from dread of that which he had no occasion to apprehend.

"Well, well, Master Kingston," replied Wolsey, "I see the matter against me, how it is framed; but if I had served God as diligently as I have served the king, *he* would not have given me over in my gray hairs. Howbeit, this is the just reward that I must receive for my worldly diligence and pains that I have had to do him service. Commend me to his majesty, beseeching him to call to his remembrance all that has passed between him and me to the present day, and most chiefly in his great matter; then shall his conscience declare whether I have offended him or no. He is a prince of royal courage, and hath a princely heart; and rather than he will miss or want part of his appetite he will hazard the loss of one half of his kingdom. I assure you I have often kneeled before him in his privy chamber, the space of an hour or two, to persuade him from his will and appetite, but I could never dissuade him." Then his words and his voice failed him. His eyes grew fixed and glazed. Incontinently the clock struck eight, and he breathed his last. "And calling to our remembrance," says Cavendish, "his words the day before, how he said that at eight of the clock we should lose our master, we stood looking upon each other, supposing he had prophesied of his departure."

As the lieutenant of the Tower had now no further charge,

and was anxious to be gone, the burial was fixed for the next day. The body was placed in a rude coffin of wood, with miter, cross, and ring, and other archiepiscopal ornaments. He lay in state until five o'clock in the afternoon, when he was carried down into the church, with great solemnity, by the abbot and convent, with many torches. Here the body rested all night in the Lady Chapel, watched by four men holding lights in their hands, while the convent chanted the old and solemn office for the dead. About four in the morning, while it was yet dark, they sung a mass. By six they had laid him in his grave, on that cold and dreary November morning, unwept and unlamented by all, except by the very few who, for the glory of human nature, amid so much of baseness, greed, ingratitude, and cruelty, remained loving and faithful to the last.

XXXI.

THE ENGLISH TERROR.—GREEN.

[After the fall of Wolsey, events marched rapidly in England. The king, impatient of the delays of the Papal Court in granting the divorce, determined to take matters into his own hand. Statute after statute was enacted in quick succession by the "Reformation Parliament" to break the connection between England and the Church of Rome. Thomas Cromwell became Henry's chief adviser, and was made "vicar-general." He forced the clergy to accept the king as Supreme Head of the Church of England, destroyed the great and wealthy monasteries, and ruled the country with an iron hand. But in 1540 he was overthrown, and executed on a charge of treason.]

WHILE the great revolution which struck down the Church was in progress, England looked silently on. In all the earlier ecclesiastical changes, in the contest over the Papal jurisdiction and Papal exactions, in the reform of the Church courts, even in the curtailment of the legislative independence of the clergy, the nation as a whole had gone with the king. But from the enslavement of the priesthood, from the gagging of the pulpits, from the suppression of the monasteries, the bulk of the nation stood aloof. There were few voices, indeed, of protest. As the royal policy disclosed itself, as the monarchy trampled under foot the tradition and reverence of ages gone by, as its figure rose bare and terrible out of the wreck of old institutions, England simply held her breath. It is only through the stray depositions of royal spies that we catch a glimpse of the wrath and hate which lay seething under this silence of the people. For the silence was a silence of terror. Before Cromwell's rise, and after his fall from power, the reign of Henry the Eighth witnessed no more than the common tyranny and bloodshed of the time. But the years of Cromwell's administration form the one period in our history which deserves the name that men have given to the rule of Robespierre. It was the English Terror. It was by terror that Cromwell mastered the king. Cranmer could plead for him at a later time with Henry as "one whose surety was only by your majesty, who loved your majesty, as I ever thought, no less than God." But the attitude of Cromwell toward the king was something more than that of absolute dependence and unquestioning devotion. He was "so vigilant to preserve your majesty from all treasons," adds the primate, "that few could be so secretly conceived but he detected the same from the beginning."

Henry, like every Tudor, was fearless of open danger, but tremulously sensitive to the lightest breath of hidden disloyalty; and it was on this dread that Cromwell based the fabric of his power. He was hardly secretary before spies were scattered broadcast over the land. Secret denunciations poured into the open ear of the minister. The air was thick with tales of plots and conspiracies, and, with the detection and suppression of each, Cromwell tightened his hold on the king. As it was by terror that he mastered the king, so it was by terror that he mastered the people.   Men felt in England, to use the figure by which Erasmus paints the time, " as if a scorpion lay sleeping under every stone."   The confessional had no secrets for Cromwell.   Men's talk with their closest friends found its way to his ear.   " Words idly spoken," the murmurs of a petulant abbot, the ravings of a moonstruck nun, were, as the nobles cried passionately at his fall, " tortured into treason."   The only chance of safety lay in silence.   " Friends who used to write and send me presents," Erasmus tells us, " now send neither letter nor gifts, nor receive any from any one, and this through fear."   But even the refuge of silence was closed by a law more infamous than any that has ever blotted the statute-book of England.   Not only was thought made treason, but men were forced to reveal their thoughts on pain of their very silence being punished with the penalties of treason.   All trust in the older bulwarks of liberty was destroyed by a policy as daring as it was unscrupulous.   The noblest institutions were degraded into instruments of terror.   Though Wolsey had strained the law to the utmost he had made no open attack on the freedom of justice.   If he shrank from assembling Parliaments, it was from his sense that they were the bulwarks of liberty.   But under Cromwell the coercion of juries and the management of judges rendered the courts mere mouth-pieces of the royal will; and where even this shadow of justice proved an obstacle to bloodshed, Parliament was brought into play to pass bill after bill of attainder.   " He shall be judged by the bloody laws he has himself made," was the cry of the Council at the moment of his fall, and, by a singular retribution, the crowning-piece of injustice which he sought to introduce even into the practice of attainder, the condemnation of a man without hearing his defense, was only practiced on himself.

But ruthless as was the Terror of Cromwell, it was of a nobler type than the Terror of France.   He never struck uselessly or capriciously, or stooped to the meaner victims of the guillotine. His blows were effective just because he chose his victims from among the noblest and the best. If he struck at the Church, it was through the Carthusians, the holiest and the most-renowned of English churchmen. If he struck at the baronage, it was through Lady Salisbury, in whose veins flowed the blood of kings. If he struck at the new learning, it was through the murder of Sir Thomas More. But no personal vindictiveness mingled with his crime. In temper, indeed, so far as we can judge from the few stories which lingered among his friends, he was a generous, kindly-hearted man, with pleasant and winning manners, which atoned for a certain awkwardness of person, and with a constancy of friendship which won him a host of devoted adherents. But no touch either of love or hate swayed him from his course. The student of Machiavelli had not studied the " Prince " in vain. He had reduced bloodshed to a system. Fragments of his papers still show us with what a business-like brevity he ticked off human lives among the casual remembrances of the day : " Item, the abbot of Reading to be sent down to be tried and executed at Reading." " Item, to know the king's pleasure touching Master More." " Item, when Master Fisher shall go to his execution, and the other." It is, indeed, this utter absence of all passion, of all personal feeling, that makes the figure of Cromwell the most terrible in our history. He has an absolute faith in the end he is pursuing, and he simply hews his way to it, as a woodman hews his way through the forest, ax in hand.

The choice of his first victim showed the ruthless precision with which Cromwell was to strike. In the general opinion of Europe, the foremost Englishman of his time was Sir Thomas More. As the policy of the divorce ended in an open rupture with Rome, he had withdrawn silently from the ministry, but his silent disapproval of the new policy was far more telling than the opposition of obscurer foes. To Cromwell there must have been something specially galling in More's attitude of reserve. The religious reforms of the new learning were being rapidly carried out, but it was plain that the man who represented the very life of the new learning believed that the sacrifice of liberty and justice was too dear a price to pay even for religious reform. In the actual changes which the divorce brought about there was nothing to move More to active or open opposition. Though he looked on the divorce and re-marriage as without religious warrant, he found no difficulty in accepting an Act of Succession passed in 1534, which declared the marriage of Anne Boleyn valid, annulled the title of Catherine's child, Mary, and declared the children of Anne the only lawful heirs to the crown. His faith in the power of Parliament over all civil matters was too complete to admit a doubt of its competence to regulate the succession to the throne. But, by the same act, an oath recognizing the succession as then arranged, was ordered to be taken by all persons; and this oath contained an acknowledgment that the marriage with Catherine was against Scripture, and invalid from the beginning. Henry had long known More's belief on this point; and the summons to take this oath was simply a summons to death. More was at his house at Chelsea when the summons called him to Lambeth, to the house where he had bandied fun with Warham and Erasmus, or bent over the easel of Holbein. For a moment there may have been some passing impulse to yield. But it was soon over. Triumphant in all else, the monarchy was to find its power stop short at the conscience of man. The great battle of spiritual freedom, the battle of the Protestant against Mary, of the Catholic against Elizabeth, of the Puritan against Charles, of the Independent against the Presbyterian, began at the moment when More refused to bend, or to deny his convictions at a king's bidding.

XXXII.

A HOLY MISSION.—Ewald.

[Henry VIII. severed England from the papacy, and yet he did not reform the English Church. Under his young son, Edward VI., England became nominally Protestant, but the religious changes were made so rapidly that they had not time to take root among the mass of the people. On the accession of Edward's half-sister, Mary, all the religious innovations made by him and his father were annulled, and England again became Catholic. Mary chose, as her chief adviser in ecclesiastical affairs, Reginald Pole, a cardinal of the Church of Rome, whom she made archbishop of Canterbury. He was of royal blood, being a Plantagenet by descent. In consequence of his opposition to the measures of Henry VIII. he had been forced to flee to the Continent to save his life, had been prominent, for many years, in Catholic councils abroad, and, it is said, once narrowly missed an election to the papal chair. In the autumn of 1554 he was at Brussels, patiently waiting to be summoned home, in order to take part in the great work of restoring England to the old Church.]

If Pole was ever to land in England, the present moment was as opportune for the purpose as any other. A messenger was, accordingly, dispatched to Brussels to arrange certain details. The legate was to pledge himself not to interfere with such church property as had been secularised in the last two reigns; and, as it was considered advisable that he should enter England, not as a legate, but as a prince of the Church and an Englishman, he was to comply with this decision. These points being settled, Pole prepared for his journey.

Lord Paget and Sir Edward Hastings crossed the Channel to escort him to England. The envoys were charmed with the cardinal. "Whensoever he shall be in England," they wrote to their queen, "believe that country shall fare the better for him, for he is the man of God, full of all godliness and virtue, ready to humble himself to all fashions that may do good." From Brussels to Calais his eminence traveled by easy stages, " for his weak body," says Paget, " can make no great journeys, and his estate is also to be considered." At Calais he was received by the governor with every honor; the bells rang, the men-of-war in the harbor fired salutes, and an enthusiastic crowd cheered his name and mission in front of his lodgings. The next day, the weather being propitious, Pole crossed over to Dover, and, having rested the night, took horse, escorted by a powerful cavalcade of neighboring gentry, to Canterbury. As the legate passed slowly along that undulating highway, trod by the feet of so many pilgrims, which leads to the famous cathedral town, not a hostile glance was leveled at him, not an irreverent remark was heard. Some looked on in silent curiosity; others knelt in the roadway, and bent their heads beneath the blessing hand; from the throats of most of them rose the cry, " God save your grace!" for, cardinal or no, he came of the proud stock of the Plantagenets, and in those days Englishmen thought far from lightly of the names which were then historical in the land. From Canterbury Pole rode slowly on to Rochester, where he became the guest of Lord Cobham. At Gravesend was moored the legate's barge, splendid in its trappings, and with the silver cross, which Pole had now received permission to exhibit, conspicuous at its prow. The cardinal sailed up the Thames, the river being crowded with gayly-dressed craft, and, after a voyage of three hours, landed at Whitehall Stairs, where he was received by Philip and Mary with every appearance of homage and affection. Lambeth Palace, now that Cranmer had been deposed, was assigned to him as his quarters.

St. Andrew's Day had been fixed for the solemn ceremony of restoring backsliding England to the apostolic fold. When the appointed time arrived the greatest excitement prevailed, and it was remarked that many of the lower classes, who hung about Lambeth and the palace gates, were in tears. Those who spoke disparagingly of what was about to take place were in the minority, and but few dared to give open expression to adverse opinions. The tone of the people was reverent, and charged with deep emotion. Parliament met in the early dusk of a November afternoon at Whitehall. On a raised dais sat the king and queen, under a canopy of cloth of gold, with the cardinal on their right, his chair slightly in advance of the royal seat. Facing the distinguished three, crowding every inch of the great hall, were the nobles and the commons, with such spectators as had obtained permission to attend. When silence had been restored, Gardyner, now lord chancellor, at the bidding of their majesties, opened the proceedings. He read from a written paper, and his words were to the effect that England, represented by her Parliament, expressed her deep repentance for her past schism and disobedience, and implored the apostolic see to receive her again into the bosom and unity of Christ's Church. The perusal finished, all eyes were fixed upon Pole. The moment that he had so long prayed for in his cell, by the waters of the Lago di Guarda, had at last arrived; the end for which he had defied sickness and fatigue had been attained; the goal of his ambition had been reached; and before him stood the once proud, rebellious England, penitent and submissive, begging grace for her misdeeds. His heart was full, and his voice trembled as he spoke a few prefatory words from his chair. England, he said, should indeed be grateful to the Almighty for bringing her to the unity of the Church and to the obedience of the see apostolic. As in the days of the primitive Church, she had been the first to be called from heathenism to Christianity, so now she was the first of the Protestant peoples to whom grace had been granted to repent her of her past heresy. If heaven, he exclaimed, rejoiced over the conversion of one penitent sinner, how great must be the celestial joy over the conversion of an entire nation! Then he rose from his seat and lifted his right hand.

The moment of reconciliation had arrived; the whole audience fell on their knees and awaited in the stillest silence, broken only now and then by the smothered sob of an emotion that could not be controlled, the removal of the ban of excommunication. " Our Lord Jesus Christ," said the legate, in tones that filled every corner of the chamber, " who has, through his most precious blood, redeemed and washed us from all our sins and iniquities, that he might purchase unto himself a glorious spouse without spot or wrinkle, whom the Father has appointed head over all his Church ; He by his mercy absolves you, and we, by apostolic authority given unto us by the Most Holy Lord Pope, Julius the Third, his vice-gerent on earth, do absolve and deliver you, and every of you, with this whole realm and the dominions thereof, from all heresy and schism, and from all and every judgment, censure, and pain for that cause incurred. And we do restore you again into the unity of our mother, the Holy Church, in the name of the Father, of the Son, and of the Holy Ghost." His words ended, there rose up from the relieved, yet awe-stricken, congregation "a spontaneous and repeated shout of Amen, Amen." Their majesties now made a move, followed by their subjects, to the palace chapel, where the organ pealed forth the jubilant strains of the *Te Deum*.

England had sworn fealty to the pope ; still, the object of the legate was twofold—to have the papal supremacy acknowledged, and to stamp out the heresies that had sprung up in the English Church. A kind and amiable man in private life, Pole was severity itself when the favorite tenet of his creed was concerned. He would use all his persuasive powers to convert the heretic from his errors ; but if such a one persistently refused to turn toward the light, let him at once be put away and cast into outer darkness. In the memorable Marian persecutions Cardinal Pole took a leading part. His voice was ever in favor of mercy, provided there seemed a prospect of a recantation from the heretic ; but when no such hope was held out, no judge was sterner or more inflexible than the legate. Hard and intolerant as he was on these occasions, his conduct was but the logical result of a sincere belief in his creed. Outside the pale of the Catholic Church he thought there was no salvation; to bring all within the fold was, therefore, the object of every true son of the Church; those who created schisms and disseminated heresies were guilty of the most awful of all crimes—the eternal destruction of immortal souls. To the man who destroyed the body the penalty of death was dealt out; was he who damned the soul to be more mercifully treated? In the eyes of Pole a heretic was the greatest enemy of God and man. " For be you assured," said he, when lecturing the citizens of London upon their sympathy with the Protestant martyrs, "there is no kind of men so pernicious to the commonwealth as these heretics be; there are no thieves, no murderers, no adulterers, nor no kind of treason to be compared to theirs, who, as it were, undermining the chief foundation of all commonwealths, which is religion, maketh an entry to all kinds of vices in the most heinous manner." The conduct of Pole, during the short period he held office in England, reveals the true nature of the creed of Rome where its actions are unfettered by the civil power. As a consistent Catholic, possessing the opportunity of enforcing his principles, the legate could not, and ought not to, have acted otherwise.

XXXIII.

CHARACTER AND POLICY OF ELIZABETH.—GREEN.

[The terrible persecution of Mary's reign, and her anti-national policy, led to a strong reaction against her. If she had lived longer, it is probable that she would have been hurled from the throne by a revolution. At her death the English people eagerly welcomed her successor. But the young queen was not inclined, at first, to play the *role* of a Protestant leader. She wished to become queen of the nation, and not of a party; and throughout her reign she followed public opinion rather than led it.]

QUEEN ELIZABETH.

To the world about her the temper of Elizabeth recalled, in its strange contrasts, the mixed blood within her veins. She was at once the daughter of Henry and of Anne Boleyn. From her father she inherited her frank and hearty address, her love of popularity and of free intercourse with the people, her dauntless courage, and her amazing self-confidence. Her harsh, manlike voice, her impetuous will, her furious outbursts of anger, came to her with her Tudor blood. She rated great nobles as if they were school-boys; she met the insolence of Lord Essex with a box on the ear; she broke now and then into the gravest deliberations to swear at her ministers like a fish-wife. Strangely in contrast with these violent outlines of her father's temper stood the sensuous, self-indulgent nature she drew from Anne Boleyn. Splendor and pleasure were with Elizabeth the very air she breathed Her delight was to move in perpetual progresses from castle to castle through a series of gorgeous pageants, fanciful and extravagant as a caliph's dream. She loved gayety, and laughter, and wit. A happy retort or a finished compliment never failed to win her favor. She hoarded jewels. Her dresses were innumerable. Her vanity remained, even to old age, the vanity of a coquette in her teens. No adulation was too fulsome for her, no flattery of her beauty too gross. She would play with her rings that her courtiers might note the delicacy of her hands; or dance a *coranto* that an embassador, hidden dexterously behind a curtain, might report her sprightliness to his master. Her levity, her frivolous laughter, her unwomanly jests, gave color to a thousand scandals. Her character, in fact, like her portraits, was utterly without shade. Of womanly reserve or self-restraint she knew nothing. No instinct of delicacy veiled the voluptuous temper which broke out in the romps of her girlhood, and showed itself almost ostentatiously through her later life. Personal beauty in a man was a sure passport to her liking. She patted handsome young squires on the neck when they knelt to kiss her hand, and fondled her "sweet Robin," Lord Leicester, in the face of the court.

It was no wonder that the statesmen whom she outwitted held Elizabeth to be little more than a frivolous woman, or that Philip of Spain wondered how " a wanton " could hold in check the policy of the Escurial. But the Elizabeth whom they saw was far from being all of Elizabeth. Wilfulness and triviality played over the surface of a nature hard as steel, a temper purely intellectual, the very type of reason untouched by imagination or passion. Luxurious and pleasure-loving as she seemed, the young queen lived simply and frugally, and she worked hard. Her vanity and caprice had no weight whatever with her in state affairs. The coquette of the presence-chamber became the coolest and hardest of politicians at the council-board   Fresh from the flattery of her courtiers, she would tolerate no flattery in the closet ; she was herself plain and downright of speech with her counselors, and she looked for a corresponding plainness of speech in return. The very choice of her advisers, indeed, showed Elizabeth's ability. She

Q

had a quick eye for merit of any sort, and a wonderful power
of enlisting its whole energy in her service. The sagacity
which chose Cecil and Walsingham was just as unerring in
its choice of the meanest of her agents. Her success, indeed,
in securing, from the beginning of her reign to its end, with
the single exception of Leicester, precisely the right men for
the work she set them to do, sprang, in great measure, from
the noblest characteristic of her intellect. If in loftiness of
aim the queen's temper fell below many of the tempers of her
time in the breadth of its range, in the universality of its sympathy it stood far above them all. Elizabeth could talk poetry with Spenser, and philosophy with Bruno; she could dis-
cuss Euphuism with Lilly, and enjoy the chivalry of Essex;
she could turn from talk of the last fashions to pore with
Cecil over dispatches and treasury-books; she could pass
from tracking traitors with Walsingham, to settle points of
doctrine with Parker, or to calculate with Frobisher the
chances of a north-west passage to the Indies. The versatil-
ity and many-sidedness of her mind enabled her to understand every phase of the intellectual movement about her,
and to fix, by a sort of instinct, on its higher representatives.

It was only on its intellectual side, indeed, that Elizabeth
touched the England of her day. All its moral aspects were
simply dead to her. It was a time when men were being
lifted into nobleness by the new moral energy which seemed
suddenly to pulse through the whole people, when honor and
enthusiasm took colors of poetic beauty, and religion became
a chivalry. But the finer sentiments of the men about her
touched Elizabeth simply as the fair tints of a picture would
have touched her. She made her market with equal indifference out of the heroism of William of Orange or the bigotry
of Philip. The noblest aims and lives were only counters on
her board. She was the one soul in her realm whom the news
of St. Bartholomew stirred to no thirst for vengeance; and
while England was thrilling with the triumph over the

Armada, its queen was coolly grumbling over the cost, and making her profit out of the spoiled provisions she had ordered for the fleet that saved her.   No womanly sympathy bound her even to those who stood closest to her life.   She loved Leicester, indeed; she was grateful to Cecil.   But for the most part she was deaf to the voices either of love or gratitude.   She accepted such services as were never rendered to any other English sovereign without a thought of return.   Walsingham spent his fortune in saving her life and her throne, and she left him to die a beggar.   But, as if by a strange irony, it was to this very lack of womanly sympathy that she owed some of the grandest features of her character. If she was without love, she was without hate.   She cherished no petty resentments; she never stooped to envy or suspicion of the men who served her.   She was indifferent to abuse.   Her good-humor was never ruffled by the charges of wantonness and cruelty with which the Jesuits filled every court in Europe.   She was insensible to fear.   Her life became at last a mark for assassin after assassin, but the thought of peril was the thought hardest to bring home to her.   Even when Catholic plots broke out in her own household she would listen to no proposals for the removal of Catholics from her court.

Nothing is more revolting, but nothing is more characteristic of the queen than her shameless mendacity.   It was an age of political lying, but in the profusion and recklessness of her lies Elizabeth stood without a peer in Christendom.   A falsehood was to her simply an intellectual means of meeting a difficulty; and the ease with which she asserted or denied whatever suited her purpose was only equaled by the cynical indifference with which she met the exposure of her lies as soon as their purpose was answered.   Her trickery, in fact, had its political value.   Ignoble and wearisome as the queen's diplomacy seems to us now, tracking it as we do through a thousand dispatches, it succeeded in its main end, for it gained time, and every year that was gained doubled Elizabeth's strength.   She made as dexterous a use of the foibles of her temper.   Her levity carried her gayly over moments of detection and embarrassment, where better women would have died of shame.   She screened her tentative and hesitating statesmanship under the natural timidity and vacillation of her sex.   She turned her very luxury and sports to good account. There were moments of grave danger in her reign when the country remained indifferent to its perils, as it saw the queen give her days to hawking and hunting, and her nights to dancing and plays.   Her vanity and affectation, her womanly fickleness and caprice, all had their part in the diplomatic comedies she played with the successive candidates for her hand.   If political necessities made her life a lonely one, she had at any rate the satisfaction of averting war and conspiracies by love sonnets and romantic interviews, or of gaining a year of tranquillity by the dexterous spinning out of a flirtation.

As we track Elizabeth through her tortuous mazes of lying and intrigue, the sense of her greatness is almost lost in a sense of contempt.   But, wrapped as they were in a cloud of mystery, the aims of her policy were, throughout, temperate and simple, and they were pursued with a rare tenacity.   The sudden acts of energy which from time to time broke her habitual hesitation proved that it was no hesitation of weakness.   Elizabeth could wait and *finesse;* but when the hour was come she could strike, and strike hard.   Her natural temper, indeed, tended to a rash self-confidence rather than to self-distrust.   "I have the heart of a king," she cried, at a moment of utter peril, and it was with a kingly unconsciousness of the dangers about her that she fronted them for fifty years.   She had, as strong natures always have, an unbounded confidence in her luck.   "Her majesty counts much on fortune," Walsingham wrote bitterly ; "I wish she would trust more in Almighty God."   The diplomatists who censured at one moment her irresolution, her delay, her changes of front, censured at the next her " obstinacy," her iron will, her defiance of what seemed to them inevitable ruin. " This woman," Philip's envoy wrote after a wasted remonstrance, " this woman is possessed by a hundred thousand devils." To her own subjects, who knew little of her maneuvers and flirtations, of her " by-ways " and " crooked ways," she seemed the embodiment of dauntless resolution. Brave as they were, the men who swept the Spanish Main or glided between the icebergs of Baffin's Bay never doubted that the palm of bravery lay with their queen.

XXXIV.

EXECUTION OF MARY STUART.—FROUDE.

[Events soon forced Elizabeth to assume the leadership of the Protestant party in England, and, to some extent, in Europe. This brought her into antagonism with Spain, the great Catholic power of the age, and it also brought her face to face with her Catholic rival, Mary Stuart, who had a strong claim to the English throne. In the summer of 1568 Mary, fleeing from her rebellious subjects in Scotland, took refuge in England, and was detained there against her will. Many conspiracies were formed to liberate her, to assassinate Elizabeth, and to place Mary on the throne. At length, after nearly twenty years of anxiety and trouble, Elizabeth and her advisers thought it necessary to put her out of the way. She was executed on a charge of treason in 1587.]

THE end had come. She had long professed to expect it, but the clearest expectation is not certainty. The scene for which she had affected to prepare she was to encounter in its dread reality, and all her busy schemes, her dreams of vengeance, her visions of a revolution, with herself ascending out of the convulsion and seating herself on her rival's throne—all were gone. She had played deep, and the dice had gone against her. . . . Her last night was a busy one. As she said herself, there was much to be done, and the time was short. A few lines to the king of France were dated two hours after midnight. They were to insist, for the last time, that she was innocent of the conspiracy, that she was dying for religion, and for having asserted her right to the crown ; and to beg that, out of the sum which he owed her, her servants' wages might be paid, and masses provided for her soul. After this she slept for three or four hours, then rose, and with the most elaborate care prepared to encounter the end.

At eight in the morning the provost-marshal knocked at the outer door which communicated with her suite of apartments. It was locked, and no one answered. He went back in some trepidation lest the fears might prove true which had been entertained the preceding evening. On his returning with the sheriff, however, a few minutes later, the door was open, and they were confronted with the tall, majestic figure of Mary Stuart standing before them in splendor. The plain, gray dress had been exchanged for a robe of black satin; her jacket was of black satin also, looped and slashed, and trimmed with velvet. Her false hair was arranged studiously with a coif, and over her head, and falling down over her back, was a white veil of delicate lawn. A crucifix of gold hung from her neck. In her hand she held a crucifix of ivory, and a number of jeweled paternosters was attached to her girdle. Led by two of Paulet's gentlemen, the sheriff walking before her, she passed to the chamber of presence in which she had been tried, where Shrewsbury, Kent, Paulet, Drury, and others were waiting to receive her.

Andrew Melville, Sir Robert's brother, who had been master of her household, was kneeling in tears. " Melville," she said, " you should rather rejoice than weep that the end of my troubles is come. Tell my friends I die a true Catholic. Commend me to my son. Tell him I have done nothing to prejudice his kingdom of Scotland, and so, good Melville, farewell." She kissed him, and turning, asked for her chaplain, Du Preau. He was not present. There had been a fear of some religious melodrama which it was thought well to avoid. Her ladies, who had attempted to follow her, had been kept back also. She could not afford to leave the account of her death to be reported by enemies and Puritans, and she required assistance for the scene which she meditated. Missing them, she asked the reason of their absence, and said she wished them to see her die. Kent said he feared they might scream or faint, or attempt, perhaps, to dip their handkerchiefs in her blood. She undertook that they should be quiet and obedient. " The queen," she said, "would never deny her so slight a request;" and when Kent still hesitated, she added, with tears, "You know I am cousin to your queen, of the blood of Henry VII., a married queen of France, and anointed queen of Scotland." It was impossible to refuse. She was allowed to take six of her own people with her, and select them herself. She chose her physician Burgoyne, Andrew Melville, the apothecary Gorion, and her surgeon, with two ladies, Elizabeth Kennedy and Curle's young wife, Barbara Mowbray, whose child she had baptized.

"*Allons donc*," she then said, "let us go," and passing out attended by the earls, and leaning on the arm of an officer of the guard, she descended the great staircase to the hall. The news had spread far through the country. Thousands of people were collected outside the walls. About three hundred knights and gentlemen of the county had been admitted to witness the execution. The tables and forms had been removed, and a great wood-fire was blazing in the chimney. At the upper end of the hall, above the fire-place, but near it, stood the scaffold, twelve feet square and two feet and a half high. It was covered with black cloth; a low rail ran round it covered with black cloth also, and the sheriff's guard of halberdiers were ranged on the floor below on the four sides, to keep off the crowd. On the scaffold was the block, black like the rest; a square black cushion was placed behind it, and behind the cushion a black chair; on the right were two other chairs for the earls. The ax leant against the rail, and two masked figures stood like mutes on either side at the back. The Queen of Scots, as she swept in, seemed as if coming to take a part in some solemn pageant. Not a muscle of her face could be seen to quiver; she ascended the scaffold with absolute composure, looked round her smiling, and sat down. Shrewsbury and Kent followed and took their places, the sheriff stood at her left hand, and Beale then mounted a platform and read the warrant aloud.

In all the assembly Mary Stuart appeared the person least interested in the words which were consigning her to death.

"Madam," said Lord Shrewsbury to her, when the reading was ended, "you hear what we are commanded to do."

"You will do your duty," she answered, and rose as if to kneel and pray.

The dean of Peterborough, Dr. Fletcher, approached the rail. "Madam," he began, with a low obeisance, "the queen's most excellent majesty—" "Madam, the queen's most excellent majesty—" Thrice he commenced his sentence, wanting words to pursue it. When he repeated the words a fourth time she cut him short.

"Mr. Dean," she said, "I am a Catholic, and must die a Catholic. It is useless to attempt to move me, and your prayers will avail me but little." "Change your opinion, madam," he cried, his tongue being loosed at last; "repent of your sins, settle your faith in Christ, by him to be saved." "Trouble not yourself further, Mr. Dean," she answered; "I am settled in my own faith, for which I mean to shed my blood." "I am sorry, madam," said Shrewsbury, "to see you so addicted to popery."

"That image of Christ you hold there," said Kent, "will not profit you if he be not engraved in your heart." She did not reply, and, turning her back on Fletcher, knelt for her own devotions. He had been evidently instructed to impair the Catholic complexion of the scene, and the Queen of Scots was determined that he should not succeed. When she knelt he commenced an extempore prayer, in which the assembly joined. As his voice sounded out in the hall she raised her own, reciting with powerful, deep-chested tones the penitential psalms in Latin, introducing English sentences at intervals, that the audience might know what she was

9*

saying, and praying with especial distinctness for her holy father, the pope.

From time to time, with conspicuous vehemence she struck the crucifix against her bosom, and then, as the dean gave up the struggle, leaving her Latin, she prayed in English wholly, still clear and loud. She prayed for the Church which she had been ready to betray, for her son whom she had disinherited, for the queen whom she had endeavored to murder. She prayed God to avert his wrath from England—that England which she had sent a last message to Philip to beseech him to invade. She forgave her enemies, whom she had invited Philip not to forget, and then, praying to the saints to intercede for her with Christ, and kissing the crucifix and crossing her own breast, " Even as thy arms, O Jesus," she cried, " were spread upon the cross, so receive me into thy mercy and forgive my sins."

With these words she rose. The black mutes stepped forward, and in the usual form begged her forgiveness. " I forgive you," she said, " for now I hope you shall end all my troubles." They offered their help in arranging her dress. " Truly, my lords," she said, with a smile, to the earls, " I never had such grooms waiting on me before." Her ladies were allowed to come up upon the scaffold to assist her; for the work to be done was considerable, and had been prepared with no common thought.

She laid her crucifix on her chair. The chief executioner took it as a perquisite, but was ordered instantly to lay it down. The lawn vail was lifted carefully off, not to disturb the hair, and was hung upon the rail. The black robe was next removed. Below it was a petticoat of crimson velvet. The black jacket followed, and under the jacket was a body of crimson satin. One of her ladies handed her a pair of crimson sleeves, with which she hastily covered her arms; and thus she stood on the black scaffold with the black figures all around her, blood-red from head to foot. Her reasons for adopting so extraordinary a costume must be left to conjecture.   It is only certain that it must have been carefully studied, and that the pictorial effect must have been appalling.

The women, whose firmness had hitherto borne the trial, began now to give way, spasmodic sobs bursting from them which they could not check.   "*Ne criez vous*," she said; "*j'ai promis pour vous*," ("Do not cry; I have promised for you.")   Struggling bravely, they crossed their breasts again and again, she crossing them in turn and bidding them pray for her.   Then she knelt on the cushion.   Barbara Mowbray bound her eyes with a handkerchief.   "Adieu," she said, smiling for the last time, and waving her hand to them, "*Adieu, au revoir*."   They stepped back from off the scaffold, and left her alone.   On her knees she repeated the psalm, "*In te, Domine, confido*," ("In thee, O Lord, have I put my trust.")   Her shoulders being exposed, two scars became visible, one on either side, and, the earls being now a little behind her, Kent pointed to them with his white wand and looked inquiringly at his companion.   Shrewsbury whispered that they were the remains of two abscesses from which she had suffered while living with him at Sheffield.

When the psalm was finished she felt for the block, and, laying down her head, muttered, "*In manus, Domine tuas, commendo animam meam*."   The hard wood seemed to hurt her, for she placed her hands under her neck.   The executioners gently removed them, lest they should deaden the blow, and then, one of them holding her slightly, the other raised the ax and struck.   The scene had been too trying even for the practiced headsman of the Tower.   His arm wandered.   The blow fell on the knot of the handkerchief and scarcely broke the skin.   She neither spoke nor moved. He struck again, this time effectively.   The head hung by a shred of skin, which he divided without withdrawing the ax; and at once a metamorphosis was witnessed strange as was

ever wrought by wand of fabled enchanter. The coif fell
off, and the false plaits. The labored illusion vanished.
The lady who had knelt before the block was in the maturity
of grace and loveliness. The executioner, when he raised
the head, as usual, to show it to the crowd, exposed the
withered features of a grizzled, wrinkled old woman.

"So perish all enemies of the queen!" said the dean of
Peterborough. A loud "Amen!" rose over the hall. "Such
end," said the earl of Kent, rising and standing over the
body, "to the queen's and the Gospel's enemies!"

Orders had been given that every thing which she had
worn should be immediately destroyed, that no relics should
be carried off to work imaginary miracles. Sentinels stood
at the doors, who allowed no one to pass out without permission; and after the first pause, the earls still keeping their
places, the body was stripped. It then appeared that a favorite lap-dog had followed its mistress unperceived, and
was concealed under her clothes. When discovered it gave
a short cry, and seated itself between the head and the neck,
from which the blood was still flowing. It was carried away
and carefully washed, and then beads, paternoster, handkerchief—each particle of dress which the blood had touched—
with the cloth on the block and on the scaffold, was burnt in
the hall-fire in the presence of the crowd. The scaffold itself was next removed; a brief account of the execution was
drawn up, with which Henry Talbot, Lord Shrewsbury's son,
was sent to London, and then every one was dismissed.
Silence settled down on Fotheringay, and the last scene of
the life of Mary Stuart, in which tragedy and melodrama
were so strangly intermingled, was over.

XXXV.

ARRIVAL OF THE ARMADA.—Ewald.

[The great effort of Spain and Philip II. to subjugate England was to have been made in favor of Mary Stuart. But Mary was destroyed before the preparations for the expedition could be completed. The attempt, therefore, when it was made, the year after Mary's death, appeared as a bald design to crush England under a foreign yoke, and the result was that every Englishman, old and young, Catholic and Protestant, rallied under the banner of the queen.]

THE summer sun was casting its lengthening shadows upon the bowling-green behind that hotel well known to all officers of her majesty's navy, the Pelican Inn, Plymouth. It was the evening of July 19, 1588. An exciting game of bowls was about to be interrupted. Standing around the bowling-alley watching the play was a little throng whose names naval warfare and the story of adventure will not easily let die. There on that memorable occasion stood Lord Howard, of Effingham, the lord high admiral of England ; Sir Robert Southwell, his son-in-law, the captain of the *Elizabeth Jorcas;* Sir Walter Raleigh and Sir Richard Grenville; Martin Frobisher and John Davis; and last, but far from least, Sir John Hawkins, "the patriarch of Plymouth seamen," lazily watching the movements of his pupil, Sir Francis Drake, vice-admiral of the fleet. Raising his form to his full height, then slowly bending forward, the better to give impetus to the swing of his right arm, Sir Francis was about to send the bowl speeding along the alley, when he suddenly stayed his hand and gazed open-mouthed at an old sailor who, with the news-fever burning hot within him, had rushed into their midst. "My lord, my lord!" cried the weather-beaten old salt to the lord high admiral, "they're coming —I saw 'em off the Lizard last night; they're coming full sail, hundreds of 'em a darkening the waters!" The cool vice-admiral turned to his chief, as he hurled the bowl along the smooth, worn planks, and said, "There will be time enough to finish the game, and then we'll go out and give the dons a thrashing!"

It was the first intimation of the arrival of the long-expected "dons." The opal even-tide was fast deepening into night when the towering hulls of the Armada were seen rounding the Lizard. At last the shores of England were before the Spaniards, and the object of their ambition was about to be attained. The weary months passed in busy preparation, the anxious nights spent amid the storms of the Atlantic, the fatigues and privations that had been endured, were now to receive their reward. The spirits of the men on board the galleons rose high, for all were convinced that success was about to crown their efforts. The moment had arrived when vengeance was to be theirs. Within sight was the England who had shown herself, on every occasion, the enemy of Spain, who had encouraged the Protestant revolt in the Low Countries, who had robbed the West Indies of their treasures, who had captured wealthy galleons bound for Cadiz or Lisbon, and brought them in triumph to the mouth of the Thames; whose famous mariners had, within the very fortifications which commmanded the Spanish forts, fallen upon the fleets of the most Catholic king, plundered them of their goods, and then left them a mass of wrecked timber. But the hour of revenge was at hand, and haughty England, who styled herself the mistress of the seas, was to be humbled on her own element, or yield her lands to the foreigners. Forming his ships in the shape of a crescent, which stretched some seven miles from horn to horn, Medina Sidonia came full sail toward Plymouth. Hastily weighing anchor, Lord Howard hurried out of the harbor to give battle to the enemy in the Channel.

Meanwhile the beacon-lights had flashed through the country the news of the arrival of the Armada. In every shire men were looking up their arms and saddling their horses, ready for any emergency. Shipping was placed at the Nore to protect both Sheppey and the Thames. A camp was formed at Tilbury to cover London; and the earl of Leicester, who had shown himself both incompetent and improvident in the Low Countries, and who owed all his advancement to the favor in which he was held by the queen, was appointed commander-in-chief. The hour of danger, however, stimulated him to unwonted activity. "Nothing must be neglected," he wrote to the Council, "to oppose this mighty enemy now knocking at our gates." The queen herself came down to the camp, rode along the lines, and exhorted her troops to remember their duty to their country and their religion. "She had come among them at this time," she cried, amid the enthusiastic cheers of the troops, "not for her sport or recreation, but being resolved, in the midst and heat of the battle, to live or die among her people—to lay down, for her God and for her kingdom, her honor and her blood even in the dust. She knew she had but the body of a weak and feeble woman, but she had the heart of a king, and of a king of England, too; and thought foul scorn that Parma, or Spain, or any prince of Europe should dare to invade the borders of her realm. Rather," she exclaimed, with all the fire of her Tudor blood, "than any dishonor should grow by her, she herself would take up arms, she herself would be their general, their judge and rewarder of every one of their virtues in the field!"

Her soldiers, however, required little pressing to go forth and attack the enemy. They burned to meet the foe who had the audacity to attempt the invasion of their country, or to dream of forcing upon Protestant England the hated creed of Rome. Stories of the terrors of the Inquisition, of the cruelties that had been practiced by Alva in the Low Countries, and of the fate that was to be in store for Englishmen, should the forces of Medina and Parma win the day, were freely circulated. It was said that the houses and parks of the English nobles were to be parceled out among the Spanish grandees, and that a list had been drawn up to that effect, which was in the pocket of every Spaniard. English women were to be spared only to be consigned to a fate worse than death. The houses of the wealthy merchants in London had been inserted in a Spanish register, and were to be divided among the squadrons of the navy for their spoil. Every galleon had hundreds of halters on board wherewith to hang the English people, while children under seven years of age were to be branded upon their faces, so as to be known hereafter as the offspring of the conquered nation. Such tales were fully credited, and goaded the patriotism of the country into a perfect frenzy of wild and vindictive hate.

On issuing from Plymouth harbor into the open Channel, Lord Howard gave orders to his men not to come to close quarters with the towering unwieldly galleons, but to pour broadside after broadside into them at a distance, and to bide their opportunity to fall upon them. They had not long to wait. One of the galleons, the *Capitana*, carrying the flag of Pedro de Valdez, ran foul of the *Santa Catalina*, and broke her bowsprit. She was disabled; it was in vain that the Spaniards tried to take her in tow, and Drake timely coming up, she struck her flag, and was tugged at the stern of the *Revenge*, a prize into Torbay. Among the prisoners was De Valdez, "the third in command of the fleet," and Juan Martinez de Recaldo, vice-admiral. As the Armada advanced up the Channel the English hung upon its rear, firing shot after shot into the lofty hulls of the galleons and galleasses, yet all the while taking excellent care to give them a wide berth. "The enemy pursue me," moans Medina Sidonia; "they fire upon me most days from morning till nightfall; but they will not close and grapple. I have purposely left ships exposed to tempt them to board, but they decline to do it ; and there is no remedy, for they are swift, and we are slow."

The Spanish captain-general was fairly nonplussed. The smart, well-handled English ships ran in and out, doing him as much damage as it was possible, always declining to come to close quarters, while his lumbering craft were useless to chase and cripple the agile enemy. Medina resolved to bear up for Calais, in hope that Parma was ready to put to sea. Shortly after the galleons had anchored in Calais roads, Lord Howard, whose ammunition and provisions, owing to the short-sighted stinginess of Elizabeth, were running terribly low, and who, consequently, was most anxious not to protract proceedings, practiced a successful *ruse* upon the Spaniards. Filling certain of his smaller ships with combustible materials, he dispatched them, one after the other, into the midst of the enemy. The Spaniards, panic-stricken, cut their cables, and, utterly demoralized, took to flight in all speed. The next morning Howard, seizing the opportunity of their confusion, fell upon them and destroyed about a dozen of their ships, besides inflicting considerable damage upon their fleet generally.

It was now evident to the most ardent Spaniard that the object of the expedition was completely frustrated. The duke of Parma declined to quit the harbor to land his forces in England unless protected by the Spanish fleet, and the Armada was now flying northward for dear life, intent far more upon seeing the coast of Spain than that of England. "God grant ye have a good eye to the duke of Parma," writes Drake cheerily to Walsingham, " for with the grace of God, if we live, I doubt not, ere it be long, so to handle the matter with the duke of Sidonia as he shall wish himself at St. Mary Port among his orange-trees." The duke must have already wished himself at his country seat. Nervous and confused by the complete collapse of the expedition, he knew not what course to pursue. He dared not return home by the Channel, for his men refused to encounter the English again in the narrow seas; it was idle for him, with his dismantled fleet and dispirited crews, to remain in the Downs; where further action was impossible, retreat became necessary; and so, after an anxious parliament with his lieutenants, it was resolved to seek Spain by way of the North Sea. Crowding all sail, and throwing overboard useless cargo, the Armada steered for the Orkneys. Howard, however, had no intention of seeing the hostile fleet sneak off like a whipped cur without receiving the full punishment she so richly deserved. Leaving Lord Henry Seymour's squadron to guard "the narrow seas," the English admiral gave chase to the Spaniard. But English courage, though capable of great efforts, requires to be supplied with the ordinary means of subsistence. A stern chase is proverbially a long chase, but it becomes infinitely longer where the crews in pursuit are decimated by scurvy and dysentery, are weakened by absolute hunger, are in want of water, and are only animated by the undying pluck of their race.

Sadder reading there is not than the piteous moans for provisions, to be met with in the State Papers of this date, from the captains of the different men-of-war then watching the Channel for the protection of England. Wages were in arrears, every farthing of extra expenditure had to be rigidly accounted for to the queen, while sailors brought on shore sick or dying had no place to receive them. "It would grieve any man's heart," writes Howard, "to see men who had served so valiantly die so miserably." Yet Elizabeth, who owed her realm to the efforts of these her gallant subjects, though she could speak brave words to them, which stirred their blood like a trumpet, would permit no lavish encroachments upon her exchequer. She doled out in miserable portions, money, food, drink, and clothes. Even her cherished favorite, Leicester, had to complain that on four thousand men coming into Tilbury, after twenty miles' march, " as forward and willing men as ever I saw," there was not "a barrel of beer nor a loaf of bread" to give them. The one cry throughout the correspondence of this period is: "Nothing can exceed the patient and willing spirit of both sailors and soldiers; but, for God's sake, send us provisions, send us powder, send us money, clothes, and drink, else we be too enfeebled to fight." Still, the miserable parsimony of the queen was deaf to all entreaties, in spite of Drake's advice, that it was an ill policy "to hazard a kingdom with saving a little charge."

The result of all this cheese-paring was now to tell its tale. Off Norfolk a storm arose; the men under Howard in pursuit of the Armada were too weak to work the ships; the admiral himself was compelled to satisfy the pangs of hunger with a few coarse beans, while the crews were forced for drink—the story can hardly be credited—to fall back upon the resources of human nature, and the chase had to be abandoned. With extreme difficulty Howard, accompanied by the largest of his ships, reached Margate; the rest of the fleet were driven into Harwich. "Our parsimony at home," writes Captain Whyte to Walsingham, "hath bereaved us of the famousest victory that ever our nation had at sea."

XXXVI.

SIR WALTER RALEIGH.—FARRAR.

[The sovereign who succeeded Elizabeth had been king of Scotland for a quarter of a century, but he had had little real power, and had busied himself with devising a scheme of absolute government which was to be tried in his new kingdom of England. Lacking tact and skill, he soon came into collision with the English House of Commons, and sowed trouble for his son to reap. He reversed the foreign policy of his predecessor by at once making peace with Spain, and through all his life he assiduously courted the favor of that power. It was mainly to the Spanish policy of James that Raleigh was sacrificed. Raleigh had grown up among the great men who had been so conspicuous as navigators and discoverers in Elizabeth's reign.]

AMONG souls so pure and noble the boy Raleigh passed his earlier years. After brilliant promise at school and college, by the age of seventeen he was fighting for Protestants in France, and beginning his many-sided career as soldier, sailor, courtier, poet, discoverer, and author. If you would understand his life, and the glorious years of Queen Elizabeth, you must remember three things—that it was the era of the Renascence, the era of the Reformation, and the era of the colonization of America.

It was the era of the Renascence. That new boyhood of life produced splendid daring. The glory of England, in that day, was as when the aloe rushes into its crimson flower. Around the queen stood men crowned with many laurels, men of strong passions, of deep feelings, of large hopes, of dauntless endurance, of ardent imagination, of magnificent purposes. Think of the day when Hooker was preaching at the Temple; and Bacon meditating on the " Novum Organum;" and Spenser writing the " Faerie Queene; " and Sidney fighting in the Netherlands; and Galileo reading the secrets of the stars; and Drake singeing the beard of the king of

Spain; and Shakspere, Marlowe, Chapman, and Ben Jonson were pouring forth all the passion of which man's heart is capable; and Milton was a little boy; when trade, art, science, learning, burst into new life; when England was acquiring the empire of the sea; and the queen was telling Mendoza—in quite her natural voice, and as though it was the most natural thing in the world, though he was the embassador of a king at whom the world trembled—that if he talked to her about Philip's threats again she would fling him into a dungeon. Yes! England was the England of Shakspere and Raleigh, and spoke in the voice of England then, because her sons were neither cynical unbelievers nor gilded effeminates, but feared God, and were noble and great and true.

And this era of the Renascence was, on the religious side, the era of the Reformation. In these our days love of popery shows itself in coquetting with dead usages, and hatred of popery has dwindled down into the feeble spite of religious newspapers; and most men, caring nothing about either tendency, walk in the cold mid region between a boundless skepticism and an unfathomable superstition. But in *those* days hatred of popery was no mere intolerance about minor religious opinions. It was, and had a right to be, a holy and mighty passion. It meant hatred of popes like Pius V., who sent his soldiers into France with the words, "Slay immediately whatever heretics fall into your hands," and who taught Englishmen to defy and plot against their queen. It meant hatred of Moloch fires which flamed through all lands; hatred of queens steeped, like Mary, in murder and adultery; hatred of generals, like Alva, reeking with the blood of saints; hatred of blood which cried to heaven from an earth which would not cover her slain. Hatred of popery meant, in that day, hatred of the sanguinary alliance between priestly usurpation and monarchic despotism; between cruel tyranny and deadly superstition. It meant hatred of burnings, tortures, butcheries; hatred of the dark, crooked devil's work of a plotting, murdering Jesuitism, which absolved the reckless perjuries of the conspirator, and consecrated the cursed dagger of the assassin; it meant hatred of the Inquisitor, wielding the sword of the tyrant and wearing the ephod of the priest. But with Raleigh—born when the fires of Smithfield were barely extinguished, reading Foxe's "Martyrs" at his mother's knee, who, as a boy, had fought against Alva in the Netherlands, and seen Condé die at Jarnac, whose ears had thrilled with the shrieks of St. Bartholomew, and who knew how Philip of Spain had laughed aloud when he heard of that awful massacre, and how Pope Gregory XIII. had struck medals and sung *Te Deums* in its honor—to Raleigh hatred of popery was, in that day, inevitably one with loyalty to Elizabeth and love of England, and passion for the primary rights, the natural liberty and free conscience of mankind. And because he was a life-long foe to popery he was a life-long foe to Spain, which was then trying to blight the whole world with the upas shadows of abhorrent absolutism.

The great men of Elizabeth knew that the triumph of Spain, the triumph of popery, would have meant the holiness of racks and the beatitude of thumbscrews. It would have meant that the England of Elizabeth would have reeked, as did the England of James II., with the odors of the charnel-house. It was this that made Raleigh fight papists in Ireland, which he called then, as it is now, "not the common weal, but the common woe;" and fight papists in France, and in the Netherlands, and on the Armada, and in the New World. It was this which made him burn the Spanish fleet in Cadiz Bay. It was this that made him tell in immortal prose, as Tennyson has told in immortal verse, that death of Sir Richard Grenville, when one English ship fought for fifteen mortal hours against fifty-three Spanish ships at the Azores. Yes, in the era of the Reformation hatred of popery meant love of truth, love of England, love of freedom, love of progress, air, and light.

But, nobly as Raleigh served the cause of England and the cause of the Reformation, it is with the New World and its colonization that his name will be most gloriously and most permanently connected. To Raleigh and the old sea worthies of England the New World meant Eldorado. But Spain, forsooth, claimed the whole of this New World by virtue of a trumpery parchment signed by a meddling Italian priest! And how did this land of promise and golden dreams fare in the hands of popery and Spain? The tale of their greed and cruelty rang through all lands. The flames woven on the banners of Cortez were the accursed emblem of the Inquisition. But they had not occupied a third, even, of the coast; and was that land of boundless wonder and beauty, of boundless fertility and wealth, to be abandoned to them? Were millions of innocent Indians to be treated like brute beasts? Were the English, whom they called "Lutheran devils," to be handed over to the rack and the galleys, if they ventured to trade, nay, if they were but shipwrecked, on those shores? Not if Raleigh could help it! His genius fixed upon, and his dauntless patience and princely munificence secured regions which had almost escaped the notice of Spain. On the colonization of Virginia he spent £40,000, and was ready to spend his whole fortune, to the last coin.

Let me for one moment glance at his life and end. If you would judge of his zenith, see him in the splendor of Durham House, his beautiful wife beside him, his noble boy at his knee, sometimes flashing about as captain of Elizabeth's guard, in his armor of enameled silver; sometimes in his "doublet of white satin, all embroidered with rich pearls, and a weighty chain of great pearls around his neck;" the friend of Sidney, the patron of Spenser, the companion of Ben Jonson and Shakspere, lord of the Stannaries, governor of Munster, governor of Jersey, rear-admiral of the fleet against the Azores; ruffling it with Leicester and Essex, their equal in manly beauty; "lording it with awful ascendency" in the fairy-land of Gloriana's Court—"a man at whom men gazed as at a star." Envy not his splendor! All the while he was struggling in a net-work of base intrigues. Long before pride and passion led him into sin, he had learned—as his poem, "The Lie," shows—how hollow and disappointing it all was. And then see the plunge right down to the very nadir of human misery and ruin. I know few tragedies to equal those last twelve years of his in the Tower of London. Elizabeth had died, "with the whole Book of Ecclesiastes written on her mighty heart," and the very basest and meanest of English kings, with no fear except to offend Spain and no money except to lavish on infamous favorites, disgraced her throne. Such a man as James naturally hated such a man as Raleigh. His fair day at once drew to evening. "I am left of all men," he wails, "that have done good to many. All my good turns forgotten, all my errors revived and expounded to all extremity of ill, all my services, hazards, and expenses for my country—plantings, discoveries, fights, counsels, and whatsoever—dire malice has now covered over." Ah! what a shipwreck of man's ingratitude! and how common on the treacherous sea of life! And then came the midnight. Imprisoned, robbed, slandered, yet enriching even his prison hours with the "History of the World;" in vain attempting suicide, betrayed by his own king, suffering from fever, losing his gallant boy in battle, and his devoted adherent by suicide; old, gray-headed, lame, worn with sickness, anguish, and watching; penniless, ruined, dishonored—finding the whole world turned for him to thorns—after being belied for a while in a hubbub of lies, he is, at a day's notice, infamously doomed to the scaffold. In all those awful fires God had purged away all his dross. He had long learned to defy death in all his ugly and misshapen forms. "O, eloquent, just, and mighty death," he wrote at the end of his

" History of the World," " whom none could advise, thou
hast persuaded ; what none hast dared, thou hast done ; and
whom the world flattered, thou hast cast out of the world
and despised ; thou hast drawn together all the far-fetched
greatness, all the pride, cruelty, and ambition of man, and
covered it all over with these two narrow words, '*hic jacet.*' "
Even such, he wrote in his cell the evening before his
execution :

> " E'en such is time—who takes in trust
> Our youth, our hopes, our all we have,
> And pays us but with earth and dust ;
> Who, in the dark and silent grave,
> When we have wandered all our ways,
> Shuts up the story of our days.
> But from this earth, this grave, this dust,
> My God shall raise me up, I trust ! "

" Prythee, let me see the ax," he says to the executioner.
" Dost thou think, man, I am afraid of it ? " " A sharp medicine, but a sound cure for all diseases." " I entreat you,"
he says, "that you will all join with me in prayer to the God
of heaven, whom I have grievously offended, being a man full
of all vanity, who have lived a sinful life, that the Almighty
Goodness will forgive ; that he will cast away my sins from
me ; that he will receive me into everlasting life. So I take
leave of you all, making my peace with God." He says but one
more word. Asked to face toward the east, he says · " If the
heart be right, it matters not which way the head lies." So
dies the most brilliant of Englishmen ; so fades all glory into
darkness, and all life into dust, that we may give God the
splendor.

10

XXXVII.

GATHERING OF THE STORM.—EWALD.

[In view of the training in absolute government which Charles had had under his father, it is no wonder that his reign ended in revolution. Under the influence of an unprincipled favorite, Buckingham, and to gratify personal whims, he plunged recklessly into foreign wars. He summoned two Parliaments in quick succession, and when they refused to vote him all the money he wanted for his useless military expeditions, which were led by incompetent commanders, he dissolved them in anger, and undertook to supply his necessities by means of forced loans. Hence "the gathering of the storm."]

In the meantime the unconstitutional proceedings instituted by Charles, though they inflamed the country with wrath and sedition, failed to replenish the coffers of his exhausted exchequer. The general loan had been well subscribed to, but all its proceeds were swallowed up by the pressing necessities of the Crown. In the expenditure of the past year there was a vast deficit. The preparations for war now amounted to a fearful total. The pay of the soldiers and the seamen was rated at some £200,000 a year, and if Rochelle was to be relieved in the spring, another £100,000 would be required. How, and from whom, were these sums to be obtained? The king was aware that the inevitable must be boldly faced, and he summoned his memorable third Parliament. We all remember the scenes that took place. The Commons, conscious of their power and of the justness of the grievances they complained of, refused to be brow-beaten, or to yield one jot of their demands. Five subsidies were voted, but before they were handed to the king the representatives of the people determined to obtain a guarantee against the abuses of the past. The Petition of Right was drawn up. Charles was asked to pledge himself that he would never raise loans or levy taxes without the consent of

Parliament; that his subjects should be free from arbitrary imprisonment; that soldiers should not be billeted upon the people; and that martial law should be abolished. The king attempted to evade the clauses of the Petition. Instead of pronouncing the usual words which signify the royal assent to a bill, he, inspired by Buckingham, replied: "The king willeth that right be done according to the laws and customs of the realm, and that the statutes be put into execution; that his subjects may have no cause to complain of any wrong or oppression contrary to their just rights and liberties, to the preservation whereof he holds himself in conscience as much obliged as of his own prerogative." The Commons were not to be hoodwinked by so elastic an answer; they did not want the statutes confirmed by simple words, but interpreted according to the hard and fast limits they had assigned to them. For a time the king refused to return any other answer, and threatened the House with instant dissolution. Then, after some delay, advised by Buckingham, who had been concerned at the fierce censure poured upon his conduct by the Commons, and pressed by a joint application from the two Chambers, Charles came down to Westminster and agreed to the terms of the Petition, by pronouncing the usual form, "Let it be law as is desired."

"The king came to the House at two o'clock," writes Secretary Conway, "and gave an answer which begat such an acclamation as made the House ring several times. I never saw a more general joy in all faces than spread itself suddenly and broke out into ringing of bells and bonfires miraculously." "It is not possible," writes Sir Francis Nethersole to the queen of Bohemia, "to express with what joy this answer was heard, nor what joy it causes in all the city, where they are making bonfires at every door, such as were never seen but upon his majesty's return from Spain." This frantic delight was, however, soon checked. In the struggle between the inquisitorial power of Parliament and the despotism of prerogative the Commons had been victorious. Flushed with success, they now pressed the Crown still further with their demands. They requested that the penal laws against the Catholics should be fully enforced, that the Arminians should be silenced, and that the duke of Buckingham should be removed. To satisfy the religious prejudices of the Commons the king had no objection, but to dismiss the duke from his councils was an interference with the royal prerogative which Charles declined to entertain for a moment. Irritated at this refusal, the Lower House now proceeded in a spirit of mischievous intrusion, to meddle with the grant of tonnage and poundage (the duties on exports and imports), which ever since the days of our sixth Henry had been voted by Parliament during the life-time of each successive monarch, on the ground that the king had relinquished his claim to this taxation by his assent to the Petition of Right. Charles loudly raised his voice against this strained interpretation of the favors he had recently granted; and seeing that the position of affairs was now reversed, that it was the Commons who were encroaching upon the rights of the Crown, and not the sovereign upon the rights of the subject, he hastily prorogued the Parliament.

And now he who had been the head and front of all the evils under which the country was then laboring was to fall a victim, not to the vengeance of a justly angered legislature, but to the hand of an unknown assassin. The duke of Buckingham had gone down to Portsmouth to superintend the preparations for an expedition to relieve Rochelle. While engaged in conversation with one of his colonels, a man, who had long been on the watch for his opportunity, suddenly pressed against him and stabbed him in the breast. The blow had been well directed; the duke unsheathed the knife from his wound, crying out, " Villain! " and attempted to pursue his murderer; but he was mortally struck, and after an unsuccessful effort to steady himself fell to the ground a dead man. The assassin was John Felton, a young Puritan officer, who had conceived a deadly hatred against Buckingham on account of having been disappointed of his promotion when serving in the expedition against Rhé. "Our noble duke," writes Lord Dorchester, " in the greatest joy and alacrity I ever saw him in my life, at news received about eight o'clock in the morning of Saturday last, of the relief of Rochelle, wherewith he was hastening to the king, who had that morning sent for him by me, at his going out of a lower parlor, in presence of many standers-by, was stabbed into the breast with a knife by one Felton, a reformed lieutenant, who hastening out of the door, and the duke having pulled out the knife and following him out of the parlor into the hall, with his hand put to his sword, there fell down dead with much effusion of blood. The Lady Anglesea, then looking down into the hall, went immediately with a cry into the duchess's chamber, who was in bed, and there fell down on the floor. The murderer in the midst of the noise and tumult slipped out into the kitchen, when a voice being current in the court, ' A Frenchman! a Frenchman!' his guilty conscience making him believe it was ' Felton! Felton!' he came out of the kitchen, said, 'I am the man,' and rendered himself to the company."

So terrible a tragedy, its victim the foremost man in the kingdom, created a profound sensation, and not a detail respecting the history of the murderer, the sorrow of the king, the grief of the widow, the burial of the duke, and the sentiments of the nation upon the dread event is omitted in the State Papers before us. There we learn how Felton had come " from London expressly the Wednesday, arriving at Portsmouth the very morning, not above half an hour before he committed the deed; " how " he gloried in his act the first day, but when told that he was the first assassin of an Englishman, a gentleman, a soldier, and a Protestant, he shrank at it, and is now grown penitent; how it was wished to have him racked, should the law sanction such punishment, to find out his accomplices;" how "he confessed his offense to 'be a fearful and crying sin,' and requested that he might do some public penance before his death, in sackcloth, with ashes on his head and ropes about his neck;" how verses were written in his honor, and how he was hanged at Tyburn, and the body then carried to Portsmouth to be suspended in chains. There we read how "the king took the duke's death very heavily, keeping his chamber all that day, as is well to be believed; but the base multitude in London drink health to Felton, and there are infinitely more cheerful than sad faces of bitter degree;" how "there never was greater demonstration of affection than his majesty showed to the deceased duke in all which concerns his honor, estate, friends, and enemies, whom he cannot well look upon if any come in his way;" how "the king omitted nothing which may in any way concern the doing honor to the body of the duke," and how the corpse was privately interred in the Abbey to escape the fury of the mob; and how passionate was the sorrow of the bereaved duchess. Still in the nation at large, though it regretted the act of the assassin, few beyond the king and the widow mourned the death of the duke. "The stone of offense being now removed by the hand of God," writes a courtier, "it is to be hoped that the king and his people will come to a perfect unity."

The vacancy left in the councils of the king by the murder of Buckingham was soon to be filled up by a far more dangerous favorite, Thomas Wentworth, later earl of Strafford. In the first three Parliaments summoned by Charles he had sided with the popular party, not because he was opposed to the policy of the Crown, but because he detested, with a malignity which knew no rest, the man who was then the adviser of the king and the sole minister of the nation. He is the first on the list of those English statesmen who have gone into factious opposition, not because they disapprove of the measures of the government, but because they hate the minister who suggests them.

It is absurd to class Wentworth in the same category with the leaders of the popular party, with Eliot, with Pym, with Hampden. He was no friend to democracy; he had no wish to see the prerogative domineered over by the Parliament; if there was to be a battle between the sovereign and the subject, he did not desire to see the latter supreme. In his sympathies, in his prejudices, in his views of government, he was thoroughly the aristocrat. When he stood forward as the opponent of the Crown, he was always most careful to distinguish between the acts of the sovereign and the acts of the minister. After the passing of the Petition of Right, he severed himself entirely from his colleagues. He had no sympathy with the course the House of Commons was then pursuing. He made overtures to the Court, which were accepted; the death of Buckingham removed the great bar to his progress, and henceforth the chief author of the Petition of Right was to be the firm friend and confidential adviser of the king.

XXXVIII.

TRIAL OF STRAFFORD.—Mozley.

[After the dissolution of his third Parliament the king entered upon a course of absolute power. For eleven years he refused to summon the representatives of the nation. Ably seconded by Strafford and Laud, he attempted to establish an "enlightened despotism," and at one time it seemed as if he might succeed. But the petty ecclesiastical measures of Laud not only roused strong opposition in England, but so exasperated the Scots that they rose in rebellion. Attempts to pacify them failed, and in the spring of 1640 Charles was forced to call a Parliament. He quarreled with it, however, and sent it home in disgrace. But the Scotch difficulty was increasing, the king was unable to meet it, and so he reluctantly summoned his fifth Parliament. This was the famous Long Parliament; and it proceeded at once to call the king's ministers to account. In its eyes Strafford was the arch criminal.]

STRAFFORD came up to town late on Monday, rested on Tuesday, came to Parliament on Wednesday, and that very night was in the Tower. The Lower House closed their doors, and the speaker kept the keys till the debate was over, when Pym, attended by a number of members, went up to the Upper House, and, in a short speech, accused, in the name of the Commons of England, Thomas, earl of Strafford and lord-lieutenant of Ireland, of high treason. The sudden step astounded the Lords; word went to Strafford, who was just then closeted with the king; he returned instantly to the House, called loudly at the door for Maxwell (keeper of the black rod) to open, and, with firm step and proudly darkened countenance, marched straight up to his place at the board head. A host of voices immediately forced him to the door again. The consultation over, he was called back and stood before the House. "Kneel, kneel," he was told; he knelt, and on his knees was delivered into the custody of the black rod, to be a prisoner till cleared of the Common's charges. He offered to speak, but was commanded to be gone without a word.

The black rod bore off his great charge, and apparently felt his importance on the occasion. "In the outer room," says Baillie, "James Maxwell required him, as a prisoner, to give up his sword. When he had got it he cried with a loud voice for his man to carry my lord-lieutenant's sword. This done, he makes through a number of people toward his coach, all gazing, no man capping to him before whom that morning the greatest of England would have stood discovered; all crying, "What is the matter?" He said, "A small matter I warrant you." They replied, "Yes, indeed, high treason is a small matter." Coming to the place where he expected his coach, it was not there, so he behoved to return that same way, through a world of gazing people. When at last he found his coach, and was entering, James Maxwell told him, "Your lordship is my prisoner, and must go in my coach." This great step taken, the Commons were all activity. Pursuivants dispatched to Ireland and the north sounded the trumpet, and summoned all who had any complaint against the lord-deputy and president to appear at the approaching trial. Strafford was busily employed with his counsel in the Tower preparing his defense.

Four months passed, and the two sides met to encounter in the court of justice, before they tried their strength at Marston Moor and Worcester. On the 21st of March, Westminster Hall, railed and platformed, and benched, and scaffolded up to the roof, showed an ascending crowd of heads—judges, lawyers, peers of Parliament, Scotch commissioners, aggrieved gentlemen from the north, incensed Irish lords; the look of strife, of curiosity, and here and there of affection and pity, turned, in the excitement of the opening trial, on the illustrious prisoner. From a high scaffold at the north end an empty throne looked disconsolately over the scene, a chair for the prince on one side of it, which he occupied during the proceedings. "Before it"—the accurate and characteristic account of an eye-witness shall continue the description—
10*

"lay a large wool-sack, covered with green, for my lord steward, the earl of Arundel. Beneath it lay two other sacks for the lord keeper and the judges, with the rest of the Chancery, all in their red robes. Beneath this, a little table for four or five clerks of the Parliament, in their black gowns. Round about these some forms covered with green frieze, whereupon the earls and lords did sit in their red robes of the same fashion, lined with the same white ermine skin, as ye see the robes of our lords when they ride to Parliament. Behind the forms, where the lords sit, there is a bar covered with green. At the one end stands the committee of eight or ten gentlemen appointed by the House of Commons to pursue. At the midst there is a little desk, where the prisoner stands or sits as he pleases, together with his keeper, Sir William Balfour, the lieutenant of the Tower. This is the order of the House below on the floor; the same that is used daily in the higher House. Upon the two sides of the House, east and west, there arose a stage of eleven ranks of forms, the highest almost touching the roof; every one of these forms went from the one end of the room to the other, and contained about forty men; the two highest were divided from the rest by a rail, and a rail at every end cut off some seats. The gentlemen of the Lower House sat within the rails, others without. All the doors were kept very straitly with guards. We always behoved to be there a little after five in the morning. Lord Willoughby, earl of Lindsey, lord-chamberlain of England (Pembroke is chamberlain of the court) ordered the House with great difficulty. James Maxwell, black rod, was great usher; a number of other servants, gentlemen, and knights, assisted. The House was full daily before seven; the lords, in their robes, were set about eight. The king was usually half an hour before them. He came not into his throne, for that would have marred the action; for it is the order of England, when the king appears, he speaks what he will, but no other speaks in his presence. At the back of the throne were two rooms on the two sides. In the one duke de Vanden, duke de Valler, and other French nobles, sat; in the other, the king, queen, princess Mary, the prince elector, and other court ladies. The tirlies, that made them to be secret, the king brake down with his own hands, so that they sat in the eyes of all; but little more regarded than if they had been absent, for the lords sat all covered. Those of the Lower House, and all others, except the French noblemen, sat discovered when the lords came, not else. A number of ladies were in boxes above the rails, for which they paid much money." Private persons of place and distinction were admitted to place among the Commons; one of whom was Baillie, principal of the University of Glasgow, and one of the commissioners from Scotland, from whose letters we borrow this description. By the force of a clear, strong mind, the intellectual Scotchman proceeds, in spite of himself, to describe, in Strafford, a fallen greatness, before which the noisy bustling scene sank into vulgarity; and, while his hatred of the champion of Church and king is as intense as ever, his intellect bows to the nobleness and grandeur of the man.

At eight o'clock the lieutenant and a guard brought up Strafford in a barge from the Tower; the lord-chamberlain and black rod met him at the door of the court. On his entrance he made a low courtesy, when he had proceeded a little way a second, and, on coming to his place, a third; he then kneeled, with his forehead upon his desk, rose quickly, saluted both sides of the court, and sat down; some few of the lords lifted their hats to him. Every day he was attired in the same deep suit of black. Four secretaries sat at a desk just behind him, whom he kept busily employed reading and writing, arranging and handing him his papers; and behind them his counsel, five or six able lawyers, who were not permitted to argue upon matters of fact, but only on points of law.

A day or two were occupied in preambles and general

statements, and a declamatory speech from Pym gave a sketch of all the charges against Strafford, and endeavored to destroy all the merit of those parts of his administration which the accused could appeal to. The regular business of the court followed; twenty-eight charges of treason and mal-administration were formally preferred against Strafford; every high proceeding and act of power, every harshness, and every case of grievance of the subject, noble and aristo-cratical, that they thought could tell upon the court; all the knots and rough spots and corners that an administration of unparalleled activity had, in the full swing and impetus of its course, contracted, were brought up, singly and isolatedly enlarged upon, and exhibited in the very worst color. Straf-ford was asserted to have done every thing with a view to the most selfish ends, to establish his own tyranny, oppression, and extortion; and the very idea of a respectable *intention* in what he did, of any view to public good, mistaken, irregular, as they might think it, but still real, was not alluded to.

Strafford was fully equal to the emergency, and played off his host of papers with all the self-possession and dexterity possible. No knowledge of what a thread his life hung by ever unsteadied for a moment his thorough coolness and pres-ence of mind; no unfair play, time after time, throughout the trial, put him the least out of temper; he let nothing pass without a struggle, he fought for a point of law or court prac-tice stoutly, determinately; when decided against him, the fine, well-tempered spirit was passive again, took, with a *nil admirari*, what it could not help, and worked upon the bad ground as if it were its own choice. A charge was made with every skillful exaggeration and embellishment; he simply asked time to get up his reply—it was refused; without " sign of repining "—it is the unconsciously beautiful expression of Baillie—he turned round and conferred with his counsel. For a few minutes a little nucleus of heads, amid the general tur-moil, were seen in earnest consultation, eyes bent downward,

and hands shuffling and picking out papers: the defense
arranged with that concentrated attention which shortness of
time and necessity inspire, Strafford was ready again, and
faced the court. Great was the contrast of the rest of the
scene; these pauses were the immediate signal for a regular
noise and hubbub, and it was with laughing, chattering, walking about, eating and drinking, close to him and echoed from
all sides, that the tall, black figure of Strafford was seen, " serious with his secretaries," and life and death were at work in
his small isolated knot. The general behavior in court
throughout was gross and vulgar in the extreme, and scandalized Baillie. There was a continual noise, movement, and
confusion of people leaving and returning, doors slamming,
and enormous eating and drinking; bread and meat and
confections were dispatched greedily; the bottle went round
from mouth to mouth, and the assembled company manifested by the freest signs their enjoyment of the occasion.

XXXIX.

ATTEMPT TO ARREST THE FIVE MEMBERS.—Gardiner.

[Strafford was condemned and executed in May of 1641. In the summer
of that year Charles visited his northern capital. His plan was to make
peace with the Scots, which he did by yielding all the points in dispute,
and then to turn upon and crush the English opposition. Returning to
London toward the close of the year, he brought a charge of high treason
against five of the leaders of the House of Commons. There were constitutional methods by which these men might have been arrested, and, if
guilty, punished. But Charles disdained constitutional ways and chose to
resort to force. He grossly violated the privileges of the Parliament by
going to the House of Commons at the head of a body of armed men and
attempting to arrest his enemies in their places in the House.]

If the blow had not already fallen, it was because Charles
had been involved in his usual vacillation. According to a

not improbable account, he had that morning sought out the queen, and had given strong reasons against the execution of the plan. Henrietta Maria was in no mood to accept excuses. "Go, you coward!" she cried, "and pull these rogues out by the ears, or never see my face more." Charles bowed to fate and his high-spirited wife, and left her, resolved to hang back no longer. Again there was delay, perhaps on account of the adjournment at midday; and before Charles actually left Whitehall the queen had trusted the secret to her ill-chosen confidante, Lady Carlisle, and Lady Carlisle at once conveyed the news to Essex.

Before dinner was over the five accused members received a message from Essex, telling them that the king was coming in person to seize them, and recommending them to withdraw. They could not make up their minds as yet to fly. In truth, Charles was still hesitating, in his usual fashion, and it might be that he would never accomplish his design. When the House met again at one, satisfactory replies were received from the inns of court. The lawyers said that they had gone to Whitehall, because they were bound to defend the king's person, but that they were also ready to defend the Parliament. The Lords, too, had shown themselves resolute, and had agreed to join the Commons in styling the attorney-general's articles a scandalous paper.

It may be that the contemptuous term applied to the accusation which he had authorized had at last goaded Charles to action. Late — but, as she fondly hoped, not too late— the queen had her way. About three o'clock Charles, taking with him the elector palatine, hurried down stairs, calling out, "Let my faithful subjects and soldiers follow me." Throwing himself into a coach, which happened to be near the door, he drove off, followed by some three or four hundred armed men.

Such a number could not march at any great speed. A Frenchman, named Langres, who had probably been set to watch by the embassador, La Ferté, pushed through the crowd, and ran swiftly to the House of Commons. He at once called out Fiennes and told him what he had seen. The five members were at once required to withdraw. Pym, Hampden, Hazlerigg, and Holles took the course which prudence directed. Strode, always impetuous, insisted on remaining to face the worst, till Erle seized him by the cloak and dragged him off to the river-side, where boats were always to be found. The five were all conveyed in safety to the city.

It was high time for them to be gone. Charles's fierce retinue struck terror as it passed. The shopkeepers in the mean buildings which had been run up against the north end of Westminster Hall hastily closed their windows. Charles alighted and strode rapidly through the Hall between the ranks of the armed throng. As he mounted the steps which led to the House of Commons he gave the signal to them to await his return there. About eighty of them, however, probably in consequence of previous orders, pressed after him into the lobby, and it was afterward noticed that "divers of the late army in the north, and other desperate ruffians" had been selected for this post.

Charles did his best to maintain a show of decency. He sent a message to the House, informing them of his arrival. As he entered, with the young elector palatine at his side, he bade his followers on their lives to remain outside. But he clearly wished it to be known that he was prepared to use force if it were necessary. The earl of Roxburgh leaned against the door, keeping it open so that the members might see what they had to expect in case of resistance. By Roxburgh's side stood Captain David Hyde, one of the greatest scoundrels in England. The rest were armed with swords and pistols, and many of them had left their cloaks in the Hall, with the evident intention of leaving the sword-arm free.

As Charles stepped through the door, which none of his predecessors had ever passed, he was, little as he thought it, formally acknowledging that power had passed into new hands. The revolution, which his shrewd father had descried when he bade his attendants to set stools for the deputies of the Commons as for the embassadors of a king, was now a reality before him. He had come to the Commons because they would no longer come to him. To Charles the new constitutional fact was merely a temporary interruption of established order. In his eyes there was visible no more than a mortal duel between King Charles and King Pym. As he moved forward, the members standing bare-headed on either side, his glance, perhaps involuntarily, sought the place on the right-hand side near the bar which was usually occupied by Pym. That seat was empty. It was the one thing for which he was unprepared. "By your leave, Mr. Speaker," he said, as he reached the upper end of the House, "I must borrow your chair a little." Standing in front of it, he cast his eyes around, seeking for those who were by this time far away.

"Gentlemen," he said at last, "I am sorry for this occasion of coming unto you. Yesterday I sent a sergeant-at-arms upon a very important occasion to apprehend some that by my command were accused of high treason, whereunto I did expect obedience, and not a message ; and I must declare unto you here that, albeit no king that ever was in England shall be more careful of your privileges to maintain them to the uttermost of his power than I shall be, yet you must know that in cases of treason no person hath a privilege; and, therefore, I am come to know if any of these persons that were accused are here."

Once more he cast his eyes around. " I do not see any of them," he muttered, "I think I should know them." "For I must tell you, gentlemen," he went on to say, in continuation of his interrupted address, "that so long as those persons that I have accused—for no slight crime, but for treason —are here, I cannot expect that this House can be in the right way that I do heartily wish it. Therefore, I am come to tell you that I must have them wheresoever I find them."

Then, hoping against hope that he had not come in vain, he put the question, " Is Mr. Pym here ?" There was no re- ply, and a demand for Holles was no less fruitless. Charles turned to Lenthall. "Are any of these persons in the House ?" he asked. "Do you see any of them ? Where are they ?" Lenthall was not a great or heroic man, but he knew what his duty was. He now gave voice, in words of singular force and dexterity, to the common feeling that no individual expression of the intentions or opinions of the House was permissible. "May it please your majesty," he said, falling on his knee before the king, "I have neither eyes to see, nor tongue to speak, in this place but as this House is pleased to direct me, whose servant I am here; and I humbly beg your majesty's pardon that I cannot give any other answer than this to what your majesty is pleased to demand of me."

" Well," replied Charles, assuming a cheerfulness which he can hardly have felt, "I think my eyes are as good as an- other's." Once more he looked carefully along the benches. " Well," he said, "I see all the birds are flown. I do expect from you that you shall send them unto me as soon as they return hither. If not, I will seek them myself, for their trea- son is foul, and such a one as you will thank me to discover. But I assure you, on the word of a king, I never did intend any force, but shall proceed against them in a legal and fair way, for I never meant any other. I see I cannot do what I came for. I think this is no unfit occasion to repeat what I have said formerly, that whatsoever I have done in favor, and to the good of my subjects, I do mean to maintain it."

So Charles spoke, and so, no doubt, he thought. He did not intend to assassinate the five whom he accused, any more than Pym had a year before intended to assassinate Strafford.   But he meant again to be king of England, as he and his father before him had understood kingship.   It would not be his fault if resistance brought bloodshed with it.

He knew now that, for the time at least, he was baffled. As he left the House, with gloom on his brow, he could hear the cries of "Privilege ! Privilege !" raised behind him.   His armed followers were exasperated at his failure.   Those minutes of waiting had sadly tried their patience.   Strange words had fallen from the lips of some of them.   "I warrant you," said one, cocking his pistol, "I am a good marksman, I will hit sure."   "A pox take the House of Commons," growled another, "let them be hanged if they will."   When the king re-appeared, there was a general cry for the word which was to let them loose.   "How strong is the House of Commons?" asked one.   "Zounds !" cried another, as soon as the absence of the five was known, "they are gone, and now we are never the better for our coming."   The general feeling of these men was doubtless expressed by an officer on the following day. He and his comrades, he said, had come, "because they heard that the House of Commons would not obey the king, and therefore they came to force them to it; and he believed, in the posture that they were set, that if the word had been given, they should certainly have fallen upon the House of Commons."

Such was the shape which Charles's legal and peaceable action took in the eyes of those whom he had called on to execute his design.   The Commons at once adjourned, with the sense that they had but just escaped a massacre.

Charles could not afford to acknowledge that he had failed. The next day he set out for the city, hoping to obtain there what he had not obtained at Westminster.   He took with him in his coach, Hamilton, Essex, Holland, and Newport, perhaps with the idea of sheltering himself under their popularity.   The rumor spread that he was carrying them with him in order to imprison them in the Tower.   Multitudes poured into the streets in no gentle humor.   At last he reached Guildhall, and made his demand to the common council. After he had spoken there was a long silence, broken at last by shouts of "Parliament! Privileges of Parliament!" The meeting was, however, not unanimous. Cries as loud of "God bless the king" were heard. Charles asked that those who had any thing to say should speak their minds. "It is the vote of this court," cried one, "that your majesty hear the advice of your Parliament." "It is not the vote of this court," cried another, "it is your own vote." "Who is it," asked the king, "that says I do not take the advice of my Parliament? I do take their advice; but I must distinguish between the Parliament and some traitors in it. Those I would bring to a legal trial." On this a man sprang on a form and shouted out, "Privileges of Parliament!" Charles repeated what he had said, in a slightly altered form. "I have and will observe all privileges of Parliament, but no privileges can protect a traitor from a legal trial." In spite of the division of opinion, it was evident that there would be no surrender of the members. As the king passed out, there was a loud shout of "Privileges of Parliament!" from the crowd outside. He stopped to dine with one of the sheriffs. On his way back to Whitehall the streets rang with the cry of "Privileges of Parliament." One bold man threw into his coach a paper, on which was written, "To your tents, O Israel!" The allusion to Rehoboam's deposition was one which Charles could not fail to understand.

XL.

EXECUTION OF CHARLES THE FIRST.—GUIZOT.

[The attempt upon the five members resulted in a triumph for them, and the country rapidly drifted into civil war. During the first eighteen months of the struggle the advantage lay with the king, owing chiefly to his superiority in cavalry. But the formation of Cromwell's famous "Ironsides" turned the scale in favor of the Parliament. At Marston Moor the royalist army, under Rupert, was disastrously defeated in July of 1644, and the king himself was overthrown at Naseby in June of 1645. Charles took refuge with the Scots, who had joined the side of the Parliament in the war ; the Scots, failing to convert him to their creed, delivered him over to the English Presbyterians, and from the hands of the latter he passed into the keeping of the army, which was composed chiefly of Independents, and whose ruling spirit was Cromwell. The king played a shuffling game with all parties. · In 1648 a reaction took place in his favor. The Scots and the English royalists and Presbyterians united against the Independent army to place him back upon the throne. The army crushed the movement, and resolved to call the king to account for the blood that had been shed. He was tried and condemned by a tribunal, which was virtually a court-martial.]

THE king, after a few hours of tranquil sleep, left his bed. "I have a great affair to terminate," he said to Herbert, "I must get up immediately ; " and he went to his toilet. Herbert was agitated, and did not comb his hair with his usual care. "I pray you," said Charles, "take as much pains as usual; though my head is not to remain long upon my shoulders, I will be dressed like a bridegroom to-day." As he was dressing he asked for a second shirt; "the season is so cold," he said, "that I might tremble; some people would attribute it to fear, and I would not have such a supposition possible." As soon as day dawned the bishop arrived, and began his pious office; as he read, in the twenty-seventh chapter of the Gospel according to St. Matthew, the passion of Jesus Christ, the king asked him, "My lord, did you choose this chapter as applicable to my situation?"   "I beg your majesty to observe," said the bishop, "that it is the gospel of the day, as the calendar indicates."   The king appeared deeply affected, and continued his devotions with greater fervor.   At about ten a gentle knock was heard at the door; Herbert paid no heed to it; a second, rather louder, though still gentle knock succeeded.   "Go," said the king, "and see who is there."   It was Hacker.   "Tell him to come in," said the king.   "Sir," said the colonel, with a low and trembling voice, "it is time to go to Whitehall; your majesty will still have an hour there to compose yourself."   "I will go directly," answered Charles; "leave me."   Hacker went out; the king bent for a few moments more in silent prayer; and then, taking the bishop by the hand, "Come," he said, "let us go; Herbert, open the door, Hacker knocks again;" and he went down into the park, through which he was to pass on his way to Whitehall.

Several companies of infantry awaited him, forming a double line on each side of his road; a detachment of halberdiers marched on before, with banners flying; the drums beat; not a voice could be heard for the noise.   On the right of the king was the bishop; on the left, with his head uncovered, was Colonel Tomlinson, the commander of the guard, whom Charles, touched by his attentions, had requested not to leave him till his last moment.   He talked with him, as they advanced, of his funeral, of the persons to whom he wished the care of it to be intrusted, with a serene air, a beaming eye, a firm step, walking even faster than the troops, and wondering at their slowness.   One of the officers on duty, probably thinking to confuse him, asked him whether he had not concurred with the late duke of Buckingham in causing the death of his father.   "My friend," answered Charles, with gentle contempt, "if I had no other sin than that, I call God to witness that I should not have any need to beg his forgiveness."   Arrived at Whitehall, he ascended the stairs with a light step, passed through the long gallery, and gained his bedroom, where he was left alone with the bishop, who was preparing to give him the communion. A few Independent ministers, Nye and Goodwin among the rest, came and knocked at the door, saying that they wished to offer their services to the king. " The king is at prayers," answered Juxon; yet they still insisted. " Well, then," said Charles to the bishop, " thank them in my name for their offer; but tell them frankly that after having so often prayed against me, and without any reason, they shall not pray with me in my agony. They can, if they like, pray for me; for that I shall be grateful." They thereupon retired ; and the king knelt down, received the communion from the hands of the bishop, and then, rising with alacrity, said: " Now let these rascals come; I have forgiven them from my heart, and I am prepared for all that I have to go through." His dinner had been prepared, but he refused to eat any of it. " Sir," said Juxon, " your majesty has long been fasting; the weather is so cold, perhaps on the scaffold some fainting . . ." " You are right," interrupted the king, and he took a piece of bread and drank a glass of wine. It was then one o'clock; Hacker knocked at the door. Juxon and Herbert fell on their knees; " Rise, my old friend," said Charles, holding out his hand to the bishop. Hacker knocked again, and Charles ordered the door to be opened. " Go on," he said to the colonel, " I will follow you." He advanced through the banqueting hall, still between a double line of soldiers; a multitude of men and women, who had rushed in at the peril of their lives, stood motionless behind the guard, praying for the king as he passed; the soldiers themselves were silent, and did not insult him. At the farther end of the hall an opening had been made in the wall leading immediately to the scaffold, which was entirely covered with black. Two men, dressed as sailors and both wearing masks, stood by the block. The king arrived, carrying his head erect, and looking on all sides for the people to speak to them; but, seeing that only soldiers filled the place, and that none could approach, he

Execution of King Charles.

turned toward Juxon and Tomlinson, and said, "I cannot be heard by many but yourselves, therefore to you I will speak a few words;" and he delivered to them a short speech which he had prepared, and which was calm and grave to coldness, and merely intended to maintain that he had been right; that contempt of the rights of the sovereign was the true cause of the people's misfortunes; that the people ought not to take any part in government; that upon this condition only would the country ever regain peace and its liberties. While he was speaking, some one touched the ax; he turned hastily, saying, "Do not spoil the ax, it would hurt me more;" and when he had finished his speech, some one again approaching it, "Take care of the ax, take care!" he repeated, in a tone of terror. The most profound silence reigned; he put a silk cap on his head, and, addressing the executioner, said: "Is my hair in the way?" "I beg your majesty to push it more under your cap," replied the man, bowing. The king, with the help of the bishop, pushed his hair aside. As he was doing this he said: "I have on my side a good cause, and a merciful God." "Yes, sir," said the bishop, "there is but one stage more, which, though turbulent and troublesome, is yet a very short one. Consider, it will soon carry you a great way; it will carry you from earth to heaven!" "I go," replied the king, "from a corruptible to an incorruptible crown, where no disturbance can take place!" and, turning toward the executioner, "Is my hair now right?" he said. He took off his cloak and George, gave the George to Juxon, saying, "Remember!" He then took off his coat, put on his cloak again, and, looking at the block, said to the executioner, "Place it so that it will not shake." "It is firm, sir," replied the man. The king said: "I shall say a short prayer, and when I hold out my hands, then . . ."

He stood in meditation, said a few words to himself, raised his eyes to heaven, knelt down, and laid his head upon the block; the executioner touched his hair to push it still farther under his cap; the king thought he was going to strike. "Wait for the signal," he said. "I shall wait for it, sir, with the good pleasure of your majesty." In about a minute the king held out his hands; the executioner struck; the head was severed at a blow. "This is the head of a traitor," he cried, as he held it up to the people; a long, deep murmur spread around Whitehall; many persons rushed to the scaffold to dip their handkerchiefs in the king's blood. Two troops of horse, advancing in different directions, slowly dispersed the crowd. When the scaffold was at length clear, the body was taken away; it was already inclosed in the coffin when Cromwell wished to see it. He considered it attentively, and, taking up the head in his hands, as if to make sure that it was severed from the body. said: "This was a well-constituted frame and promised a long life."

XLI.

THE DECISION AT WORCESTER.—FORSTER.

[The execution of Charles was followed by the overthrow of the monarchy and the establishment of a republic or "commonwealth." But the new state was forced at once to enter upon a struggle for existence. Widespread disaffection existed in England ; in Scotland, the son of the "martyr-king" was called to the throne ; in Ireland there was open rebellion. Cromwell's vigorous campaign restored order in Ireland, and in the summer of 1650 he was sent against the Scots. He defeated them disastrously at Dunbar, but they rallied the next year, and staked all on an invasion of England. Cromwell followed and overtook them at Worcester.]

WITH the advance of winter an attack of ague seized Cromwell, but after severe suffering he rallied, and in time for that ill-judged movement of the young king of Scots which brought on the battle of Worcester.

The Presbyterian army, restored to a numerous and most effective force, now held a strong position near Stirling.

Charles II. commanded it in person. Taught by the fatal experience of Dunbar, however, he kept acting on the defensive, and could not be drawn from his well-selected ground. As a last effort with this view, Cromwell, with singular daring, transported his army into Fife, and proceeded toward Perth, which he captured after a siege of two days. The stratagem succeeded, in one sense, but, besides moving the Scots from their stronghold, it had also induced Charles to adopt the plan of marching into England. It is said that in this he yielded to the advice of his English followers, who overruled the more prudent Argyle, looked with contempt upon the Parliament, and counted upon the numerical majority of the English nation as unquestionably in his favor. On the 31st of July he broke up his camp near the Torwood, and on the 6th of August reached Carlisle.

Cromwell was engaged in the superintendence of a new citadel by means of which he designed to hold Perth in subjection, when the news reached him of the movement of the Presbyterians and the king. His spirit rose to that crisis with a renewal of the excitement which men noted in him at Dunbar. He wrote at once to London to give all necessary courage and confidence to the council and citizens. After informing them of the meditated invasion hanging over them, he observed that it " was not out of choice on our part; " and did not conceal his fear that it would trouble some men's thoughts, and occasion some inconvenience. But, he adds, " this is our comfort, that, in simplicity of heart as to God, we have done to the best of our judgments, knowing that, if some issue were not put to this business, it would occasion another winter's war, to the ruin of your soldiery, for whom the Scots are too hard in respect of enduring the winter difficulties of this country, and have been under the endless expense of the treasury of England in prosecuting this war. It may be supposed we might have kept the enemy from this by interposing between him and England, which I truly

11

believe we might; *but how to remove him out of this place without doing what we have done,* unless we had a commanding army on both sides of the river of Forth, is not clear to us, or how to answer the inconveniences afore-mentioned, we understand not." He then entreats that the council of state would collect what forces they could without loss of time, to give the enemy some check, until he should be able to overtake them. Meantime, he sent Lambert at the head of the cavalry, who, upon joining with Harrison, whose forces were at Newcastle, was ordered to advance through the western parts of Northumberland, to intercept the Scots in their progress through Lancashire, to watch their motions, straiten their quarters, impede their progress in every way, but not to risk a battle.

Charles, meanwhile, with but sorry success, had pushed on by Kendal and Preston to Warrington, where, at the bridge, he received a momentary check from Lambert and Harrison. He still forced his way, summoned Shrewsbury in passing, but without effect, and at last made for Worcester, where he was proclaimed, according to Clarendon, king of England, Scotland, France, and Ireland.

London, anticipating his entry almost every hour, gave way to fearful alarms. Even Bradshaw himself, it is said, lion-hearted as he was, could not among his private friends conceal his fears. Some raged against Cromwell, and uttered deep suspicions of his fidelity. No one could understand his intentions, nor where he was, nor why he had allowed an enemy to enter the land when there were no troops to oppose him. Both the city and the country, says Mrs. Hutchinson, were all amazed, and doubtful of their own and the commonwealth's safety. Some could not hide very pale and unmanly fears, and were in such distraction of spirit as much disturbed their counsels.

Yet truly there was little need. The genius of Cromwell had already saved them. He had collected a tremendous force—nearly thirty thousand men—and on the 28th of August had them all in position within two miles of Worcester. The Presbyterian force was greatly inferior, but the almost impregnable site of the city of Worcester was an ample set-off against that circumstance.

Built along the right bank of the Severn, it defied immediate assault, and Charles's officers had, of course, done their best to increase its already splendid resources of resistance and defense. Cromwell found the bridges broken above and below, every boat removed—not even a punt to be seen—and, in the extensive line of fires above, saw how strongly the heights of the place were occupied. But not for a moment did he hesitate. Inspired by the genius which had served him so often, and never failed him yet, he took the sudden and daring resolve of throwing his army astride upon two rivers—of forcing at their higher transits a passage across both the Severn and the Teme—and of coming down at once upon the enemy from the eastern and western heights overlooking Worcester!

The preparations for this daring exploit were completed on the 2d of September, for Cromwell had, moreover, determined to fight this decisive battle for the possession of three disputed kingdoms on what he called his *fortunate day*—his day of Dunbar. Skirmishes meanwhile took place between the out-posts on both sides of the river, and before the morning of the 3d a desperate struggle had passed at the half-broken Upton bridge, between Lambert and its gallant defender, Massey. Lambert carried it at last, repaired the broken arch, and conducted across ten thousand men, who took their ground along the course of the Teme.

It was now the morning of the 3d. The Presbyterians had the day before, in alarm at Lambert's movement, destroyed every bridge upon that river. Yet Cromwell, not caring to husband life at any time, and still less now when his superior numbers gave him so many lives to play with—sent out an

order to Fleetwood to force, at any loss, his detached corps
across the Teme. Cromwell at the same moment threw a
bridge of boats over the Severn at Bunshill, near the conflu-
ence of the two rivers, and restored the communication that
had been partially cut off. A hot fire near Powick—so sudden were these movements—was the first thing that attracted
the attention of Charles, who, from one of the towers of the
cathedral, was examining the positions of the enemy, when,
finding that an attack was begun in that quarter, he instantly
dispatched a re-enforcement of horse and foot to the spot,
and gave instructions to the commanding officer to prevent, if
possible, the formation of the bridge. But a similar addition
had been made to the detachment under Fleetwood, who
again outnumbered his opponents, and pressed them with
great vivacity toward Worcester. "The Scots, in the hope
that, by occupying so large a force, they might afford to their
countrymen on the other side of the Severn an opportunity of
breaking the regiments under Cromwell, maintained the most
obstinate resistance." They disputed every inch of ground
which presented the slightest advantage; fought from hedge
to hedge, and frequently charged with the pike, to check the
advance of the enemy.

For an instant this rolled the tide of battle back toward
the Teme; but fresh battalion after battalion arrived to the
support of Fleetwood, who then bore the Scots by fair force
of numbers even across the bridge.

Cromwell was meanwhile deciding the battle under the
walls of the town ; and here, or on both sides of the river,
from two o'clock in the morning till night-fall, had this terrible contest raged with unceasing fury. The main body of
the enemy's infantry had advanced out of the city against the
renowned chief of the Ironsides, and the conflict upon one
spot in this quarter, Cromwell wrote in his dispatch, lasted
three hours. It was closed by the veteran regiment which
had so often closed the battles of the Parliament, and which

now, for the last time, advanced at the word of Cromwell. The victory was complete—gloriously complete, as the lord-general exultingly wrote, and " gained after as stiff a contest for many hours—including both sides of the river "—as he had ever seen. The fort having been summoned, and Colonel Drummond still refusing to surrender it, it was carried, in all the wild triumph of the victory, by a furious storm, wherein fifteen hundred men were put to the sword. Charles, flying through the streets in piteous despair, in vain attempted to rally his troops, and, finding they would no longer move, is said to have cried out, with a burst of passionate tears, " Then shoot me dead, rather than let me live to see the sad consequences of this day." A crown had vanished from his grasp.

On another man, who still stood upon that field, a crown was now descending. He stood there, some time after the day was won, in a state of uncontrollable emotion. Then, calling Fleetwood and Lambert to his side, he told them, with a fit of boisterous laughter, that he would knight them, as heroes of old were knighted (he did not say by kings), on the field where they had achieved their glory. The excitement subdued, he retired to his tent, and there, at "ten o'clock at night," "weary, and scarce able to write," he yet wrote to the Parliament of England these memorable words : " The dimensions of this mercy are above my thoughts. It is for aught I know a crowning mercy."

XLII.

DISSOLUTION OF THE LONG PARLIAMENT.—GARDINER.

[The Long Parliament, or what was left of it, was now the highest legitimate authority in the land. In the course of the revolution, however, it
had been weeded out several times, and, in its present maimed and
shrunken form, could not pretend to represent the public sentiment of the
country. Nevertheless it clung to power, and steadily refused to make
way for a new Parliament, freely chosen. For this reason Cromwell drove
it out.]

" PEACE," sung Milton, in his sonnet to Cromwell, " hath
her victories no less renowned than war." Peace, too, has
her forlorn hopes, her stout battling for a cause lost by anticipation, and destined only to re-appear in other days when
the standard shall have been intrusted to arms more fortunate, if not more stalwart. Cromwell and the higher officers
in the army, Sir Henry Vane and the nobler spirits yet remaining in the Parliament, were alike bent upon realizing the
same high object—a free state governed in accordance with
the resolutions of its elected representatives, and offering
guarantees for individual liberty of thought and speech, without which Parliamentary government is only another name for
tyranny. But their powers were not equal to their wishes.
The revolutionary force in the country had been spent long
before the execution of Charles ; and now that his possible
successor was a youth of whom no harm was known, the
Royalist flood was mounting steadily. Even the original
feeling of the nation had not been against royalty, but against
the particular way in which the king had acted ; and the necessity for dethronement, and the supposed necessity for execution, had been founded upon reasoning which had never
stirred the popular heart. The nation at large did not really
care for a commonwealth, did not care for religious liberty.
The violent suppression of the Episcopalian worship had

alienated as many as had been alienated by Laud's injudicious resuscitation of obsolete forms. Most Englishmen would have been quite content if they could have got a king who would have shown some reasonable respect for the wishes of Parliament, and who would abstain from open illegality.

In short, the leaders of the commonwealth found themselves, in some sort, in the same position as that in which Laud found himself in 1629. They had an ideal of their own, which they believed to be really good for the nation, and they hoped that, by habituating the nation to that which they thought best, they could at last bring it to a right frame of mind. If their experiment and its failure is more interesting than Laud's experiment and its failure, it is because their ideal was far higher than his. It broke down, not because they were wrong, but because the nation was not as yet ripe for acceptance of any thing so good.

The difference of opinion which slowly grew up between army leaders and Parliamentary leaders was only the natural result of the tacit acknowledgment of this rock ahead, which was none the less felt because both parties shrank from avowing it. A free Parliament would, perhaps, be a Royalist Parliament. In that case it would probably care nothing about liberty, and would certainly care nothing about Puritanism. How was the danger to be met? The fifty or sixty men who called themselves a Parliament had their own remedy for the disease. Let there be new elections to the vacant seats, but let their own seats not be vacated. Let these old members have power to reject such new members as seemed to them unfit to serve in Parliament. There would be something that looked like a free Parliament, and yet it would not be a free Parliament at all. Those only would be admitted who were thought by the old members to be the right sort of persons to influence the nation.

The scheme, in fact, was a sham, and Cromwell disliked shams. He had another objection equally strong. If there was one thing for which he and his soldiers had fought and bled, it was for the sake of religious liberty, a liberty which was real enough as far as it went, even if it was much less comprehensive than that which has been accepted in later times. No security was offered for religious liberty under the new-old Parliament. There was nothing to prevent it from abolishing all that existed at any moment it pleased.

As often happens, moral repugnance came to the help of logical reasoning. Not a few of the members of Parliament were conducting themselves in such a way as to forfeit the respect of all honest men. Against foreign foes, indeed, the commonwealth had been successful. The navy, reorganized by Vane, had cleared the seas of Royalist privateers. Commercial jealousy against the Dutch had mingled with the tide of political ill-feeling. In 1651 the Navigation Act was aimed at the Dutch carrying trade, which had flourished simply because the Dutch vessels were better built, and long experience had enabled them to transport goods from one country to another more cheaply than the merchants of other nations. Henceforth English vessels alone were to be allowed to import goods into England, excepting in the case of vessels belonging to the country in which the goods were produced.

War was the result. In January, 1652, the seizure of Dutch ships began. The two sturdy antagonists were well matched. There were no decisive victories; but, on the whole, the English had the upper hand.

Such a war was expensive. Royalists were forced to compound for their estates, forfeited by their adoption of the king's cause. Even if this measure had been fairly carried out, the attempt to make one part of the nation pay for the expenses of the whole was more likely to create dissension than to heal it. But it was not fairly carried out. Members of Parliament took bribes to let this man and that man off more easily than those who were less able to pay. The effects of unlimited power were daily becoming more manifest.

To be the son or a nephew of one of the holders of authority was a sure passport to the public service. Forms of justice were disregarded, and the nation turned with vexation upon its so-called liberators, whose yoke was as heavy to bear as that which had been shaken off.

Of this dissatisfaction Cromwell made himself the mouthpiece. His remedy for the evil, which both sides dreaded, was not the perpetuation of a Parliament which did not represent the nation, but the establishment of constitutional securities which would limit the powers of a freely elected Parliament. He and his officers proposed that a committee, formed of members of Parliament and officers, should be nominated to deliberate on the requisite securities.

On April 19 he was assured, or believed himself to be assured, by one of the leading members that nothing would be done in a hurry. On the morning of the 20th he was told that Parliament was hurriedly passing its own bill, in defiance of his objections. Going at once to the House, he waited till the decisive question was put to vote. Then he rose. The Parliament, he said, had done well in their pains and care for the public good. But it had been stained with "injustice, delays of justice, self-interest." Then, when a member interrupted him, he blazed up into anger. "Come, come! we have had enough of this. I will put an end to this. It is not fit you should sit here any longer." Calling in his soldiers, he bade them clear the House, following the members with words of obloquy as they were driven out. "What shall we do with this bauble?" he said, taking up the mace. "Take it away." Then, as if feeling the burden of the work which he was doing pressing upon him, he sought to excuse himself, as he had sought to excuse himself after the slaughter of Drogheda. "It is you," he said, "that have forced me to do this. I have sought the Lord night and day that he would rather slay me than put me upon the doing of this work."

11*

XLIII.

LAST DAYS OF CROMWELL.—MASSON.

[Cromwell was now virtually supreme. In December, 1653, he was made Lord Protector of the three kingdoms, and entered, with characteristic energy, upon the herculean task of establishing a permanent civil organism, and of securing recognition for his government abroad. Both his home and his foreign policy were exceedingly brilliant, challenging the admiration even of his enemies ; but he was constantly harassed by factions, was often compelled to resort to force when he would have ruled constitutionally, and at last broke down under a burden which proved to be greater than even he could bear.]

THOUGH but in his sixtieth year, and with his prodigious powers of will, intellect, heart, and humor unimpaired visibly in the least atom, his frame had for some time been giving way under the pressure of his ceaseless burden. For a year or two his handwriting, though statelier and more deliberate than at first, had been singularly tremulous, and to those closest about him there had been other signs of physical breaking up. Not till late in July, however, or early in August, was there any serious cause for alarm; and then in consequence of the terrible effects upon his highness of his close attendance on the death-bed of his second daughter, the much-loved Lady Claypole. She had been lingeringly ill for some time of a most painful internal disease, aggravated by the death of her youngest boy, Oliver. Hampton Court had received her as a dying invalid, "tortured by frequent and long convulsion-fits;" and here, through a great part of July, the fond father had been hanging about her, broken-hearted and unfit for business.

Before her death his grief had passed into an indefinite illness, described as "of the gout and other distempers ;" and though he was able to come to London on the 10th of August, he returned to Hampton Court greatly the worse. But, after four or five days of confinement, he was out again for an hour

Oliver Cromwell.

on the 17th; and thence till Friday, the 20th, he seemed so much better that Thurloe and others thought the danger past. From the public at large the fact of his illness had been hitherto concealed as much as possible; and hence it may have been, that on two or three of those days of convalescence, he showed himself, as usual, riding with his life-guards in Hampton Court Park. It was on one of them, most probably Friday, the 20th, that George Fox had that final meeting with him, which he describes in his journal. The good, but obtrusive, Quaker had been writing letters of condolence and mystical religious advice to Lady Claypole in her illness, and had recently sent one of mixed condolence and rebuke to Cromwell himself, and now, not knowing of Cromwell's own illness, he had come to have a talk with him about the sufferings of the Friends. "Before I came to him, as he rode at the head of his life-guard," says Fox, "I saw and felt a waft of death go forth against him; and, when I came to him, he looked like a dead man." Fox, nevertheless, had his conversation with the protector, who told him to come again. Next day, Saturday, August 21, when Fox went to Hampton Court Palace to keep his appointment, he could not be admitted. Harvey, the groom of the bed-chamber, told him that . his highness was very ill, with his physicians about him, and must be kept quiet. That morning his distemper had developed itself distinctly into "an ague;" which ague proved, within the next few days, to be of the kind called by the physicians "a bastard tertian," that is, an ague with the cold and hot shivering fits recurring most violently every third day, but with the intervals also troublesome. The physicians, thinking the London air better for the malady than that of Hampton Court, his highness was removed to Whitehall on Tuesday, the 24th.

Saturday, the 28th, was a day of marked crisis. The ague had then changed into a "double tertian," with two fits in the twenty-four hours, both extremely weakening. So Sunday passed, with prayers in all the churches; and then came that extraordinary Monday, August 30, which lovers of coincidence have taken care to remember as the day of most tremendous hurricane that ever blew over London and England. From morning to night the wind raged and howled, emptying the streets, unroofing houses, tearing up trees in the parks, foundering ships at sea, and taking even Flanders and the coasts of France within its angry whirl. The storm was felt, within England, as far as Lincolnshire, where, in the vicinity of an old manor-house, a boy of fifteen years of age, named Isaac Newton, was turning it to account, as he afterward remembered, by jumping first with the wind, and then against it, and computing its force by the difference of the distances. Through all this storm, as it shuddered round Whitehall, shaking the doors and windows, the sovereign patient had lain on, passing from fit to fit, but talking in the intervals with the lady protectress, or with his physicians, while Owen, Thomas Goodwin, Sterry, or some other of the preachers that were in attendance, went and came between the chamber and an adjoining room. A certain belief that he would recover, which he had several times before expressed to the lady protectress and others, had not yet left him, and had communicated itself to the preachers as an assurance that their prayers were heard. Writing to Henry Cromwell at nine o'clock that night, Thurloe could say: "The doctors are yet hopeful that he may struggle through it, though their hopes are mingled with much fear." Even the next day, Tuesday, August 31, Cromwell was still himself, still consciously the lord protector. Through the storm of the preceding day, Ludlow had made a journey to London from Essex, on family business, beaten back in the morning by a wind against which two horses could not make way, but contriving late at night to push on as far as Epping. "By this means," he says, "I arrived not at Westminster till Tuesday about noon, when, passing by Whitehall, notice was immediately given to Cromwell that I was come to town. Where-upon he sent for Lieutenant-General Fleetwood, and ordered him to inquire concerning the reason of my coming at such haste and at such a time." At the end of the day, Fleet-wood, writing to Henry Cromwell, reported: "The Lord is pleased to give some little reviving this evening; after few slumbering sleeps, his pulse is better." As near as can be guessed, it was that same night that Cromwell himself uttered the well-known short prayer, the words of which, or as nearly as possible the very words, were preserved by the pious care of his chamber-attendant, Harvey. It is to the same authority that we owe the most authentic record of the religious de-meanor of the protector from the beginning of his illness. Very beautifully and simply Harvey tells us of his " holy ex-pressions," his fervid references to Scripture texts, and his repetitions of some texts in particular, such repetitions "usu-ally being very weighty, and with great vehemency of spirit." One of them was: "It is a fearful thing to fall into the hands of the living God." Three times he repeated this; but the texts of promise and of Christian triumph had all along been more frequently on his lips. All in all, his single short prayer, which Harvey places " two or three days before his end," may be read as the summary of all we need to know of the dying Puritan in these eternal respects. "Lord," he muttered, "though I am a miserable and wretched creature, I am in covenant with Thee through grace, and I may, I will, come to Thee. For Thy people, Thou hast made me, though very unworthy, a mean instrument to do them some good, and Thee service; and many of them have set too high a value upon me, though others wish and would be glad of my death. But, Lord, however Thou dost dispose of me, continue and go on to do good for them. Give them consi tency of judg-ment, one heart, and mutual love; and go on to deliver them, and with the work of reformation; and make the name of Christ glorious in the world. Teach those who look too much upon Thy instruments to depend more upon Thyself; pardon such as desire to trample upon the dust of a poor worm, for they are Thy people too; and pardon the folly of this short prayer, even for Jesus Christ's sake; and give us a good night, if it be Thy pleasure."

Wednesday, September 1, passed unmarked, unless it may be for the delivery to the lady protectress, in her watch over Cromwell, of a letter dated that day, and addressed to her and her children, from the Quaker, Edward Burrough. It was long and wordy, but substantially an assurance that the Lord had sent this affliction upon the protector's house, on account of the unjust sufferings of the Quakers. " Will not their sufferings lie upon you ? For many hundreds have suffered cruel and great things, and some the loss of life (though not by, yet in the name of, the protector); and about a hundred at this present day lie in holes, and dungeons, and prisons, up and down the nation." The letter, we may suppose, was not read to Cromwell, and the Wednesday went by. On Thursday, September 2, there was an unusually full council meeting, close to his chamber, at which order was given for the removal of Lords Lauderdale and Sinclair from Windsor Castle to Warwick Castle, to make more room at Windsor for the duke of Buckingham. That night Harvey sat up with his highness, and again noted some of his sayings. One was, " Truly, God is good; indeed He is; He will not—" He did not complete the sentence. " His speech failed him," says Harvey; " but, as I apprehended, it was, ' He will not " leave me.' This saying, that God was good, he frequently " used all along, and would speak it with much cheerfulness " and fervor of spirit in the midst of his pain. Again, he said, " ' I would be willing to live to be further serviceable to God " and His people; but my work is done.' He was very rest- " less most part of the night, speaking often to himself. And, " there being something to drink offered him, he was desired " to take the same, and endeavor to sleep; unto which he an-

" swered, 'It is not my design to drink or to sleep, but my
" design is to make what haste I can to be gone.' Afterward,
" toward morning, using divers holy expressions, implying
" much inward consolation and peace, among the rest, he spake .
" some exceeding self-debasing words, annihilating and judg-
" ing himself." This is the last. The next day, Friday, was
his twice victorious 3d of September, the anniversary of
Dunbar and Worcester. That morning he was speechless;
and, though the prayers in Whitehall, and in all London and
the suburbs, did not cease for him, people in the houses and
passers in the streets knew that hope was over, and Oliver at
the point of death.

LXIV.

THE RESTORATION.--Guizot.

[Two troublous years came after Cromwell's death. Though his
son Richard quietly succeeded to the office of protector, it soon became
apparent that the protectorate must fall. Only another Oliver could have
upheld it, and there was none at hand. The sentiment in favor of calling
back the banished Stuarts was too strong to be resisted. For a few months
Richard's tottering authority was upheld by the influence of his father's
name. Then came a brief succession of factions, and then the inevitable—
the Restoration. The tardy action of General Monk was scarcely more
than incidental.]

AT day-break the army, more than thirty thousand strong,
was drawn out in battle-array on Blackheath, where it silently
awaited the coming of the king. It was sad and disquieted
but resigned to its fate ; it had seen all the governments that
it loved—the commonwealth, Cromwell, and its own dominion—fall one after another ; among its leaders, the majority, and those the greatest of them all, had gone over to
the royal cause ; others, still popular among the rank and
file, were proscribed and compelled to fly, for having formerly maintained a deadly conflict against the king. The

republican spirit, military pride, and religious zeal were still powerful in the army; but it no longer had confidence either in those who commanded it or in itself; and bowing its head beneath the secret consciousness of its errors, it accepted the restoration of the monarchy as a necessity, regarded submission to the civil power as a duty, and devoted itself to the maintenance of public order and the preservation of private interests. The king arrived, accompanied by his brothers, and attended by his staff, with Monk at its head, and by a brilliant cavalcade of volunteers elegantly dressed, and adorned with plumes and scarfs. As they pranced about in every direction, an officer, bending toward Monk, whispered in his ear, "You had none of these at Coldstream; but grasshoppers and butterflies never come abroad in frosty weather." Many men in the ranks shared in this feeling of ill-humor. But Charles was young, vivacious, and affable; he presented himself gracefully to the army; and, singularly enough, it was the anniversary of his birthday; he was just thirty years of age. He was well received. Colonel Knight, on behalf of all the regiments, presented to him an address full of the utmost protestations of loyalty, which the soldiers confirmed rather by their submissive· countenance than by their acclamations. The king left Blackheath, delighted at having got through this ordeal satisfactorily. On arriving at St. George's Fields, he met the lord mayor, aldermen, and common council of the city of London, who were awaiting him in a richly decorated tent, to offer him their address and a collation. He halted there for a few moments, and was more cordially received and felt more at his ease among the throng of citizens than among the ranks of the army. His road from St. George's Fields to Whitehall was one continued ovation. He was preceded and followed by numerous squadrons of mounted guards and volunteers, magnificently dressed and caparisoned; the train-bands of the city and of Westminster, and the various corporations with their banners, formed a double line through which he passed; the sheriffs, the aldermen, and all the municipal officers of the city, with a host of servants in splendid liveries, crowded around him ; the lord mayor, with Monk on his right hand and the duke of Buckingham on his left, bore the sword before him ; five regiments of cavalry formed his escort; the streets were strewn with boughs and flowers, the houses hung with flags, the windows, balconies, and roofs crowded with innumerable spectators, men and women, nobles and citizens, all in their gayest attire ; the cannon of the Tower, the bells of the churches, the bands of the regiments, and the shouts of the crowd, filled the air with a deafening and joyous sound. "I stood in the strand and beheld it, and blessed God," says an eye-witness. "All this was done without one drop of bloodshed, and by that very army that rebelled against him ; but it was the Lord's doing, for such a restoration was never mentioned in any history, ancient or modern, since the return of the Jews from the Babylonish captivity; ror was so joyful a day and so bright ever seen in this nation, this happening when to expect or effect it was past all human policy."

Charles himself expressed his delight and surprise with some little irony. "I doubt not," he said, "it has been my own fault I was absent so long, for I see no one who does not protest he has ever wished for my return."

He arrived at Whitehall somewhat later than he had announced, for it was nearly seven o'clock when he reached the palace. The two Houses were awaiting him. He received them each in turn, the Lords in the great hall of the palace, and the Commons in that same banqueting hall through which, eleven years before, the king, his father, had walked on his way to the scaffold. The two speakers, the earl of Manchester and Sir Harbottle Grimstone, addressed the king in speeches at once pompous and sincere, expressing, in terms of somewhat labored eloquence, enthusiasm for monarchy and attachment to the religion and liberties of the country. Lord Manchester more particularly explained his views with firm frankness. "Great king," he said, "permit me to speak the confidence as well as the desires of the peers of England. Be you the powerful defender of the true Protestant faith, the just asserter and maintainer of the laws and liberties of your subjects; so shall judgment run down like a river, and justice like a mighty stream." Charles was, doubtless, struck by this expression; for, in replying to Manchester, he repeated it almost literally. "I am so disordered by my journey," he said, "and with the noise still sounding in my ears, which I confess was pleasing to me because it expressed the affections of my people, that I am unfit at the present to make such a reply as I desire. Yet thus much I shall say unto you, that I take no greater satisfaction to myself in this my change than that I find my heart really set to endeavor by all means the restoring of this nation to freedom and happiness, and I hope by the advice of my Parliament to effect it. Of this also you may be confident, that next to the honor of God, from whom principally I shall ever own this restoration to my crown, I shall study the welfare of my people, and shall not only be a true defender of the faith, but a just asserter of the laws and liberties of my subjects." The king's answer to the House of Commons was very similar, but somewhat shorter; and he excused himself from further discourse with them on the ground of extreme fatigue. The two Houses took their leave. The king was, in fact, so utterly wearied that he was unable to proceed, as he had intended, to Westminster Abbey, on that day, in order to take part in a solemn thanksgiving service; and he ended the day which had witnessed the re-establishment of monarchy in England, by offering up his prayers to God in the reception-room at Whitehall.

At the same moment, throughout the kingdom, thousands of hearts, full of joy, were also raising themselves in thanks to the Almighty and praying him to bless the king whom he had restored to his people. The restoration of Charles the Second was not the consequence, but the cause, of a passionate outburst of the monarchical spirit. Decimated by the civil war, ruined by confiscations, baffled in all its attempts at insurrection and conspiracy, conquered in turn by all its enemies, by the Presbyterians, the Republicans, the Cromwellians, and the soldiers, the Royalist party had given up the conflict, but had not renounced its opinions or its hopes. At once inactive and persevering, it had endured the rule of all successive tyrannies, whether strong or weak, glorious or disgraceful, watching them pass with anger or contempt, and waiting until God and necessity should put the king once more in the place of this chaos. While thus waiting, the Royalists found themselves joined by most of their former adversaries in succession; from conviction, from passion, from resignation, or from personal interest, the Presbyterians, the political reformers, who would not be and did not think themselves revolutionists, a great many Cromwellians, both civilians and soldiers, and even some Republicans, took advantage of one conjuncture or another to range themselves beneath the banner of monarchy. And what was still more important, that portion of the population which had held aloof from all parties, those innumerable and unknown spectators who merely look on at political struggles, and derive from them only their emotions and their fate, this vast mass of the people could now see safety and find hope only in the re-establishment of the monarchy. On the 29th of May, 1660, the Royalist party, which had not conquered, which had not even fought, was nevertheless national and all-powerful. It was England.

XLV.

EXECUTION OF MONMOUTH.—MACAULAY.

[Charles the Second was easy, good-natured, and popular in his ways, but he was unprincipled and utterly selfish. His chief aim was to avoid trouble, so that he might pursue his pleasures unmolested. Almost from the outset he played into the hands of the French king, Louis XIV., and enabled that monarch to build up a power which proved dangerous to Europe. As Charles had no legitimate children, his lawful heir was his brother James, who was a Catholic. There were many in England who thought that a Catholic king should not be allowed to rule, and they made a determined effort to have a law enacted excluding James from the succession. But the measure failed, and, on the death of Charles, in 1683, James became king.

He was exceedingly unpopular, and his first acts made him still more so. So strong was the feeling against him that the duke of Monmouth, the eldest of Charles's illegitimate children, and a Protestant, believed that he could be dethroned by force. In 1685 Monmouth invaded the kingdom; but he had mistaken the temper of the English people. They refused to support the claim of a bastard, and the duke was defeated and captured at the battle of Sedgemoor.]

THE king cannot be blamed for determining that Monmouth should suffer death. Every man who heads a rebellion against an established government stakes his life on the event; and rebellion was the smallest part of Monmouth's crime. He had declared against his uncle a war without quarter. In the manifesto put forth at Lyme, James had been held up to execration as an incendiary, as an assassin, who had strangled one innocent man and cut the throat of another, and, lastly, as the poisoner of his own brother. To spare an enemy who had not scrupled to resort to such extremities would have been an act of rare, perhaps of blamable, generosity. But to see him and not to spare him was an outrage on humanity and decency. This outrage the king resolved to commit. The arms of the prisoner were bound behind him with a silken cord; and, thus secured, he was ushered into the presence of the implacable kinsman whom he had wronged.

Then Monmouth threw himself on the ground, and crawled to the king's feet. He wept. He tried to embrace his uncle's knees with his pinioned arms. He begged for life, only life, life at any price. He owned that he had been guilty of a great crime, but tried to throw the blame on others, particularly on Argyle, who would rather have put his legs into the boots than have saved his own life by such baseness. By the ties of kindred, by the memory of the late king, who had been the best and truest of brothers, the unhappy man adjured James to show some mercy. James gravely replied that this repentance was of the latest; that he was sorry for the misery which the prisoner had brought on himself; but that the case was not one for lenity. A declaration, filled with atrocious calumnies, had been put forth. The regal title had been assumed. For treasons so aggravated there could be no pardon on this side of the grave. The poor, terrified duke vowed that he had never wished to take the crown, but had been led into that fatal error by others. As to the declaration, he had not written it; he had not read it; he had signed it without looking at it; it was all the work of Ferguson, that bloody villain, Ferguson. "Do you expect me to believe," said James, with contempt but too well merited, "that you set your hand to a paper of such moment without knowing what it contained?" One depth of infamy only remained, and even to that the prisoner descended. He was pre-eminently the champion of the Protestant religion. The interest of that religion had been his plea for conspiring against the government of his father, and for bringing on his country the miseries of civil war; yet he was not ashamed to hint that he was inclined to be reconciled to the Church of Rome. The king eagerly offered him spiritual assistance, but said nothing of pardon or respite. "Is there, then, no hope?" asked Monmouth. James turned away in silence. Then Monmouth strove to rally his courage, rose from his knees, and retired with a firmness which he had not shown since his overthrow.

The hour drew near, all hope was over, and Monmouth had passed from pusillanimous fear to the apathy of despair. His children were brought to his room that he might take leave of them, and were followed by his wife. He spoke to her kindly, but without emotion. Though she was a woman of great strength of mind, and had little cause to love him, her misery was such that none of the by-standers could refrain from weeping. He alone was unmoved.

It was ten o'clock. The coach of the lieutenant of the Tower was ready. Monmouth requested his spiritual advisers to accompany him to the place of execution, and they consented; but they told him that, in their judgment, he was about to die in a perilous state of mind, and that, if they attended him, it would be their duty to exhort him to the last. As he passed along the ranks of the guards he saluted them with a smile; and he mounted the scaffold with a firm tread. Tower Hill was crowded, up to the chimney-tops, with an innumerable multitude of gazers, who, in awful silence, broken only by sighs and the noise of weeping, listened for the last accents of the darling of the people. "I shall say little," he began. "I come here not to speak, but to die. I die a Protestant of the Church of England." The bishops interrupted him, and told him that, unless he acknowledged resistance to be sinful, he was no member of their Church. He went on to speak of his Henrietta.* She was, he said, a young lady of virtue and honor. He loved her to the last, and he could not die without giving utterance to his feelings.

The bishops again interfered, and begged him not to use such language. Some altercation followed. The divines have been accused of dealing harshly with the dying man.

* Henrietta, Baroness Wentworth, had followed Monmouth to Holland, and had sacrificed her jewels to provide funds for his expedition.

But they appear to have only discharged what, in their view, was a sacred duty. Monmouth knew their principles, and, if he wished to avoid their importunity, should have dispensed with their attendance. Their general arguments against resistance had no effect on him. But when they reminded him of the ruin which he had brought on his brave and loving followers, of the blood which had been shed, of the souls which had been sent unprepared to the great account, he was touched, and said, in a softened voice, "I do own that. I am sorry that it ever happened." They prayed with him long and fervently; and he joined in their petitions till they invoked a blessing on the king. He remained silent. "Sir," said one of the bishops, "do you not pray for the king with us?" Monmouth paused some time, and, after an internal struggle, exclaimed, "Amen." But it was in vain that the prelates implored him to address to the soldiers and to the people a few words on the duty of obedience to the government. "I will make no speeches," he exclaimed. "Only ten words, my lord." He turned away, called his servant, and put into the man's hand a tooth-pick case, the last token of ill-starred love. "Give it," he said, "to that person." He then accosted John Ketch, the executioner, a wretch who had butchered many brave and noble victims, and whose name has, during a century and a half, been vulgarly given to all who have succeeded him in his odious office. "Here," said the duke, "are six guineas for you. Do not hack me as you did my Lord Russell. I have heard that you struck him three or four times. My servant will give you some more gold if you do the work well." He then undressed, felt the edge of the ax, expressed some fear that it was not sharp enough, and laid his head on the block. The divines in the meantime continued to ejaculate with great energy: "God accept your repentance! God accept your imperfect repentance!"

The hangman addressed himself to his office; but he had been disconcerted by what the duke had said. The first blow inflicted only a slight wound. The duke struggled, rose from the block, and looked reproachfully at the executioner. The head sank down once more. The stroke was repeated again and again; but still the neck was not severed, and the body continued to move. Yells of rage and horror rose from the crowd. Ketch flung down the ax with a curse. "I cannot do it," he said; "my heart fails me." "Take up the ax, man," cried the sheriff. "Fling him over the rails!" roared the mob. At length the ax was taken up. Two more blows extinguished the last remains of life; but a knife was used to separate the head from the shoulders. The crowd was wrought up to such an ecstasy of rage that the executioner was in danger of being torn in pieces, and was conveyed away under a strong guard.

In the mean time many handkerchiefs were dipped in the duke's blood; for, by a large part of the multitude, he was regarded as a martyr who had died for the Protestant religion. The head and body were placed in a coffin covered with black velvet, and were laid privately under the communion table of St. Peter's Chapel, in the Tower. Within four years the pavement of the chancel was again disturbed, and hard by the remains of Monmouth were laid the remains of Jeffreys. In truth, there is no sadder spot on earth than that little cemetery. Death is there associated, not, as in Westminster Abbey and St. Paul's, with genius and virtue, with public veneration and imperishable renown; not, as in our humblest churches and church-yards, with every thing that is most endearing in social and domestic charities; but with whatever is darkest in human nature and in human destiny, with the savage triumph of implacable enemies, with the inconstancy, the ingratitude, the cowardice of friends, with all the miseries of fallen greatness and of blighted fame. Thither have been carried, through successive ages, by the rude hands of jailers, without one mourner following, the bleeding relics of men who had been the captains of armies, the leaders of parties, the oracles of senates, and the ornaments of courts. Thither was borne, before the window where Jane Grey was praying, the mangled corpse of Guilford Dudley. Edward Seymour, duke of Somerset, and protector of the realm, reposes there by the brother whom he murdered. There has moldered away the headless trunk of John Fisher, bishop of Rochester and cardinal of St. Vitalis, a man worthy to have lived in a better age, and to have died in a better cause. There are laid John Dudley, duke of Northumberland, lord high admiral; and Thomas Cromwell, earl of Essex, lord high treasurer. There, too, is another Essex, on whom nature and fortune had lavished all their bounties in vain, and whom valor, grace, genius, royal favor, popular applause, conducted to an early and ignominious doom. Not far off sleep two chiefs of the great house of Howard—Thomas, fourth duke of Norfolk, and Philip, eleventh earl of Arundel. Here and there, among the thick graves of unquiet and aspiring statesmen, lie more delicate sufferers : Margaret of Salisbury, the last of the proud name of Plantagenet, and those two fair queens who perished by the jealous rage of Henry. Such was the dust with which the dust of Monmouth mingled.

Yet a few months, and the quiet village of Toddington, in Bedfordshire, witnessed a still sadder funeral. Near that village stood an ancient and stately hall, the seat of the Wentworths. The transept of the parish church had long been their burial-place. To that burial-place, in the spring which followed the death of Monmouth, was borne the coffin of the young Baroness Wentworth of Nettlestede. Her family reared a sumptuous mausoleum over her remains; but a less costly memorial of her was long contemplated with far deeper interest. Her name, carved by the hand of him whom she loved too well, was, a few years ago, still discernible on a tree in the adjoining park.

12

XLVI.

EXIT JAMES THE SECOND.—COOKE.

[James went on from bad to worse, and in the end succeeded in alienating nearly all classes of his subjects. In this state of affairs some of the most prominent party leaders entered into negotiations with William, prince of Orange, and secretly invited him to invade the country. The prince had married James's elder daughter, Mary, and he had, besides, an eventual claim to the crown in his own right, for he was a grandson of Charles the First. He accepted the invitation, and, on his landing, in 1688, James's army melted away, his friends deserted him, and he fled in terror to the Continent. Parliament met, of course without the sanction of the king, declared the throne vacant, and elected William and Mary as joint sovereigns of England.]

JAMES II.

THE desertions which immediately ensued have been recorded as examples of the blackest ingratitude, and, in too many instances, the imputation cannot be denied. Men who had owed their whole advancement to James, now promised fidelity, were trusted, and betrayed him. No consideration can make us regard with pleasure the dissimulation of Ormond or Drumlawrig, or read without strong reprobation the refined treachery of Churchill. It must, however, be remembered that those who are most prominent in the catalogue of traitors could have procured, upon the condition of their conversion, far higher honors under James than any they could hope to receive from the prince of Orange. Whether the crusade which James had commenced against all who continued steadfast to the English Church had absolved him from all ties of gratitude, was a question which the casuistry of a courtier would probably solve in the affirmative ; and since he was persecuted for his religion, he might easily persuade himself that he was justified in joining a prince who treated the report that he had a design upon the crown as a calumny, and stated his object to be, not the dethronement of the monarch, but the protection of the religion and liberty of the subject.

That many of those who now forsook the king had no further intention than the redress of grievances is proved by their after-conduct. Among the present partisans of the prince appear the most illustrious of those names which were afterward reckoned among the party of the Jacobites and in the muster-rolls of the Pretenders. These observations apply only to individuals of the Tory party. The Whigs had no favors to requite ; in too many instances they had wrongs to revenge.

Upon the landing of the prince it became immediately evident how impotent the priests behind the throne were to avert the ruin they had called down. Petre* had obtained the disgrace of Sunderland, who, dismissed from all his offices, and, perhaps, trembling for his head, declared to his former dependents that he merely retired because it was, at present, inexpedient to employ Catholics. For a moment Petre and his fellow-laborer, the earl of Melford, held the ascendency, but James, alarmed by the suddenness and magnitude of his danger, was now really aware of their incapacity, and turned for advice to those of the Protestants who were still with him. These, however, could already read the signs of the times. They had nothing to expect from his success, every thing from his failure. Halifax and Rochester now intrigued, not for the honor of serving, but for the opportunity of betraying, him. Halifax was the successful competitor ; joined with Nottingham, who had refused to sit at the council-board, and, with Godolphin, who had already changed his

* Petre was James's clerk of the closet.

allegiance, in a commission to treat with the king, he, at his first meeting with the confidential agent of the prince, expressed his determination to use his powers as he might direct. After an interview with the prince he wrote to the king, declaring that he thought there was a design against his person, and Godolphin seconded the intrigue by a letter of advice to withdraw, and within a year his people would invite him back upon their knees.

It was, doubtless, this letter from Halifax which caused James's suddenly conceived and rapidly executed project of flight. The services of that nobleman in bringing about the revolution were so great, that we could wish to remove from him that stigma of treachery which renders deeds that were the salvation of his country, the dishonor of the man.

The sufferings of James were now, doubtless, great; deserted by all those who had been accustomed to deem themselves honored by his slightest command, a terrified fugitive, stealing under the cover of darkness and disguise from his capital and his kingdom, then a captive in the hands of the rabble of a small fishing-town, cringing, entreating, and imploring his life from these ignoble masters of his fate, while the nobles of his council sought, in affected ignorance of his situation, an excuse for conniving at his destruction; then again, when for a moment installed in his former dignity, and when beginning to remember the language of command, banished at midnight from his palace by the voice of the man he had confided in as his embassador, reduced to the necessity of borrowing so small a sum as a hundred guineas from a subject; and, lastly, obtaining, by favor of his enemy, an ignominious safety in a second secret flight; these were sufferings which, having none of the dignity that commonly ennobles the reverses of royalty, must have borne with tenfold weight upon the haughty spirit of the last of the Stuart kings. Yet, amid all this misfortune, he must be possessed of a very morbid sensibility who can pity James. When we picture him kneeling and crying before the hooting rabble, we see, also, Monmouth kneeling at his feet; the rude jests which assailed James from the fishermen of Feversham, were not nearly so savage as the cool denial of mercy with which the duke was dismissed from the presence-chamber to the scaffold. What suffering, which James underwent, can we compare with the horrors which he jested of as Jeffreys's campaign in the West? No one ever thought of pitying the fate which now overtook that instrument of human butchery; why, then, should we waste commiseration upon him who was the real author of all the other's crimes, and who superadded to them the diabolical deeds which he personally perpetrated in the torture-chamber in Scotland?

In the midst of all his distress one act in the dark catalogue of his crimes was brought before him with its full force. Previous to his flight he called together those nobles who were within reach of his summons, to advise with them upon his affairs. The earl of Bedford, whom age and despondency had long secluded from public business, came among the rest. "You, my lord," said James, to this popular nobleman, as he sat at the council-board, "could do much for me in this extremity." The earl replied that he was now old and incapable of exertion; "but," he added, with a sigh, "I once had a son who might have been of infinite service to your majesty at this moment." It is said that James was pale and confounded at the reply. It was the rebuke of a father to the murderer of his son.

Even the treachery of which James was the victim was, in many instances, of a character to excite only disapprobation of the traitors, not commiseration for the betrayed. Their master had rivaled them all in ingratitude. Hyde, earl of Rochester, at one time his chief, at all times his devoted supporter, who had served him faithfully through his difficult and apparently hopeless struggle for the crown, was cast aside like a worn garment, when success had rendered him unnecessary. The eloquence of Halifax, to which he was not less indebted for his throne, could not protect him from similar treatment; and not the most unconditional compliance, even to the abandonment of his religion, could preserve Sunderland, when he halted for a moment in the course he was given to run.

The king arrived in France on the last day of the year 1688.

XLVII.

KILLIECRANKIE.—Scott.

[William came as a mediator between parties, and his influence told beneficially in nearly all directions. The Catholics of Ireland and the Catholic Highlanders of Scotland, however, refused to submit to his authority, and both had to be reduced by force. The Highland clans gathered under Viscount Dundee as leader, and defeated the royal army at Killiecrankie, where Dundee was slain. But if Dundee had lived, the ultimate result would have been practically the same. A Highland army was never so little to be feared as the day after a victory, for the clans were wont to disperse at once to their homes to secure the booty they had won.]

In this celebrated defile, called the Pass of Killiecrankie, the road runs for several miles along the banks of a furious river, called the Garry, which rages below, among cataracts and water-falls which the eye can scarcely discern, while a series of precipices and wooded mountains rise on the other hand; the road itself is the only mode of access through the glen, and along the valley which lies at its northern extremity. The path was then much more inaccessible than at the present day, as it ran close to the bed of the river, and was narrower and more rudely formed.

A defile of such difficulty was capable of being defended to the last extremity by a small number against a considerable army; and considering how well adapted his followers were for such mountain warfare, many of the Highland chiefs were of opinion that Dundee ought to content himself with guarding the pass against Mackay's superior army, until a rendezvous, which they had appointed, should assemble a stronger force of their countrymen. But Dundee was of a different opinion, and resolved to suffer Mackay to march through the pass without opposition, and then to fight him in the open valley, at the northern extremity. He chose this bold measure, both because it promised a decisive result to the combat which his ardent temper desired; and also because he preferred fighting Mackay before that general was joined by a considerable body of English horse who were expected, and of whom the Highlanders had at that time some dread.

On the 17th of June, 1689, General Mackay, with his troops, entered the pass, which, to their astonishment, they found unoccupied by the enemy. His forces were partly English and Dutch regiments, who, with many of the Lowland Scots themselves, were struck with awe, and even fear, at finding themselves introduced by such a magnificent and, at the same time, formidable avenue, to the presence of their enemies, the inhabitants of these tremendous mountains, into whose recesses they were penetrating. But besides the effect produced on their minds by the magnificence of natural scenery, to which they were wholly unaccustomed, the consideration must have hung heavy on them, that if a general of Dundee's talents suffered them to march unopposed through a pass so difficult, it must be because he was conscious of possessing strength sufficient to attack and destroy them at the farther extremity; when their only retreat would lie through the narrow and perilous path by which they were now advancing.

Midday was passed ere Mackay's men were extricated from the defile, when their general drew them up in one line three deep, without any reserve, along the southern extremity of the narrow valley into which the pass opens. A hill on the north side of the valley, covered with dwarf trees and bushes, formed the position of Dundee's army, which, divided into columns, formed by the different clans, was greatly outflanked by Mackay's troops.

The armies shouted when they came within sight of each other; but the enthusiasm of Mackay's soldiers being damped by the circumstances we have observed, their military shout made but a dull and sullen sound compared to the yell of the Highlanders, which rang far and shrill from all the hills around them. Sir Evan Cameron of Lochiel called on those around him to attend to this circumstance, saying, that in all his battles he observed victory had ever been on the side o' those whose shout before joining seemed most sprightly and confident. It was accounted a less favorable augury by some of the old Highlanders that Dundee at this moment, to render his person less distinguishable, put on a sad-colored buff-coat above the scarlet cassock and bright cuirass in which he had hitherto appeared.

It was some time ere Dundee had completed his preparations for the assault which he meditated, and only a few dropping shots were exchanged, while, in order to prevent the risk of being outflanked, he increased the intervals between the columns with which he designed to charge, insomuch that he had scarce men enough left in the center. About an hour before sunset he sent word to Mackay that he was about to attack him, and gave the signal to charge.

The Highlanders stripped themselves to their shirts and doublets, threw away every thing that could impede the fury of their onset, and then put themselves in motion, accompanying with a dreadful yell the discordant sound of their war-pipes. As they advanced, the clansmen fired their pieces, each column thus pouring in a well-aimed though irregular volley, when, throwing down their fusees, without waiting to reload, they drew their swords, and, increasing their pace to the utmost speed, pierced through and broke the thin line which was opposed to them, and profited by their superior activity, and the nature of their weapons, to make a great havoc among the regular troops. When thus mingled with each other, hand to hand, the advantages of superior discipline on the part of the

Lowland soldier were lost—agility and strength were on the side of the mountaineers. Some accounts of the battle give a terrific account of the blows struck by the Highlanders, which cleft heads down to the breast, cut steel head-pieces asunder as night-caps, and slashed through pikes like willows. Two of Mackay's English regiments in the center stood fast, the interval between the attacking columns being so great that none were placed opposite to them. The rest of King William's army were totally routed, and driven headlong into the river.

Dundee himself, contrary to the advice of the Highland chiefs, was in front of the battle, and fatally conspicuous. By a desperate attack, he possessed himself of Mackay's artillery, and then led his handful of cavalry, about fifty men, against two troops of horse, which fled without fighting. Observing the stand made by the two English regiments already mentioned, he galloped toward the clan of MacDonald, and was in the act of bringing them to the charge, with his right arm elevated as if pointing the way to victory, when he was struck by a bullet beneath the arm-pit, where he was unprotected by his cuirass. He tried to ride on, but being unable to keep the saddle, fell mortally wounded, and died in the course of the night.

It was impossible for a victory to be more complete than that gained by the Highlanders at Killiecrankie. The cannon, baggage, and stores of Mackay's army fell into their hands. The two regiments which kept their ground suffered so much in their attempt to retreat through the pass, now occupied by the Athole-men, in their rear, that they might be considered as destroyed. Two thousand of Mackay's army were killed or taken, and the general himself escaped with difficulty to Stirling, at the head of a few horse. The Highlanders, whose dense columns, as they came down to the attack, underwent three successive volleys from Mackay's line, had eight hundred men slain.

But all other losses were unimportant compared to that of

Dundee, with whom were forfeited all the fruits of that bloody victory. Mackay, when he found himself free from pursuit, declared his conviction that his opponent had fallen in the battle. And such was the opinion of Dundee's talents and courage, and the general sense of the peculiar crisis at which his death took place, that the common people of the low country cannot, even now, be persuaded that he died an ordinary death. They say that a servant of his own, shocked at the severities which, if triumphant, his master was likely to accomplish against the Presbyterians, and giving way to the popular prejudice about his having a charm against the effect of lead balls, shot him, in the tumult of the battle, with a silver button taken from his livery coat. The Jacobites and the Episcopal party, on the other hand, lamented the deceased victor, as the last of the Scots, the last of the Grahams, and the last of all that was great in his native country.

XLVIII.

DOWNFALL OF MARLBOROUGH.—LECKY.

[While William, by his wise statesmanship, conferred great benefits upon England, he rendered still greater service to the Continental states in checkmating the ambition of Louis XIV. Death came to him, however, before the struggle with Louis was over, and the work which he had begun was committed to other hands. John Churchill, earl of Marlborough, was appointed by William's successor, Queen Anne, commander-in-chief of the army. By a series of remarkably brilliant campaigns which proved him to be the greatest general of his age, he forced the French king to sue for peace. But, as the proffered terms were rejected through Marlborough's influence, it was thought that he was prolonging the war for his own advantage. Therefore, the Tories, who strongly opposed the war, and who hated Marlborough because of his great successes, determined to accomplish his ruin.]

MEANWHILE the government at home had been pressing on the peace by measures of almost unparalleled violence.

Supported by a large majority in the House of Commons, it resolved to silence or crush all opposition. The first and most conspicuous victim was Marlborough. It was alleged, and alleged with truth, that, while commanding in the Netherlands, he had during several years received an annual pension of about £6,000 from the contractor who supplied his army with bread, and also that he had appropriated two and a half per cent. of the money which had been voted by Parliament for paying the subsidized troops, and on these grounds he was accused of peculation. The answer, however, in ordinary times would have been accepted as conclusive. It was shown that the former sum was a perquisite always granted to the commander in the Netherlands, and employed by him for obtaining that secret intelligence which is absolutely essential to a general, and which was never more complete than under Marlborough, and that the deduction from the subsidies was expressly authorized by the foreign powers who were subsidized, and by a royal warrant which granted it to the commander-in-chief "for extraordinary contingent expenses." Whatever irregularity there might be in providing by these means a supply of secret-service money, it was of old standing ; there was no reason whatever to believe that the fund was misappropriated, though from its very nature it could not be accounted for in detail, and it was proved that the expenditure of secret-service money in the campaigns of Marlborough was considerably smaller than it had been in the incomparably less successful campaigns of William. Prince Eugene afterward very candidly declared that he had himself given for intelligence three times as much as Marlborough was charged with on that head.

The object of the dominant party, however, was, at all costs, to discredit Marlborough. He was dismissed from all his employments, pronounced guilty by a party vote of the House of Commons, and exposed to a storm of mendacious obloquy. When Eugene came over to England in order to use his influence against the peace in January of 1711–12, he perceived, with no little generous indignation, that every effort was made to extol his military talents at the expense of the great English commander. Marlborough was assailed as he drove through the streets with cries of "Stop thief!" He was grossly insulted in the House of Lords. He was accused of the most atrocious plots against the queen and against the state. The scurrilous pens of Mrs. Manley and of a host of other libelers were employed against him. Ballads, describing him as the basest of men, were sung publicly in the highways. The funds which the queen had hitherto provided for the construction of Blenheim were stopped, and the tide of calumny and vituperation ran so strongly that he thought it advisable to abandon the country, and accordingly proceeded, in November, 1712, almost alone, to Flanders, and soon after to Germany. He was received in both countries with a respect and an enthusiasm that contrasted strangely with his treatment at home, and he at the same time invested £50,000 in Holland, in case the state of home politics should exclude him forever from his country.

English history contains no more striking instance of the sudden revulsion of popular feeling. Beyond comparison, the greatest of English generals, Marlborough, had raised his country to a height of military glory such as it had never attained since the days of Poitiers and Agincourt, and his victories appeared all the more dazzling after the ignominious reigns of the last two Stuarts, and after the many failures that checkered the enterprises of William. His military genius, though once bitterly decried by party malignity, will now be universally acknowledged, and it was sufficient to place him among the greatest captains who have ever lived. Hardly any other modern general combined to an equal degree the three great attributes of daring, caution, and sagacity, or conducted military enterprises of equal magnitude and duration without losing a single battle, or failing in a single siege. He was

one of the very few commanders who appear to have shown
equal skill in directing a campaign, in winning a battle, and
in improving a victory. It cannot, indeed, be said of him, as
it may be said of Frederick the Great, that he was at the head
of a small power, with almost all Europe in arms against it,
and that nearly every victory he won was snatched from an
army enormously outnumbering his own. Nor did the circumstances of Marlborough admit of a military career of the same
brilliancy, variety, and magnitude of enterprise as that of
Napoleon. But both Frederick and Napoleon experienced
crushing disasters, and both of them had some advantages
which Marlborough did not possess. Frederick was the absolute ruler of a state which had for many years been governed
exclusively on the military principle, in which the first and
almost the sole object of the government had been to train
and discipline the largest and most perfect army the nation
could support. Napoleon was the absolute ruler of the foremost military power on the Continent, at a time when the enthusiasm of a great revolution had given it an unparalleled
energy, when the destruction of the old hierarchy of rank
and the opening of all posts to talent, had brought an extraordinary amount of ability to the forefront, and when the
military administrations of surrounding nations were singularly decrepit and corrupt. Marlborough, on the other hand,
commanded armies consisting, in a great degree, of confederates and mercenaries of many different nationalities, and
under many different rulers. He was thwarted at every step
by political obstacles, and by the much graver obstacles arising from divided command and personal or national
jealousies; he contended against the first military nation of
the Continent, at a time when its military organization had
attained the highest perfection, and when a long succession
of brilliant wars had given it a school of officers of consum-
mate skill.

But, great as were his military gifts, they would have been

insufficient had they not been allied with other qualities, well fitted to win the admiration of men. Adam Smith has said, with scarcely an exaggeration, that "it is a characteristic almost peculiar to the great duke of Marlborough, that ten years of such uninterrupted and such splendid successes as scarce any other general could boast of, never betrayed him into a single rash action, scarcely into a single rash word or expression." Nothing in his career is more admirable than the unwearied patience, the inimitable skill, the courtesy, the tact, the self-command with which he employed himself during many years in reconciling the incessant differences, overcoming the incessant opposition, and soothing the incessant jealousies of those with whom he was compelled to co-operate. His private correspondence abundantly shows how gross was the provocation he endured, how keenly he felt it, how nobly he bore it. As a negotiator, he ranks with the most skillful diplomatists of his age, and it was, no doubt, his great tact in managing men that induced his old rival Bolingbroke, in one of his latest writings, to describe him as not only the greatest general, but also "the greatest minister our country or any other has produced." Chesterfield, while absurdly depreciating his intellect, admitted that "his manner was irresistible," and he added that, of all men he had ever known, Marlborough "possessed the graces in the highest degree."

Nor was his character without its softer side. Though he cannot, I think, be acquitted of a desire to prolong war, in the interests of his personal or political ambition, it is at least true that no general ever studied more, by admirable discipline and by uniform humanity, to mitigate its horrors. Very few friendships, among great political or military leaders, have been as constant, or as unclouded by any shade of jealousy, as the friendship between Marlborough and Godolphin, and between Marlborough and Eugene. His conjugal fidelity, in a time of great laxity, and under temptations and provocations of no common order, was beyond reproach. His attachment to the

Church of England was at one time the great obstacle to his advancement. It appears never to have wavered through all the vicissitudes of his life; and no one who reads his most private letters with candor, can fail to perceive that a certain vein of genuine piety ran through his nature, however inconsistent it may appear with some portions of his career.

Yet it may be questioned whether, even in the zenith of his fame, he was really popular. He had grave vices, and they were precisely of that kind which is most fatal to public men. His extreme rapacity in acquiring, and his extreme avarice in hoarding money, contrasted forcibly with the lavish generosity of Ormond, and alone gave weight to the charges of peculation that were brought against him. It is true that this, like all his passions, was under control. Torcy soon found that it was useless to attempt to bribe him, and he declined, as we have seen, with little hesitation, the enormously lucrative post of governor of the Austrian Netherlands, when he found that the appointment aroused the strong and dangerous hostility of the Dutch. In these cases, his keen and far-seeing judgment perceived clearly his true interest, and he had sufficient resolution to follow it. Yet still, like many men who have risen from great poverty to great wealth, avarice was the passion of his life, and the rapacity, both of himself and of his wife, was insatiable. Besides immense grants for Blenheim, and marriage portions given by the queen to their daughters, they at one time received between them an annual income of public money of more than £64,000.

Nor can he be acquitted of very gross and aggravated treachery to those he served. It is, indeed, not easy to form a fair estimate in this respect of the conduct of public men at the period of the Revolution. Historians rarely make sufficient allowance for the degree in which the judgments and dispositions even of the best men are colored by the moral tone of the age, society, or profession in which they live, or for the temptations of men of great genius and of natural ambition in times when no highly scrupulous man could possibly succeed in public life.   Marlborough struggled into greatness from a very humble position, in one of the most profligate periods of English politics, and he lived-through a long period when the ultimate succession of the crown was very doubtful.   A very large proportion of the leading statesmen, during this long season of suspense, made such overtures to the deposed dynasty as would at least secure them from absolute ruin in the event of a change ; and their conduct is surely susceptible of much palliation.   The apparent interests and the apparent wishes of the nation hung so evenly, and oscillated so frequently, that strong convictions were rare, and even good men might often be in doubt.

But the obligations of Marlborough to James were of no common order, and his treachery was of no common dye.   He had been raised by the special favor of his sovereign from the position of a page to the peerage, to great wealth, to high command in the army.   He had been trusted by him with the most absolute trust.   He not only abandoned him in the crisis of his fate, with circumstances of the most deliberate and aggravated treachery, but also employed his influence over the daughter of his benefactor to induce her to fly from her father, and to array herself with his enemies.   Such conduct, if it had indeed been dictated, as he alleged, solely by a regard for the interests of Protestantism, would have been certainly, in the words of Hume, "a signal sacrifice to public virtue of every duty in private life ; " and it "required ever after the most upright, disinterested, and public-spirited behavior, to render it justifiable."   How little the later career of Marlborough fulfilled this condition is well known.   When we find that, having been loaded under the new government with titles, honors, and wealth, having been placed in the inner council and intrusted with the most important state secrets, he was one of the first Englishmen to enter into negotiations with the exiled king; that he purchased his pardon from James by betraying important military secrets to the enemies of his country, and that during a great part of his subsequent career, while holding office under the government, he was secretly negotiating with the pretender, it is difficult not to place the worst construction upon his public life. It is probable, indeed, that his negotiations with the Jacobites were never sincere, that he had no real desire for a restoration, and that his guiding motive was much less ambition than a desire to secure what he possessed; but these considerations only slightly palliate his conduct. At the period of his downfall his later acts of treason were, for the most part, unknown; but his conduct toward James weighed heavily upon his reputation, and his intercourse with the pretender, though not proved, was suspected by many. Neither Hanoverians nor Jacobites trusted him; neither Whigs nor Tories could regard him, without reserve, as their own.

And with this feeling of distrust there was mingled a strong element of fear. In the latter years of Queen Anne the shadow of Cromwell fell darkly across the path of Marlborough. The profound horror of military despotism, which is one of the strongest and most salutary of English sentiments, has been, perhaps, the most valuable legacy of the commonwealth. In Marlborough, for the first time since the Restoration, men saw a possible Cromwell, and they looked forward with alarm to the death of the queen as a period peculiarly propitious to military usurpation.

These considerations help to explain the completeness of the downfall of Marlborough.

XLIX.

WALPOLE AS A PEACE MINISTER.—GREEN.

[By a law enacted during the life-time of William it was settled that, if neither he and Queen Mary, nor Queen Anne, left any children, the crown should go to the German branch of the Stuart family. The head of this branch, at the time of Queen Anne's death, was George, elector of Hanover, and he accordingly became the first English king of the house of Hanover, or Brunswick, as it is often called. As he was a foreigner, ignorant of English politics, and even of the English language, it was almost inevitable that the administration of affairs should fall into the hands of his ministers. Among these Sir Robert Walpole soon rose to prominence, and became prime minister in 1721. From that time on until his retirement, in 1742, his history is the history of the nation.]

GEORGE I.

BUT it was no mere chance or good luck which maintained Walpole at the head of affairs for more than twenty years. If no minister has fared worse at the hand of poets or historians, there are few whose greatness has been more impartially recognized by practical statesmen. His qualities, indeed, were such as a practical statesman can alone do full justice to. There is nothing to charm in the outer aspect of the man; nor is there any thing picturesque in the work which he set himself to do, or in the means by which he succeeded in doing it. But picturesque or no, the work of keeping England quiet, and of giving quiet to Europe, was in itself a noble one ; and it is the temper with which he carried on this work, the sagacity with which he discerned the means by which alone it could be done, and the stubborn, indomitable will with which he faced every difficulty in the doing it, which gives Walpole his place

among English statesmen.   He was the first and he was the
most successful of our peace ministers.   "The most pernicious
circumstances," he said, "in which this country can be are
those of war; as we must be losers while it lasts, and cannot
be great gainers when it ends."   It was not that the honor or
influence of England suffered in Walpole's hands, for he won
victories by the firmness of his policy and the skill of his negotiations as effectual as any that are won by arms.   But up
to the very end of his ministry, when the frenzy of the nation
at last forced his hand, in spite of every varying complication
of foreign affairs, and a never-ceasing pressure alike from the
opposition and the court, it is the glory of Walpole that he
resolutely kept England at peace.   And as he was the first of
our peace ministers, so he was the first of our financiers.   He
was far indeed from discerning the powers which later statesmen have shown to exist in a sound finance—powers of pro-
ducing both national development and international amity;
but he had the sense to see, what no minister till then had
seen, that the only help a statesman can give to industry or
commerce is to remove all obstacles in the way of their natural growth, and that beyond this the best course he can take
in presence of a great increase in national energy and national wealth is to look quietly on and to let it alone.   At the outset of his rule he declared in a speech from the throne that
nothing would more conduce to the extension of commerce
"than to make the exportation of our own manufactures, and
the importation of the commodities used in the manufacturing of them, as practicable and easy as may be."

The first act of his financial administration was to take off
the duties from more than a hundred British exports, and
nearly forty articles of importation.   In 1730 he broke, in the
same enlightened spirit, through the prejudice which re-
stricted the commerce of the colonies to the mother country
alone, by allowing Georgia and the Carolinas to export their
rice directly to any part of Europe.   The result was, that

the rice of America soon drove that of Italy and Egypt from the market. His excise bill, defective as it was, was the first measure in which an English minister showed any real grasp of the principles of taxation. The wisdom of Walpole was rewarded by a quick up-growth of prosperity. The material progress of the country was such as England had never seen before. Our exports, which were only six millions in value at the beginning of the century, had reached the value of twelve millions by the middle of it. It was, above all, the trade with the colonies which began to give England a new wealth. The whole colonial trade at the time of the battle of Blenheim (1704) was no greater than the trade with the single isle of Jamaica at the opening of the American war. At the accession of George the Second the exports to Pennsylvania were valued at £15,000. At his death they reached half a million. In the middle of the eighteenth century the profits of Great Britain from the trade with the colonies were estimated at two millions a year. And with the growth of wealth came a quick growth in population. That of Manchester and Birmingham, whose manufactures were now becoming of importance, doubled in thirty years. Bristol, the chief seat of the West Indian trade, rose into new prosperity. Liverpool, which owes its creation to the new trade with the West, sprang up from a little country town into the third port of the kingdom. With peace and security, and the wealth that they brought with them, the value of land, and with it the rental of every country gentleman, rose fast. "Estates which were rented at two thousand a year threescore years ago," said Burke, in 1766, "are at three thousand at present."

Nothing shows more clearly the soundness of his political intellect than the fact that this up-growth of wealth around him never made Walpole swerve from a rigid economy, from a steady reduction of the debt, or a diminution of fiscal duties. Even before the death of George the First the public burdens were reduced by twenty millions. It was, indeed, in economy alone that his best work could be done. In finance, as in other fields of statesmanship, Walpole was forbidden from taking more than tentative steps toward a wiser system by the needs of the work he had specially to do. To this work every thing gave way. He withdrew his excise bill rather than suffer the agitation it roused to break the quiet which was reconciling the country to the system of the revolution. His hatred of religious intolerance, or the support he hoped for from the dissenters, never swayed him to rouse the spirit of popular bigotry, which he knew to be ready to burst out at the slightest challenge, by any effort to repeal the laws against non-conformity. His temper was naturally vigorous and active, and yet the years of his power are years without parallel in our annals for political stagnation. His long administration, indeed, is almost without a history. All legislative and political action seemed to cease with his entry into office. Year after year passed by without a change. In the third year of Walpole's ministry there was but one division in the House of Commons. Such an inaction gives little scope for the historian; but it fell in with the temper of the nation at large. It was popular with the class which commonly presses for political activity. The energy of the trading class was absorbed, for the time, in the rapid extension of commerce and accumulation of wealth. So long as the country was justly and temperately governed the merchant and shopkeeper were content to leave government in the hands that held it. All they asked was to be let alone to enjoy their new freedom and develop their new industries. And Walpole let them alone.

On the other hand, the forces which opposed the revolution lost, year by year, somewhat of their energy. The fervor which breeds revolt died down among the Jacobites as their swords rusted idly in their scabbards. The Tories sulked in their country houses; but their wrath against the house of

Hanover ebbed away for want of opportunities of exerting itself. And, meanwhile, on opponents as on friends, the freedom which the revolution had brought with it was doing its work.

It was to the patient influence of this freedom that Walpole trusted; and it was the special mark of his administration that, in spite of every temptation, he gave it full play. Though he dared not touch the laws that oppressed the Catholic or the dissenter, he took care that they should remain inoperative. Catholic worship went on unhindered. Yearly bills of indemnity exempted the non-conformists from the consequences of their infringement of the test act. There was no tampering with public justice or with personal liberty. Thought and action were alike left free. No minister was ever more foully slandered by journalists and pamphleteers, but Walpole never meddled with the press.

-------•-------

L.

THE PREACHING OF WHITEFIELD.—Lecky.

[The great Methodist revival dates from the later years of Walpole's ministry. The Church of England was in a state of great stagnation, and a group of Oxford students, among whom John and Charles Wesley were the most prominent, determined to regenerate it. But the wonderful preaching of Whitefield was the main instrument in spreading the movement, especially among the lower classes.]

His eloquence had nothing of that chaste and polished beauty which was displayed in the discourses of the great French preachers, and which, in the present century, has led so many men of fastidious taste to hang spell-bound around the pulpit of Robert Hall. It had none of that force of reasoning, that originality of thought, or that splendor of language, which constituted the great charm of the sermons of

Chalmers. Yet, while exercising a power which has, probably never been equaled on the most ignorant and the most vicious, Whitefield was quite capable of fascinating the most refined audiences in London, and he extorted the tribute of warm admiration from such critics as Hume and Franklin, from such orators as Bolingbroke and Chesterfield. His preaching combined almost the highest perfection of acting with the most burning fervor of conviction. No man ever exhibited more wonderfully that strange power which great histrionic talent exercises over the human mind—investing words which are, in truth, the emptiest bombast with all the glow of the most majestic eloquence, and imparting, for a moment at least, to confident assertions more than the weight of the most convincing arguments. His gestures were faultless in their beauty and propriety, while his voice was so powerful that Franklin, who was the most accurate of men, ascertained by experiment that it could be heard distinctly in the open air by 30,000 persons. It was, at the same time, eminently sweet, musical, and varied, and it was managed with perfect skill. Garrick is reported to have said, with a pardonable exaggeration, that Whitefield could pronounce the word Mesopotamia in such a way as to move an audience to tears. With the exception of a slight squint of one eye, which was much dwelt on by his satirists, his person was unusually graceful and imposing, and, like Chatham, the piercing glance of a singularly brilliant eye contributed, in no small measure, to the force of his appeals.

To these gifts we must add a large command of vivid, homely, and picturesque English, and an extraordinary measure of the tact which enables a practiced orator to adapt himself to the character and dispositions of his audience. We must add, above all, a contagious fervor of enthusiasm, which, like a resistless torrent, bore down every obstacle. Of no other preacher could it be more truly said that he preached "as a dying man to dying men." His favorite maxim was that "a preacher, whenever he entered the pulpit, should look upon it as the last time he might preach, and the last time his people might hear." To his vivid imagination heaven and hell, death and judgment, appeared palpably present. His voice was sometimes choked with tears; he stamped vehemently on the pulpit floor; every nerve was strained; his whole frame was convulsed with passion. One who heard him described how, during the whole remainder of his life, he was haunted by the recollection of the tone of piercing pathos with which Whitefield once interrupted the course of his remarks, as if overpowered by a sudden thought: "O, my hearers, the wrath to come! the wrath to come!"

One of the great peculiarities of the Methodist preachers was the personal application they gave to their exhortations. It was their main object, by gesture, by look, by the constant use of the singular pronoun, to preach so that each member of the congregation might imagine the whole force of the denunciations or of the pleadings of the preacher was directed individually to himself. In this art Whitefield especially excelled, and he sometimes carried it to strange lengths, and employed it with strange effects. On one occasion he saw the actor Shuter, who was then attracting much notice in the part of Ramble in the "Rambler," seated in a front pew of the gallery. He at once turned toward him and exclaimed, "And thou, too, poor Ramble, who hast rambled so far from him, O! cease thy ramblings, and come to Jesus." On another, when appealing to a Negro congregation, he asked whether they did not desire to go to heaven, the audience was amused by an old Negro audibly exclaiming, "Yes, sir." "The gentleman put the question once or twice," he afterward explained, "till at last he seemed to point to me, and I was ashamed that nobody should answer him, and, therefore, I did." Very frequently, by his glance, he singled out, or appeared to single out, one member of his vast congregation, and a great part of the tremendous power which his appeals exercised over some minds is ascribed to this habit.

He delighted in strokes of dramatic oratory, which, with an ordinary man, would have appeared simply ludicrous or intolerably tawdry, but to which his transcendent power of acting never failed to impart an extraordinary power. On one occasion— the scene is described by no less a person than David Hume —"after a solemn pause, he thus addressed the audience : ' The attendant angel is just about to leave the threshold of this sanctuary, and ascend to heaven. And shall he ascend and not bear with him the news of one sinner among all this multitude reclaimed from the error of his way ?' To give the greater effect to this exclamation, Whitefield stamped with his foot, lifted up his hands and eyes to heaven, and cried aloud, ' Stop, Gabriel, stop, ere you enter the sacred portals, and yet carry with you the news of one sinner converted to God !' " " This address," adds Hume, " was accompanied by such animated yet natural action, that it surpassed any thing I ever saw or heard in any other preacher." He was fond of painting the denial by Peter, and when he came to describe the apostle as going out and weeping bitterly, he had always ready a fold of his gown in which to bury his face. Sometimes he would visit a court of justice, and afterward reproduce the condemnation scene in the pulpit. With his eyes full of tears, and his voice trembling with pity, he would begin, after a momentary pause: "I am now going to put on the condemning cap. Sinner, I must do it. I must pronounce sentence upon you." Then changing his tone, he thundered over his awe-struck congregation the solemn words, "Depart from me, ye cursed, into everlasting fire !" Of the vehemence of his manner, and the extraordinary effect which that vehemence produced, it is difficult, from any example of our own day, to form a conception. " I hardly ever knew him to go through a sermon," wrote one who knew him well, " without weeping more or less, and I truly believe his were

13

the tears of sincerity. His voice was often interrupted by his affection, and I have heard him say in the pulpit, 'You blame me for weeping, but how can I help it when you will not weep for yourselves, though your immortal souls are on the verge of destruction, and, for aught you know, you are hearing your last sermon.' " "God always makes use of strong passions," he was accustomed to say, "for a great work," and it was his object to rouse such passions by his eloquence to the highest point. Hume describes almost the whole assembly as weeping, and, though himself one of the most delicate of critics, and one of the coldest and most skeptical of men, he pronounced Whitefield the most ingenious preacher he had ever heard, and declared that it was worth going twenty miles to hear him.

The account which Franklin has given of the effects of the eloquence of Whitefield, though well known, is too characteristic to be omitted. Franklin, strongly disapproving of the scheme of building an orphanage in Georgia, which was but thinly populated, and where workmen and materials were scarce, instead of at Philadelphia, determined not to support it. "I happened soon after," he tells us, "to attend one of his sermons, in the course of which I perceived he intended to finish with a collection, and I silently resolved he should get nothing from me. I had in my pocket a handful of copper money, three or four silver dollars, and five pistoles in gold. As he proceeded I began to soften, and concluded to give the copper. Another stroke of his oratory made me ashamed of that, and determined me to give the silver, and he finished so admirably that I emptied my pocket wholly into the collector's dish, gold and all. At this sermon there was also one of our club, who, being of my sentiments respecting the building in Georgia, and suspecting a collection might be intended, had, by precaution, emptied his pockets before he came from home. Toward the conclusion of the discourse, however, he felt a strong inclination to give, and applied to a neighbor, who stood near him, to lend him some money for the purpose. The request was made to, perhaps, the only man in the company who had the firmness not to be affected by the preacher. His answer was, ' At any other time, friend Hopkinson, I would lend thee freely, but not now, for thee seems to me to be out of thy right senses.'"

The effect of this style of preaching was greatly enhanced by an extreme variety of gesture, intonation, and manner. Considering the very small number of his ideas, it is a remarkable proof of the oratorical talents of Whitefield that his sermons were never charged with monotony. He frequently interspersed the more serious passages with anecdotes or illustrations. He sometimes even relieved them by a jest. Often, when the audience had been strung to the highest pitch of excitement, he would suddenly make a long, solemn, and dramatic pause. He painted scenes as if they were visibly present to the eye, with all the fire and the animation of the most perfect actor. On one occasion, when illustrating the peril of sinners, he described, with such admirable power, an old blind man, deserted by his dog, tottering feebly over the desolate moor, endeavoring in vain to feel his way with his staff, and gradually drawing nearer and nearer to the verge of a dizzy precipice, that when he arrived at the final catastrophe, no less a person than Lord Chesterfield lost all self-possession, and was heard audibly exclaiming, " Good God ! he is gone." On another occasion, preaching before seamen at New York, he adopted a nautical tone. " Well, my boys, we have a clear sky, and are making fine headway over a smooth sea before a light breeze, and we shall soon lose sight of land. But what means this sudden lowering of the heavens, and that dark cloud arising from beneath the western horizon ? Hark ! Don't you hear distant thunder ? Don't you see those flashes of lightning ? There is a storm gathering ! Every man to his duty ! How the waves arise and dash against the ship ! The air is dark ! The tempest rages ! Our masts are gone ! The ship is on her beam-ends! What next ?" "The long boat, take to the long boat !" shouted his excited hearers.

A very great part of his influence depended, no doubt, upon the matter of his discourses. He avoided all abstract reflections, all trains of reasoning, every thing that could fatigue the attention, or rouse the intellect to question or oppose. His preaching was based upon the most confident assertions, and it dealt almost exclusively with topics which, if firmly believed, could hardly fail to have a deep influence upon men. The utter depravity of human nature—the eternal tortures which are the doom of every unconverted man—the free salvation by Christ—the imminence of death—the necessity to salvation of a complete, supernatural change of character and emotions, were the subjects upon which he continually dilated. It is easy to understand that such topics, urged by a great orator, at a time when some of them were by no means familiar, should have exercised a far deeper influence than any dissertation upon the duties of man, or the authority of revelation. Besides this, Whitefield was perpetually changing his audience. His style was never suffered to pall upon his hearers. The same sermon was again and again repeated, and at every repetition, passages which appeared ineffective were retrenched, and a greater perfection of emphasis and intonation was acquired. Garrick and Foote declared that he never reached his highest perfection till the fortieth repetition. The picturesque scenes and the striking contrasts which out-of-door preaching furnished, added to the effect, and the great multitude who were attracted by his eloquence gave in turn to that eloquence an additional power. A contagion of excitement was aroused, and an irresistible wave of sympathetic feeling rolled through the mighty host.

I have dwelt at some length upon the preaching of Whitefield, for it was of vital importance to the religious revival of the eighteenth century. But for the simultaneous appearance of a great orator and a great statesman, Methodism would probably have smoldered, and at last perished, like the very similar religious societies of the preceding century. Whitefield was utterly destitute of the organizing skill which could alone give a permanence to the movement, and no talent is naturally more ephemeral than popular oratory; while Wesley, though a great and impressive preacher, could scarcely have kindled a general enthusiasm had he not been assisted by an orator who had an unrivaled power of moving the passions of the ignorant. The institution of field-preaching by Whitefield, in the February of 1739, carried the impulse through the great masses of the poor, while the foundation by Wesley, in the May of the same year, of the first Methodist chapel, was the beginning of an organized body capable of securing and perpetuating the results that had been achieved.

LI.

AFTER CULLODEN.—Stanhope.

[While the Church of England was being stirred to its depths by the preaching of Whitefield and his associates, Prince Charles Edward Stuart, the young pretender, as he was called, made an attempt to recover his ancestral throne. Landing in Scotland, in 1745, with only six companions, he rallied many of the Highland clans around him, and gained brilliant successes at Preston Pans and at Falkirk, but was disastrously defeated at Culloden. After wandering for five months as a fugitive in the Highlands, he succeeded in making his escape to France.]

But where was he, the young and princely chief of this ill-fated enterprise, the new Charles of this second Worcester? His followers dismissed to seek safety as they could for themselves, he sometimes alone, sometimes with a single Highlander as his guide and companion, sometimes begirt with strange faces, of whose fidelity he had no assurance, a price set upon his head, hunted from mountain to island, and from island to mountain, pinched with famine, tossed by storms, and unsheltered from the rains--such was now the object of so many long-cherished and lately towering hopes! In the five months of his weary wanderings—from April to November—almost every day might afford its own tale of hardship, danger, and alarm, and a mere outline must suffice for the general historian. It is much to Charles's honor, that, as one of his chance attendants declares, " he used to say that the fatigues and distresses he underwent signified nothing at all, because he was only a single person, but when he reflected upon the many brave fellows who suffered in his cause, that, he behoved to own, did strike him to the heart, and did sink very deep within him." But most of all entitled to praise appear the common Highlanders around him. Though in the course of these five months the secrets of his concealment became intrusted to several hundred persons, most of them poor and lowly, not one of them was ever tempted by the prize of £30,000 to break faith, and betray the suppliant fugitive, and, when destitute of other help and nearly, as it seemed, run to bay, he was saved by the generous self-devotion of a woman.

In the hope of finding a French ship to convey him, Charles had embarked, only eight days after Culloden, for that remote cluster of isles, to which the common name of Long Island is applied. Driven from place to place by contrary winds and storms, and having sometimes no other food than oatmeal and water, he at length gained South Uist, where his wants were in some degree relieved by the elder Clanranald. But his course being tracked or suspected, a large body of militia and regular troops, to the number of two thousand men, landed on the island, and commenced an eager search, while the shores were surrounded by small vessels of war. Concealment or escape seemed alike impossible, and so they must have proved, but for Miss Flora Macdonald, a name, says Dr. Johnson, which will forever live in history. This young lady was then on a visit to Clanranald's family, and was step-daughter of a captain in the hostile militia which occupied the island. Being appealed to in Charles's behalf, she nobly undertook to save him at all hazards to herself. She obtained from her step-father a passport to proceed to Skye, for herself, a man-servant, and a maid who was termed Betty Burke, the part of Betty to be played by the chevalier. When Lady Clanranald and Flora sought him out, bringing with them a female dress, they found him alone in a little hut upon the shore, employed in roasting the heart of a sheep upon a wooden spit. They could not forbear from shedding tears at his desolate situation, but Charles observed, with a smile, that it would be well, perhaps, for all kings if they had to pass through such an ordeal as he was now enduring. On the same evening he took advantage of the passport, embarking in his new attire, with Flora and a faithful Highlander, Neil MacEachan, who acted as their servant. The dawn of the next day found them far at sea in their open boat, without any land in view ; soon, however, the dark mountains of Skye rose on the horizon. Approaching the coast at Waternish, they were received with a volley of musketry from the soldiers stationed there, but none of the balls took effect, and the rowers, vigorously plying their oars, bore them away from that scene of danger, and enabled them to disembark on another point.

Charles was now in the country of Sir Alexander Macdonald, at first a waverer in the contest, but of late a decided foe. When the prudent chief saw the Jacobite cause decline, he had been induced to levy his clan against it, and was now on the main-land in attendance upon the duke of Cumberland. Yet it was of his wife, Lady Margaret, a daughter of the earl of Eglinton, that Flora determined to implore assistance, having no other resource, and knowing from herself the courageous pity of a female heart. Lady Margaret received the news with pain and surprise, but did not disappoint Flora's firm reliance ; her own house was filled with militia officers, but she intrusted Charles, with earnest injunctions for his safety, to the charge of Macdonald of Kingsburgh, the kinsman and factor of her husband. As they walked to Kingsburgh's house, Charles still in woman's disguise, they had several streams to pass, and the prince held up his petticoats so high as to excite the surprise and laughter of some country people on the road. Being admonished by his attendants, he promised to take better care for the future, and accordingly, on passing the next stream, allowed the skirts to hang down and float upon the water. "Your enemies," said Kingsburgh, "call you a pretender, but if you be, I can tell you, you are the worst of your trade I ever saw!"

' Next day, at Portree, Charles took leave of the noble-minded Flora with warm expressions of his gratitude, and passed over to the Isle of Rasay, under the less inconvenient disguise of a male servant, and the name of Lewis Caw. His preservers soon afterward paid the penalty of their compassion, both Kingsburgh and Flora Macdonald being arrested and conveyed in custody, the former to Edinburgh, the latter to London. The conduct of Lady Margaret likewise was much inveighed against at court, but once, when it provoked some such censure from the princess of Wales, "And would not you, madam," asked Frederick, with a generous spirit, "would not you in like circumstances have done the same? I hope, I am sure you would!" It was at the intercession, it is said, of his royal highness, that Flora was released from prison after a twelvemonth's confinement. A collection was made for her among the Jacobite ladies in London, to the amount of nearly fifteen hundred pounds. She then married Kingsburgh's son, and many years afterward went with him to North America, but both returned during the civil war, and died in their native Isle of Skye.

From Rasay Charles again made his way to the main-land, where he lay for two days cooped up within a line of sentinels, who covered each other upon their posts, so that he could only crouch among the heather, without daring to light a fire, or to dress his food. From this new danger he at length escaped, by creeping at night down a narrow glen, the bed of a winter stream, between two of the stations. Another vicissitude in his wanderings brought him to a mountain cave, where seven robbers had taken their abode; and with these men he remained for nearly three weeks. Fierce and lawless as they were, they never thought for an instant of earning "the price of blood;" on the contrary, they most earnestly applied themselves to secure his safety and supply his wants. Sometimes they used singly, and in various disguises, to repair to the neighboring Fort Augustus, and obtain for Charles a newspaper or the current reports of the day. On one occasion they brought back to the prince, with much exultation, the choicest dainty they had ever heard of—a pennyworth of gingerbread!

On leaving these generous outlaws, and after other perils and adventures, Charles effected a junction with his faithful adherents, Cluny and Lochiel, who was lame,from his wound. There he found a rude plenty to which he had long been unused. "Now, gentlemen, I live like a prince!" cried he, on his first arrival, as he eagerly devoured some collops out of a saucepan with a silver spoon. For some time they resided in a singular retreat called the Cage, on the side of Mount Benalder; it was concealed by a close thicket, and half-suspended in the air. At this place Charles received intelligence that two French vessels, sent out expressly for his deliverance, under the direction of Colonel Warren, of Dillon's regiment, and with that officer on board, had anchored in Lochnanuagh. Immediately setting off for that place, but traveling only by night, he embarked on the 20th of September, attended by Lochiel, Colonel Roy Stuart, and about one hundred other persons, who had gathered at the news. It was the very same spot where Charles had landed fourteen months before, but how changed since that time both his fate and his feelings! With what different emotions must he have

13*

gazed upon these desolate mountains, when stepping from his ship in the ardor of hope and coming victory; and now, when he saw them fade away in the blue distance, and bade them an everlasting farewell! Rapidly did his vessel bear him from the Scottish shores; concealed by a fog, he sailed through the midst of the English fleet; and he safely landed at the little port of Roscoff, near Morlaix, on the 29th of September.

He went—but not with him departed his remembrance from the Highlanders. For years and years did his name continue enshrined in their hearts and familiar to their tongues; their plaintive ditties resounding with his exploits, and inviting his return. ·Again, in these strains do they declare themselves ready to risk life and fortune for his cause ; and even maternal fondness—the strongest, perhaps, of all human feelings—yields to the passionate devotion to " Prince Charlie."

> " I ance had sons, but now hae nane,
> I bred them toiling sairly ;
> And I wad bear them a' again
> And lose them a' for Charlie ! "

. LII.

PITT AS A WAR MINISTER —MACAULAY.

[The expedition of Prince Charles to Scotland had been countenanced by France, and was an episode of the war in which England, in alliance with Austria and Holland, was at that time engaged against France, Spain, and Prussia. This war, which was causeless, so far as England was concerned, was terminated by the peace of Aix la Chapelle, in 1748; but this treaty did not settle the conflicting claims of England and France in India and in America. Both in the East and in the West these two powers were striving for the mastery. In 1756 England, now in alliance with Prussia, entered into the struggle known as the Seven Years' War, and William Pitt, who, since Walpole's retirement, had risen rapidly into prominence, was summoned to conduct it. Early in 1757 he was made first secretary of state and virtually prime minister ; and he guided the destinies of England through the war with signal ability and success.]

PITT desired power ; and he desired it, we really believe, from high and generous motives. He was, in the strict sense of the word, a patriot. He had none of that philanthropy which the great French writers of his time preached to all the nations of Europe. He loved England as an Athenian loved the city of the Violet Crown, as a Roman loved the City of the Seven Hills. He saw his country insulted and defeated. He saw the national spirit sinking. Yet he knew what the resources of the empire, vigorously employed, could effect ; and he felt that he was the man to employ them vigorously. " My lord," he said to the duke of Devonshire, " I am sure that I can save this country, and nobody else can."

Desiring, then, to be in power, and feeling that his abilities and the public confidence were not alone sufficient to keep him in power against the wishes of the court and of the aristocracy, he began to think of a coalition with Newcastle.

Newcastle was equally disposed to a reconciliation. He, too, had profited by his recent experience. He had found that the court and the aristocracy, though powerful, were not every thing in the state. A strong oligarchical connection, a great borough interest, ample patronage, and secret-service money might, in quiet times, be all that a minister needed ; but it was unsafe to trust wholly to such support in time of war, of discontent, and of agitation. The composition of the House of Commons was not wholly aristocratical ; and, whatever be the composition of large deliberative assemblies, their spirit is always, in some degree, popular. Where there are free debates, eloquence must have admirers, and reason must make converts. Where there is a free press, the governors must live in constant awe of the opinions of the governed.

Thus these two men, so unlike in character, so lately mortal enemies, were necessary to each other. Newcastle had fallen in November, for want of that public confidence which Pitt possessed, and of that parliamentary support which Pitt was better qualified than any man of his time to give. Pitt had fallen in April, for want of that species of influence which Newcastle had spent his whole life in acquiring and hoarding. Neither of them had power enough to support himself. Each of them had power enough to overturn the other. Their union would be irresistible. Neither the king nor any party in the state would be able to stand against them.

The first acts of the new administration were characterized rather by vigor than by judgment. Expeditions were sent against different parts of the French coast with little success. The small island of Aix was taken, Rochefort threatened, a few ships burned in the harbor of St. Malo, and a few guns and mortars brought home as trophies from the fortifications of Cherbourg. But soon conquests of a very different kind filled the kingdom with pride and rejoicing. A succession of victories undoubtedly brilliant, and, as it was thought, not barren, raised to the highest point the fame of the minister to whom the conduct of the war had been intrusted. In July, 1758, Louisburg fell. The whole island of Cape Breton was reduced. The fleet to which the court of Versailles had confided the defense of French ·America was destroyed. The captured standards were borne in triumph from Kensington Palace to the city, and were suspended in St. Paul's Church amid the roar of guns and kettle-drums, and the shouts of an immense multitude. Addresses of congratulation came in from all the great towns of England. Parliament met only to decree thanks and monuments, and to bestow, without one murmur, supplies more than double of those which had been given during the war of the Grand Alliance.

The year 1759 opened with the conquest of Goree. Next fell Guadaloupe ; then Ticonderoga ; then Niagara. The Toulon squadron was completely defeated by Boscawen off Cape Lagos. But the greatest exploit of the year was the achievement of Wolfe on the heights of Abraham. The news of his glorious death and of the fall of Quebec reached London in the very week in which the Houses met. All was joy and triumph. Envy and faction were forced to join in the general applause. Whigs and Tories vied with each other in extolling the genius and energy of Pitt. His colleagues were never talked of or thought of. The House of Commons, the nation, the colonies, our allies, our enemies, had their eyes fixed on him alone.

Scarcely had Parliament voted a monument to Wolfe, when another great event called for fresh rejoicings. The Brest fleet, under the command of Conflans, had put out to sea. It was overtaken by an English squadron under Hawke. Conflans attempted to take shelter close under the French coast. The shore was rocky ; the night was black ; the wind was furious; the waves of the Bay of Biscay ran high. But Pitt had infused into every branch of the service a spirit which had long been unknown. No British seaman was disposed to err on the same side with Byng. The pilot told Hawke that the attack could not be made without the greatest danger. "You have done your duty in remonstrating," answered Hawke; "I will answer for every thing. I command you to lay me along-side the French admiral." Two French ships of the line struck. Four were destroyed. The rest hid themselves in the rivers of Brittany.

The year 1760 came, and still triumph followed triumph. Montreal was taken; the whole province of Canada was subjugated; the French fleets underwent a succession of disasters in the seas of Europe and America.

On the continent of Europe the odds were against England. We had but one important ally, the king of Prussia, and he was attacked, not only by France, but also by Russia and Austria. Yet even on the continent the energy of Pitt triumphed over all difficulties. Vehemently as he had condemned the practice of subsidizing foreign princes, he now carried that practice further than Carteret himself would have ventured to do. The active and able sovereign of Prussia received such pecuniary assistance as enabled him to maintain the conflict on equal terms against his powerful enemies. On no subject had Pitt ever spoken with so much eloquence and ardor as on the mischiefs of the Hanoverian connection. He now declared, not without much show of reason, that it would be unworthy of the English people to suffer their king to be deprived of his electoral dominions in an English quarrel. He assured his countrymen that they should be no losers, and that he would conquer America for them in Germany. By taking this line, he conciliated the king, and lost no part of his influence with the nation. In Parliament, such was the ascendency which his eloqence, his success, his high situation, his pride, and his intrepidity had obtained for him, that he took liberties with the House of which there had been no example, and which have never since been imitated. No orator could there venture to reproach him with inconsistency. One unfortunate man made the attempt, and was so much disconcerted by the scornful demeanor of the minister that he stammered, stopped, and sat down. Even the old Tory country gentlemen, to whom the very name of Hanover had been odious, gave their hearty *ayes* to subsidy after subsidy. In a lively contemporary satire, much more lively, indeed, than delicate, this remarkable conversion is not unhappily described :

> " No more they make a fiddle-faddle
> About a Hessian horse or saddle.
> No more of continental measures ;
> No more of wasting British treasures.
> Ten millions and a vote of credit—
> 'Tis right. He can't be wrong who did it."

The success of Pitt's continental measures was such as might have been expected from their vigor. When he came into power Hanover was in imminent danger; and before he had been in office three months the whole electorate was in the hands of France. But the face of affairs was speedily changed. The invaders were driven out. An army, partly English, partly Hanoverian, partly composed of soldiers furnished by the petty princes of Germany, was placed under the command of Prince Ferdinand of Brunswick. The French were beaten in 1758 at Crevelt. In 1759 they received a still more complete and humiliating defeat at Minden.

In the meantime the nation exhibited all the signs of wealth and prosperity. The merchants of London had never been more thriving. The importance of several great commercial and manufacturing towns, of Glasgow in particular, dates from this period. The fine inscription on the monument of Lord Chatham, in Guildhall, records the general opinion of the citizens of London, that under his administration commerce had been " united with and made to flourish by war."

It must be owned, however, that these signs of prosperity were in some degree delusive. Even as a war minister, Pitt is scarcely entitled to all the praise which his contemporaries lavished on him. We, perhaps from ignorance, cannot discern in his arrangements any appearance of profound or dexterous combination. Several of his expeditions, particularly those which were sent to the coast of France, were at once costly and absurd. Our Indian conquests, though they add to the splendor of the period during which he was at the head of affairs, were not planned by him. He had undoubtedly great energy, great determination, great means at his command. His temper was enterprising; and, situated as he was, he had only to follow his temper. The wealth of a rich nation, the valor of a brave nation, were ready to support him in every attempt.

In one respect, however, he deserved all the praise that he has ever received. The success of our arms was, perhaps, owing less to the skill of his dispositions than to the national resources and the national spirit. But that the national spirit rose to the emergency, that the national resources were contributed with unexampled cheerfulness, this was undoubtedly his work. The ardor of his soul had set the whole kingdom on fire. It inflamed every soldier who dragged the cannon up the heights of Quebec, and every sailor who boarded the French ships among the rocks of Brittany. The minister, before he had been long in office, had imparted to the commanders whom he employed his own impetuous, adventurous, and defying character. They, like him, were disposed to risk every thing, to play double or quits to the last, to think nothing done while any thing remained undone, to fail rather than not to attempt. For the errors of rashness there might be indulgence. For over-caution, for faults like those of Lord George Sackville, there was no mercy. In other times, and against other enemies, this mode of warfare might have failed. But the state of the French government and of the French nation gave every advantage to Pitt. The fops and intriguers of Versailles were appalled and bewildered by his vigor. A panic spread through all ranks of society. Our enemies soon considered it as a settled thing that they were always to be beaten. Thus victory begot victory till, at last, wherever the forces of the two nations met, they met with disdainful confidence on the one side, and with a craven fear on the other.

The situation which Pitt occupied at the close of the reign of George the Second was the most enviable ever occupied by any public man in English history. He had conciliated the king; he domineered over the House of Commons; he was adored by the people; he was admired by all Europe. He was the first Englishman of his time, and he had made England the first country in the world. The Great Commoner, the name by which he was often designated, might look down with scorn on coronets and garters. The nation was drunk with joy and pride. The Parliament was as quiet as it had been under Pelham. The o'd party distinctions were almost effaced; nor was their place yet supplied by distinctions of a still more important kind. - A new generation of country squires and rectors had arisen who knew not the Stuarts. The Dissenters were tolerated; the Catholics not cruelly persecuted. The Church was drowsy and indulgent. The great civil and religious conflict which began at the Reformation seemed to have terminated in universal repose. Whigs and Tories, Churchmen and Puritans, spoke with equal reverence of the Constitution, and with equal enthusiasm of the talents, virtues, and services of the minister.

A few years sufficed to change the whole aspect of affairs. A nation convulsed by faction, a throne assailed by the fiercest invective, a House of Commons hated and despised by the nation, England set against Scotland, Britain set against America, a rival legislature sitting beyond the Atlantic, English blood shed by English bayonets, our armies capitulating, our conquests wrested from us, our enemies hastening to take vengeance for past humiliation, our flag scarcely able to maintain itself in our own seas, such was the spectacle which Pitt lived to see. But the history of this great revolution requires far more space than we can at present bestow. We leave the Great Commoner in the zenith of his glory.

LIII.

AN EMPIRE WON IN THE EAST.—MACAULAY.

[It was the good fortune of Pitt that, at the beginning of his ministry, and without any direct agency of his own, a great triumph of the English arms in India came to enhance the glory of his triumphs in Europe and America. Robert Clive, who had already distinguished himself in the service of the East India Company,* was appointed governor of Fort St. David by the Company in 1757. Entering into negotiations with the disaffected subjects of the nabob, or nawab, of Bengal, he won the battle of Plassey over the native army, on the 23d of June. This victory firmly established the hitherto wavering British power in the East, and enabled it to enter upon the career of conquest which has since given it the whole of India.]

THE nabob had feared and hated the English, even while he was still able to oppose to them their French rivals. The French were now vanquished, and he began to regard the English with still greater fear and still greater hatred. His weak and unprincipled mind oscillated between servility and insolence. One day he sent a large sum to Calcutta, as a part of the compensation due for the wrongs which he had committed. The next day he sent a present of jewels to Bussy, exhorting that distinguished officer to hasten to protect Bengal "against Clive, the daring in war, on whom," says his highness, "may all bad fortune attend." He ordered his army to march against the English. He countermanded his orders. He tore Clive's letters. He then sent answers in the most florid language of compliment. He ordered Watts out of his presence, and threatened to impale him. He again sent for Watts, and begged pardon for the insult. In the mean time his wretched maladministration, his folly, his dissolute manners, and his love of the lowest company, had disgusted all classes of his subjects—soldiers, traders, civil functionaries, the proud and ostentatious Mohammedans, the

* A company of London merchants who, in 1600, had acquired, by charter, a monopoly of the trade with India.

timid, subtle, and parsimonious Hindus. A formidable confederacy was formed against him, in which were included Roydullub, the minister of finance ; Meer Jaffier, the principal commander of the troops; and Jugget Seit, the richest banker in India. The plot was confided to the English agents, and a communication was opened between the malcontents at Moorshedabad and the committee at Calcutta.

In the committee there was much hesitation ; but Clive's voice was given in favor of the conspirators, and his vigor and firmness bore down all opposition. It was determined that the English should lend their powerful assistance to depose Surajah Dowlah, and to place Meer Jaffier on the throne of Bengal. In return, Meer Jaffier promised ample compensation to the Company and its servants, and a liberal donative to the army, the navy, and the committee. The odious vices of Surajah Dowlah, the wrongs which the English had suffered at his hands, the dangers to which our trade must have been exposed, had he continued to reign, appear to us fully to justify the resolution of deposing him. But nothing can justify the dissimulation which Clive stooped to practice. He wrote to Surajah Dowlah in terms so affectionate that they, for a time, lulled that weak prince into perfect security. The same courier who carried this " soothing letter," as Clive calls it, to the nabob, carried to Mr. Watts a letter in the following terms: "Tell Meer Jaffier to fear nothing. I will join him with five thousand men who never turned their backs. Assure him I will march night and day to his assistance, and stand by him as long as I have a man left."

It was impossible that a plot which had so many ramifications should long remain entirely concealed. Enough reached the ears of the nabob to arouse his suspicions. But he was soon quieted by the fictions and artifices which the inventive genius of Omichund* produced with miraculous readiness.

* A native merchant, once very wealthy, who, together with Mr. Watts, was employed by Clive to negotiate with the nabob.

All was going well; the plot was nearly ripe, when Clive learned that Omichund was likely to play false. The artful Bengalee had been promised a liberal compensation for all that he had lost at Calcutta. But this would not satisfy him. His services had been great. He held the thread of the whole intrigue. By one word breathed in the ear of Surajah Dowlah he could undo all that he had done. The lives of Watts, of Meer Jaffier, of all the conspirators, were at his mercy, and he determined to take advantage of his situation, and to make his own terms. He demanded three hundred thousand pounds sterling as the price of his secrecy and of his assistance. The committee, incensed by the treachery and appalled by the danger, knew not what course to take. But Clive was more than Omichund's match in Omichund's own arts. The man, he said, was a villain. Any artifice which would defeat such knavery was justifiable. The best course would be to promise what he asked. Omichund would soon be at their mercy; and then they might punish him by withholding from him, not only the bribe which he now demanded, but also the compensation which all the other sufferers of Calcutta were to receive.

His advice was taken. But how was this wary and sagacious Hindu to be deceived? He had demanded that an article touching his claims should be inserted in the treaty between Meer Jaffier and the English, and he would not be satisfied unless he saw it with his own eyes. 'Clive had an expedient ready. Two treaties were drawn up, one on white paper, the other on red—the former real, the latter fictitious. In the former Omichund's name was not mentioned ; the latter, which was to be shown to him, contained a stipulation in his favor.

But another difficulty arose. Admiral Watson had scruples about signing the red treaty. Omichund's vigilance and acuteness were such that the absence of so important a name would, probably, awaken his suspicions. But Clive was not a man to do any thing by halves. We almost blush to write it. He forged Admiral Watson's name.

All was now ready for action. Mr. Watts fled secretly from Moorshedabad. Clive put his troops in motion, and wrote to the nabob in a tone very different from that of his previous letters. He set forth all the wrongs which the British had suffered, offered to submit the points in dispute to the arbitration of Meer Jaffier, and concluded by announcing that, as the rains were about to set in, he and his men would do themselves the honor of waiting on his highness for an answer.

Surajah Dowlah instantly assembled his whole force, and marched to encounter the English. It had been agreed that Meer Jaffier should separate himself from the nabob, and carry over his division to Clive. But, as the decisive moment approached, the fears of the conspirator overpowered his ambition. Clive had advanced to Cossimbuzar; the nabob lay, with a mighty power, a few miles off at Plassey; and still Meer Jaffier delayed to fulfill his engagements, and returned evasive answers to the earnest remonstrances of the English general.

Clive was in a painfully anxious situation. He could place no confidence in the sincerity or in the courage of his confederate; and, whatever confidence he might place in his own military talents and in the valor and discipline of his troops, it was no light thing to engage an army twenty times as numerous as his own. Before him lay a river over which it was easy to advance, but over which, if things went ill, not one of his little band would ever return. On this occasion, for the first and for the last time, his dauntless spirit, during a few hours, shrank from the fearful responsibility of making a decision. He called a council of war. The majority pronounced against fighting, and Clive declared his concurrence with the majority. Long afterward he said that he had never called but one council of war, and that, if he had taken the advice of that council, the British would never have been masters of Bengal. But scarcely had the meeting broken up when he was himself again. He retired alone under the shade of some trees, and passed near an hour there in thought. He came back determined to put every thing to the hazard, and gave orders that all should be in readiness for passing the river on the morrow.

The river was passed; and, at the close of a toilsome day's march, the army, long after sunset, took up its quarters in a grove of mango-trees near Plassey, within a mile of the enemy. Clive was unable to sleep; he heard, through the whole night, the sound of drums and cymbals from the vast camp of the nabob. It is not strange that even his stout heart should now and then have sunk when he reflected against what odds, and for what a prize, he was in a few hours to contend

Nor was the rest of Surajah Dowlah more peaceful. His mind, at once weak and stormy, was distracted by wild and horrible apprehensions. Appalled by the greatness and nearness of the crisis, distrusting his captains, dreading every one who approached him, dreading to be left alone, he sat gloomily in his tent, haunted, a Greek poet would have said, by the furies of those who had cursed him with their last breath in the Black Hole.

The day broke, the day which was to decide the fate of India. At sunrise the army of the nabob, pouring through many openings from the camp, began to move toward the grove where the English lay. Forty thousand infantry, armed with firelocks, pikes, swords, bows and arrows, covered the plain. They were accompanied by fifty pieces of ordnance of the largest size, each tugged by a long team of white oxen, and each pushed on from behind by an elephant. Some smaller guns, under the direction of a few French auxiliaries, were, perhaps, more formidable. The cavalry were fifteen thousand, drawn not from the effeminate population of Bengal, but from the bolder race which inhabits the northern provinces; and the practiced eye of Clive could perceive that both the men and the horses were more powerful than those of the Carnatic. The force which he hadt o oppose to this great multitude consisted of only three thousand men. But of these nearly a thousand were English, and all were led by English officers, and trained in the English discipline. Conspicuous in the ranks of the little army were the men of the Thirty-ninth Regiment, which still bears on its colors, amidst many honorable additions, won under Wellington in Spain and Gascony, the name of Plassey, and the proud motto, *Primus in Indis*.

The battle commenced with a cannonade in which the artillery of the nabob did scarcely any execution, while the few field-pieces of the English produced great effect. Several of the most distinguished officers in Surajah Dowlah's service fell. Disorder began to spread through his ranks. His own terror increased every moment. One of the conspirators urged on him the expediency of retreating. The insidious advice, agreeing, as it did, with what his own terrors suggested was readily received. He ordered his army to fall back, and this order decided his fate. Clive snatched the moment, and ordered his troops to advance. The confused and dispirited multitude gave way before the onset of disciplined valor. No mob attacked by regular soldiers was ever more completely routed. The little band of Frenchmen, who alone ventured to confront the English, were swept down the stream of fugitives. In an hour the forces of Surajah Dowlah were dispersed, never to re-assemble. Only five hundred of the vanquished were slain. But their camp, their guns, their baggage, innumerable wagons, innumerable cattle, remained in the power of the conquerors. With the loss of twenty-two soldiers killed and fifty wounded, Clive had scattered an army of near sixty thousand men, and subdued an empire larger and more populous than Great Britain.

LIV.

AN EMPIRE LOST IN THE WEST.—STANHOPE.

[Soon after the great success of Clive in the East, General Wolfe, whom Pitt had appointed commander-in-chief of the British forces in America, succeeded in wresting Canada from the French by the capture of Quebec. In the treaty of peace which closed the Seven Years' War France was forced to cede to England nearly all her colonial possessions in America. But this great gain to England led directly to a far greater loss. So long as the French power in America remained as a rival to that of Britain, the Anglo-American colonies were forced to rely upon the mother-country to maintain themselves against it; when that power was broken the colonists became practically independent. The narrow and selfish policy pursued by George III. and his ministers toward the colonies gradually weakened their feeling of loyalty, and at length drove them to rebellion. The struggle which led to a separation was virtually ended by the surrender of the British army, under Cornwallis, at Yorktown.

GEORGE III.

MEANWHILE it was determined to press the operations against Lord Cornwallis with the utmost vigor. The net, indeed, was rapidly closing around the English earl. During the month of August he had relinquished Portsmouth and taken post at Yorktown, in pursuance of some instructions from Sir Henry Clinton, which Sir Henry meant as permission, but which Cornwallis understood as peremptory. Yorktown, as Cornwallis afterward declared, was not, in his judgment, well adapted for defense. It is a small village, about twelve miles from Williamsburg, built upon a high bank, the southern one, of York River. There the long peninsula, extending between the rivers York and James, is little more than eight miles broad. There the river York itself is one mile in width; and, on a point of land projecting from the northern bank, lies Gloucester, another small village, which Cornwallis also held. Both posts, but more especially York-town as the larger, he had fortified as best he might, with redoubts and intrenchments; and these unfinished works he was now to maintain with seven thousand men against a force which by degrees grew to eighteen thousand. His position was not really perilous, so long as the English retained the superiority at sea; but the great fleet of De Grasse was now interposing, and cut off his retreat.

Cornwallis is admitted to have shown most undaunted resolution. The officers under him, and the troops, German and English, all did their duty well. For some weeks they had labored hard and unremittingly in raising their defenses; and they were now prepared, with equal spirit, to maintain their half-completed works. But, besides the enemy without, they had another foe within—an epidemic sickness that stretched many hundreds helpless on their pallet-beds. Nor could they hinder Washington from completing his first parallel, and opening his fire upon them on the evening of the 9th of October For two days the fire was incessant from heavy cannon, and from mortars and howitzers, throwing shells in showers on the town, until, says Cornwallis, all our guns on the left were silenced, our works much damaged, and our loss of men considerable. By these shells, also, the *Charon*, a ship of forty-four guns, together with three British transports in the river, were set in flames and consumed. On the night of the 11th the enemy began their second parallel at about three hundred yards; that is, at only half the distance of the former. Cornwallis did all in his power to delay, for prevent he could not, the progress of this work, by opening new embrasures for guns, and keeping up a constant fire with all the howitzers and small mortars that he could man.

In their approaches the enemy were also, in some degree, impeded by two redoubts which the British had constructed
14

in advance to cover their left flank. These Washington resolved to storm; and, for the sake of exciting emulation, he
intrusted the attack of the one to the Americans, and of the
other to the French. Both attacks were made in the night
of the 14th, and with full success; and, by the unwearied
exertions of the enemy, both redoubts were included in their
second parallel by day-break the next morning.

[On the 16th the English general made an ineffectual
attempt to escape by way of Gloucester.]

Meanwhile, as Cornwallis had expected, the enemy's
batteries before Yorktown had opened fire at day-break.
Nothing now remained for him but to obtain the best terms
he could. On that morning, then, the 17th of October, he
sent a flag of truce to Washington, proposing a cessation of
arms, and a treaty for the capitulation of his post. Washington, in reply, required him to state within two hours the
terms which he demanded. In a second letter hereupon
Cornwallis asked that the garrisons of Yorktown and Gloucester, though laying down their arms as prisoners of war,
should be sent home—the Britons to Britain, and the Germans to Germany, under engagement not to serve against
France, America, or their allies, until in due form exchanged.
The American general declared these terms to be inadmissi-
ble, and the earl then agreed to waive them. It appears
probable, indeed, that they were proposed only for the sake
of form or show.

On this basis, then—as yielded by Cornwallis, on the morning of the 18th of October—a cessation of arms was continued, and a negotiation began. The commissioners, two
field-officers being named on either side, conferred together,
and discussed the terms that same day. All the artillery
and public stores in the two forts, together with the shipping
and boats in the two harbors, were to be surrendered by the
English. On the other hand, private property of every kind
was to be respected by the Americans and French. The

garrisons of Yorktown and Gloucester were to march out with the same honors of war as had been granted by Sir Henry Clinton at Charleston; the land forces to remain prisoners of the United States, and the naval forces prisoners of France. The soldiers were to be kept in Virginia, Maryland, or Pennsylvania, and as much by regiments as possible. The general, staff, and other officers not left with the troops, to be permitted to go to New York or to Europe on parole.

"It is remarkable," says an American historian, "that while Colonel Laurens, the officer employed by General Washington (in conjunction with the Vicomte de Noailles) was drawing up these articles, his father was closely confined in the Tower of London, of which Lord Cornwallis was constable. By this singular combination of circumstances, his lordship became a prisoner to the son of his own prisoner!"

The articles of capitulation, having been finally fixed by Washington and accepted by Cornwallis, were signed by the respective generals on the morning of the 19th of October. On the British side about five hundred men had been killed or wounded during the progress of the siege. At its close, the British and German troops, exclusive of the seamen, amounted to six thousand; but so great was the number of the sick and the disabled, that there remained less than four thousand fit for duty. At two o'clock that afternoon, as agreed in the capitulation, the Yorktown troops marched out with their drums beating, their arms shouldered, and their colors cased, to lay down their arms before the enemy, Americans and French, drawn out in line. The officer specially appointed to receive them was General Lincoln, the chief of their captives at Charleston, in the preceding year. Yet Washington, with his usual lofty spirit, had no desire to aggravate the anguish and humiliation of honorable foes. On the contrary, he bade all mere spectators keep aloof from the ceremony, and suppressed all public signs of exultation.

The scene which ensued is described by an eye-witness, a

French chaplain of the Comte de Rochambeau. The two lines of the allied army, says Abbé Robin, were drawn out for upward of a mile, the Americans having the right. The disproportion of heights and of ages in their men, and their soiled and ragged clothing, might be unfavorably contrasted with the neater and more soldierly appearance of the French. Yet, under such circumstances, the personal disadvantages of a raw militia should rather be looked upon as an enhancement of the triumph they had gained. The abbé was struck at seeing, from several indications, how much keener were at that time the animosity between the English and Americans than between the English and French. Thus, the English officers, when they laid down their arms, and were passing along the enemy's line, courteously saluted every French officer, even of the lowest rank—a compliment which they withheld from every American, even of the highest.

With the surrender of Lord Cornwallis the American war may be said to have concluded; so far, at least, as its active military operations were concerned. It was a war by no means, as we sometimes hear alleged of it, founded on any plain or palpable injustice in point of law, since, at the outset, when the taxes were first imposed, the English ministers might point to nearly all the highest authorities as affirming the abstract right of taxation we possessed. But beyond all doubt, it was a war proceeding on the grossest impolicy, from the moment it was seen how much resentment the exercise of that right provoked. For the mere barren assertion of that right—for a mere peppercorn of rent—we alienated and, as it were, in wantonness, flung from us provinces which, at the peace of 1763, had been as contented and loyal as the shires along the Severn or the Thames. We grew wiser, but too late. Earnest and more earnest overtures, larger and then larger concessions, were tendered, from time to time, to the uprisen colonies, but always a few weeks or a few months beyond the period when they might yet have healed the wound. The same utter want of policy which provoked the war was shown in its first direction. Our most skillful commanders, our most daring enterprises, seemed to be reserved for the conclusion of the conflict, when skill could no more avail us, and when enterprise led only to disaster. While the opportunity was still ours—while France and Spain, so soon to combine against us, still kept aloof—while Washington's army, for example, was in full flight, or Gates's army was not yet formed, then it was that we find General Howe content to bound his conquests at the Delaware, and General Burgoyne refrain a whole month from his advance to Albany.

Such was the system in the cabinet, against which our greatest statesmen warned the ministry in vain. Such were the errors in the field, which even the occasional skill of our officers, and the constant bravery of our troops, could not retrieve. Thus did we alienate a people with whom we might, perhaps, to this very day, have kept united; with them resolutely upholding peace among all other nations; with them, the leaders of the world in temperate liberty and Christian progress. They might have been both our brother freemen and our fellow-subjects, free with their own assemblies, as we are free with ours, yet bound to us beneath the golden circle of the crown. Or if even, with their growing numbers, that golden circle had seemed to them to press, it might have been gently and quietly unloosed. We might have parted as friends and kinsmen part, not have torn asunder with a bleeding gash on either side.

LV.

THE TERRIBLE PENAL CODE.—LECKY.

[The success of the American revolutionists gave a new impulse to the spirit of rebellion in Ireland, and led to a renewal of the attempts which had been made there from time to time to throw off the yoke of English oppression. In 1693, when nine tenths of the people of Ireland were Catholics, the English Parliament passed a law which excluded Catholics from the Irish Parliament. The latter body then began the enactment of the infamous series of statutes known as the Irish Penal Code. Since the days of Walpole, some provisions of the code had been relaxed; but now, in response to the fierce demands of the Irish, England was compelled to make further concessions. The entire code, however, was not swept away until 1829.]

IT required, indeed, four or five reigns to elaborate a system so ingeniously contrived to demoralize, to degrade, and to impoverish the people of Ireland. By this code the Roman Catholics were absolutely excluded from the Parliament, from the magistracy, from the corporations, from the bench, and from the bar. They could not vote at Parliamentary elections or at vestries. They could not act as constables, or sheriffs, or jurymen, or serve in the army or navy, or become solicitors, or even hold the positions of gamekeeper or watchman. Schools were established to bring up their children as Protestants; and if they refused to avail themselves of these, they were deliberately consigned to hopeless ignorance, being excluded from the university, and debarred, under crushing penalties, from acting as school-masters, as ushers or as private tutors, or from sending their children abroad to obtain the instruction they were refused at home. They could not marry Protestants; and if such a marriage were celebrated it was annulled by law, and the priest who officiated might be hung. They could not buy land, or inherit or receive it as a gift from Protestants, or hold life annuities, or leases for more than thirty-one years, or any lease on such terms that the profits of the land exceeded one third of the rent. If any Catholic lease-holder by his industry so increased his profits that they exceeded this proportion, and did not immediately make a corresponding increase in his payments, any Protestant who gave the information could enter into possession of his farm. If any Catholic had secretly purchased his old forfeited estate, or any other land, any Protestant who informed against him might become the proprietor.

The few Catholic land-holders who remained were deprived of the right which all other classes possessed of bequeathing their lands as they pleased. If their sons continued Catholics, it was divided equally between them. If, however, the eldest son consented to apostatize, the estate was settled upon him; the father from that hour became only a life-tenant, and lost all power of selling, mortgaging, or otherwise disposing of it. If the wife of a Catholic abandoned the religion of her husband, she was immediately free from his control, and the chancellor was empowered to assign to her a certain proportion of her husband's property. If any child, however young, professed itself a Protestant, it was at once taken from the father's care, and the chancellor could oblige the father to declare, upon oath, the value of his property, both real and personal, and could assign for the present maintenance and future portion of the converted child such proportion of that property as the court might decree. No Catholic could be guardian either to his own children, or to those of another person; and, therefore, a Catholic who died while his children were minors had the bitterness of reflecting upon his deathbed that they must pass into the care of Protestants. An annuity of from twenty to forty pounds was provided as a bribe for every priest who would become a Protestant. To convert a Protestant to Catholicism was a capital offense.

In every walk of life the Catholic was pursued by persecution or restriction. Except in the linen trade, he could not have more than two apprentices. He could not possess a horse of the value of more than five pounds, and any Protestant, on giving him five pounds, could take his horse. He was compelled to pay double to the militia. He was forbidden, except under particular conditions, to live in Galway or Limerick. In case of war with a Catholic power, the Catholics were required to reimburse the damage done by the enemy's privateers. The Legislature, it is true, did not venture absolutely to suppress their worship, but it existed only by a doubtful connivance—stigmatized as if it were a species of licensed prostitution, and subject to conditions which, if they had been enforced, would have rendered its continuance impossible. An old law which prohibited it, and another which enjoined attendance at the Anglican worship, remained unrepealed, and might at any time be revived ; and the former was, in fact, enforced during the Scotch rebellion of 1715. The parish priests, who alone were allowed to officiate, were compelled to be registered, and were forbidden to keep curates, or to officiate anywhere except in their own parishes. The chapels might not have bells or steeples. No crosses might be publicly erected. Pilgrimages to the holy wells were forbidden. Not only all monks and friars, but also all Catholic archbishops, bishops, deacons, and other dignitaries, were ordered by a certain day to leave the country ; and if, after that date, they were found in Ireland, they were liable to be first imprisoned, and then banished; and if, after that banishment, they returned to discharge their duty in their dioceses, they were liable to the punishment of death. To facilitate the discovery of offenses against the code, two justices of the peace might at any time compel any Catholic of eighteen years of age to declare when and where he last heard mass, what persons were present, and who officiated ; and, if he refused to give evidence, they might imprison him for twelve months, or until he paid a fine of twenty pounds. Any one who harbored ecclesiastics from beyond the seas was subject to fines which, for the third offense, amounted to the confiscation of all his goods. A graduated scale of rewards was offered for the discovery of Catholic bishops, priests, and school-masters ; and a resolution of the House of Commons pronounced "the prosecuting and informing against Papists" "an honorable service to the government."

Such were the principal articles of this famous code— a code which Burke truly described as "well digested and well disposed in all its parts ; a machine of wise and elaborate contrivance, and as well fitted for the oppression, impoverishment, and degradation of a people, and the debasement in them of human nature itself, as ever proceeded from the perverted ingenuity of man." It was framed by a small minority of the nation for the oppression of the majority, who remained faithful to the religion of their fathers. It was framed by men who boasted that their creed rested upon private judgment, and whose descendants are never weary of declaiming upon the intolerance of popery; and it was directed, in many of its provisions, against mere religious observances ; and was in all its parts so strictly a code of religious persecution, that any Catholic might be exempted from its operation by simply forsaking his religion. It was framed and enforced, although by the treaty of Limerick the Catholics had been guaranteed such privileges in the exercise of their religion as they enjoyed in the reign of Charles II., although the sovereign at the same time promised, as soon as his affairs would permit, "to summon a Parliament in this kingdom, and to endeavor to procure the said Roman Catholics such further security in that particular as may preserve them from any disturbance on account of their religion, although not a single overt act of treason was proved against them, and although they remained passive spectators of two

14*

rebellions which menaced the very existence of the Protestant dynasty in England.

The economical and moral effects of the penal laws were
profoundly disastrous.   The productive energies of the nation
were fatally diminished.   Almost all Catholics of energy and
talent who refused to abandon their faith emigrated to foreign
lands.   The relation of classes was permanently vitiated, for
almost all of the land-holders of the country belonged to one
religion, while the great majority of their tenants were of another.   The Catholics, excluded from almost every possibil-
ity of eminence, and consigned by the Legislature to utter
ignorance, soon sank into the condition of broken and dispirited helots.   A total absence of industrial virtues, a cow-
ering and abject deference to authority, a recklessness about
the future, a love of secret illegal combinations, became general among them.   Above all, they learned to regard law as
merely the expression of force, and its moral weight was
utterly destroyed.   For the greater part of a century the
main object of the Legislature was to extirpate a religion by
the encouragement of some of the worst and the punishment of some of the best qualities of our nature.   Its rewards
were reserved for the informer, for the hypocrite, for the undutiful son, or for the faithless wife.   Its penalties were directed against religious constancy and the honest discharge of
ecclesiastical duty.   It would, indeed, be scarcely possible to
conceive a more infamous system of legal tyranny than that
which in the middle of the eighteenth century crushed every
class and almost every interest in Ireland.

The history of the penal laws should furnish a lasting warning to persecutors of all religions.   Arthur Young asserts that
the numerical proportion of the Roman Catholics in Ireland
was not even diminished, if any thing, the reverse; and that
it was admitted, by those who asserted the contrary, that it
would take four thousand years, according to the then rate of
progress, to convert them.   It was stated in Parliament that

only four thousand and fifty-five had conformed in seventy-one years under the system ; and what little the religion may have lost in number it gained in intensity. The poorer classes in Ireland emerged from their long ordeal, penetrated with an attachment to their religion almost unparalleled in Europe. With the exception of the inhabitants of Bavaria and the Tyrol, there is, perhaps, no nation in Europe whose character has been so completely molded and permeated by it, or in which skeptical doubts are more completely unknown.

The code perished at last by its own atrocity. It became, after a time, so out of harmony with the prevailing tone of Irish opinion that it ceased to be enforced, and the Irish Protestants took the initiative in obtaining its mitigation.

LVI.

IMPEACHMENT OF HASTINGS.—MACAULAY.

[Ireland was still in a state of agitation when the attention of the English Parliament became absorbed in one of the most remarkable of modern criminal trials. In 1773 Warren Hastings was made the first governor-general of India. During the twelve years of his administration he rendered inestimable service in extending and consolidating England's power in the East, but his glory was sullied by many crimes. Soon after his retirement from office he was impeached (1788) by the House of Commons, before the bar of the Lords, on charges of misgovernment in India. The trial dragged on for eight years, and, in the end, Hastings was acquitted ; but the object for which the impeachment had been begun was attained. The crimes of Hastings have never been repeated, even by the worst of his successors.]

IN the mean time the preparations for the trial had proceeded rapidly, and, on the 13th of February, 1788, the sittings of the court commenced. There have been spectacles more dazzling to the eye, more gorgeous with jewelry and cloth of gold, more attractive to grown-up children than that which was then exhibited at Westminster; but, perhaps, there never was a spectacle so well calculated to strike a highly cultivated, a reflecting, an imaginative mind. All the various kinds of interest which belong to the near and to the distant, to the present and to the past, were collected on one spot, and in one hour. All the talents and all the accomplishments which are developed by liberty and civilization were now displayed, with every advantage that could be derived from co-operation and from contrast. Every step in the proceedings carried the mind either backward, through many troubled centuries, to the days when the foundations of our constitution were laid, or far away, over boundless seas and deserts, to dusky nations living under strange stars, worshiping strange gods, and writing strange characters from right to left. The High Court of Parliament was to sit, according to forms handed down from the days of the Plantagenets, on an Englishman accused of exercising tyranny over the lord of the holy city of Benares, and over the ladies of the princely house of Oude.

The place was worthy of such a trial. It was the great hall of William Rufus, the hall which had resounded with acclamations at the inauguration of thirty kings, the hall which had witnessed the just sentence of Bacon and the just absolution of Somers, the hall where the eloquence of Strafford had for a moment awed and melted a victorious party inflamed with just resentment, the hall where Charles had confronted the High Court of Justice with the placid courage which has half-redeemed his fame. Neither military nor civil pomp was wanting. The avenues were lined with grenadiers. The streets were kept clear by cavalry. The peers, robed in gold and ermine, were marshaled by the heralds under garter king-at-arms. The judges, in their vestments of state, attended to give advice on points of law. Near a hundred and seventy lords, three fourths of the Upper House, as the Upper House then was, walked in solemn order from their usual place of assembling to the tribunal. The junior baron present led the way, George Eliott, Lord Heathfield, recently ennobled for his memorable defense of Gibraltar against the fleets and armies of France and Spain. The long procession was closed by the duke of Norfolk, earl-marshal of the realm, by the great dignitaries, and by the brothers and sons of the king. Last of all came the prince of Wales, conspicuous by his fine person and noble bearing. The gray old walls were hung with scarlet. The long galleries were crowded by an audience such as has rarely excited the fears or the emulation of an orator. There were gathered together, from all parts of a great, free, enlightened, and prosperous empire, grace and female loveliness, wit and learning, the representatives of every science and of every art. There were seated round the queen the fair-haired young daughters of the house of Brunswick. There the embassadors of great kings and commonwealths gazed with admiration on a spectacle which no other country in the world could present. There Siddons, in the prime of her majestic beauty, looked with emotion on a scene surpassing all the imitations of the stage. There the historian of the Roman Empire thought of the days when Cicero pleaded the cause of Sicily against Verres, and when, before a senate which still retained some show of freedom, Tacitus thundered against the oppressor of Africa. There were seen, side by side, the greatest painter and the greatest scholar of the age. The spectacle had allured Reynolds from that easel which has preserved to us the thoughtful foreheads of so many writers and statesmen, and the sweet smiles of so many noble matrons. It had induced Parr to suspend his labors in that dark and profound mine from which he had extracted a vast treasure of erudition, a treasure too often buried in the earth, too often paraded with injudicious and inelegant ostentation, but still precious, massive, and splendid. There appeared the voluptuous charms of her * to whom the heir of the throne had in secret plighted his faith. There, too, was she, † the beautiful mother of a beautiful race, the St. Cecilia, whose delicate features, lighted up by love and music, art has rescued from the common decay. There were the members of that brilliant society which quoted, criticized, and exchanged repartees under the rich peacock-hangings of Mrs. Montague. And there the ladies —whose lips, more persuasive than those of Fox himself, had carried the Westminster election against palace and treasury —shone round Georgiana, duchess of Devonshire.

The sergeants made proclamation. Hastings advanced to the bar and bent his knee. The culprit was, indeed, not unworthy of that great presence. He had ruled an extensive and populous country, had made laws and treaties, had sent forth armies, had set up and pulled down princes. And in his high place he had so borne himself that all had feared him, that most had loved him, and that hatred itself could deny him no title to glory, except virtue. He looked like a great man, and not like a bad man. A person small and emaciated, yet deriving dignity from a carriage which, while it indicated deference to the court, indicated also habitual self-possession and self respect ; a high and intellectual forehead; a brow pensive, but not gloomy; a mouth of inflexible decision ; a face pale and worn, but serene, on which was written, as legibly as under the picture in the council-chamber at Calcutta, *Mens aequa in arduis ;* such was the aspect with which the great pro-consul presented himself to his judges.

His counsel accompanied him—men all of whom were afterward raised, by their talents and learning, to the highest posts in their profession—the bold and strong-minded Law, afterward chief-justice of the King's Bench ; the more humane and eloquent Dallas, afterward chief-justice of the Common Pleas; and Plomer, who, near twenty years later, successfully conducted, in the same high court, the defense

* Mrs. Fitzherbert.   † Mrs. Sheridan.

of Lord Melville, and subsequently became vice-chancellor and master of the rolls.

But neither the culprit nor his advocates attracted so much notice as the accusers. In the midst of the blaze of red drapery a space had been fitted up with green benches and tables for the Commons. The managers, with Burke at their head, appeared in full dress. The collectors of gossip did not fail to remark that even Fox, generally so regardless of his appearance, had paid to the illustrious tribunal the compliment of wearing a bag and sword. Pitt had refused to be one of the conductors of the impeachment; and his commanding, copious, and sonorous eloquence was wanting to that great muster of various talents. Age and blindness had unfitted Lord North for the duties of a public prosecutor; and his friends were left without the help of his excellent sense, his tact, and his urbanity. But, in spite of the absence of these two distinguished members of the Lower House, the box in which the managers stood contained an array of speakers such as, perhaps, had not appeared together since the great age of Athenian eloquence. There were Fox and Sheridan, the English Demosthenes and the English Hyperides. There was Burke, ignorant, indeed, or negligent, of the art of adapting his reasonings and his style to the capacity and taste of his hearers, but in amplitude of comprehension and richness of imagination superior to every orator, ancient or modern. There, with eyes reverentially fixed on Burke, appeared the finest gentleman of the age, his form developed by every manly exercise, his face beaming with intelligence and spirit, the ingenious, the chivalrous, the high-souled Windham. Nor, though surrounded by such men, did the youngest manager pass unnoticed. At an age when most of those who distinguish themselves in life are still contending for prizes and fellowships at college, he had won for himself a conspicuous place in Parliament. No advantage of fortune or connection was wanting that could set off to the height his splendid talents and his unblemished honor. At twenty-three he had been thought worthy to be ranked with the veteran statesmen who appeared as the delegates of the British Commons at the bar of the British nobility. All who stood at that bar, save him alone, are gone—culprit, advocates, accusers. To the generation which is now in the vigor of life he is the sole representative of a great age which has passed away. But those who, within the last ten years, have listened with delight, till the morning sun shone on the tapestries of the House of Lords, to the lofty and animated eloquence of Charles, Earl Grey,* are able to form some estimate of the powers of a race of men among whom he was not the foremost.

The charges and the answers of Hastings were first read. The ceremony occupied two whole days, and was rendered less tedious than it would otherwise have been by the silver voice and just emphasis of Cowper, the clerk of the court, a near relation of the amiable poet. On the third day Burke rose. Four sittings were occupied by his opening speech, which was intended to be a general introduction to all the charges. With an exuberance of thought and a splendor of diction which more than satisfied the highly raised expectation of the audience, he described the character and institutions of the natives of India, recounted the circumstances in which the Asiatic empire of Britain had originated, and set forth the constitution of the Company and of the English presidencies. Having thus attempted to communicate to his hearers an idea of Eastern society as vivid as that which existed in his own mind, he proceeded to arraign the administration of Hastings as systematically conducted in defiance of morality and public law. The energy and pathos of the great orator extorted expressions of unwonted admiration from the stern and hostile chancellor, and, for a moment, seemed to pierce even the resolute heart of the defendant.

* Earl Grey died in 1845.

At length the orator concluded. Raising his voice till the old arches of Irish oak resounded, " Therefore," said he, " hath it with all confidence been ordered by the Commons of Great Britain, that I impeach Warren Hastings of high crimes and misdemeanors. I impeach him in the name of the Commons' House of Parliament, whose trust he has betrayed. I impeach him in the name of the English nation, whose ancient honor he has sullied. I impeach him in the name of the people of India, whose rights he has trodden under foot, and whose country he has turned into a desert. Lastly, in the name of human nature itself, in the name of both sexes, in the name of every age, in the name of every rank, I impeach the common enemy and oppressor of all."

LVII.

TRAFALGAR—DEATH OF NELSON.—Southey.

[The trial of Hastings had but just begun when the world was startled by the outbreak of the French Revolution of 1789—the greatest event of modern history.   In France, after the monarchy had been overthrown and the members of the royal family had been either put to death or driven from the country, a republic was established, which passed through various phases, and at length ended in a military despotism. Napoleon Bonaparte, the most successful soldier of the revolution, became first consul of France in 1799, and in 1804 he took the title of emperor as Napoleon the First.

England entered the contest in 1793, and ultimately became the chief rival of Napoleon. One great object, therefore, of the French emperor was to cripple or destroy England ; and he labored long and earnestly in the hope of breaking her maritime supremacy. But all his plans in this direction were brought to naught by the battle of Trafalgar, by which, though England lost her ablest seaman, the combined fleets of France and Spain were annihilated, and England's naval power became greater than ever.]

The enemy continued to fire a gun at a time at the *Victory*, till they saw that a shot had passed through her main-topgallant-sail ; then they opened their broadsides, aiming chiefly at her rigging, in the hope of disabling her before she could close with them. Nelson, as usual, had hoisted several flags, lest one should be shot away. The enemy showed no colors until late in the action, when they began to feel the necessity of having them to strike. For this reason the *Santissima Trinidad*, Nelson's old acquaintance, as he used to call her, was distinguishable only by her four decks; and to the bow of this opponent he ordered the *Victory* to be steered. Meantime an incessant raking fire was kept up upon the *Victory*. The admiral's secretary was one of the first who fell; he was killed by a cannon-shot while conversing with Hardy. Captain Adair, of the marines, with the help of a sailor, endeavored to remove the body from Nelson's sight, who had a great regard for Mr. Scott; but he anxiously asked : " Is that poor Scott that's gone ? " and being informed that it was indeed so, exclaimed, " Poor fellow ! " Presently a double-headed shot struck a party of marines, who were drawn up on the poop, and killed eight of them; upon which Nelson immediately desired Captain Adair to disperse his men round the ship, that they might not suffer so much from being together. A few minutes afterward a shot struck the fore brace bits on the quarter deck, and passed between Nelson and Hardy, a splinter from the bit tearing off Hardy's buckle and bruising his foot. Both stopped, and looked anxiously at each other, each supposing the other to be wounded. Nelson then smiled, and said, " This is too warm work, Hardy, to last long."

The *Victory* had not yet returned a single gun; fifty of her men had been by this time killed or wounded, and her main-topmast, with all her studding-sails and her booms, shot away. Nelson declared that, in all his battles, he had seen nothing which surpassed the cool courage of his crew on this occasion. At four minutes after twelve she opened her fire from both sides of her deck. It was not possible to break the enemy's line without running on board one of their ships. Hardy informed him of this, and asked him which he would prefer. Nelson replied, "Take your choice, Hardy, it does not signify much." The master was ordered to put the helm to port, and the *Victory* ran on board the *Redoubtable*, just as her tiller ropes were shot away. The French ship received her with a broadside; then instantly let down her lower-deck ports, for fear of being boarded through them, and never afterward fired a great gun during the action. Her tops, like those of all the enemy's ships, were filled with riflemen. Nelson never placed musketry in his tops; he had a strong dislike to the practice, not merely because it endangers setting fire to the sails, but also because it is a murderous sort of warfare by which individuals may suffer, and a commander now and then be picked off, but which never can decide the fate of a general engagement.

Captain Harvey, in the *Téméraire*, fell on board the *Redoubtable* on the other side. Another enemy was in like manner on board the *Téméraire ;* so that these four ships formed as compact a tier as if they had been moored together, their heads lying all the same way. The lieutenants of the *Victory*, seeing this, depressed their guns of the middle and lower decks, and fired with a diminished charge, lest the shot should pass through, and injure the *Téméraire.* And because there was danger that the *Redoubtable* might take fire from the lower deck guns, the muzzles of which touched her sides when they were run out, the fireman of each gun stood ready with a bucket of water, which, as soon as the gun was discharged, he dashed into the hole made by the shot. An incessant fire was kept up from the *Victory* from both sides; her larboard guns playing upon the *Bucentaure* and the huge *Santissima Trinidad.*

It had been part of Nelson's prayer that the British fleet might be distinguished by humanity in the victory which he expected. Setting an example himself, he twice gave orders to cease firing upon the *Redoubtable*, supposing that she had struck because her great guns were silent; for, as she carried no flag, there was no means of instantly ascertaining the fact. From this ship, which he had thus twice spared, he received his death. A ball fired from her mizzen-top, which, in the then situation of the two vessels, was not more than fifteen yards from that part of the deck where he was standing, struck the epaulette on his left shoulder, about a quarter after one, just in the heat of action. He fell upon his face, on the spot which was covered by his poor secretary's blood. Hardy, who was a few steps from him, turning round, saw three men raising him up. "They have done for me at last, Hardy," said he. "I hope not," cried Hardy. "Yes!" he replied; "my back-bone is shot through." Yet even now, not for a moment losing his presence of mind, he observed, as they were carrying him down the ladder, that the tiller-ropes, which had been shot away, were not yet replaced, and ordered that new ones should be rove immediately; then, that he might not be seen by the crew, he took out his handkerchief, and covered his face and his stars. Had he but concealed these badges of honor from the enemy, England, perhaps, would not have had cause to receive with sorrow the news of the battle of Trafalgar. The cockpit was crowded with wounded and dying men, over whose bodies he was with some difficulty conveyed, and laid upon a pallet in the midshipmen's berth. It was soon perceived, upon examination, that the wound was mortal. This, however, was concealed from all except Captain Hardy, the chaplain, and the medical attendants. He himself being certain, from the sensation in his back, and the gush of blood he felt momently within his breast, that no human care could avail him, insisted that the surgeon should leave him, and attend to those to whom he might be useful; "for," said he, "you can do nothing for me." All that could be done was to fan him with paper, and frequently to give him lemonade to alleviate his intense thirst. He was in great pain, and expressed much anxiety for the event of the action, which now began to declare itself. As often as a ship struck, the crew of the *Victory* huzzaed; and at every huzza, a visible expression of joy gleamed in the eyes and marked the countenance of the dying hero. But he became impatient to see Captain Hardy; and, as that officer, though often sent for, could not leave the deck, Nelson feared that some fatal cause prevented him, and repeatedly cried, "Will no one bring Hardy to me? He must be killed! He is surely dead!" An hour and ten minutes elapsed from the time when Nelson received his wound before Hardy could come to him. They shook hands in silence, Hardy in vain struggling to suppress the feelings of that most painful and yet sublimest moment. "Well, Hardy," said Nelson, "how goes the day with us?" "Very well," replied Hardy; "ten ships have struck, but five of the van have tacked, and show an intention to bear down upon the *Victory*. I have called two or three of our fresh ships around, and have no doubt of giving them a drubbing." "I hope," said Nelson, "none of our ships have struck." Hardy answered, "There was no fear of that." Then, and not till then, Nelson spoke of himself. "I am a dead man, Hardy," said he; "I am going fast; it will be all over with me, soon. Come nearer to me. Let my dear Lady Hamilton have my hair, and all other things belonging to me." Hardy observed that he hoped Mr. Beatty could yet hold out some prospect of life. "O, no!" he replied; "it is impossible. My back is shot through; Beatty will tell you so." Captain Hardy then once more shook hands with him; and, with a heart almost bursting, hastened upon deck.

By this time all feeling below the breast was gone; and Nelson, having made the surgeon ascertain this, said to him, "You know I am gone; I know it. I feel something rising in my breast"—putting his hand on his left side—"which tells me so." And, upon Beatty's inquiring whether his pain was very great, he replied, so great that he wished he was dead. "Yet," said he, in a lower voice, "one would like to live a little longer, too." And, after a few minutes, in the same undertone, he added, "What would become of poor Lady Hamilton, if she knew my situation!" Next to his country she occupied his thoughts. Captain Hardy, some fifty minutes after he had left the cockpit, returned; and, again taking the hand of his dying friend and commander, congratulated him on having gained a complete victory. How many of the enemy were taken he did not know, as it was impossible to perceive them distinctly; but fourteen or fifteen, at least. "That's well," cried Nelson, "but I bargained for twenty." And then, in a stronger voice, he said, "Anchor, Hardy, anchor." Hardy, upon this, hinted that Admiral Collingwood would take upon himself the direction of affairs. "Not while I live, Hardy," said the dying Nelson, ineffectually endeavoring to raise himself from the bed; "do you anchor." His previous order for preparing to anchor had shown how clearly he foresaw the necessity of this. Presently, calling Hardy back, he said to him, in a low voice. "Don't throw me overboard;" and he desired that he might be buried by his parents, unless it should please the king to order otherwise. Then, reverting to private feelings, "Take care of my dear Lady Hamilton, Hardy; take care of poor Lady Hamilton. Kiss me, Hardy," said he. Hardy knelt down, and kissed his cheek, and Nelson said, "Now I am satisfied. Thank God, I have done my duty." Hardy stood over him in silence for a moment or two, then knelt again, and kissed his forehead. "Who is that?" said Nelson; and, being informed, he replied, "God bless you, Hardy." And Hardy then left him—forever.

Nelson now desired to be turned upon his right side, and said, "I wish I had not left the deck, for I shall soon be gone." Death was, indeed, rapidly approaching. He said to the chaplain, "Doctor, I have *not* been a *great* sinner;" and after a short pause, "Remember that I leave Lady Hamilton and my daughter Horatia as a legacy to my country."

His articulation now became difficult; but he was distinctly heard to say, "Thank God, I have done my duty." These words he repeatedly pronounced; and they were the last words which he uttered. He expired at thirty minutes after four—three hours and a quarter after he had received his wound.

LVIII.

BOMBARDMENT OF COPENHAGEN.—FYFFE.

[As the war went on, after Trafalgar, it developed more and more into a gigantic duel between the two great rivals, England and Napoleon, and was conducted on both sides with an utter disregard of the rights of neutral nations. One of the best illustrations of the outrageous treatment to which neutrals were subjected was the attack of the English fleet on Copenhagen, the capital of a neutral power, in the summer of 1807. In that year Napoleon had entered into a treaty with Alexander of Russia, the object of which was practically to divide the Continent between them.]

SUCH was this vast and threatening scheme, conceived by the man whose whole career had been one consistent struggle for personal domination, accepted by the man who, among the rulers of the Continent, had hitherto shown the greatest power of acting for a European end, and of interesting himself in a cause not directly his own. In the imagination of Napoleon the national forces of the western continent had now ceased to exist. Austria excepted, there was no state upon the main-land whose army and navy were not prospectively in the hands of himself and his new ally. The commerce of Great Britain, already excluded from the greater part of Europe, was now to be shut out from all the rest; the armies which had hitherto fought under British subsidies for the independence of Europe, the navies which had preserved their existence by neutrality or by friendship with England, were soon to be thrown without distinction against that last foe. If, even at this moment, an English statesman who had learned the secret agreement of Tilsit might have

looked without fear to the future of his country, it was not
from any imperfection in the structure of continental tyranny.   The fleets of Denmark and Portugal might be of little
real avail against English seamen ; the homes of the English
people might still be as secure from foreign invasion as when
Nelson guarded the seas ; but it was not from any vestige of
political honor surviving in the Emperor Alexander.   Where
Alexander's action was really of decisive importance, in his
mediation between France and Prussia, he threw himself
without scruple on to the side of oppression.   It lay within his
power to gain terms of peace for Prussia as lenient as those
which Austria had gained at Campo Formio and at Lunéville ;
he sacrificed Prussia, as he allied himself against the last up-
holders of national independence in Europe, in order that he
might himself receive Finland and the Danubian Provinces.

Two days before the signature of the treaty of Tilsit the
British troops, which had once been so anxiously expected
by the czar, landed in the island of Rügen.   The struggle in
which they were intended to take their part was over.   Sweden alone remained in arms, and even the Quixotic pugnacity
of King Gustavus was unable to save Stralsund from a speedy
capitulation.   But the troops of Great Britain were not destined to return without striking a blow.   While the negotiations between Napoleon and Alexander were still in
progress the government of England received secret intelligence of their purport.   It became known in London that the
fleet of Denmark was to be seized by the two emperors, and
forced to fight against Great Britain.   The ministry acted
with the promptitude that seldom failed the British government when it could effect its object by the fleet alone.   It
determined to anticipate Napoleon's violation of Danish
neutrality, and to seize upon the navy which would otherwise
be seized by France and Russia.

On the 28th of July a fleet, with 20,000 men on board, set
sail from the British coast.   The troops landed in Denmark

in the middle of August, and united with the corps which had already been dispatched to Rügen. The Danish government was summoned to place its navy in the hands of Great Britain, in order that it might remain as a deposit in some British port until the conclusion of peace. While demanding this sacrifice of Danish neutrality, England undertook to protect the Danish nation and colonies from the hostility of Napoleon, and to place at the disposal of the government every means of naval and military defense. Failing the surrender of the fleet, the English declared that they would bombard Copenhagen. The reply given to this summons was such as might be expected from a courageous nation exasperated against Great Britain by its harsh treatment of neutral ships of commerce, and inclined to submit to the despot of the Continent rather than to the tyrant of the seas. "More honor," the crown-prince is reported to have answered, "is to be expected from the pirates of Barbary than from the British government. Your allies, vainly expecting your succors for an entire year, have taught us what is the worth of English friendship." Negotiations proved fruitless, and, on the 2d of September, the English opened fire on Copenhagen. For three days and nights the city underwent a bombardment of cruel efficiency. Eighteen hundred houses were leveled, the town was set on fire in several places, and a large number of inhabitants lost their lives. At length the commander found himself compelled to capitulate. The fleet was handed over to Great Britain, with all the stores in the arsenal at Copenhagen. It was brought to England, no longer under the terms of a friendly neutrality, but as a prize of war.

The captors themselves were ashamed of their spoil. England received an armament which had been taken from a people who were not our enemies, and by an attack which was not war, with more misgiving than applause.* In Europe

---

* Yet the House of Commons approved of the action of the ministry by a vote of more than two to one.

15

the seemingly unprovoked assault upon a weak neutral state
excited the utmost indignation. The British ministry, who
were prevented from making public the evidence which they
had received of the intention of the two emperors, were believed to have invented the story of the secret treaty. The
Danish government denied that Napoleon had demanded
their co-operation; Napoleon and Alexander themselves assumed the air of indignant astonishment. But the facts alleged by Canning and his colleagues were correct. The
conspiracy of the two emperors was no fiction. The only
question still remaining open relates to the engagements entered into by the Danish government itself. Napoleon, in
his correspondence of this date, alludes to certain promises
made to him by the court of Denmark, but he also com-
plains that these promises had not been fulfilled; and the
context of the letter renders it almost cer ain that nothing
more was promised than that the ports of Denmark should be
closed to English vessels. If the British cabinet possessed
evidence of the determination of the Danish government to
transfer its fleet to Napoleon without resistance, the attack
upon Denmark, considered as virtually an act of war, was not
unjust. If no such evidence existed, the conspiracy of the
emperors against Danish neutrality was no sufficient ground
for an action on the part of Great Britain which went so far
beyond the mere frustration of their designs. The surrender
of the Danish fleet demanded by England would have been
an unqualified act of war on the part of Denmark against
Napoleon; it was no mere guarantee for a continued neutrality. Nor had the British government the last excuse
of an urgent and overwhelming necessity. Nineteen Danish
men-of-war would not have turned the scale against England.
The memory of Trafalgar might well have given a British
ministry courage to meet its enemies by the ordinary methods
of war. Had the forces of Denmark been far larger than
they actually were, the peril of Great Britain was not so ex-

treme as to excuse the wrong done to mankind by an example encouraging all future belligerents to anticipate one another in forcing neutrals to take part with themselves.

<hr>

LIX.

BATTLE OF WATERLOO—Creasy.

[The failure of his attempt to subjugate Spain, which was made in the
year following the humiliation of Denmark by England, marked the turn-
ing-point in Napoleon's career. Fortune, indeed, did not desert him in his
brilliant campaign against Austria, in 1809; but his insane invasion of
Russia, in 1812, and the obstinacy with which he rejected all overtures of
peace during the campaigns/of 1813 and 1814 led to his downfall in the
latter year, in spite of the almost superhuman activity and energy he displayed.   By the treaty of Paris (1814) the island of Elba was assigned to
him as a place of residence ; but in the spring of 1815, while the congress
of Vienna was busy in re-arranging the map of Europe, he escaped from
the island. France welcomed him, Europe combined against him, and
he was finally overthrown by the English and Prussian armies on the field
of Waterloo. The crisis of the battle is described below.]

BETWEEN seven and eight
o'clock the infantry of the Old
Guard was formed into two
columns, on the declivity near
La Belle Alliance. Ney was
placed at their head. Napoleon himself rode forward
to a spot by which his veterans
were to pass; and as they approached he raised his arm,
and pointed to the position of
the allies, as if to tell them
that their path lay there.

DUKE OF WELLINGTON.

They answered with loud cries of " Vive l'Empereur ! " and
descended the hill from their own side into that " valley of

the shadow of death," while their batteries thundered with redoubled vigor over their heads upon the British line. The line of march of the columns of the Guard was directed between Hougoumont and La Haye Sainte, against the British right center; and at the same time, Donzelot and the French who had possession of La Haye Sainte, commenced a fierce attack upon the British center, a little more to its left. This part of the battle has drawn less attention than the celebrated attack of the Old Guard; but it formed the most perilous crisis for the allied army; and if the Young Guard had been there to support Donzelot, instead of being engaged with the Prussians at Planchenoit, the consequences to the allies in that part of the field must have been most serious. The French *tirailleurs*, who were posted in clouds in La Haye Sainte, and the sheltered spots near it, completely disabled the artillery-men of the English batteries near them; and, taking advantage of the crippled state of the English guns, the French brought some field-pieces up to La Haye Sainte, and commenced firing grape from them on the infantry of the allies, at a distance of not more than a hundred paces. The allied infantry here consisted of some German brigades, who were formed in squares, as it was believed that Donzelot had cavalry ready behind La Haye Sainte to charge them with, if they left that order of formation. In this state the Germans remained for some time with heroic fortitude, though the grape-shot was tearing gaps in their ranks, and the side of one square was literally blown away by one tremendous volley which the French gunners poured into it. The prince of Orange in vain endeavored to lead some Nassau troops to their aid. The Nassauers would not or could not face the French; and some battalions of Brunswickers, whom the duke of Wellington had ordered up as a re-enforcement, at first fell back, until the duke in person rallied them and led them on. The duke then galloped off to the right to lead his men who were exposed to the attack of the Imperial Guard. He had saved one part of his center from being routed; but the French had gained ground here, and the pressure on the allied line was severe, until it was relieved by the decisive success which the British in the right center achieved over the columns of the Guard.

The British troops on the crest of that part of the position, which the first column of Napoleon's Guard assailed, were Maitland's brigade of British Guards, having Adam's brigade on their right. Maitland's men were lying down, in order to avoid, as far as possible, the destructive effect of the French artillery, which kept up an unremitting fire from the opposite heights, until the first column of the Imperial Guard had advanced so far up the slope toward the British position that any further firing of the French artillery-men would endanger their own comrades. Meanwhile, the British guns were not idle; but shot and shell plowed fast through the ranks of the stately array of veterans that still moved imposingly on. Several of the French superior officers were at its head. Ney's horse was shot under him, but he still led the way on foot, sword in hand. The front of the massive column now was on the ridge of the hill. To their surprise they saw no troops before them. All they could discern through the smoke was a small band of mounted officers. One of these was the duke himself. The French advanced to about fifty yards from where the British Guards were lying down, when the voice of one of the band of British officers was heard calling, as if to the ground before him, " Up, Guards, and at them! " It was the duke who gave the order; and at the words, as if by magic, up started before them a line of the British Guards four deep, and in the most compact and perfect order. They poured an instantaneous volley upon the head of the French column, by which no less than three hundred of those chosen veterans are said to have fallen. The French officers rushed forward, and, conspicuous in front of their men, attempted to deploy them into a more extended line, so as to enable them to reply with effect to the British fire. But Maitland's brigade kept showering in volley after volley with deadly rapidity. The decimated column grew disordered in its vain efforts to expand itself into a more efficient formation. The right word was given at the right moment to the British for the bayonet-charge, and the brigade sprang forward with a loud cheer against their dismayed antagonists. In an instant the compact mass of the French spread out into a rabble, and they fled back down the hill, pursued by Maitland's men, who, however, returned to their position in time to take part in the repulse of the second column of the Imperial Guard. [This column also advanced with great spirit and firmness but met with such strenuous opposition that it, like its predecessor, broke and fled.]

But the battle was not yet won. Napoleon had still some battalions in reserve near La Belle Alliance. He was rapidly rallying the remains of the first column of his Guards, and he had collected into one body the remnants of the various corps of cavalry, which had suffered so severely in the earlier part of the day. The duke instantly formed the bold resolution of now himself becoming the assailant, and leading his successful, though enfeebled, army forward, while the disheartening effect of the repulse of the Imperial Guard on the French army was still strong, and before Napoleon and Ney could rally the beaten veterans themselves for another and a fiercer charge. As the close approach of the Prussians now completely protected the duke's left, he had drawn some reserves of horse from that quarter, and he had a brigade of Hussars, under Vivian, fresh and ready at hand. Without a moment's hesitation, he launched these against the cavalry near La Belle Alliance. The charge was as successful as it was daring; and as there was now no hostile cavalry to check the British infantry in a forward movement, the duke gave the long-wished-for command for a general advance of the army along the whole line upon the foe.

It was now past eight o'clock, and for nine deadly hour. had the British and German regiments stood unflinching under the fire of artillery, the charge of cavalry, and every variety of assault that the compact columns or the scattered *tirailleurs* of the enemy's infantry could inflict. As they joyously sprang forward against the discomfited masses of the French, the setting sun broke through the clouds, which had obscured the sky during the greater part of the day, and glittered on the bayonets of the allies, while they in turn poured down into the valley and toward the heights that were held by the foe. Almost the whole of the French host was now in irretrievable confusion. The Prussian army was coming more and more rapidly forward on their right, and the Young Guard, which had held Planchenoit so bravely, was at last compelled to give way. Some regiments of the Old Guard in vain endeavored to form in squares. They were swept away to the rear; and then Napoleon himself fled from the last of his many fields, to become, in a few weeks, a captive and an exile.

The battle was lost by France past all recovery. The victorious armies of England and Prussia, meeting on the scene of their triumph, continued to press forward and overwhelm every attempt that was made to stem the tide of ruin. The British army, exhausted by its toils and suffering during that dreadful day, did not urge the pursuit beyond the heights which the enemy had occupied. But the Prussians drove the fugitives before them throughout the night. And of the magnificent host which had that morning cheered their emperor in confident expectation of victory, very few were ever assembled again in arms. Their loss, both in the field and in the pursuit, was immense ; and the greater number of those who escaped, dispersed as soon as they crossed the frontier.

The army under the duke of Wellington lost nearly fifteen thousand men in killed and wounded on this terrible day of battle.   The loss of the Prussian army was nearly seven thousand more.   At such a fearful price was the deliverance of Europe purchased.

LX.

CORONATION OF QUEEN VICTORIA.—GREVILLE.

[At the close of the Napoleonic wars a long era of peace and prosperity dawned for England.   While many of the continental countries were convulsed by revolution during the decade, from 1820 to 1830, in England the causes of popular discontent were to a great degree removed by wise legislation and a skillful foreign policy.   The period is well characterized by such measures as the great Catholic Emancipation Act of 1829. and the still more important Reform Bill of 1832.   The latter measure, it is true, was not as thorough as the Radical party desired ; but their dissatisfaction was not great enough to mar the general and genuine enthusiasm with which the nation welcomed its young queen to the throne.]

June 27th, 1838.—There never was any thing seen like the state of this town ; it is as if the population had been on a sudden quintupled ; the uproar, the confusion, the crowd, the noise, are indescribable.   Horsemen, footmen, carriages squeezed, jammed, intermingled, the pavement blocked up with timbers, hammering and knocking, and falling fragments stunning the ears and threatening the head ; not a mob here and there, but the town all mob, thronging, bustling, gaping, and gazing at every thing, at any thing, or at nothing ; the park one vast encampment, with banners floating on the tops of the tents ; and still the roads are covered, the railroads loaded with arriving multitudes.   From one end of the route of the royal procession to the other, from the top of Piccadilly to Westminster Abbey, there is a vast line of scaffolding ; the noise, the movement, the restlessness are incessant and universal ; in short, it is very curious, but uncommonly tiresome, and the sooner it is over the better.   There has been a grand bother about the embassadors forming part of the royal procession. They all detest it, think they ought not to have been called upon to assist, and the poor representatives of the smaller courts do not at all fancy the expense of fine equipages, or the mortification of exhibiting mean ones. This arrangement was matter of negotiation for several days, and (the Lord knows why) the government pertinaciously insisted on it. Public opinion has declared against it, and now they begin to see that they have done a very foolish thing, odious to the *corps diplomatique* and unpleasing to the people.

June 29th.—The coronation (which, thank God, is over) went off very well. The day was fine, without heat or rain—the innumerable multitude which thronged the streets orderly and satisfied. The appearance of the abbey was beautiful, particularly the benches of the peeresses, who were blazing with diamonds. The entry of Soult* was striking. He was saluted with a murmur of curiosity and applause as he passed through the nave, and nearly the same as he advanced along the choir. His appearance is that of a veteran warrior, and he walked alone, with his numerous suite following at a respectful distance, preceded by heralds and ushers, who received him with marked attention, more certainly than any of the other embassadors. The queen looked very diminutive, and the effect of the procession itself was spoiled by being too crowded ; there was not interval enough between the queen and the lords and others going before her. The bishop of London (Blomfield) preached a very good sermon. The different actors in the ceremonial were very imperfect in their parts, and had neglected to rehearse them. Lord John Thynne, who officiated for the dean of Westminster, told me that nobody knew what was to be done except the archbishop and himself (who had rehearsed), Lord Willoughby (who is experienced in such matters), and the duke of Wellington,

* Marshal Soult, once the antagonist of Wellington in Spain, represented the king of the French on this occasion.

15*

and, consequently, there was a continual difficulty and embarrassment, and the queen never knew what she was to do next. They made her leave her chair and enter into St. Edward's Chapel before the prayers were concluded, much to the discomfiture of the archbishop. She said to John Thynne, " Pray tell me what I am to do, for they don't know; " and at the end, when the orb was put into her hand, she said to him, " What am I to do with it ? " " Your majesty is to carry it, if you please, in your hand." " Am I ? " she said ; " it is very heavy." The ruby ring was made for her little finger instead of the fourth, on which the rubric prescribes that it should be put. When the archbishop was to put it on, she extended the former, but he said it must be on the latter. She said it was too small, and she could not get it on. He said it was right to put it there, and, as he insisted, she yielded, but had first to take off her other rings, and then this was forced on ; but it hurt her very much, and as soon as the ceremony was over, she was obliged to bathe her finger in iced water in order to get it off.

The noise and confusion were very great when the medals were thrown about by Lord Surrey, every body scrambling with all their might, and none more vigorously than the maids of honor. There was a great demonstration of applause when the duke of Wellington did homage. Lord Rolle, who is between eighty and ninety, fell down as he was getting up the steps of the throne. Her first impulse was to rise, and when afterward he came again to do homage, she said : " May I not get up and meet him ? " and then rose from the throne, and advanced down one or two of the steps to prevent his coming up, an act of graciousness and kindness which made a great sensation. It is, in fact, the remarkable union of *naïveté*, kindness, nature, good nature, with propriety and dignity, which makes her so admirable and so endearing to those about her, as she certainly is. I have been repeatedly told that they are all warmly attached to her, but that all feel the impossibility of for a moment losing sight of the respect which they owe her. She never ceases to be a queen, but is always the most charming, cheerful, obliging, unaffected queen in the world. The procession was very handsome, and the extraordinary embassadors produced some gorgeous equipages. This sort of procession is incomparably better than the old ceremonial which so much fuss was made about, for the banquet would only have benefited the privileged few and the rich, and for one person who would have witnessed the procession on the platform, five hundred enjoyed the sight of this. In fact, the thing best worth seeing was the town itself, and the countless multitudes through which the procession passed. The chancellor of the exchequer told me that he had been informed £200,000 had been paid for seats alone, and the number of people who have flocked into London has been estimated at five hundred thousand. It is said that a million have had sight of the show in one way or another. These numbers are possibly exaggerated, but they really were prodigious. From Buckingham Palace to Westminster Abbey, by the way they took, which must be two or three miles in length, there was a dense mass of people; the seats and benches were all full, every window was occupied, the roofs of the houses were covered with spectators, for the most part well dressed, and, from the great space through which they were distributed, there was no extraordinary pressure, and consequently no room for violence or ill-humor. In the evening I met Prince Esterhazy, and asked him what the foreigners said. He replied that they admired it all very much: " Strogonoff and the others don't like you, but they feel it, and it makes a great impression on them; in fact, nothing can be seen like it in any other country." I went into the park, where the fair was going on; a vast multitude, but all of the lower orders; not very amusing. The great merit of this coronation is, that so much has been done for the people; to amuse and interest *them* seems to have been the principal object.

LXI.

BATTLE OF THE ALMA.—McCarthy.

[The peace of Victoria's reign was not seriously interrupted until the outbreak of the Crimean war, in 1854. The natural desire of Russia to extend her power to the Dardanelles, and to open a way for her commerce
into the Mediterranean by encroaching upon the Turkish dominions, both
in Europe and Asia, aroused the jealousy of the Western Powers, and led
England and France to combine against her. The war was carried on
principally around Sebastopol, a powerful fortress in the peninsula of the
Crimea, in southern Russia, and the battle of the Alma was the first of a
series of battles which were fought for the possession of that fortress.]

THE invasion of the Crimea, however, was not a soldier's
project. It was not welcomed by the English or the French
commander. It was undertaken by Lord Raglan out of deference to the recommendations of the government; and by
Marshal St. Arnaud out of deference to the emperor of the
French, and because Lord Raglan did not see his way to decline the responsibility of it. The allied forces were therefore conveyed to the south-western shore of the Crimea, and
effected a landing in Kalamita Bay, a short distance north of
the point at which the river Alma runs into the sea. Sebastopol itself lies about thirty miles to the south; and then more
southward still, divided by the bulk of a' jutting promontory
from Sebastopol, is the harbor of Balaklava. The disembar-
kation began on the morning of September 14, 1854; it was
completed on the fifth day; and there were then some 27,000
English, 30,000 French, and 7,000 Turks, landed on the shores
of Catherine the Great's Crimea. The landing was effected
without any opposition from the Russians. On September
19 the allies marched out of their encampments, and moved
southward in the direction of Sebastopol. They had a skir-
mish or two with a reconnoitering force of Russian cavalry and
Cossacks; but they had no business of genuine war until they
reached the nearer bank of the Alma. The Russians, in great

strength, had taken up a splendid position on the heights that fringed the other side of the river. The allied forces reached the Alma about noon on September 20. They found that they had to cross the river in the face of the Russian batteries, armed with heavy guns on the highest point of the hills or bluffs, of scattered artillery, and of dense masses of infantry which covered the hills. The Russians were under the command of Prince Mentschikoff. It is certain that Prince Mentschikoff believed his position unassailable, and was convinced that his enemies were delivered into his hands when he saw the allies approach, and attempt to effect the crossing of the river. He had allowed them, of deliberate purpose, to approach thus far. He might have attacked them on their landing, or on their two days' march toward the river. But he did not choose to do any thing of the kind. He had carefully sought out a strong, and what he considered an impregnable, position. He had found it, as he believed, on the south bank of the Alma; and there he was simply biding his time. His idea was that he could hold his ground for some days against the allies with ease; that he would keep them there, play with them, until the great re-enforcements he was expecting could come to him; and then he would suddenly take the offensive and crush the enemy. He proposed to make of the Alma and its banks the grave of the invaders. But, with characteristic arrogance and lack of care, he had neglected some of the very precautions which were essentially necessary to secure any position, however strong. He had not taken the pains to make himself certain that every easy access to his position was closed against the attack of the enemy. The attack was made with desperate courage on the part of the allies, but without any great skill of leadership or tenacity of discipline. It was rather a pell-mell sort of fight in which the headlong courage and the indomitable obstinacy of the English and French troops carried all before them at last.

A study of the battle is of little profit to the ordinary

reader. It was an heroic scramble. There was little coherence of action between the allied forces. But there was, happily, an almost total absence of generalship on the part of the Russians. The soldiers of the Czar fought stoutly and stubbornly, as they always have done; but they could not stand up against the blended vehemence and obstinacy of the English and French. The river was crossed, the opposite heights were mounted, Prince Mentschikoff's great redoubt was carried, the Russians were driven from the field, the allies occupied their ground; the victory was to the Western powers. Indeed, it would not be unfair to say that the victory was to the English; owing to whatever cause, the French did not take that share in the heat of the battle which their strength and their military genius might have led men to expect. ·St. Arnaud, their commander-in-chief, was in wretched health, on the point of death, in fact; he was in no condition to guide the battle; a brilliant enterprise of General Bosquet was ill-supported, and had nearly proved a failure; and Prince Napoleon's division got hopelessly jammed up and confused. Perhaps it would be fairer to say that, in the confusion and scramble of the whole affair, we were more lucky than the French. If a number of men are rushing headlong, and in the dark, toward some distant point, one may run against an unthought-of obstacle, and fall down, and so lose his chance, while his comrade happens to meet with no such stumbling-block, and goes right on. Perhaps this illustration may not unfairly distribute the parts taken in the battle. It would be superfluous to say that the French fought splendidly where they had any real chance of fighting. But the luck of the day was not with them. On all sides the battle was fought without generalship. On all sides the bravery of the officers and men was worthy of any general. Our men were the luckiest. They saw the heights; they saw the enemy there; they made for him; they got at him; they would not go back; and so he had to give way. That was the history of the day. The big scramble was all over in a few hours. The first field was fought, and we had won.

The Russians ought to have been pursued. They themselves fully expected a pursuit. They retreated in something like utter confusion, eager to put the Katcha river, which runs south of the Alma, and with a somewhat similar course, between them and the imaginary pursuers. Had they been followed to the Katcha they might have been all made prisoners or destroyed. But there was no pursuit. Lord Raglan was eager to follow up the victory; but the French had as yet hardly any cavalry, and Marshal St. Arnaud would not agree to any further enterprise that day. Lord Raglan believed that he ought not to persist; and nothing was done. The Russians were unable at first to believe in their good fortune. It seemed to them for a long time impossible that any commanders in the world could have failed, under conditions so tempting, to follow a flying and disordered enemy.

Except for the bravery of those who fought, the battle was not much to boast of. The allies altogether considerably outnumbered the Russians, although, from the causes we have mentioned, the Englishmen were left throughout the greater part of the day to encounter an enemy numerically superior, posted on difficult and commanding heights. But it was the first great battle which for nearly forty years our soldiers had fought with a civilized enemy. The military authorities and the country were well disposed to make the most of it. At this distance of time it is almost touching to read some of the heroic contemporaneous descriptions of the great scramble of the Alma. It might almost seem as if, in the imaginings of the enthusiastic historians, Englishmen had never mounted heights and defeated superior numbers before. The sublime triumphs against every adverse condition which had been won by a Marlborough or a Wellington could not have been celebrated in language of more exalted dithyrambic pomp.

The gallant medley on the banks of the Alma, and the fruit-less interval of inaction that followed it, were told of as if men were speaking of some battle of the gods.

LXII.

THE STORY OF CAWNPORE.—KAYE.

[It was largely the fear that Russia, by getting control of the eastern Mediterranean, might throw herself across the most direct route between England and her great empire in the East, that induced the latter power to enter the Crimean war. But England little dreamed, at the close of the war, that a far greater danger to her power existed in India itself. For many years, and from a variety of causes, a smoldering discontent had existed among the populations of India, and it now (1857) broke out into open mutiny. The siege of Cawnpore by Nana Sahib, whose ambition was to restore the old empire of the Moguls, together with the subsequent surrender and massacre of the little English garrison, was one of the most thrilling incidents in the whole history of the mutiny. After the siege had lasted three weeks, the Nana offered conditions of surrender, one of which was that he would provide boats to convey the garrison down the river Ganges to a place of safety.]

THAT the boats were ready at the river-side had been ascertained by a committee of our own people; and when the dreary procession reached the appointed place of embarkation, the uncouth vessels were seen a little way in the stream, in shallow water, for it was the close of the dry season, and the river was at its lowest. The boats were the ordinary eight-oared budgerows of the country—ungainly structures with thatched roofs, looking at a distance like floating hay-stacks, and into these our people now began to crowd without order or method, even the women with children in their arms, with but little help from others, wading knee-deep in the water, and scrambling as they best could up the sides of the vessels. It was nine o'clock before the whole were embarked, and some—Heaven only knows, for their voices are sealed—may have breathed more freely as they awaited the friendly order to push off and to drop down the stream toward the great goal of ultimate deliverance. But there were those on the river banks—those even in the boats themselves—who had far other thoughts, far other expectations. Every boat that had been prepared for our people was intended to be a human slaughter-house. They had not gone down to the banks of a friendly river that was to float them to a place of safety. They had been lured to the appointed shambles, there to be given up to cruel death.

No sooner were our people on board the boats than the foul design became apparent. The sound of a bugle was heard. The native boatmen clambered over the sides of the vessels, and sought the shore. Then a murderous fire of grape-shot and musket-balls was opened upon the wretched passengers from both banks of the river; and presently the thatch of the budgerows, cunningly ignited by hot cinders, burst into a blaze. There was then only a choice of cruel deaths for our dear Christian people. The men, or the foremost among them, strenuous in action to the last, leaped overboard, and strove, with shoulders to the hulls of the boats, to push them into mid-channel. But the bulk of the fleet remained immovable, and the conflagration was spreading. The sick and wounded were burnt to death, or more mercifully suffocated by the smoke ; while the stronger women, with children in their arms, took to the river, to be shot down in the water, to be sabered in the stream by the mounted troopers, who rode in after them, to be bayoneted on reaching land, or to be made captives, and reserved for a later and more cruel immolation. The fewest words are here the best. I should have little taste to tell the foul details of this foul slaughter, even if authentic particulars were before me. It is better that they should remain in the obscurity of an uncertain whole ; enough that no aspect of Christian humanity, not the sight of the old general, who had nearly numbered his fourscore years, nor of the little babe still on its mother's breast, raised any feeling of compunction or of pity in these butchers on the river side.   It sufficed that there was Christian blood to be shed.

While this terrible scene was being acted at the Ghaut, the Nana Sahib, having full faith in the malevolent activity of his lieutenants on the river bank, was awaiting the issue in his tent on the cantonment plain.   It is related of him that, unquiet in mind, he moved about, passing hither and thither, in spite of the indolence of his habits and the obesity of his frame.   After a while, tidings of the progress of the massacre were brought to him by a wounded trooper.   What had been passing within him during those morning hours no human pen can reveal.   Perhaps some slight spasm of remorse may have come upon him, or he may have thought that better use might be made of some of our people alive than dead.   But whether moved by pity or by craft, he sent orders back by the messenger that no more women and childen should be slain, but that not an Englishman should be left alive.   So the murderers, after butchering, or trying to butcher, the remnant of our fighting men, stayed their hands and ceased from the slaughter ; and a number of weaker victims, computed with probable accuracy at a hundred and twenty-five, some sorely wounded, some half-drowned, all dripping with the water of the Ganges and begrimed with its mud, were carried back in custody to Cawnpore, by the way they had come, envying, perhaps, those whose destiny had been already accomplished.

But among the men—survivors of the Cawnpore garrison —were some who battled bravely for their lives, and sold them dearly.   Strong swimmers took to the river, but often sunk in the reddened water beneath the fire of their pursuers ; while others, making toward the land lower down the stream, stood at bay on bank or islet, and made vain but gallant use of the cherished revolver in the last grim energies of death. There was nothing strange, perhaps, in the fact that the foremost heroes of the defense were the last even now to yield up their lives to the fury of the enemy. One boat held Moore and Vibart, Whiting and Mowbray-Thomson, Ashe, Delafosse, Bolton, and others, who had been conspicuous in the annals of that heroic defense. By some accident or oversight the thatch had escaped ignition. Lighter, too, than the rest, or perhaps more vigorously propelled by the shoulders of these strong men, it drifted down the stream; but Moore was shot through the heart in the act of propulsion, and Ashe and Bolton perished while engaged in the same work. The grape and round-shot from the Oude bank of the river ere long began to complete the massacre. The dying and the dead lay thickly together entangled in the bottom of the boat, and for the living there was not a mouthful of food.

As the day waned it was clear that the activity of the enemy had not abated. That one drifting boat, on the dark waters of the Ganges, without boatman, without oars, without a rudder, was not to be left alone with such sorry chance of escape; so a blazing budgerow was sent down the river after it, and burning arrows were discharged at its roof. Still, however, the boat was true to its occupants; and with the new day, now grounding on sand-banks, now pushed off again into the stream, it made weary progress between the two hostile banks, every hour lighter, for every hour brought more messengers of death. At sunset a pursuing boat from Cawnpore, with fifty or sixty armed natives on board, came after our people, with orders to board and destroy them. But the pursuers also grounded on a sand-bank; and then there was one of those last grand spasms of courage even in death which are seldom absent from the story of English heroism. Exhausted, famishing, sick and wounded, as they were, they would not wait to be attacked. A little party of officers and soldiers armed themselves to the teeth, and fell heavily upon the people who had come down to destroy them. Very few of the pursuers returned to tell the story of their pursuit. This was the last victory of the hero-martyrs of Cawnpore. They took the enemy's boat, and found in it good stores of ammunition. They would rather have found a little food. Victors as they were, they returned to the cover of the boat only to wrestle with a more formidable enemy. For starvation was staring them in the face.

Sleep fell upon the survivors; and when they woke the wind had risen, and the boat was drifting down the stream—in the darkness they knew not whither; and some even then had waking dreams of a coming deliverance. But with the first glimmer of the morning despair came upon them. The boat had been carried out of the main channel of the river into a creek or siding, where the enemy soon discerned it, and poured a shower of musket balls upon its miserable inmates. Then Vibart, who lay helpless, with both arms shot through, issued his last orders. It was a forlorn hope. But while there was a sound arm among them, that could load and fire, or thrust with a bayonet, still the great game of the English was to go to the front and smite the enemy, as a race that seldom waited to be smitten. So Mowbray-Thomson and Delafosse, with a little band of European soldiers of the Thirty-second and the Eighty-fourth, landed to attack their assailants. The fierce energy of desperation drove them forward. Sepoys and villagers, armed and unarmed, surged around them, but they charged through the astonished multitude, and made their way back again through the crowd of blacks to the point from which they had started. Then they saw that the boat was gone. The fourteen were left upon the pitiless land, while their doomed companions floated down the pitiless water.

There was one more stand to be made by Mowbray-Thomson and his comrades. As they returned along the bank of the river, seeing after a while no chance of overtaking the boat, they made for a Hindu temple, which had caught the eye of their leader, and defended the door-way with fixed bayonets. After a little time they stood behind a rampart of black and bloody corpses, and fired, with comparative security, over this bulwark of human flesh. A little putrid water found in the temple gave our people new strength, and they held the door-way so gallantly, and so destructively to the enemy, that there seemed to be no hope of expelling them by force of arms. So while word went back to Nana Sahib, that the remnant of the English army was not to be conquered, the assailants, huddling round the temple, brought leaves and fagots, which they piled up beneath the walls, and strove to burn out the little garrison. Then Providence came to their help in their sorest need. The wind blew smoke and fire away from the temple. But the malice of the enemy had a new device in store. They threw bags of powder on the burning embers. There was now nothing left for our people but flight. Precipitating themselves into the midst of the raging multitude, they fired a volley and then charged with the bayonet. Seven of the fourteen carried their lives with them, and little else, to the bank of the river. There they took to the stream ; but presently two of the swimmers were shot through the head, while a third, well-nigh exhausted, making for a sand-bank, had his skull battered in as soon as he landed. But the surviving four, being strong swimmers, and with heroic power in doing and in suffering, struck down the stream, and aided by the current, evaded their pursuers. Mowbray-Thomson and Delafosse, with privates Murphy and Sullivan, reached alive the territory of a friendly Oude rajah, and survived to tell the story of Cawnpore.

CHRONOLOGICAL TABLE OF ENGLISH SOVEREIGNS

FROM ECGBERHT TO VICTORIA.

SAXON PERIOD.—802-1066.

802–839.	Ecgberht—first king of all Englishmen in Britain.
839–857.	Æthelwulf, son of Ecgberht.
857–860.	Æthelbald,
860–866.	Æthelberht,
866–871.	Æthelred I.,
871–901.	Ælfred (the Great),

sons of Æthelwulf.

901–924.	Eadward I., the Elder, son of Ælfred.
924–940.	Æthelstan,
940–946.	Eadmund I.,
946–955.	Eadred,

sons of Eadward I.

955–959.	Eadwig,
959–975.	Eadgar,

sons of Eadmund I.

975–978.	Eadward II., the Martyr,
978–1013.	Æthelred II., the Unready,

sons of Eadgar.

1013–Feb., 1014.	Swein (Swegen), the first Danish king.
1014–April, 1016.	Æthelred II., the Unready. (Restored.)
April–Nov., 1016.	Eadmund II., Ironsides, son of Æthelred II.
1016–1035.	Cnut, son of Swein.
1035–1040	Harold I., Harefoot,
1040–1042.	Harthacnut,

sons of Cnut.

1042–1066.	Eadward III., the Confessor, son of Æthelred II., the Unready.
Jan.–Oct., 1066.	Harold II., son of Godwine, brother-in-law of Eadward III.

NORMAN PERIOD.—1066-1154.

1066–1087.	William the Conqueror, duke of Normandy.
1087–1100.	William II., Rufus, second son of the Conqueror.
1100–1135.	Henry I., Beauclerc, youngest son of the Conqueror.
1135–1154.	Stephen, count of Blois, son of Adela, fourth daughter of the Conqueror. Matilda, daughter of Henry I., disputes with him the crown.

PLANTAGENETS.

1154–1189. Henry II., son of Matilda, daughter of Henry I., and Geoffrey, count of Anjou.
1189–1199. Richard I., Cœur de Lion, son of Henry II.
1199–1216. John, youngest son of Henry II.
1216–1272. Henry III., son of John.
1272–1307. Edward I., son of Henry III.
1307–1327. Edward II., son of Edward I. (Deposed.)
1327–1377. Edward III., son of Edward II.
1377–1399. Richard II., son of Edward the Black Prince, grandson of Edward III. (Deposed.)

PLANTAGENETS.—House of Lancaster ("Red Rose").—
1399–1461.

1399–1413. Henry IV., son of John, duke of Lancaster, who was the third son of Edward III.
1413–1422. Henry V., son of Henry IV.
1422–1461. Henry VI., son of Henry V. (Deposed.)

PLANTAGENETS.—House of York ("White Rose").—1461–1485.

1461–1483. Edward IV., great-grandson of Edmund, duke of York, fourth son of Edward III. ; and also great-great-great grandson of Lionel, duke of Clarence, second son of Edward III.
April–June, 1483. Edward V., son of Edward IV. (Deposed and murdered.)
1483–1485. Richard III., brother of Edward IV. (Defeated and slain in battle.)

HOUSE OF TUDOR.—1485–1603.

1485–1509. Henry VII., son of Edmund Tudor, earl of Richmond, and Margaret Beaufort, an illegitimate descendant of John, duke of Lancaster, third son of Edward III.
1509–1547. Henry VIII., second son of Henry VII.
1547–1553. Edward VI., son of Henry VIII. and his third queen, Jane Seymour.
1553–1558. Mary I., daughter of Henry VIII. and his first queen, Catherine of Aragon.
1558–1603. Elizabeth, daughter of Henry VIII. and his second queen, Anne Boleyn.

HOUSE OF STUART—First Period.—1603–1649.

1603–1625. James I., great-grandson of Margaret, elder daughter of Henry VII., and James IV. Stuart, king of Scotland.
1625–1649. Charles I., son of James I. (Deposed and beheaded.)

INTERREGNUM.—1649–1660.

1649–1653.   Commonwealth.   Council of State and Parliament.
1653–1658.   Oliver Cromwell, Protector.
1658–1659.   Richard Cromwell, Protector, son of Oliver.
1659–1660.   Commonwealth restored.

HOUSE OF STUART—Second Period.—1660–1688.

1660–1685.   Charles II., son of Charles I.
1685–1688.   James II., second son of Charles I.   ("Abdicated.")

INTERREGNUM.—Dec. 11, 1688–Feb. 13, 1689.

HOUSES OF ORANGE AND STUART.—1689–1702.

1689–1702.   William III. and Mary II., elected king and queen.
             William III., prince of Orange-Nassau, was the
             son of William II., prince of Orange-Nassau,
             and Mary, daughter of Charles I.   He married
             (1677) his cousin, Mary, daughter of James, duke
             of York, later James II.   He was, then, both
             nephew and son-in-law of James II.   William and
             Mary had no children.

HOUSE OF STUART—Third Period.—1702–1714.

1702–1714.   Anne, second daughter of James II.   Married Prince
             George of Denmark.   None of her numerous chil-
             dren survived her.

HOUSE OF HANOVER.—1714 ——.

1714–1727.   George I., elector of Hanover, great-grandson of
             James I.   Elizabeth, daughter of James I., mar-
             ried Frederick V., elector palatine.   Their daugh-
             ter, Sophia, married Ernest Augustus, first elector
             of Hanover.   George Lewis, elector of Hanover—
             George I. of England—was the son of this marriage.
1727–1760.   George II., son of George I.
1760–1820.   George III., son of Frederick, prince of Wales, and
             grandson of George II.
1820–1830.   George IV., son of George III.   His only child, a
             daughter, died before him and left no children.
1830–1837.   William IV., third son of George III.   No children.
1837 ——.   Victoria, daughter of Edward, duke of Kent, fourth
             son of George III.

CHAUTAUQUA ATLAS

— OF —

ENGLISH HISTORY

SELECTED FROM "THE NEW HISTORICAL ATLAS AND
GENERAL HISTORY," BY ROBERT H. LABBERTON,
1 VOL., ROYAL 8°, 200 MAPS, CLOTH, $2.00.

....

LIST OF MAPS.

I. Celtic Britain about the Birth of Christ.

II. Roman Britain about 369 A.D.

III. Britain about 500 A. D.
N.E. Part of Kent about 450 A.D.

IV. Britain after 577 A.D.
Theatre of War between Britains and West Saxons about 577 A.D.

V. Britain in 626 A.D.
The Battlefield near the River Idle.

VI. Britain in 658 A.D.
The New Settlements in Central Britain about 666 A. D.

VII. Britain in 795 A.D.
S. W. Britain about 800 A.D.

VIII. Britain in 827 A. D.
London about 800 A.D.

IX. Britain in 878 A.D.
Scene of the Defeat, Wanderings and Victory of Alfred the Great.

X. Britain about 975 A.D.
The Realm of Cnut the Great, 1028–1035 A.D.

XI. Britain in 1064.
Neighborhood of York.

XII. Britain from 1066 to 1070 A.D.
Eastern Part of Coast of Sussex.

XIII. England and France in 1180.

XIV. England and France in 1223.

XV. England and France about 1360.

NOTE: Celtic Names. *Latin Names.* *Old English.* *Modern Names.*

CELTIC BRITAIN
ABOUT THE BIRTH OF CHRIST.
Ivernians
Goidels or Gaels
Brythans or Gauls
Caledonii
Vacomagi
Spey R.
Dee R.
Don R.
Firth of Tay
Firth of Forth
Otadini
Tweed R.
Damnonii
Novantae
Selgovae
Tyne R.
Solway Firth
Tees R.
Dalriada
Parisii
IVERNIA
Boyne R.
Mersey R.
Dee R.
Brigantes
The Humber
Liffey R.
Ordovices
Cornavii
Coritavi
The Wash
Iceni
Catuvellauni
Demetae
Wye R.
Usk R.
Trinovantes
Silures
Atrebates
Thames R.
Severn R.
Avebury
Cantion
Belgae
Stonehenge
Regni
Parret R.
Exe R.
Damnonii
Stour R.
Bolerium
Tamar R.

ROMAN BRITAIN
ABOUT 369 A.D.
VALENTIA
Vallum Antonini
Graham's Dyke
Clota
Bodotria Aest.
Alaunus
Vallum Hadriani
Tina
Luguvallium
Carlisle
Ituna Aest.
Tisa
MAXIMA
Monoeda
Man
CAESARIENSIS
Eburacum
York
Abus
Mona
Anglesey
Deva
Chester
Lindum
Lincoln
Metaris Aest.
FLAVIA
Str.
Viroconium
Wroxeter
Hermia
Venta Icenorum
Caistor
BRITANNIA SECUNDA
The Fosse
Hermia
Vennonae
Icknield Str.
Str.
Sitomagus
Dunwich
Limes Saxonicus
CAESARIENSIS
Glevum
Gloucester
Watling St.
Camalodunum
Colchester
Corinium
Cirencester
Londinium
London
Tamesis Aest.
Sabrina Aest.
Fosse
The
BRITANNIA PRIMA
Durovernum
Canterbury
Dubris
Dover
Venta Belgarum
Winchester
Isca Damnoniorum
Exeter
Seaton
Vectis
Wight
Limes Saxonicus
BRITANNIA

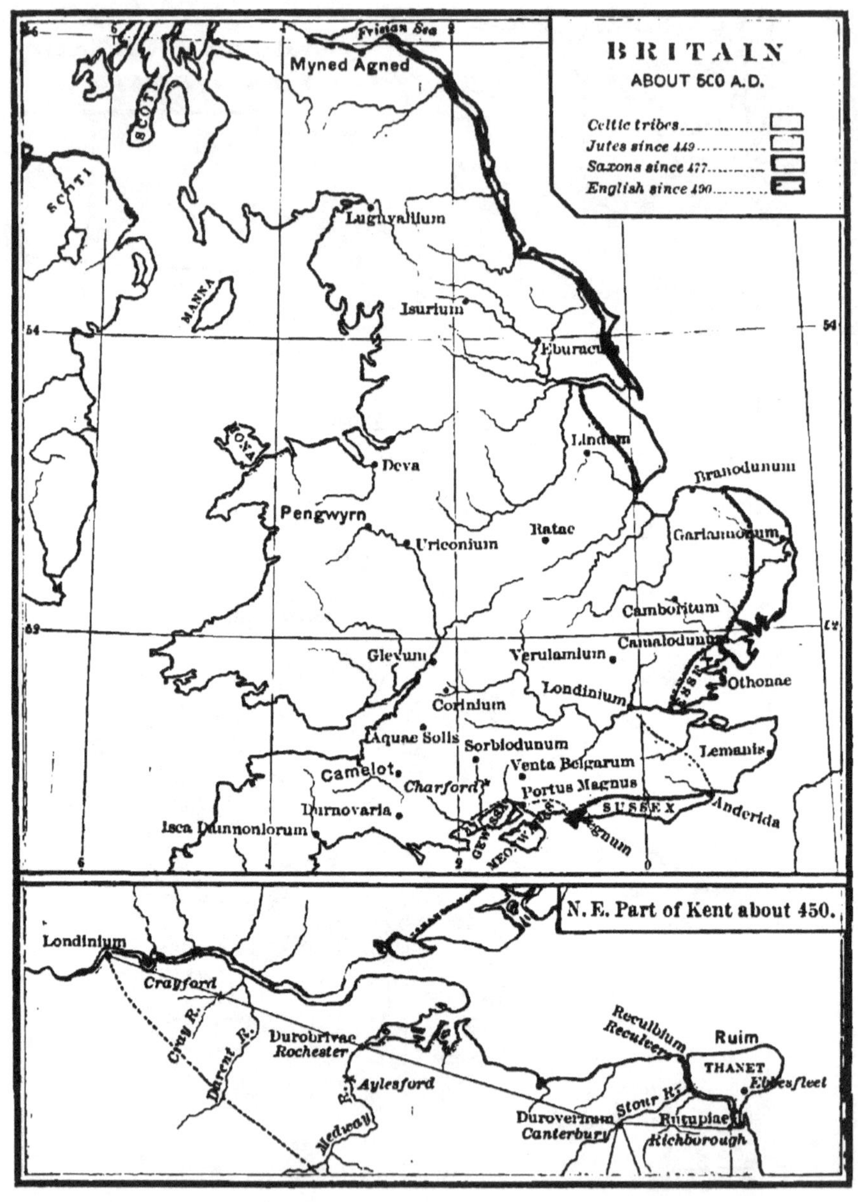
BRITAIN
ABOUT 500 A.D.
Celtic tribes
Jutes since 449
Saxons since 477
English since 490
Frisian Sea
Myned Agned
SCOTI
SCOTI
Luguvallium
MANNA
Isurium
Eburacum
MONA
Lindum
Deva
Branodunum
Pengwyrn
Gariannonum
Uriconium
Ratae
Camboritum
Camalodunum
Glevum
Verulamium
Othonae
Londinium
Corinium
Aquae Sulis
Lemanis
Sorbiodunum
Camelot
Venta Belgarum
Charford
Portus Magnus
SUSSEX
Anderida
Durnovaria
Magnus
Isca Dunnoniorum
GEWISSE
MEON WARE
N. E. Part of Kent about 450.
Londinium
Crayford
Reculbium
Reculver
Ruim
Cray R.
Durobrivae
Rochester
THANET
Darent R.
Aylesford
Ebbsfleet
Durovernum
Canterbury
Stour R.
Rutupiae
Richborough
Medway

BRITAIN
AFTER 577 A.D.

Celtic tribes
Jutic tribes
Saxons tribes
English tribes

SCOTI
PICTI
Mynod Agned
DERNICIA
Bamborough
STRATHCLYDE
PICTI
CUMBRIA
Luguvallium
Tyne R.
DEIRA
HOLDERNESS
MANNA
Humber R.
IONA
PECSAETAN
The Wash
Deva
Snottinga
MERCIANS
LINDISWARA
Faddiley
Pengwyrn
MIDDLE
ENGLE
GYRWAS
EAST ENGLE
Uriconium
SOUTH
ENGLE
NORTH WALES
HWICCAS
ESSEX
Stour R.
MIDDLESEX
Londonburh
Thames R.
Camelot
Creggan Ford
KENT
ANDREDSWEALD
WESSEX
SUSSEX
Andredes
Ceaster
WEST WALES
Chichester

Theatre of War between Britains
and West Saxons about 577.

Lenborough
Glevum
Gloucester
Egonesham
Oxford
Cherwell R.
Usk R.
Wye R.
Windrush R.
Thames R. Aylesburg
Corinium
Cirencester
Thames R.
Dennington
Wanborough
Wallingford
River Severn
Avon R.
Deorham
Ilanbury Hill
Baydon Hill
Exe R.
Aquae Solis
Bath
Cunetio
Marlborough
Kennet R.
Thames R.
Calleva
Silchester

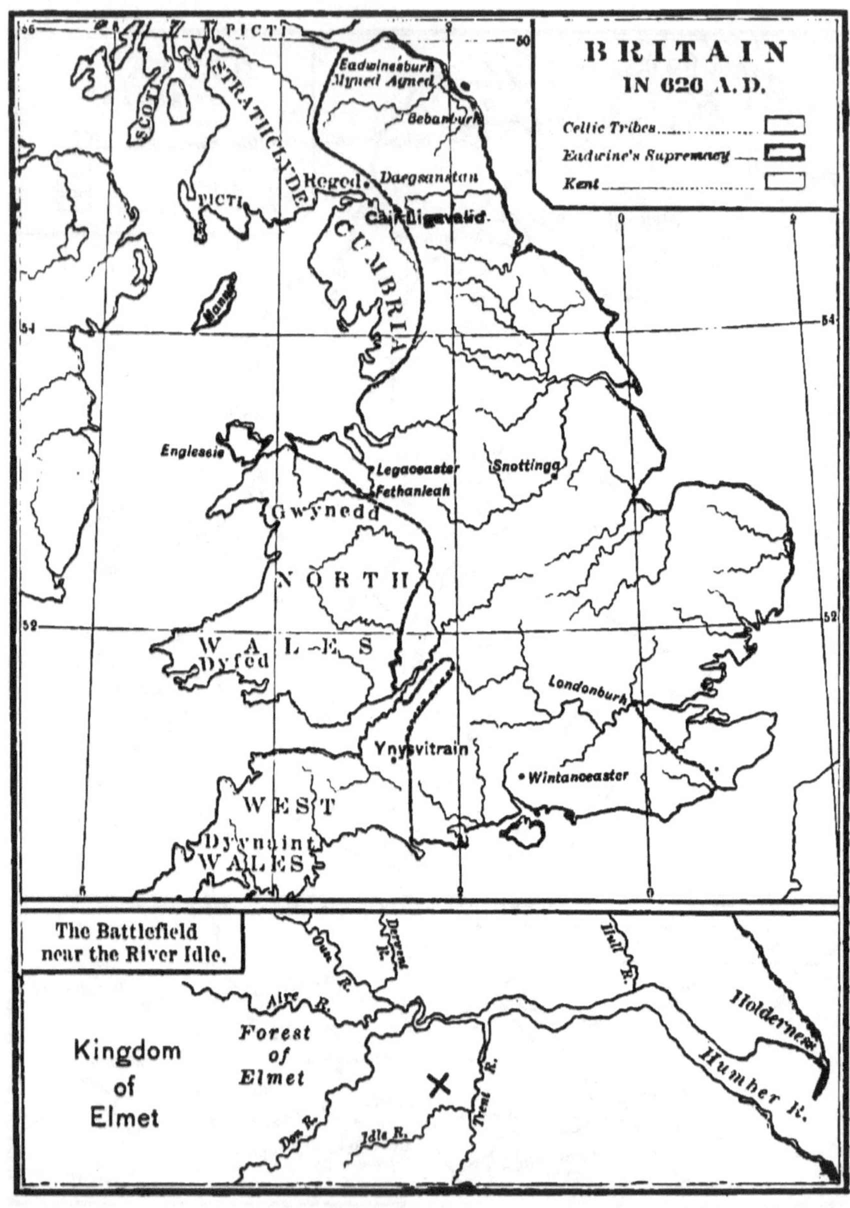

BRITAIN
IN 626 A.D.

Celtic Tribes
Eadwine's Supremacy
Kent

PICTI
SCOTI
STRATHCLYDE
Eadwinesburh
Mynedd Agned
Bebanburh
Reged
Daegsanstan
Cair Ligualid
PICTI
CUMBRIA
Manau
Englescie
Legaceaster
Fethanleah
Snottingg
Gwynedd
NORTH
WALES
Dyfed
Londonburh
Ynysvitrain
Wintanceaster
WEST
Dyvnaint
WALES

The Battlefield
near the River Idle.

Ouse R.
Derwent R.
Hull R.
Aire R.
Holderness
Forest
of
Elmet
Humber R.
Kingdom
of
Elmet
Don R.
Idle R.
Trent R.

BRITAIN
IN 658 A.D.

The Supremacy of Oswin
Kent — Jutes
Wessex — Saxons

STRATHCLYDE
CUMBRIA
PICTI
Reged
Aleluyd
Sadwine'sburh
Lindisfarena
Bebanburh
Heavenfeld
Cair Ligavalid
Manaw
Streoneshaloh
Eoforwic
Winni field
Heathfield
Engleseie
Legaceaster
Snottinga
Deorham
Gwynedd
NORTH
NORTHFOLK
Maserfield
Beormingaham
Dunevyic
Evesham
SOUTHFOLK
WALES
Dyfed
Heortford
Cirenceaster
Dorenceaster
Maidulfsburh
Bathanceaster
Londonburh
Cantwaraburh
Ynysvitrain
WEST
WALES
Dyvnhint
Wintanceaster

The New Settlements in
Central Britain about
666 A.D.

Northwearth
Derby
Snottinga
Nottingham
Botholphstun
Boston
Trent R.
Repton
Glen R.
Croyland
Severn R.
Wolverhampton
Medeshamstead
Petersborough
Beormingaham
Birmingham
Ouse R.
Huntandun
Huntingdon
Teme R.
Eligburh
Ely
Kenilworth
Avon R.
Wearingawick
Warwick
Leamington
Nen R.
Crantanbrucye
Cambridge
Wigormaceaster
Worcester
Evesham
Evesham
Stratford
Stratford
Tofeceaster
Towcester
Bedigan ford
Bedford
Cam R.

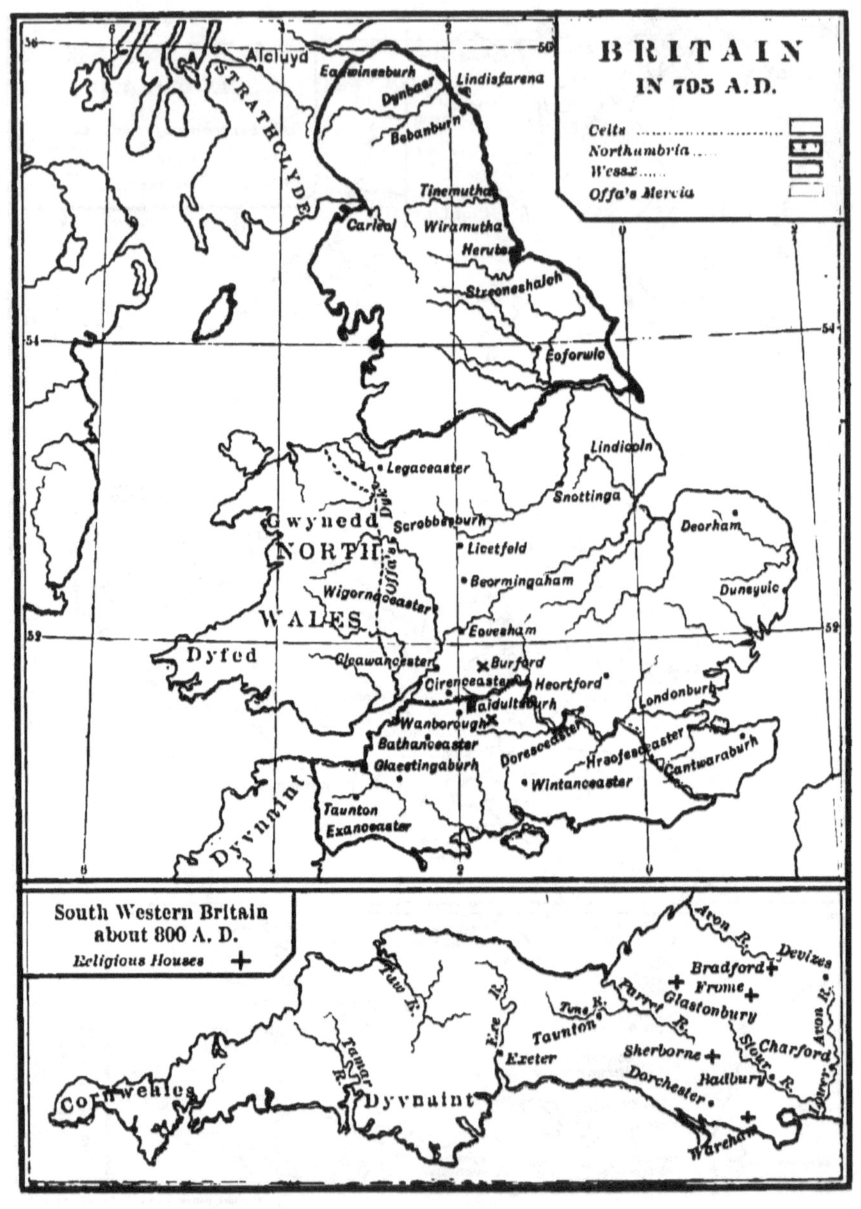

BRITAIN
IN 705 A.D.
Celts
Northumbria
Wessex
Offa's Mercia
STRATHCLYDE
Alcluyd
Eadwinesburh
Dynbaer
Lindisfarena
Bebanburh
Tinemutha
Carleal
Wiramutha
Heruteu
Streoneshalch
Eoforwic
Lindicoln
Legaceaster
Snottinga
Deorham
Gwynedd
Scrobbesburh
NORTH
Licetfeld
Beormingaham
Dunsyuic
Wigornceaster
WALES
Eouesham
Dyfed
Gleawanceaster
Burford
Cirenceaster
Heortford
Baidultsburh
Londonburh
Wanborough
Bathanceaster
Dorcesceaster
Hraofesceaster
Cantwaraburh
Glaestingaburh
Wintanceaster
Dyvnint
Taunton
Exanceaster
South Western Britain
about 800 A.D.
Religious Houses
Avon R.
Devizes
Bradford
Frome
Taw R.
Parret R.
Glastonbury
Exe R.
Tone R.
Taunton
Charford
Sherborne
Stour R.
Cornwealas
Tamar R.
Exeter
Dorchester
Hadbury
Lower Avon R.
Dyvnaint
Wareham

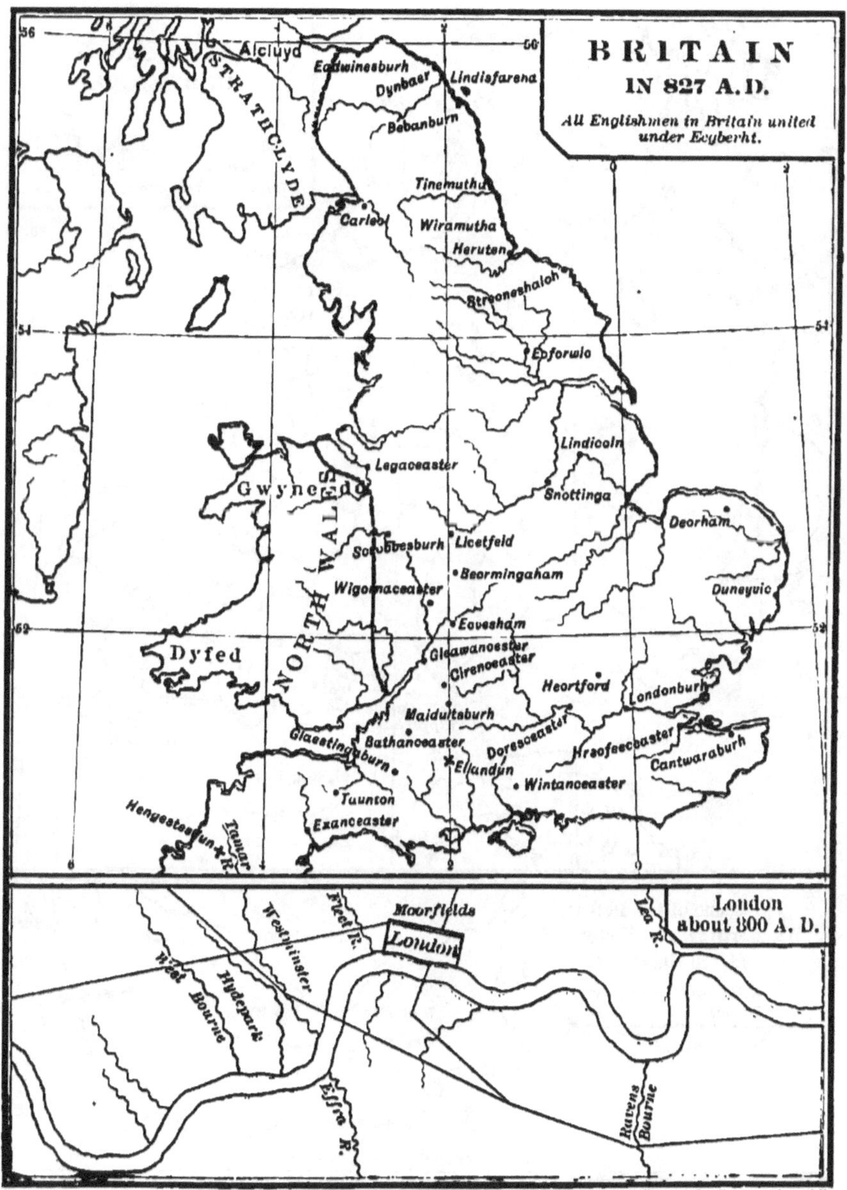

BRITAIN
IN 827 A.D.

All Englishmen in Britain united
under Ecgberht.

STRATHCLYDE
Alcluyd
Eadwinesburh
Dynbaer
Lindisfarena
Bebanburh
Tinemutha
Carleol
Wiramutha
Heruten
Streoneshaloh
Eoforwic
Lindicoln
Legaceaster
Gwynedd
Snottinga
Deorham
NORTH WALES
Scrobbesburh
Licetfeld
Duneyuic
Wigoraceaster
Beormingaham
Eovesham
Dyfed
Gleawanceaster
Cirenceaster
Heortford
Londonburh
Maidultaburh
Glaestingaburh
Bathanceaster
Doresceaster
Hraofeecoaster
Cantwaraburh
Ellandun
Wintanceaster
Tuunton
Hengestesdun
Tamar R.
Exanceaster

London
about 800 A. D.
Moorfields
London
Westminster
Fleet R.
Lea R.
West Bourne
Hydepark
Effra R.
Ravens Bourne

BRITAIN IN 878 A. D.
Celts
Danes
English
Wessex with dependencies
ALBANIA
Edinburgh
Clyde R.
Forth
Tweed R.
BERNICIA
Bamborough
Carlisle
Tyne R.
Tees R.
Armagh
Whitby
DANISH NORTHUMBRIA
Eoforwic
Dublin
Humber R.
WALES
Chester
ENGLISH MERCIA
DANISH MERCIA
Wexford
KINGDOM OF GUTHRUM
Gloucester
Wantage
London
Thames R.
Farringdon
Chippenham
Wells
WESSEX
KINGDOM OF KENT
Winchester
WEST WALES
Exeter
The Scene of the Defeat, Wanderings, and Victory of Alfred the Great.
Religious Houses
Battles
Axe R.
Ethandune
Frome
Wedmore
Wells
Frome R.
Brue R.
Carey R.
Glastonbury
Parret R.
Sedge Moor
Isle of Athelney
Aller Moor
Somerton

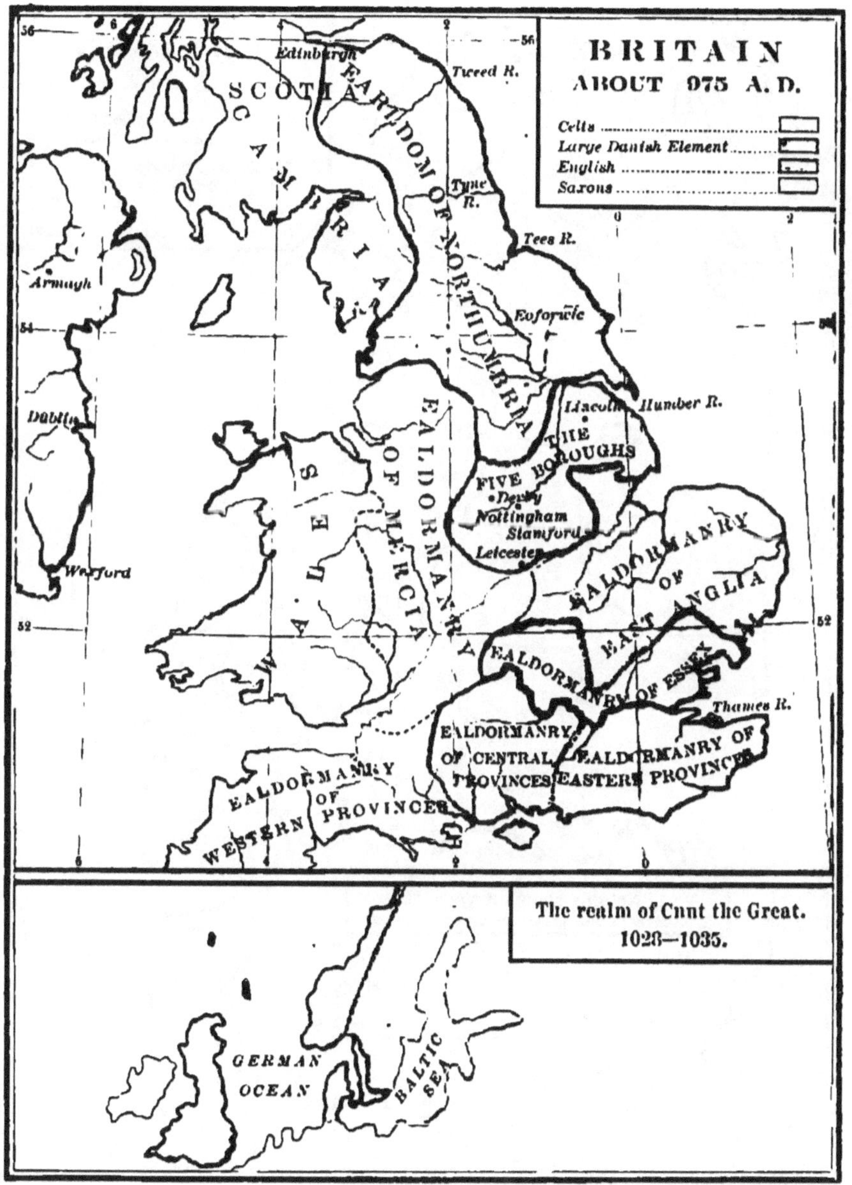

BRITAIN ABOUT 975 A.D.
Celts
Large Danish Element
English
Saxons
Edinburgh
Tweed R.
SCOTLAND
CUMBRIA
EARLDOM OF NORTHUMBRIA
Tyne R.
Tees R.
Armagh
Eoforwic
Lincoln
Humber R.
Dublin
THE FIVE BOROUGHS
EALDORMANRY OF MERCIA
Derby
Nottingham
Stamford
Leicester
Wexford
WALES
EALDORMANRY OF EAST ANGLIA
EALDORMANRY OF ESSEX
Thames R.
EALDORMANRY OF CENTRAL PROVINCES
EALDORMANRY OF EASTERN PROVINCES
EALDORMANRY OF WESTERN PROVINCES
The realm of Cnut the Great.
1028—1035.
GERMAN OCEAN
BALTIC SEA

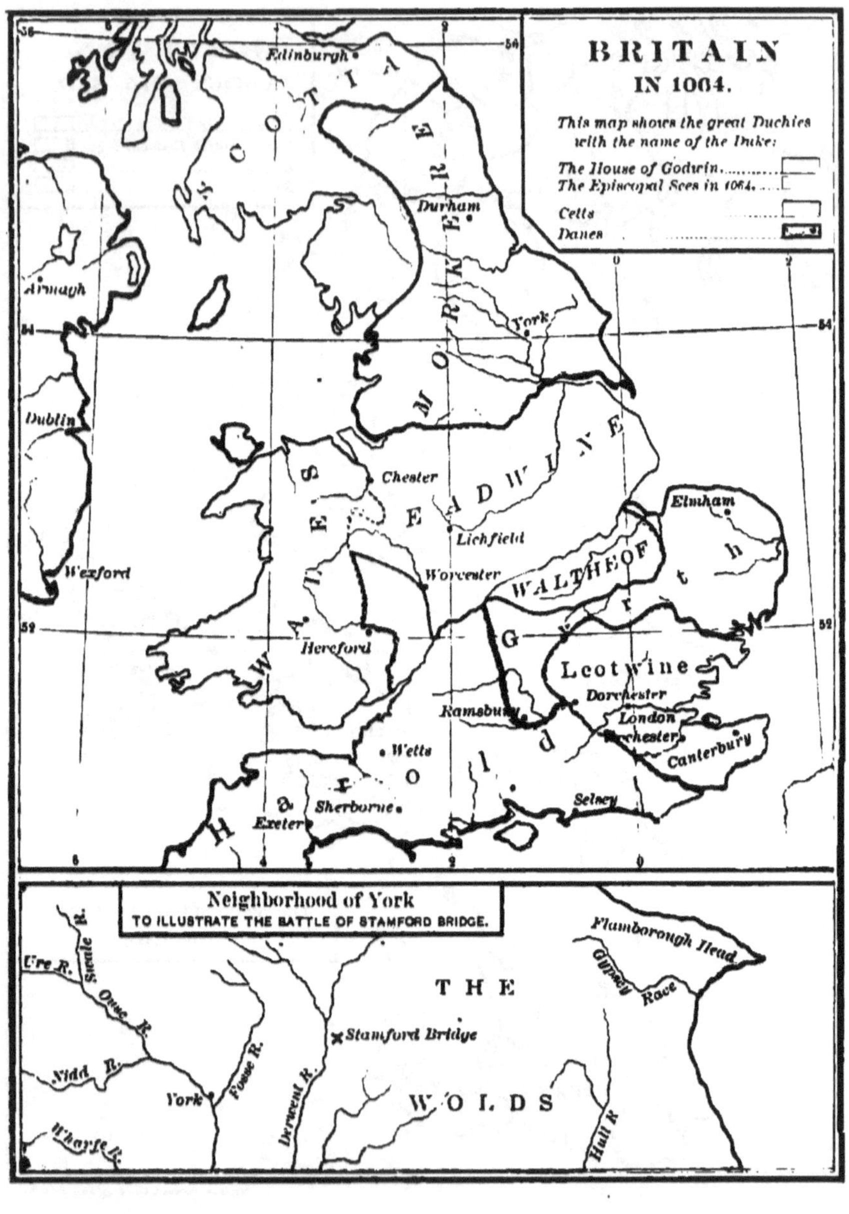

BRITAIN
IN 1064.

This map shows the great Duchies
with the name of the Duke:

The House of Godwin
The Episcopal Sees in 1064.
Celts
Danes

Edinburgh
Durham
York
Armagh
Dublin
Wexford
Chester
Elmham
Lichfield
Worcester
WALTHEOF
Hereford
Leotwine
Dorchester
Ramsbury
London
Winchester
Wells
Canterbury
Sherborne
Selsey
Exeter
SCOTIA
MORKERE
EADWINE
WALES

Neighborhood of York
TO ILLUSTRATE THE BATTLE OF STAMFORD BRIDGE.

Ure R.
Swale R.
Ouse R.
Nidd R.
Foss R.
York
Wharfe R.
Derwent R.
Stamford Bridge
THE
WOLDS
Flamborough Head
Gipsey Race
Hull R.

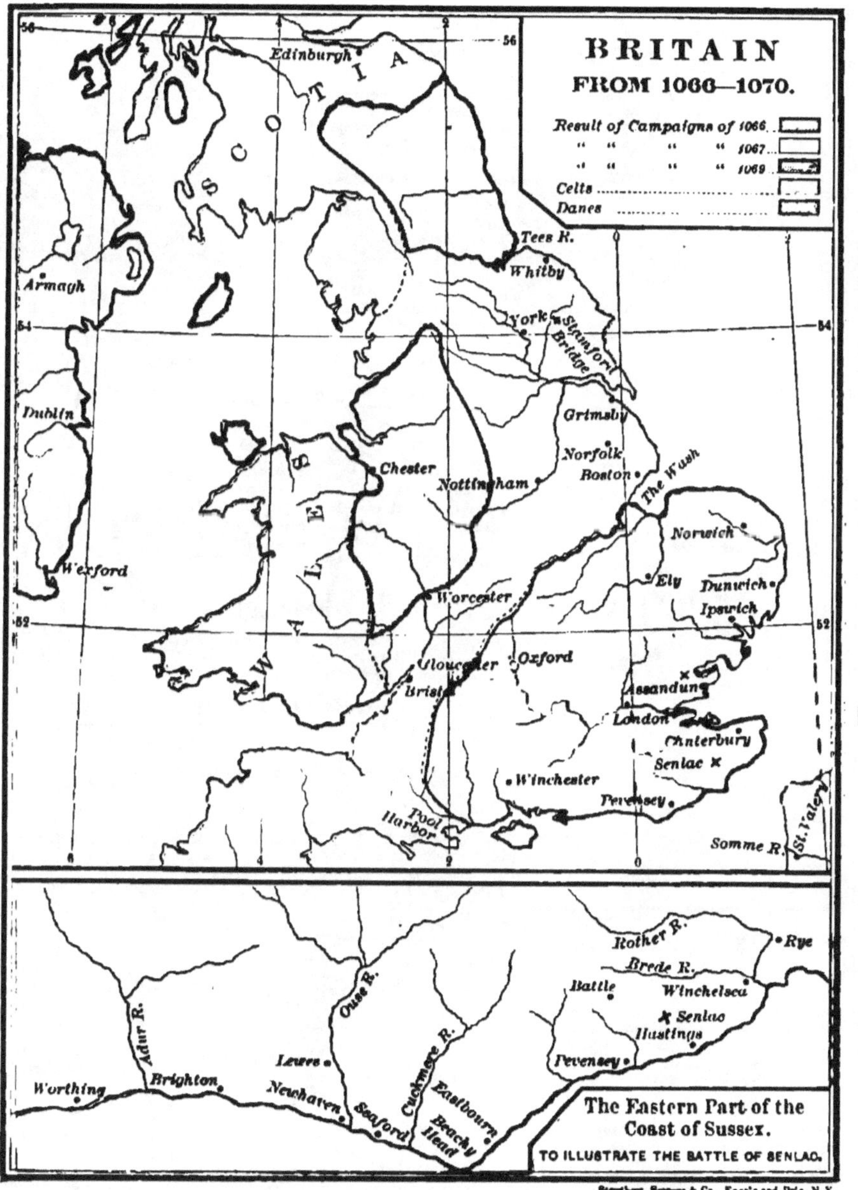

BRITAIN
FROM 1066—1070.
Result of Campaigns of 1066
" " " " 1067
" " " " 1069
Celts
Danes
Edinburgh
SCOTIA
Armagh
Dublin
Tees R.
Whitby
York
Stamford Bridge
Grimsby
Chester
Nottingham
Norfolk
Boston
The Wash
WALES
Norwich
Ely
Dunwich
Ipswich
Worcester
Gloucester
Oxford
Assandun
Bristol
London
Canterbury
Senlac
Winchester
Pevensey
St. Valery
Pool Harbor
Somme R.
Wexford
Rother R.
Rye
Brede R.
Battle
Winchelsea
Senlac
Hastings
Pevensey
Adur R.
Ouse R.
Cuckmere R.
Lewes
Worthing
Brighton
Newhaven
Seaford
Eastbourne
Beachy Head
The Eastern Part of the
Coast of Sussex.
TO ILLUSTRATE THE BATTLE OF SENLAC.

Dublin
Rhuddlan
Chester
Coleshill
Lincoln
Shrewsbury
Stamford
Bridgenorth
Rockingham
Norwich
Worcester
Evesham
Cambridge
Gloucester
Woodstock
Colchester
Oxford
London
Runnymede
Rochester
Canterbury
Winchester
Dover
Salisbury
Hastings
Clarendon
New Forest
Lewes
Exeter
Wales
Holland
Brabant
Antwerp
Flanders
Picardy
Bouvines
50
Arques
Rouen
Tournay
Vexin
Gisors
Caen
Beaumont
Isle of
Normandy
St.
Falaise
Evreux
Denis
Montmirail
Paris
Mortain
France
Champagne
Alençon
Maine
Vireuil
Brittany
Touraine
Fretehil
Orleannois
Sens
Veseldi
Nantes
Saumur
Loches
Nevers
Azai
Fontevrault
Burgundy
Poitou
Bourbonnais
Saintonge
La Marche
46
Angoumois
Lyonnais
Limoges
Auvergne
Lyons
Limousin
Chalus
Vivarais
Aquitaine
Bordeaux
Auvergne
Quercy
Mirabel
Gascony
Toulouse
Toulouse

ENGLAND AND FRANCE
AT THE ACCESSION OF PHILIP AUGUSTUS IN 1180.
The Empire of the Plantagenets
The royal domains of Philip Augustus
Territory inherited by Henry II. is shown
by the following lettering:
From his father .... Picardy
From his mother .... Anjou
Acquired from his Queen .... Gascony
Brittany, 1171-1202, Plantagenet Dukes.

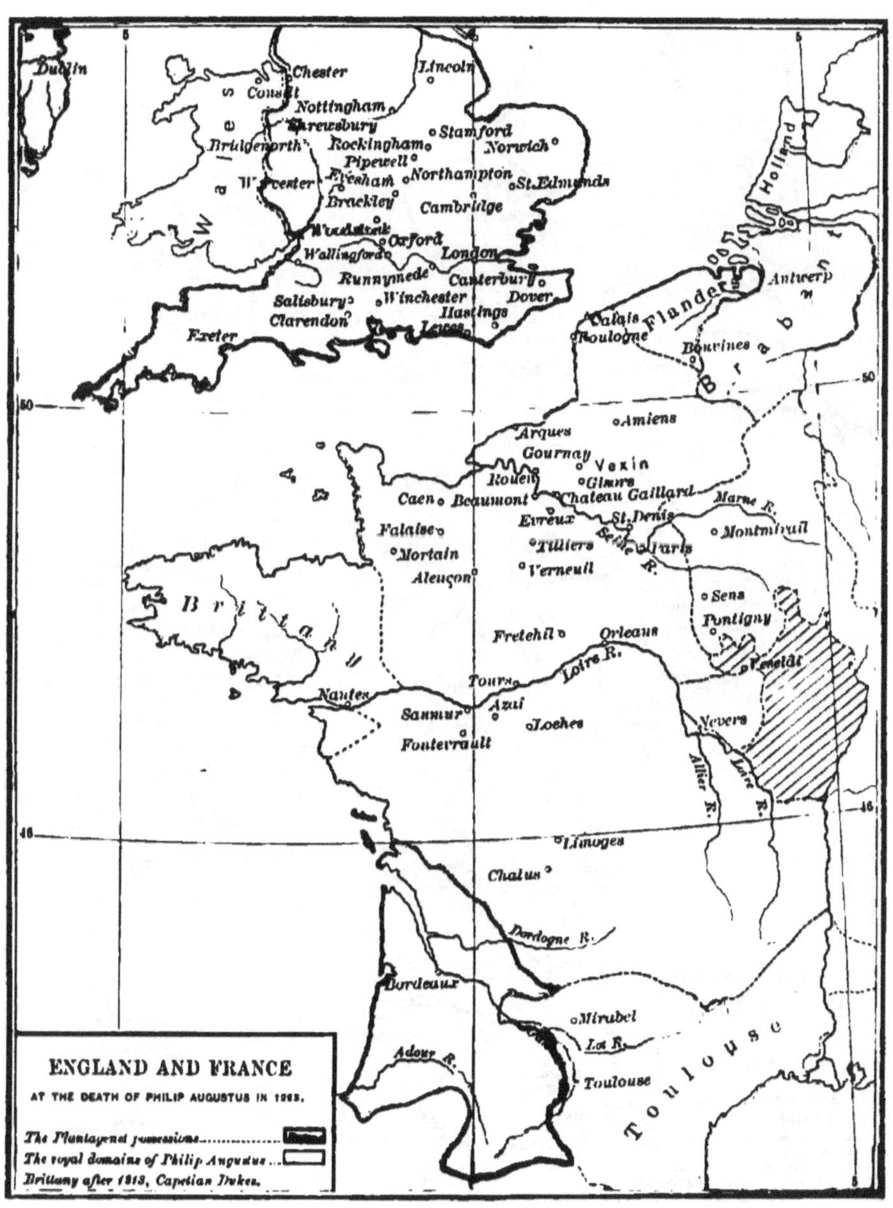

Dublin
Chester
Lincoln
Consett
Nottingham
Shrewsbury
Stamford
Bridgenorth
Rockingham
Norwich
Pipewell
Worcester
Feckham
Northampton
St. Edmunds
Brackley
Cambridge
Woodstock
Oxford
Wallingford
London
Runnymede
Canterbury
Salisbury
Winchester
Dover
Clarendon
Hastings
Lewes
Exeter
Holland
Flanders
Antwerp
Calais
Boulogne
Bourines
Brabant
Amiens
Arques
Gournay
Vexin
Rouen
Glisors
Caen
Beaumont
Chateau Gaillard
Marne R.
Evreux
St. Denis
Falaise
Tilliers
Seine R.
Paris
Montmirail
Mortain
Verneuil
Alençon
Sens
Pontigny
Brittany
Fretehil
Orleans
Vezelai
Loire R.
Tours
Nantes
Azai
Nevers
Saumur
Loches
Fontevrault
Allier R.
Loire R.
Limoges
Chalus
Dordogne R.
Bordeaux
Mirabel
Lot R.
Adour R.
Toulouse
Toulouse
ENGLAND AND FRANCE
AT THE DEATH OF PHILIP AUGUSTUS IN 1223.
The Plantagenet possessions
The royal domains of Philip Augustus
Brittany after 1213, Capetian Dukes.

Lancaster
Towton
York
Wakefield
Pomfret
Flint
More Heath
Shrewsbury
Kenilworth
Bosworth
Ludlow
Northampton
Mortimers Cross
Tewkesbury
St. Albans
Oxford
Barnet
Berkeley Cas.
London
Runnymede
Black Heath
Seven Oaks
Beaulieu
Hastings
Exeter
Dartmouth
Winchelsea
Dover
Calais
Sluys
Anticerp
Bruges
Courtray
Ghent
Brussels
Flanders
Azincourt
Namur
Cologne
Arras
Crecy
Abbeville
Scheldt R.
Sambre R.
Coblentz
50
La Hague
Somme R.
Luxemburg
Trèves
Harfleur
Aisne
Bayeux
Jumieges
Rouen
Coucy
Formigny
Soissons
Metz
Caen
Seine R.
Oise
Compiegne
Rheims
Faucouleurs
St. Lo
Falaise
Breteuil
Paris
Marne R.
Strassburg
Tenchbray
Verneuil
Vincennes
Domremy
Brest
Dinan
Mayenne
Bretigny
Montfort
Montereau
Sens
Troyes
Muhlhausen
Josselin
Rennes
Sarth R.
Orleans
Chatillon
Basle
Auray
Blois
Loire R.
Nantes
Angers
County of Burgundy
Fontevrault
Tours R.
Chinon
Nevers
Poitiers
Bourges
Maupertuis
Bourbon
Vienne R.
Moulins
Allier R.
Geneva
Taillebourg
Limoges
Lyons
45
Saintes
Chaluz
Clermont
Bordeaux
Dordogne R.
Montbrison
Le Puy
Rhone R.
Privas
Lot R.
Cahors
Adour R.
Montauban
Alais
Orange
Bayonne
Nimes
Avignon
Durance R.
Toulouse
Montpellier
Marseilles
Oleron
Beziers
Narbonne
Holland
Meuse R.
Rhine R.
Ems R.
Moselle R.

ENGLAND
AND
FRANCE
DURING THE FIRST ENGLISH
INVASION OF FRANCE.
English realm
French realm
German Empire
English realm by the treaty of Bretigny

Strothers, Servoss & Co., Engr's   N.Y.